What people are saying about

Blowing on Dandelions

"*Blowing on Dandelions* is a fun read with a beautiful setting in 1880s Baker City, Oregon. Ferrell has created characters you'll root for, and the attitudes feel appropriate for the time in this tender romance. The relationships of mothers and daughters in this story speak deeply of the need for acceptance, love, and respect from one's parents."

Susan Page Davis, award-winning author of
the Prairie Dreams and Texas Trails series

"As soft and gentle as the wisps of snowy seeds for which it is named, *Blowing on Dandelions* is an achingly tender love story that will lift your spirits—and your heart—high on a gentle breeze through the Oregon mountain valleys."

Julie Lessman, award-winning author of The
Daughters of Boston and Winds of Change series

"Miralee Ferrell's writing style is always a delight, even as her stories are captivating. *Blowing on Dandelions* is no exception. From the opening scene the reader is drawn into Katherine Galloway's life, and we care about her from that moment on. This is more than a heart-tugging romance—though it is that; it is also a mind-challenging read that will leave us in a different place from when we began."

"In Katherine Galloway, Miralee Ferrell has created a woman who models grace. As the story unfolds, readers see Katherine's faith lived out in a way that is authentic, challenging, and encouraging. A book you won't want to put down ... and a story you won't want to end."

"*Blowing on Dandelions* is an amazing, deeply emotional story. Each of the characters is so sympathetic and well drawn that it was impossible to put the book down. Ferrell is a wonderful writer who handles the pain of physical and emotional trauma beautifully. Her characters are appealing, with a touching and believable faith journey, and the romance is lovely. My only regret was reaching the final page! Miralee Ferrell's future books will be automatic purchases from now on!"

"In *Blowing on Dandelions*, Miralee Ferrell gives us an engaging story with strong characters who have hidden depths. The theme of the story is universal and will touch hearts and help heal longtime hurts. As with all of her books, Miralee weaves a satisfying romance through these pages. What else could a reader ask for?"

Lena Nelson Dooley, speaker and author of the 2012 Selah Award winner *Maggie's Journey, Mary's Blessing,* and the 2011 Will Rogers Medallion Award winner, *Love Finds You in Golden, New Mexico*

"In *Blowing on Dandelions,* Miralee Ferrell has an excellent way of keeping the words flowing, keeping the reader following, and investing in the characters. I particularly love the redemption she shows, where not all offensive people are evil, but merely hurting. Of course, the love story makes for a perfectly satisfying ending. Very well done!"

Hannah Alexander, award-winning author of the Hideaway Series

"Miralee Ferrell's *Blowing on Dandelions* is a deeply inspiring story about family conflict and the transforming power of rekindled love. A richly written story chock full of nuggets of divine wisdom, this book was, for me, a genuinely satisfying read."

Walt Larimore, bestselling author of *Hazel Creek* and *Sugar Fork*

"Miralee Ferrell delves deeply into the issues of bitterness and family discord and shines a bright light on God's path to reconciliation for every hurting heart. You won't be able to read this book without shedding a tear as you identify with one or more of these true-to-life characters."

Louise M. Gouge, award-winning author

"The relationship between a mom and her daughter can be complicated. In *Blowing on Dandelions*, Miralee Ferrell writes a compelling novel about a single mother trying to raise two girls even as she works to mend the relationship with her own mother. Miralee's story takes place more than a hundred years ago, but the poignant themes of friendship, healing, and forgiveness will inspire readers today."

Melanie Dobson, award-winning author of *Love Finds You in Liberty, Indiana* and *The Silent Order*

"An interesting combination of the classic Western and prairie romances. No cowboys but a hero who loves his son and a heroine who loves her daughters. Mix in a boardinghouse, a mysterious boarder, and two matriarchs marking their territory. Katherine Galloway is a heroine to root for! And Miralee Ferrell is an author to watch!"

Lyn Cote, author of *La Belle Christiane*

"With characters who will both delight and dismay, Miralee Ferrell's compelling style has created a story that explores relationships and the deeper emotions behind the conflicts of ordinary people in extraordinary circumstances."

Martha Rogers, Texas Christian Writers Conference 2009 Writer of the Year

Blowing on Dandelions

MIRALEE
FERRELL

A NOVEL

Blowing on Dandelions

Love Blossoms in Oregon

David C Cook®

transforming lives together

BLOWING ON DANDELIONS
Published by David C Cook
4050 Lee Vance View
Colorado Springs, CO 80918 U.S.A.

David C Cook Distribution Canada
55 Woodslee Avenue, Paris, Ontario, Canada N3L 3E5

David C Cook U.K., Kingsway Communications
Eastbourne, East Sussex BN23 6NT, England

The graphic circle C logo is a registered trademark of David C Cook.

The website addresses recommended throughout this book are offered as a
resource to you. These websites are not intended in any way to be or imply an
endorsement on the part of David C Cook, nor do we vouch for their content.

This story is a work of fiction. All characters and events are the product of the author's
imagination. Any resemblance to any person, living or dead, is coincidental.

Scripture quotations are taken from the King James
Version of the Bible. (Public Domain.)

LCCN 2013934365
ISBN 978-0-7814-0808-0
eISBN 978-1-4347-0603-4

Published in association with Tamela Hancock Murray of The Steve
Laube Agency, 5025 N. Central Ave., #635, Phoenix, AZ 85012.

The Team: Don Pape, Ingrid Beck, Ramona Cramer Tucker, Caitlyn
Carlson, Tonya Osterhouse, Karen Athen, and Karen Stoller
Cover Design: DogEared Design, Kirk DouPonce
Cover Photo: iStockPhoto

Printed in the United States of America

First Edition 2013

1 2 3 4 5 6 7 8 9 10

030113

Love Blossoms in Oregon Series

Blowing on Dandelions

Wishing on Buttercups

Dreaming on Daisies

To every woman
whose heart has been wounded
by someone she loved.
And most of all, to the woman
who inspired this story
when she shared a small part of
her broken heart with me.

He that dwelleth in the secret
place of the most High
shall abide under the shadow of the Almighty.
I will say of the LORD, He is my
refuge and my fortress:
my God; in him will I trust.

—Psalm 91:1–2

Acknowledgments

So many people worked to make this book a success that I'm afraid I might forget someone. However, I'll do my best here to give honor and thanks where it's due. First, all glory goes to: God, my Father; Jesus, my best Friend; and the Holy Spirit, my Guide and Comforter. Without the three-in-one Godhead, I'd be unable to accomplish anything worthwhile. God gives me the strength to get through each day and the creativity to put the words on paper. I write for Him first. If He's satisfied, I know the rest will fall in place.

My biggest thanks goes to my family—most especially my husband—for being patient as I work through my deadlines while being supportive of my book chatter, travel, and all it takes to bring a new book into the world. My children, Marnee and Brian, Steven and Hannah, my mother, Sylvia Gould, who is one of my closest friends, and my husband's parents, Chuck and Dolores—all have offered encouragement and support. Also a special thanks to my church family who remember to pray as I write each new story and eagerly await each new one. You are special to me.

The writing of a book is never just about the author; it takes a team working behind the scenes to bring it to life. First are my critique partners, who brainstorm with me, then help me hone and polish my work. I've been honored to work with Kimberly Johnson, Sherry Kyle, and Karen O'Connor for almost three years now. Sherri Sand and Judy Vandiver also read and critiqued my manuscript when it was finished. Sherri spent several hours showing my husband and me around Baker City, Oregon, pointing out historical landmarks, and answering numerous questions that have contributed greatly to the setting of the book. Two advance readers, Tammy Marks and Kristy Gamet, who have been with me since my first book released, eagerly await each new manuscript and devour it, giving me valuable feedback. Wilburta Arrowood, Kimberly Johnson, and Stephanie Whitson spent time on the phone brainstorming the story line, and Colleen Reece and Janice Olson assisted with title suggestions. I love all these wonderful ladies, who are an integral part of my team. In addition, many thanks go to the women who answered my call to fill out a questionnaire about their own relationship with their mother. These women were a tremendous asset.

My publishing team starts with my agent, Tamela Hancock Murray, who champions my work and helps find it the best possible home. Tamela, a friend as well as a business associate, works diligently to make my career succeed.

This is my first book with my new publisher, David C Cook, and I'm beyond excited to work with them. They graciously accepted my request to assign Ramona Tucker, the editor who worked on my last three books. I love this woman and highly value her expertise and editing. I'm so blessed to partner with her on all three books in this series. Most of my early contacts at Cook have been with Ingrid Beck, who welcomed me and made me feel part of the Cook family right from the start. I look forward to getting to know more of the quality people at my new "home."

And, last, to my readers—I value each and every email I receive, as well as the posts on Facebook, Twitter, Goodreads, and Pinterest, and I'd love to have you drop by. Thank you for your faithful support!

- My Facebook Fan Page: https://www.facebook.com/miraleeferrell
- Twitter: https://twitter.com/#!/MiraleeFerrell
- My personal website: www.miraleeferrell.com View pictures of my book research and travels, family photos, upcoming speaking event updates (via my blog link), and find announcements about future books.
- You can also drop me a note at miraleef@gmail.com.

Chapter One

Baker City, Oregon
Late May, 1880

Katherine Galloway's soft exhale sent the dandelion fluff dancing on the warm current of air, but it didn't bring the anticipated relief. Gripping the stem, she sat in the grassy field with her eyes closed and waited. Why didn't it come? It had always appeared years ago when she needed it. How long had it been since her mind had drifted away to a place where nothing could hurt her? Fifteen years? Twenty?

She shook her head, and an errant curl tickled her cheek.

More. Many more. But always her memory returned to those times when the dandelion fluff had carried her away to a place where mothers were loving and kind, and little girls didn't need to be afraid of cutting words or sharp voices.

Had she ever known a time like that, other than in her dreams? Katherine had thought she did, but now she knew: it was all an illusion, like the sunbeams glinting off the bits of white that were settling to the ground. Seeds—that's all they were. Seeds that brought unwanted weeds when they matured. Just like her life.

Unwanted. Unwelcome. Unsung.

At least by the one person who had mattered the most while she was growing up.

Katherine pushed to her feet, letting the dandelion stem dangle from her fingers. There was no fantasy world where thirty-two-year-old women—or little girls for that matter—could ride the dandelion fluff and become someone they weren't. No. It was time to put the past behind her. Mama was coming to stay at her house tomorrow, and somehow Katherine had to survive.

An hour later a wagon rumbling down the dirt road churned out a billowing cloud of powdery dust. Katherine waved a hand in front of her face and coughed. Time to face the future and try to forget the past. School would be dismissed soon, and she'd need her two daughters, Lucy and Amanda, to help ready the house for Mama's arrival.

Katherine clutched her dark blue skirt and lifted it a couple inches as she moved from the grass onto the road. If only Daniel were alive … He'd always known how to deal with Mama's irascible behavior.

Katherine pushed aside the pain that threatened to swamp her. After almost three years of widowhood, she should be able to move on, but so far it hadn't happened, and she doubted it ever would. Katherine struck off down the road, barely noticing the sun that glimmered on the unfurling green leaves of the oak trees or the birds that sang in the branches above her head. Late spring had arrived, and her heart longed to soar with the larks, but the thought of Mama's arrival slowed her steps.

June, Katherine's unmarried older sister, had been Mama's companion all of June's adult life, but her sudden passing several weeks earlier had left Mama alone and unattended. Not that she really needed tending. If anything, her sickly half sister had required more care than her mother did, but June had never allowed her frail condition to get in the way of ministering to their mother. Katherine sighed, saddened anew over the loss of her only sibling.

"Ma!" Her sweet, six-year-old Amanda's voice trilled a high note, and the patter of feet on the hard-packed dirt road drew Katherine to a halt. She pivoted, watching her younger daughter fly toward her.

A glance beyond Mandy didn't reveal thirteen-year-old Lucy. Katherine had instructed both her girls to head straight home after school. Of course, Lucy might have allowed Mandy to come alone, seeing how the schoolhouse was such a short distance.

Katherine held her arms out to the golden-haired girl, knowing her daughter would launch into the air when barely within reach.

Sure enough, Amanda giggled and leapt forward, landing in her arms. "Swing me in a circle, Ma!"

Katherine peered around but saw no one watching who might judge her unkindly. *Stop that.* She didn't care for the direction her thoughts had taken her. Mama always worried what others might think. Katherine had resolved early on that if God blessed her with children, they'd get all the hugs, kisses, and laughter she'd longed for.

She stiffened her spine. It mattered not one whit if anyone watched. She spun the little girl another time, Mandy's giggles flying as wide as the skirt she wore and beyond.

Then Katherine pressed a long kiss onto Amanda's pink cheek. "Where's your sister?"

The sweet smile faded. "Don't know."

."Is she still at school, or did she go home?"

The little girl shrugged. "She ran off, so I came to find you."

"Ran off where?" Katherine placed a finger under Amanda's chin and lifted it. "Are you hiding something, Daughter?"

Amanda's deep blue eyes dropped. "She told me not to tell, or she'd whip me later when you're not looking."

"Lucy is *not* going to whip you. I'll see to that. Now tell me what she's up to."

A huge sigh followed. "I suppose I have to, or *you'll* whip me."

Katherine's mouth dropped open. "Where in the world is all this whipping nonsense coming from?"

"Mary Jane Winters says that when she grows up, she's going to whip her children every day, even if they aren't naughty."

"Whatever for?"

Her daughter squinted up against the bright sun. "Because they probably *want* to be naughty, and if you whip them ahead of time, it will stop them from doing something bad."

"And how old is Mary Jane Winters to have such great wisdom?"

"Nine, and she's going to have at least a dozen babies when she gets married, so they can do all the chores, and she can sit and eat candy." A smile broke her solemn features. "I guess you shoulda had more babies, Ma. They could do some of the chores at the boardinghouse."

Katherine quirked an eyebrow. "Honey, more children often mean more work. Besides, God gave your father and me what He wanted us to have. Now quit changing the subject and tell me where your sister went."

"Yes, ma'am." Amanda scuffed her black boot against the dirt, covering it with dust. "She ran off with a *boy*." She made the word sound like her sister had disappeared with a two-headed monster.

Katherine would've laughed if alarm bells weren't ringing in her head. "Which boy? Where?"

"Zachary, some new boy at school. I think she's sweet on him. I saw them sitting together at dinnertime under a tree, and she shared her food with him." Mandy tugged at her mother's arm and skipped in place. "Come on, Ma. I'm hungry."

Katherine blew air out in a puff. "Let's get you home. If Lucy doesn't arrive soon, I'll go look for her. Did you see what direction they took?"

"I think to Snider's General Store. I heard the boy say he brought money, and he'd buy her a treat."

"All right." Katherine stroked her daughter's blond curls. "Thank you for telling me, even though your sister asked you not to."

Amanda raised troubled eyes. "I'm not in trouble?"

"No, darling, but your big sister will be when she gets home." Katherine took her daughter's slender hand in hers and stepped out at a brisk pace. Her arm swung in a wide arc as Mandy hopped and skipped beside her, kicking up dust as she went.

God had blessed her when He birthed this little girl into their family. Strong-willed Lucy was a blessing as well, but she'd always been more of a challenge. This newest episode was one of several recently and not something Katherine cared to deal with right now.

For the thousandth time she wished Daniel hadn't died and left her alone. He'd know what to say to Lucy and how to deal with Mama when she arrived....

Katherine tilted her chin up. No more self-pity nonsense today. Tomorrow would bring enough troubles, and she wouldn't borrow against that time. She'd make the most of this beautiful day and pray that somehow Mama had changed in the past two years.

Chapter Two

That boy was late again. Micah Jacobs hefted a bag of grain onto his left shoulder and stepped out of the feed store facing the main street of Baker City, Oregon. He squinted against the harsh glare of the late-spring sun and tugged the brim of his hat with his free hand. School had been out for at least thirty minutes, more than enough time for his son to arrive at the store and help load the grain for the livery.

Micah had hoped that moving here from the city and buying a business would interest Zachary. At nearly fifteen, the boy only had two more years of schooling. He should be planning how to make his way in the world, not mooning over books. Their family had a history of working with their hands—his father and grandfather before him had carved out a living in a smithy—but Zachary hadn't shown an interest in shoeing, working as a wheelwright, *or* helping at the livery.

Micah slammed another bag of grain onto the pile and shook his head. Zachary's sight would be damaged if he continued to pore over those schoolbooks hours on end. Books had never done Micah any good, and they wouldn't earn a living for his son. Maybe things would've been different if his wife, Emma, had lived, but regret wouldn't pay the bills.

He stepped onto the wheel of the buckboard and swung onto the seat, settling down and unwinding the reins from the brake handle. "Let's go, Charlie. Get along there, Mable." Cracking the reins against the black rumps of his mules, he turned them toward the livery. After three weeks, he'd hoped profits would've been better. The mining boom had seemed to promise prosperity to any who ventured to this town, which was situated not far from the Oregon Trail, but so far it hadn't happened.

A flash of gold registered on the edge of his vision. Micah swiveled just in time to see a little girl with blond curls escape her mother's hold and dash across the dusty road—right into the path of his mules.

Katherine stopped in front of Connors' Mercantile and gazed at a lace-edged tablecloth. Did she have enough money for something so extravagant? Mama probably wouldn't approve.

Amanda tugged her hand free, and Katherine pivoted to call her back, then froze. Mandy had bounded off the boardwalk and right into the path of an oncoming wagon.

Katherine's heart stuck in her throat. With handfuls of her skirt clutched in her fists, she finally managed to gasp, "Amanda. Stop!"

The driver of the team hauled back on his reins the instant Amanda appeared to register Katherine's words and halted her flight. The black-bay mules slowed to a stop, snorting their displeasure and pawing the ground.

Katherine reached her daughter and scooped her into her arms, wanting to shake her and hug her at the same time. "What were you thinking? That wagon almost ran over you."

The driver jumped down and strode to where they stood. "Is your little girl all right?" Concern laced the gruff edge of his voice.

"Yes, I think so." She raised her eyes, and a jolt hit her heart. Beneath a wide forehead, brows were drawn over intense green eyes, and a hat was pushed down over his dark brown hair. A firm jawline gave him a no-nonsense look, but his kind gaze belied the frown tugging at his mouth.

"I'm sorry, ma'am. Guess I had my mind on something other than my driving."

Gratitude swelled in her chest. This stranger could have easily berated her for allowing Amanda to escape her care, but he'd chosen to take responsibility for the near mishap. "Thank you, but I should've kept a tighter grip on her hand. She was anxious to visit the store across the street, and I was distracted due to my older daughter not returning home." Realizing she was rambling, Katherine set Amanda back on the ground and leaned over to the child's level. "You need to apologize to Mister ..." She gazed up at the man.

He tipped his hat, and a smile broke the serious plane of his face. "Jacobs, ma'am. Micah Jacobs, late of Seattle, Washington."

"That's a long way to travel, Mr. Jacobs. What brought you to our fair city?"

"The need for a change. I purchased the livery and smithy three weeks ago."

"Ah, a fellow businessman. I wondered what would happen to the livery when Mr. Sykes decided to pull up stakes and leave."

"*Fellow* businessman? Do you and your husband run an establishment in Baker City?"

She extended her hand while keeping a firm hold on Amanda with the other. "I apologize. I'm Katherine Galloway. My husband passed away nearly three years ago, but I own the boardinghouse on the far edge of town." She tipped her head to the south. "My older daughter, Lucy, helps me when she's not in school, and Amanda here keeps me on my toes when she's home."

"I see. Well, I won't keep you, Mrs. Galloway. I'll walk you to the boardwalk, then I'd best get this grain to the livery and unloaded. I need to track down my son."

"You and your wife have children as well? I imagine they must attend school with my girls."

A cloud passed across his handsome features, leaving them cold and withdrawn. "My son and I are here alone. Good day to you, ma'am, and again, I'm sorry for the scare to you and your daughter." He settled his hat down further on his head, climbed up onto the buckboard seat, and picked up the reins.

As the team surged forward, Katherine stared after them. What in the world had she said that soured him all of a sudden? She watched for a full minute, but the man didn't look back.

Micah slapped the reins against the mules' haunches and suppressed a shudder. He'd come so close to running down that little girl—Amanda, her mother called her. Why hadn't he been more alert and noticed that she'd dashed into the road? One tragedy in the past two years was enough for a lifetime. He certainly didn't need his poor fortune to spill over onto someone else's life.

Mrs. Galloway had handled the scare well, not shrieking or threatening to faint like some city women he'd known. Even his dear Emma would've been swooning and unable to function after such a scare. *Emma*. His heart lurched as memories of his beloved wife washed over him. He had been unbearably lonely since her passing eighteen months earlier, and only the needs of their son, Zachary, had kept him from sliding into a dark place. The past couple months had been easier, but pain still rammed its fist into his gut at unexpected times.

Admiration for Mrs. Galloway once more tickled his imagination, but he shoved it away, irritated at the unfair comparison he'd made to his Emma. He started to swivel his head to get one more glimpse of the woman but steeled himself and stared straight ahead instead. She'd been perfectly safe on the far side of the road the last time he'd looked.

He clucked to his mules again.

Women had no place in his life anymore. Not at the present nor any time in the future. Zachary was his entire world now, and Micah would do well to remember that fact.

Katherine had almost hustled her daughter home without the promised treat until she realized that's exactly what her mother would've done to her as a child. Mandy hadn't exactly disobeyed her, as she hadn't instructed her daughter to keep hold of her hand; the girl had only acted out of excitement at the promised treat. Becoming a replica of her mother by constantly chiding her children was not something Katherine intended to do, so Katherine had purchased Amanda a peppermint stick at the nearby hardware store.

A memory of Micah Jacobs's deep green eyes now swam to the fore of her thoughts as she opened the front door of her house and stepped inside. She exhaled. No time to think of anything right now except preparing for Mama's arrival.

As soon as they entered, Mandy darted off. Katherine raised her voice. "You need to wash that sticky candy off your hands before you touch anything, Amanda Lee."

"Yes, ma'am." The fairy-like voice drifted back on the quiet air. Light footsteps broke the stillness behind her.

Katherine whirled. "Lucy! Where have you been?"

Her tawny-haired daughter stood inside the open door, avoiding her gaze. "Nowhere special."

Katherine crossed her arms. "You were supposed to come straight home from school."

Lucy wrinkled her nose. "Sorry, Ma."

"So where were you?"

"I walked to the general store. I guess I forgot."

"Shut the door, please." Katherine waited until Lucy did as she asked, then beckoned the girl into the parlor. "Take a seat."

Lucy bit her lower lip and glanced at the stairway leading to her room. "I need to do my schoolwork. Could we talk later?"

"No." Katherine pointed to an upright horsehair chair. "Sit."

Her elder daughter sank onto the stiff seat but didn't settle back. "Am I in trouble?"

"I'm not sure yet, but you might be. Where did you go? More importantly, who were you with?"

Lucy bristled, her back straightening. "I suppose Mandy tattled on me?"

"This has nothing to do with your sister, young lady. You disobeyed me *and* asked your sister to lie. Now out with it."

Lucy slumped in her chair, the rebellion melting from her expression. "I'm sorry, Ma. I met a new friend, and well, he wanted to pick up something at the store, that's all."

"A new friend. Does this friend have a name?"

Her daughter ducked her head. "Zachary."

"A boy."

"Yes, ma'am."

"How old is this Zachary?"

Lucy raised her head. "Fourteen. We're in the same reader at school. He's really nice."

"Why haven't you mentioned him before?"

"There wasn't anything to say. He's new to town." She clasped her hands in her lap. "I can talk to him. Really talk to him. He's not like some of the other kids. He listens to me, and I listen to him."

Katherine drew in a deep breath and let it out slowly, working to control her emotions. "You're too young to be courted, Lucy."

"Courted!" Pink spots blossomed in Lucy's cheeks. "He's not *courting* me. I told you, he's a friend. That's all."

Katherine stared at her daughter for a full minute, trying to read the truth in her clear gaze. She saw no hint of deception there, and the girl never wavered. "All right, I believe you. But from now on, when I tell you to come straight home, you're to do so. Understand?"

"Yes, Ma."

"Good. Now we need to get to work. Your grandmother is coming tomorrow, and her room isn't ready."

Lucy blew out an exasperated breath. "I forgot. How long is she staying?"

"I'm not sure, but it's possible she'll be here for several weeks, if not longer. Grandma has no one to take care of her, and she's alone."

"I wish Aunt June hadn't died." Lucy pouted. "It's not that I don't love Grandma. I do. But sometimes she's mean to you, and I don't like it."

"We must forgive and love her in spite of herself, honey, even when it's difficult."

"I know, but it's not right God made her that way."

"Lucy! God didn't make her that way. She's a grown woman and makes her own choices."

"But He could change her if He wanted to, and He hasn't."

Katherine struggled to find the words to comfort and reassure her daughter, but what could she say? She'd had the same thoughts most of her life and had shoved them aside time after time, trying to believe it wasn't God's fault the way she was raised. She couldn't blame Lucy for her feelings, although she hated that her daughter might grow up with the same resentments and doubts that had plagued her for so many years. "God knows what He's doing, sweetie. Grandma is … different, that's all."

As much as it pained her to make excuses for Mama, Katherine couldn't permit her daughters to find fault with their grandmother. Better that she set aside her own feelings and teach Amanda and Lucy respect for their elders. "We have to make allowances." She got up and patted Lucy's shoulder.

Lucy shrugged. "I suppose, but I hope she doesn't stay long, or I might just run away." She flounced down the hall and stomped up the stairs.

Chapter Three

Jeffery Tucker approached the door of the boardinghouse and glanced over his shoulder. Should he walk in or knock? Caution won out, and he rapped against the doorframe. When no one answered, he opened the door and stepped inside the long, narrow foyer that ran the full width of the three-story home. A desk built into a corner stood empty, and no voices echoed from the rooms beyond. Plucking the metal bell off the polished counter of the desk, he rang the thing, wondering how long it would take someone to arrive.

Removing his pocket watch from his vest, he noted the time. He'd had more than his share of waiting from folks who put little stock in courtesy and good manners.

Footsteps tapped down the hall, and the door to the foyer swung open. A slender woman with dark blond hair walked in. "Good day, sir. May I help you?"

He removed his hat and bowed. "Yes, ma'am. My name is Jeffery Tucker. The proprietor at the general store assured me your establishment serves fine meals, has clean linens, and is quite reputable. I'd like to inquire after a room, if I may."

She stepped behind the desk. "I'm Katherine Galloway. I'm pleased Mr. Snider gave us such a high recommendation, and I hope we'll live up to your expectations. How long were you planning on staying, Mr. Tucker?"

"That's yet to be determined, but at least a month, possibly longer. I'm not sure how long my business will keep me in town." He swept a gaze around the foyer and through the open doorway. "Is that acceptable?"

"We have four rooms available on the second floor, each with a single bed, dresser, small desk, washstand, and window, or a larger room with a full-size bed on the first floor. We also have two small rooms on the third floor, but it tends to get warm in the summer."

He twisted his hat in his hands. As much as he'd prefer a cooler space, he'd wager the larger ones would cost more. "I assume a smaller room might be the least expensive? If so, I'll take it."

"That's correct." She placed a book and pencil where he could reach it. "Would you sign the register?"

"Certainly. Might I ask if your husband will be home in the evening, or if you have other male boarders, Mrs. Galloway?"

The woman shook her head. "I'm a widow, Mr. Tucker, and right now it's my two children, my mother—when she arrives—and myself who live here full time." She accepted the pencil he held out and slid the book back into its slot. "By the way, breakfast and supper come with the room." She motioned toward the staircase. "Would you care to see where you'll be staying?"

"Thank you, I would."

He followed her up two flights of stairs, listening as she gave him the schedule for the meals and her home's simple rules. Satisfaction burrowed into his chest. Nothing too difficult and certainly nothing that would stand in the way of the business that brought him to town. Besides, Mrs. Galloway was an attractive woman, even though she appeared to be several years his senior. He might even enjoy his stay in this back-of-nowhere town more than he'd expected.

Micah slapped his gelding on the rump and stepped out of the stall. He'd hoped the physical effort required to unhitch and groom his mules would drive away the vision of Katherine Galloway's fear-filled eyes. His first glimpse into those blue, anguished depths—beautiful, even when brimming with agony—had lingered. Now guilt and disgust pushed the thought aside. Emma had only been dead for a year and a half. How could he be so callous as to notice another woman, regardless of the circumstances?

Loneliness … that must account for it. He'd had only Zachary's company for a while now, choosing to live as much of a hermit's life as possible, rather than chance the pity of his friends. Another reason he'd left Seattle. Too many people—all of them intent on bringing him out of his self-imposed exile. Living in the wilderness and staying away from nosey neighbors would be his preference for a peaceful existence, but he couldn't do that to his son.

So what if he hadn't attended church after Emma's death? It didn't mean he no longer believed in God. He was just—angry. Yes, *anger* described his feelings quite well. Why hadn't God kept that wheel from breaking as Emma drove her buggy down that steep hill? The Bible told all sorts of tales about angels. Couldn't He have spared one to save his wife when the buggy rolled and pinned her beneath its weight, crushing the life from her? His only consolation was that Zachary, who should've been with her that day, stayed home from school with a fever.

Micah walked up the stairs located at the back of the livery to the small, dark rooms he and his son called home. No cheerful voice greeted him. No fragrance of a home-cooked meal tickled his senses. Nothing but sadness, regret, and memories whispered in the deep reaches of night when he couldn't sleep.

He grabbed a pan from a hook and slapped it onto the stove, then gathered kindling and a match. Cooking wasn't his strong suit, but he could slice potatoes and onions and make a tolerable hash topped by a couple of eggs.

A whistle reached his ears right before the door at the top of the landing opened and his son sauntered into the room, a broad smile stretching his freckled cheeks. "Hi, Pa. Dinner almost ready?"

Micah thumped a bag of potatoes onto the table and pointed at his son. "You're late. You were supposed to help me load the grain bags after school. That was over an hour ago. Where've you been?"

The bright smile faded. "Sorry, Pa. Guess I forgot. I'll do better tomorrow."

"I don't have grain to haul tomorrow. You didn't answer my question." He jerked his head toward the bag. "Wash these spuds and slice them while I get the stove going."

"Yes, sir." Zachary tumbled some potatoes into the basin, poured a bucket of water over the spuds, then grabbed a cloth and scrubbed the dirt from the skins. "I was talking to … a friend … and we went to the store."

Micah heard the hesitation in his son's voice. He struck a match against the side of the stove and placed the flame beneath the newspaper he'd crammed under the dry kindling. The fire flared up, took hold, and gave a satisfying crackle. Swinging the door shut, he focused his full attention on Zachary. Not that Micah minded the boy making friends. He was glad his son didn't want to stick his head in the sand like his pa to try to escape the world. But it grated on him that Zachary had chosen to do so when chores waited. "Does this *friend* have a name?"

Zachary turned toward his father, his face scrunched and wary. "Lucy Galloway. She lives with her ma at the boardinghouse, and she's close to my age."

Something akin to a rock settled in Micah's stomach. *Galloway.* The pretty woman with the little girl was Mrs. Galloway. She'd mentioned a daughter who hadn't returned home. *Wonderful.* First, he nearly ran down her younger child, and now Zachary added to the problem by disappearing with the other one.

Chapter Four

Katherine willed her hands to stop shaking the next day as she glanced at the clock on her bureau for the tenth time in as many minutes. At least both girls were in school, and she wouldn't have to worry about them when Mama arrived. There was no help for it—putting off the trip to meet the stage wouldn't keep the inevitable from happening. She had thirty minutes before the coach pulled in, so she'd best comb her hair and hurry to town.

She'd need to stiffen her spine and stand up against Mama's pushy ways now that Daniel wasn't here to provide a buffer. Thank God for a father who had loved her and hadn't been afraid to show it. But he'd gone to heaven shortly after her thirteenth birthday and, if anything, Mama grew harsher after his death.

Katherine brushed her hair, taking careful note of her appearance in the oval mirror hanging above her bureau. Leave it to Mama to find a strand out of place and comment on it in public. She lifted her chin. She would *not* be intimidated by Mama. With a quick twist and a couple of pins, she secured her hair on top of her head, swiveling both directions to check for any wayward curls. Plucking her hat off a nearby peg, she carefully positioned it and then gathered her courage. When she realized her muscles were bunched, she shook herself, trying to relax. She was a grown woman, for goodness' sake.

She made her way downstairs, thankful no one was around at the moment. That new man—what was his name? Oh yes, Jeffery Tucker. Something about him intrigued her. Polite, tidy, and handsome in a rather austere fashion, he held a certain appeal, although he only appeared to be in his mid- to late-twenties.

Another face flashed … one much more rugged and down-to-earth than Mr. Tucker's. Micah Jacobs, who'd nearly run over Amanda with his team of mules. The man had barely spoken three sentences, and they'd been brusque at best. Why was she thinking of him?

Daniel had been the exact opposite. Studious but talkative, her husband had always offered a ready word of encouragement to anyone in need. Reading had been his passion. He'd laughingly admitted he wasn't good with his hands and was thankful the good Lord saw fit to make him a teacher, or they'd probably have starved, although he'd found extra work in the mines during the summer. A shudder shook her. She didn't want to go to that dark place in her soul.

What was she doing thinking of men at a time like this? Mama was enough of a challenge without dredging up more.

Katherine reached for the knob and jerked back in surprise when the door opened.

A diminutive woman in a gray cloak and matching hat with a dust veil drawn over her face stood outside on the stoop. Clutching a valise with one hand, she flipped up the veil with the other and frowned.

Katherine blinked. "Mama! What are you doing here?"

Her mother swept into the foyer, plunking her valise on the floor. She swung to face Katherine, her blue eyes snapping. "Since you didn't see fit to meet me at the station, I obtained directions and walked."

Katherine felt like wilting at the biting tone and withering glance but instead gathered her mother into a hug. "I'm sorry. I thought I had time before the coach arrived. I was headed there right now."

The embrace ended abruptly as the older woman pulled back and adjusted her hat, tucking a gray curl, which still showed an occasional glimmer of gold, under the dust veil. "Humph. Well, I'm glad to be off that rattletrap of a conveyance. Where are my grand-daughters? I've missed them."

Katherine briefly closed her eyes. Just like Mama. Not a single pleasant word for her younger daughter. At least her mother loved the girls and treated them well. Katherine could be thankful for that blessing, even if it didn't extend to her. "They're in school, but they'll be home directly. Would you care to sit for a while and have a cup of tea?"

"I've been sitting in that confounded coach for the past six hours, and every bone in my body is bruised. I'd like to go to my room."

"Of course." Katherine motioned toward the valise. "Surely you brought another bag? You can't have packed all you need for your visit in that."

Mama snorted. "Visit? Didn't you get my letter?"

Katherine's heart skipped a beat, then raced forward like a run-away team. "Only the one letting me know what day you'd arrive."

"I sent another a couple of days later. I sold your sister's house." She waved her hand in the air. "You have a large home, and I'm sure you could use help with Lucy and Amanda. The rest of my trunks and bags are down at the station, waiting to be picked up as soon as you can hire a wagon. Now take me to my room so I can be rested when the girls arrive."

Katherine set her hand against the doorframe to steady herself against what she feared was to come.

"I'm moving in with you permanently, Katherine. Your mama is here to stay."

Frances Connors waited until her daughter left the room before sinking onto the edge of the bed. She slipped off one shoe, then the other, rubbing her aching feet. It had been all she could do not to reveal the pain in front of Katherine. *Recurring gout*—that's what the doctor called it. Whatever it was, the throbbing had become nearly intolerable. But she wasn't one to complain and didn't care to burden Katherine with her problems. Based on the occasional letters she'd received since her son-in-law's death nearly three years ago, Frances had been able to glean that the girl had more than her own share of problems.

Frances carefully removed her hatpins and laid her headpiece on the nearby nightstand. A short nap might relieve the ache. Somehow she'd never envisioned growing older. In her thoughts she still swept through life as the beautiful seventeen-year-old she'd been when she'd married Ben, the love of her life. Of course, fifty-seven wasn't ancient, but the gray in her hair far eclipsed the blond, and her wrinkles were decidedly pronounced. Aches had sprung up in muscles and joints, and nothing seemed as easy as in her younger days.

Frances struggled daily with the consuming grief brought on by her daughter June's passing. They had shared a special bond.

And then there was Katherine. Frances sank against the feather pillow on the bed. Sharp edges, prickles, and Katherine's high expectations marked the relationship with her only surviving child. When young, the girl had been timid, so Frances had done her best to toughen her against the realities of life. Katherine needed to be more decisive and not allow so much to slip through her hands. Not meeting Frances at the stage was a prime example. Her daughter had obviously gotten distracted and allowed trifling concerns to get in the way.

Frances scowled. Weak women wouldn't survive in this hard country. She'd discovered that when Ben died. Marrying Katherine's father saved her and June from a life of destitution and misery, but he'd had his own issues. Yes, he treated the girls well, but some of his habits—well, no need to dwell on *that* with him long in the grave.

Rolling onto her side, she stuffed the memories where they belonged—far in the past, not in the present or future. She'd do everything she could to ensure Katherine survived on her own. Her daughter wouldn't make the same mistake she'd made, remarrying out of desperate need. Not if Frances had anything to say about it.

Katherine wandered through the house, her emotions flittering about like a hummingbird—hovering first on one problem, then another, and never quite landing on a solution. She'd almost forgotten how much turmoil Mama could create by her very presence. How would Katherine keep peace in her household and teach her daughters to respect their grandmother when practically every word out of her mother's mouth cut or demeaned?

Then there was the issue of money. The boardinghouse needed to bring in more business to pay its way, especially with another mouth to feed. A mouth that planned to stay.

Forever.

"I sold your sister's house.... I'm moving in with you permanently."

Katherine's stomach muscles tightened, and she feared she'd be ill.

She shuddered, hating that she couldn't welcome her mother's arrival and rejoice at Mama deciding to make her home with them in her final years. All Katherine could think about was the recurring pain that sliced through her every time Mama rejected her. Not that Mama would ever *say* she didn't want her—no, she viewed herself as too good a parent for that—but Katherine knew. Deep in her heart she'd always known that June was enough for Mama. Katherine had never been needed, never been wanted.

She grabbed a broom and commenced sweeping the kitchen, although she'd already given it a thorough cleaning that morning. Somehow she had to burn off her disquiet before Lucy and Amanda came home. The girls were her life ... all she had left of Daniel and the love they'd shared. She couldn't allow Mama's negative influence to touch them. They deserved peace and happiness, and she'd make sure they got it, even if it meant standing up to her mother.

Could she really stand up to Mama? For the girls' sake, she could, but the idea shook her to the core. Her stomach knotted further, and she dashed outside for some fresh air. She stood on the stoop as a wagon rumbled toward her, raising a cloud of dust in its wake.

The wagon slowed, and Katherine shielded her eyes against the sun. A tremor ran through her body as her gaze met the driver's. *Micah Jacobs.* Funny, she remembered his name so easily.

"Howdy, ma'am." He lifted a hand, smiled, but didn't stop the team.

She returned a brief nod. The man's quiet, rugged strength wrapped a mantle of peace around her spirit. Katherine allowed her lips to form a smile. "A good day to you, Mr. Jacobs."

At that moment she determined that, somehow, in spite of Mama, she'd find a way to make this a good day, come what may.

Chapter Five

A shadow fell across Micah's face, breaking his concentration. His chin jerked up, and he glanced toward the person standing in the doorway of his livery, silhouetted against the harsh glare of the early afternoon sun. Setting aside the buggy strap he'd been repairing for the grocer, he raised his hand. "Can I help you?"

A man who appeared to be nearing thirty and who was wearing dark trousers and a white shirt held his hat in one hand and extended his other. "I don't think we've met yet. I'm Pastor Seth Russell from Baker City Community Church, a couple of blocks from here."

Micah was surprised at the strength of the man's grip. "Micah Jacobs. What brought you by today? Something you need done?"

"Not a thing, thank you. I thought since you and your son are new to town, I'd make your acquaintance and invite you to join us for service. We're a small congregation but friendly. It's a good way to meet your neighbors."

Micah scrubbed his sleeve across his forehead and reached for a clean rag, stalling for time. He'd hate to offend this man, but the last place he cared to spend his Sundays was church. Not that he didn't believe in God. He did. But spending time under the scrutiny of well-meaning people who wanted to pray him through his problems didn't appeal. That used to be his way, but not since Emma's death.

He wiped his hands and face. "Sorry, I'm not really a church-going man, Pastor Russell."

"Seth, or Pastor Seth, if it's all right with you. I don't see the need to stand on formality in a small town like Baker City."

"Pastor Seth, then. And I'm Micah."

Silence stretched out, and Micah's shoulders tensed. Funny he'd have so much trouble talking to this man-of-the-cloth. At one time his pastor had been a close friend, and they'd jawed for hours on a number of subjects. Now that seemed a lifetime ago.

Pastor Seth appeared at ease, his hat tucked under his arm. With a gentle smile, he gestured around the barn. "Looks like you've made some improvements since you arrived." He nodded toward the rebuilt stall doors and the new anvil.

Surprised the pastor hadn't pursued his refusal, Micah managed, "Yes, I'm considering a bit more when I have the time and money."

"You're living upstairs?"

He nodded. "With my son, Zachary."

Silence again. Micah tried not to fidget. He needed to get back to work but didn't care to be rude. Seth Russell was being decent, and Micah owed him the same courtesy.

The pastor's smile grew slowly until it lit his countenance. "I'll be off then. I don't want to keep you." He gripped Micah's hand once more. "If there's ever anything you need—anything at all—my door is always open, whether or not you attend church."

Micah tried to keep his surprise from registering on his face. "I can't imagine I will, but thank you just the same. I appreciate the offer."

Pastor Seth headed toward the door. "God be with you, Micah Jacobs."

The words fell around Micah's shoulders like a warm blanket, but he shook them off. God hadn't been with him when he needed Him the most, and Micah didn't care to have Him start now.

Lucy slowed her pace and pivoted toward the footsteps slapping the ground behind her.

Zachary.

Pleasure shot through her at the sight of her new friend. How silly that Ma thought he was a beau. She'd been honest when she tried to explain that Zachary truly listened, unlike everyone else at school. Pa had always listened when she needed someone to talk to, but since his death, Ma seemed preoccupied and rarely spent time alone with her. Of course, Ma had her hands full with the boarding-house, and now that Grandma had arrived, Lucy knew things would get worse. She frowned and aimed a kick at a rock.

Zachary panted from running across the street to catch her. "What's the matter? You don't look happy."

"The last four days with Grandma have been hard."

"I don't have a grandma. I think you're lucky."

She hunched a shoulder. "Maybe. I guess I'm glad, but some-times she's not very nice."

"To you?" He swung his cloth lunch bag between them, keeping time with their steps.

"No, she's pleasant to me and Mandy. Mostly she's not kind to Ma."

"So was she your father's ma, then?"

"No. That's the strange thing. She's Ma's mother. But they don't get along at all." Lucy kicked a pinecone out of the way. "And Ma's never mean to Grandma. She lets her say anything she wants and never stands up for herself. Makes me mad."

"At your ma or your grandma?" Zachary cocked an eyebrow.

Lucy sighed. "I don't know. Both of them, I guess. I wish Grandma wasn't going to stay at our house forever. In the past, when she came to visit, I knew she'd leave soon … but not this time. And before, my pa helped a lot too. He knew how to talk to Grandma when she started getting upset with Ma. Now meals aren't very happy 'cause Grandma picks on Ma's cooking and the way she takes care of the boardinghouse."

"I wish I could help."

Lucy shook her head, then stopped. "Maybe you can." She grinned. "We only have one boarder right now, and he doesn't seem to notice the things Grandma says. Or he doesn't care—I'm not sure which. Anyway, if you mean it about helping, I have an idea …" Lucy began whispering in his ear.

"You did what?" Katherine planted her hands on her hips and stared at her older daughter, not certain she'd heard correctly.

"I invited Zachary and his father for supper tonight. They're new, and Zachary says they don't know hardly anybody yet. His pa hasn't even taken him to church; he works all the time."

"But why in the world would you invite them to supper? Grandma is here, and I've got my hands full."

Lucy's gaze flicked to the ceiling. "Ma, I thought you always said we're supposed to show hospitality to our neighbors and to people in need. Right?"

Katherine sighed. "Yes, but that doesn't mean—"

"Zachary doesn't have a mother. She died at least a year ago … or more … and he never gets decent meals. His pa can barely cook. Don't you think that's being in need?"

Katherine wasn't sure whether to hug her daughter for her kind heart or shake her for adding more work to her schedule without permission. Of course, it wasn't like they had many boarders right now, and their big table was less than half full most of the time, even with Mama. "I suppose."

Lucy squealed and threw her arms around her mother's neck, hugging her hard. "Thanks, Ma. You won't be sorry. Besides, you didn't like that I made friends with Zachary, so I hope you will change your mind once you meet him."

Katherine drew back. "This is the same boy you ran off with last week when you were supposed to come home and help me?"

"Y-e-s …" Lucy drew the word out with a worried tone. "You don't remember his name?"

Katherine's thoughts tumbled over each other trying to keep up. The boy Lucy had befriended was the son of the man who'd almost run over Mandy. The man who'd driven by in his wagon the day Mama arrived, who'd waved but hadn't stopped to speak. He'd lost his wife so recently? No wonder his eyes were hooded with sadness, and his conversation was short. "No. I didn't remember, but it doesn't matter. You're right. If he's a new friend, then I'd like to meet him. Especially before you spend any more time with him."

Lucy nodded. "I guess I'll go up to my room now."

"Oh no you don't, young lady. You invited guests; you're helping with supper preparations. Besides, you have regular chores, and you can't accomplish them in your room."

Lucy slumped and hung her head. "I know. Is …"—she glanced toward the kitchen—"Grandma going to help too?"

Katherine studied her daughter, wondering what was going through her young head. "I'm not sure. She's resting right now, but she may be down before supper. Why?"

"Oh, no reason." Lucy perked up and spun away. "I'll put my books in my room and be right back." She dashed for the stairs.

"Stop right there." Katherine stepped toward her. "Are you sure Zachary and his father will even come for supper without me having invited them personally?"

Lucy brightened. "Don't worry. I told Zachary to tell his father that you'd be proud to have them come meet our family and that you'd be expecting them at six."

Katherine blinked. "Expecting? You made it sound as though I invited the man! I didn't even know about the invitation until now."

Lucy's blond hair swayed with the vehemence of her head shaking. "But, Ma, you *are* expecting him, and you're always proud to have people meet your family. Right?" She bolted for the stairs, leaving Katherine rooted to the spot.

So a widower and his son were coming for dinner, and the man thought she'd invited him. Katherine placed her palms against her warm cheeks and looked down at her old housedress. Well, he'd have to take her as he found her, that's all there was to it. She was not in the market for another husband, and she'd make sure he understood that wasn't her intent before the evening was over.

Chapter Six

Micah tugged at his collar, trying to loosen it. Why had he agreed to this fool notion, anyway? All right, so he wasn't the best cook in town and a home-cooked meal didn't sound half bad. That didn't mean they should traipse over to some woman's house just because she wanted to be hospitable. Even if that woman *was* downright pretty.

His stomach rumbled, and he resisted the urge to slap it. Traitor.

Zachary had added to the insult by telling him it was high time they had something to eat besides stew, potatoes and eggs, and burned biscuits.

Micah stilled his hand. *Hospitality.* Wasn't that a word women sometimes used when they were trying to lure a man into their web?

Maybe they'd better stay home. "Zachary." He stalked out of his room and lifted his voice again. "Where are you?"

Zachary poked his curly dark head out of his room. "Right here. Why're you shouting, Pa?"

Micah scowled, then smoothed his features into a more pleasant expression. "I think we should send our regrets to Mrs. Galloway. You need to run over there and let her know we won't be coming to supper tonight."

"Why ever not?"

Blame it all, he hadn't thought that far. He ran his fingers through his hair and struggled to come up with a decent excuse.

Nothing surfaced.

Zachary, evidently sensing his hesitation, jumped into the silence. "We're supposed to be there in thirty minutes. You've always told me we shouldn't be rude to folks. I reckon Mrs. Galloway has dinner almost finished."

Zachary's common sense swept over Micah, and he slumped in defeat. There was no help for it. He didn't care to give the woman more work on their account, but if she'd already fixed the meal, it wouldn't be right to make her waste it either. "All right, we'll go. But we're not staying long." He set his hat on his head and shoved it down hard.

If Katherine Galloway thought she could set her cap for him, she'd better think again. It didn't matter that she was good looking and appeared to have a sweet, quiet nature. Appearances could be deceptive. Besides, *nobody* could take his Emma's place, and he didn't aim to let this Mrs. Galloway try. No, sir.

Frances tromped down the stairs, her head fuzzy from the late-afternoon nap. She hated needing to rest. Her joints hurt, and her body ached constantly—reminders of the advancing years. Why hadn't Katherine awakened her and asked her to help prepare supper? Her daughter had enough on her hands washing the linens for the rooms and cleaning this house, in addition to caring for Amanda and Lucy.

Dishes rattling in the kitchen drew Frances in that direction. Indeed, Katherine was busy preparing the meal without her assistance. Frances surveyed the room with grudging admiration. It was spacious and well lit during the daylight hours due to the large window set over the washbasin. It also had a water pump, a massive cook stove, and a multitude of shelves and cupboards. Most frontier towns didn't boast houses this fine. Why, Katherine hardly needed the pantry situated right behind the room. "Seems like a bit much, if you ask me."

She didn't realize she'd spoken aloud until Katherine whirled, hand over her heart. "Mama, you startled me. I didn't realize you were up."

"Been up for fifteen minutes. Thought you'd come upstairs to check on me and ask me to help you with supper, but it appears you don't need me." She turned, wounded that Katherine didn't care to include her in supper preparations.

Lucy came through the door from the pantry carrying two loaves of bread. "Hi, Grandma. You're awake. It's nice to see you."

Frances relaxed at the cheerful tone. At least someone in her family cared. "Thank you, dear. Where's your sister?"

"She's picking flowers for the table in a meadow."

Frances shot Katherine a startled look. "You allow a six-year-old child to go into the woods alone?"

Katherine reached for the bread as Lucy set it down. "I'll get this sliced, and you can put it on the table." She picked up the knife. "She doesn't need to go to the woods to find flowers, or even cross the road. This isn't the city, Mama. There's a nice stand of wildflowers blooming in a field near here. It's a short walk, and she's perfectly safe."

Frances sniffed, not especially happy with the reply, but what could she say? "What do you want me to do?" Frances looked at the pot of potatoes simmering on the stove, then opened the oven door. Waves of warm fragrance hit her, and her mouth watered.

"Why don't you sit and rest? I think Lucy and I have it under control."

"Nonsense. I'm not dead yet, and I just got up from a nap, remember? I'll make the gravy. June gave me her recipe. She always did make the best gravy."

No sense in waiting on her daughter to make up her mind. Frances opened a cupboard and withdrew a large cast-iron skillet.

Katherine turned her face away. "Fine, Mama. Have it your way. What did you mean when you came into the kitchen?"

"I don't know what you're talking about."

"You said, 'seems like a bit much.' What were you referring to?"

Frances waved her hand in the air. "This kitchen. There are more cupboards, drawers, and doodads than one woman will ever use. Seems almost sinful to have so much and certainly not necessary."

"I run a boardinghouse, Mama. I need to store a lot of staples for the times we're full."

"That's what a pantry is for. June and I ran a boardinghouse years ago. She didn't need this big of a kitchen."

"It came with the house, and I appreciate having the extra space." Katherine spun at the patter of light footfalls coming into the room. "Mandy. What did you find, honey?"

"Indian paintbrush and lupine." Her hand gripped the stems of the red and purple flowers. "Can I put them in a Mason jar?"

"Let me fill it with water first. Thank you for gathering such a pretty bouquet."

Amanda's little face beamed with delight. "You're welcome." She waited for her mother to place the jar on the table, then climbed up on a chair and carefully settled the stems into the water. "Grandma, isn't it pretty?" Amanda asked with a wide smile.

A rush of love swamped Frances's heart. "They're beautiful. You did a good job finding them."

Frances caught a brief glimpse of pain in Katherine's eyes before she turned away. Why wouldn't Katherine want her to compliment her granddaughter? Was Katherine so miserly she didn't want to share Amanda?

The front door closed, and then Mr. Tucker stood framed in the opening of the kitchen archway. "I hope I'm not late for supper, Mrs. Galloway." He held his hat in his hands, and his gaze darted from the stove to the bread Lucy was slicing.

"Not at all. You have plenty of time to wash up before we set the table."

"Good. I'd hate to miss out on your excellent cooking."

"Humph," Frances mumbled. "If you think that, you should've met my daughter June." She lifted her head. "Now *she* was a good cook."

Katherine ground her teeth to keep from saying something she'd regret. She caught Lucy's angry glance but shook her head. There was nothing to be gained by getting drawn into one of Mama's tirades. Best to let this type of comment go. Surely Mama didn't mean to be as harsh as she sounded. Katherine was determined to give her the benefit of the doubt and to try to maintain peace in her household if at all possible. But it stung, nevertheless.

"What, cat got your tongue?" Mama narrowed her eyes. "Or are you pouting again?"

"Of course not, Mama." Katherine dropped a dollop of butter into the potatoes and continued mashing. Maybe she could take her frustration out on the food. "Lucy, could you set the table, please?"

"Sure." Lucy slid a stack of china plates to the edge of the cupboard, then lifted them down and carried them to the table.

"Ma, someone knocked on the door." Mandy bounced on her toes. "May I answer it?"

Katherine wiped her damp forehead. Her heart sank. She'd forgotten about Micah Jacobs and his son, Zachary, during all the to-do with Mama. She bit back a groan. "No, Mandy, I'd better get it."

Trudging to the door, Katherine poked her hair into some semblance of order and brushed a bit of food off her apron. Their guests were early. She'd decided not to go to any trouble to make a good impression, but she hadn't planned on looking like a scullery maid. Picturing those deep green eyes again, she jerked her hand away from the knob with a growing panic.

What would Mr. Jacobs think, seeing her like this?

Chapter Seven

Shifting uneasily on the front porch, Micah snatched off his hat and gave a half-bow to the woman in the doorway. "Mrs. Galloway." He eyed her apron, then let his gaze travel up to her face. Dark blue eyes sparkled in the light of the setting sun, and loose curls tickled her flushed cheeks. She was prettier than he remembered. "I hope we're not early. Your daughter told my son …"—he nodded at the tall, gangly boy beside him—"to be here a little after six."

"You're fine, Mr. Jacobs. We eat at six-thirty." She moved to one side. "Please, come in and make yourselves at home."

He took a step back. "We can come back later. I didn't realize—"

"Nonsense. You're here, and several minutes one way or the other doesn't matter."

Micah wanted to glare at his son. Why had the boy urged him to arrive early? It was obvious she hadn't expected them yet. If only he hadn't allowed himself to be talked into this visit. "If you're sure." He pushed Zachary in front of him. "This is Zachary."

"How nice to meet you." She ushered them in, then took Micah's hat and hung it on a rack behind the door. "Why don't you and Zachary wait in the parlor while Lucy and I get the food on the table?"

"Is Lucy here, ma'am?" Zachary's face lit with an eager smile.

"Yes, she's helping in the kitchen." She seemed to hesitate, then gave a short nod. "The two of you might as well come with me. Maybe Zachary would like to help Lucy set the table."

"Sure thing, Mrs. Galloway." He bolted forward.

Micah grabbed his collar and dragged him back. "Mind your manners. Let Mrs. Galloway lead the way."

Zachary had the good grace to duck his head. "Sorry, ma'am."

She offered a tight smile. "I'm sure she'll be happy to see you, too."

Obviously his son had offended this woman. For goodness' sake. She had two children, and he doubted they used perfect manners. As soon as they ate and could free themselves of this obligation, he'd skedaddle on home whether Zachary liked it or not.

From the foyer, he traipsed down a long hall and followed her into the kitchen, scanning the spotless space. Emma had been a decent housekeeper, but nothing like this. Not a speck of dust or a single dirt smudge that he could see.

"You have a very nice home, Mrs. Galloway. Have you lived here long?"

"We purchased this four years ago, shortly before my husband died." Her lips compressed.

Micah wanted to groan. Apparently he'd brought up a painful subject. His second mistake. One more and she'd boot him out the door *without* supper. "I'm sorry. I didn't mean to bring up sorrowful memories."

She shook her head, the errant blond curls dancing next to her face. "Not at all. I'm the one who should be sorry; it's been a busy day. And since we're neighbors and our children are friends, please call me Katherine. All of my friends do."

Something fluttered in his stomach at the calm, gentle response. Maybe she wasn't upset with him after all. "I'd be happy to. And my name is Micah."

Katherine turned to an older woman sitting silently nearby, a young girl perched in the chair beside her, scribbling with a pencil on a sheet of paper.

"This is my daughter Amanda and my mother, Frances Cooper." Katherine swung her gaze back to Micah. "She's recently come to live with the girls and me."

The woman gave a sharp nod. "You can call *me* Mrs. Cooper."

Micah recoiled from the harsh tone, then quickly collected himself. "A pleasure, Mrs. Cooper."

Katherine's mother sat ramrod-straight, her eyes boring into his before they settled on her daughter. "You did not tell me you had invited guests."

Katherine visibly winced, and he thought he caught a flash of frustration—or possibly irritation—in her eyes before she averted them. "We have more than enough food, and Mr. Jacobs's son, Zachary, is a friend of Lucy's. She invited them to supper."

Mrs. Cooper seemed to relax. "Well, in that case …"—she shot an indulgent look toward the girl he assumed to be Lucy—"I'm sure it's fine."

Micah glanced at the young blond girl standing beside his son. Her fingers were curled into fists. The air was strung as tight as a bowstring ready to snap. He drew in a deep breath. "Something smells wonderful."

Katherine scurried to the oven, plucking up a cloth and opening the door. "Oh dear, I'm glad it didn't burn. With all this talk I almost forgot to remove the roast."

Mrs. Cooper crossed her arms. "June would never have allowed her meat to get dry."

"June?" Micah wondered if he'd missed something. From the closed expression on Katherine's face and the smug one on her mother's, it appeared it may have been better to change the subject.

"My elder daughter, who has gone on to her reward. That girl was the best cook in the territory, if not the country." Mrs. Cooper appeared to swell with pride. "She did her best to teach Katherine, but my younger daughter never took to culinary skills like June." She tsked. "Not that Katherine does a poor job at cooking. Her food is more than adequate and quenches one's appetite."

Micah's stomach sank at the hurt Katherine was obviously trying to hide. Mrs. Cooper seemed unaware she'd said anything wrong, and Lucy continued to stand like a statue.

Finally, the young girl broke out of her stupor and grabbed Zachary's arm. "Come on. Help me set the table. You can carry the glasses, and I'll get the flatware."

As Zachary scurried to do Lucy's bidding, Katherine bent stiffly to carve the roast.

Mrs. Cooper peered at her daughter. "I am not trying to be unkind, but your cooking does not compare to June's. There is no disgrace in that; it is a simple fact. No reason you should be upset."

Micah held out his hand for the carving knife. "I'd be happy to do that if you have something else you need to do … Katherine."

Her name felt right as it rolled off his tongue. "It looks as delicious as it smells. I can't wait to taste your fine supper."

When a tentative smile softened her face, his heart rate increased. He eyed Mrs. Cooper. The woman's brows were drawn in an angry scowl, and she looked ready to bite his head off. What had he walked into? Maybe his first instinct to hightail it out of here hadn't been such a bad one after all.

Katherine could have hugged Micah Jacobs for his kind words. They went a long way toward soothing the hurt created by her mother's blunt words. She doubted the man realized he'd stepped into the dragon's maw, but she knew well enough. Poor man. If this continued, he'd probably wish he'd stayed home and not been caught between two cantankerous women.

All right, maybe she wasn't the accomplished cook her sister had been, but did Mama have to point it out, in front of company to boot? Why did she have to be disagreeable all the time? Couldn't she compliment her just once or, if nothing else, not disparage her in some way?

But that was Mama. Katherine had heard her tell both family and friends that she was a frank, outspoken woman who said what she thought and people needed to learn to accept her. Katherine had never understood why others always must bend where Mama was concerned and why Mama couldn't temper her tongue and be more gracious. Well, it wasn't her place to criticize her elders in public, and little good it would do, anyway. She'd found it easier to let Mama's comments slide by with a smile or a laugh and pretend they didn't penetrate. Truth be told, each new one simply cut a deeper rift between them, and the scars thickened with each harsh word.

Giggling from the adjoining dining room drew her out of her thoughts, and she stepped toward the entrance. Lucy and Zachary were having a tug-of-war over one of her good cloth napkins. "Lucy! Whatever do you think you're doing?"

Her daughter whirled, consternation flooding her face. "Sorry, Ma." She took the cloth from Zachary's hands and folded it carefully, laying it on the sideboard. "We were done setting the table, and we got distracted."

"Please come dish up the potatoes and help me get the food set out." Distracted, was it? Katherine didn't care at all for where that little episode appeared to be heading. Lucy claimed the boy wasn't interested in courting, but she'd noticed the gleam in his eye. Her daughter might only be thirteen, but Zachary was over a year older, and she'd seen youngsters marry at the age of fifteen. She wanted better for her girl. Not that she didn't value marriage—she'd had a strong one herself—but Lucy was bright, and Katherine didn't want her daughter missing out on a future opportunity.

Why had she offered to let Micah use her Christian name? She didn't know him well enough for that, and it was unlikely they'd end up friends, even if they were neighbors. Guilt, that's why. He had obviously been uncomfortable when he'd arrived, so she'd done what she did with everyone—tried to make things easier for them. If she'd kept it more formal, it would be so much simpler to sever any ties the children tried to create.

Well, she knew one thing for sure. After this evening she needed to have a talk with Mr. Micah Jacobs about his son's intentions toward her daughter and let him know Lucy was too young for courting. Katherine had seen too many girls get caught up in what they believed was love … and ended in drudgery. She would see to it that did not happen to her girl.

After Micah complimented her cooking, she'd regretted her earlier irritation at having guests. Now she could see her regret was a mistake. She needed both Jacobs men to understand they had no future with the Galloway women—no matter how kind or conciliatory Micah Jacobs appeared.

Frances didn't care one whit for the events unfolding at her table. She tilted her chin in the air and sniffed. Maybe not *her* table exactly, but she *was* the eldest, and it was her home now too. Who was this man, and why would Katherine allow Lucy to invite him and his son to supper? She had enough on her plate feeding boarders who paid for their meals. Why invite two additional men who would probably eat more than their fair share of the food?

Only one reason that Frances could gather. Katherine was ready to replace dear Daniel in her heart, life, and bed. Daniel had been a saint, to Frances's way of thinking, and no man could replace him. Daniel had understood her when her own daughter hadn't noticed her needs. He'd cared for Katherine and their daughters with a tenderness that Frances had only experienced years ago with Ben. But even Ben hadn't lived up to her son-in-law. No. Another man could never take Daniel's place, no matter how handsome or seemingly cordial.

Mr. Jacobs had not liked it one bit when she'd mentioned Katherine's cooking not being up to snuff with June's. Good. Maybe Katherine's lack of culinary skills would deter him from pursuing her. After all, most men thought through their stomachs or …

Heat rose in her cheeks. That was one area she had never been comfortable with, and only by dint of wifely obedience had she conceived not one, but two children.

Frances peered at Micah Jacobs as he cast a charming smile at Katherine. The girl was attractive in her own way, Frances would give her that. It was the only place Katherine had outshone June.

But beauty was only skin deep, as the saying went. Katherine did have fine qualities beyond her somewhat good looks, but how many men would see past the external? Not many, she'd guess. It would pay to keep an eye on things.

Lucy tried to keep a sweet expression during the meal, but deep inside she was screaming. Grandma was rude, and Ma wouldn't stand up to her, no matter what she said. *Why* didn't Ma say something when Grandma made such hurtful comments? Sure, Ma preached that they needed to respect their elders and return love for evil, but Lucy didn't agree. If that was one of God's rules, He certainly wasn't fair. Having to live in this house for the next four or five years and listen to Grandma's criticism seemed an eternity.

And another thing—Ma had refused to let Zachary sit next to Lucy so they could talk. Why would Ma think he wanted to court her? Lucy almost snorted her derision. She was only thirteen, for gracious' sake! The last thing she cared about was courting.

Zachary met her eyes and smiled. He raised a forkful of potatoes in the air. "Your ma's a good cook." He cast a glance at Grandma. "At least, she's sure a whole sight better than Pa."

The remark brought a chuckle from Zachary's father and a frown from Grandma.

Mr. Jacobs leaned forward and spoke to Ma. "It's far better than my cooking, and that's a fact. Thank you again for asking us." He dabbed his mouth with the cloth napkin and placed it beside his plate.

Lucy caught movement out of the corner of her eye. Mr. Tucker was staring at Mr. Jacobs. She hadn't decided if she cared for Mr. Tucker yet, though he appeared nice enough. In some ways he reminded her of Pa, with his love of books and all. But he asked too many questions and never told anyone why he'd come to town. She and Zachary had talked about it. They figured he could be a bank robber running from the law—or maybe a professor from some big city who'd been spurned by his wife and had come here to grieve. Lucy considered that last thought again. He didn't look like he was pining for someone, so they could be wrong.

Mr. Tucker cleared his throat. "So, Mr. Jacobs, what brought you to Baker City? I understand you hail from Seattle. Have you always owned a livery?"

"No. For a time I worked in a mine but grew to dislike the dank air, so I returned to what my father taught me. Sometimes I

miss it, though—the hunt for gold or silver and the hope of strik-
ing it rich."

Lucy heard a quiet gasp from her mother. She knew exactly what
she was thinking. Pa had taken a summer job in a mine and been
killed in an accident. Ma hated anything to do with the trade. It was
a wonder they'd stayed here after Pa's death, but Ma didn't have a skill
and the boardinghouse promised to provide for their needs.

"Is that what brought you here, knowing it's a mining town?"
Mr. Tucker continued.

Mr. Jacobs lifted one shoulder. "Not really, although I'll admit
it's crossed my mind once or twice."

Great. Now Ma might never want to be friends with Mr. Jacobs.

Chapter Eight

Mama had managed to be rude again—and once more Katherine had barely slept. She rose early, not feeling a bit rested after a night spent tossing and turning. Micah Jacobs and his son excused themselves shortly after she'd served dessert, and she couldn't blame them. Between her mother's not-so-subtle comments about her cooking and her own coolness toward the pair, she was amazed they'd even agreed to stay for the meal.

She absently buttoned the front of her dress and pulled on her stockings, feeling horrible about letting her feelings toward Zachary color her behavior. Maybe if she hadn't already been so irritated with Mama it wouldn't have been such a struggle to keep her emotions hidden.

Breakfast wouldn't get made on its own, though. It was time to get to work. After starting a fire in the cookstove, she mixed a pan of biscuit dough. Maybe she was worrying overly about the two children, but the notion of Zachary and Lucy together made her tense. She didn't care for Lucy sneaking off to see the boy, nor did she approve of her inviting him for supper without her knowledge. Of course, nothing untoward happened last night, but she couldn't let it go. Katherine had hoped to speak to

Micah privately about their children, but she'd decided to let well enough alone for now. The poor man could only take so much in one evening.

As the heel of her hand flattened the dough on the floured work surface, she recalled the kindness in Micah's voice when he'd complimented her cooking, and she gave her head a brisk shake. Feelings like this were not allowed. Besides, the man stated he'd been a miner in the past and admitted he'd consider returning to it.

Then there was Jeffery Tucker. It was interesting seeing the two men together. During her first meeting with Micah, she'd assumed him to be taciturn and utterly rough, but his manners had been excellent, and he'd even held a cordial conversation.

But Jeffery Tucker was a bit of an enigma. His polished demeanor and obvious education drew her, but she'd not given *him* permission to use her first name. Something to think about, but not right now. She must hurry if she was to finish serving breakfast and arrive on time to the quilting session at the church.

Katherine worried her lip. She supposed it only right to invite Mama to attend, but she hated the idea. The small gathering of women had become her safe place—her refuge of support and friendship since Daniel's death. Allowing Mama to come would desecrate that somehow. Could she slip out of the house and not mention it? No. Her innate sense of honesty wouldn't allow that. All she could do was pray Mama refused.

Jeffery Tucker sauntered down the main street, hoping he'd find the right person. So far he hadn't turned up nearly as much information as he'd expected.

In the quiet of the early morning not many people stirred. He figured most of the men were working the mines and the women caring for their homes. Maybe late afternoon or evening would be a better time to find a vociferous soul who wouldn't be adverse to talking. He let his gaze sweep the boardwalk. A lone man sat outside the general store. Jeffery strode down the walk and stopped nearby. "I say, good morning, sir." He tipped his hat and mustered the most genial smile he could command.

A pair of shrewd gray eyes lifted. The man lowered the stick he'd been whittling but kept the knife poised right above his belt. "Same t'you, mister." He stared at Jeffery's black bowler hat and scowled. "You a city man?"

"Back East, yes. What might you be working on?" He ventured a step closer and peered at the chunk of wood the man held.

"Nothin' much. Just a play pretty fer my grandson. Cain't work in the mines no more, 'count of my bum leg." He gestured at the limb tucked under the bench.

"Ah, I see." Jeffery sized the man up. He must be at least sixty years old, with steely gray hair, a mustache, and dusty clothes. From the looks of things, he'd been working somewhere recently, even if not in the mines. "Care to share the story of what happened to your leg?"

The man glared. "Not especially. 'Tain't anyone's business but mine." He jerked his head in a semblance of a nod. "Have yerself a good day." He bowed his head back over his knife.

Jeffery had heard that people in the West were warm and hospitable, but somehow that didn't appear to extend to questions about their past or current business. At this rate, his mission here would stalemate, and he'd be stuck in this two-bit town forever. Of course, he could always move on to a city—back to the comforts he'd become accustomed to—but that wouldn't serve his purpose like this close-knit community.

Maybe move on to another small town? He shook his head. The residents would likely act the same. He'd have to keep plugging away with his questions and hope he'd find someone who'd give him the information he needed.

Micah Jacobs. He was an outsider as well. Maybe Micah could add to Jeffery's store of knowledge, limited though it was at the moment. He shouldn't be as reticent to talk about the area—that is, if he knew much about it. Jeffery's shoulders slumped. From what he understood, the man had lived here less than a month. He sauntered on down the street, keeping an eye open for any other likely candidates.

So far he hadn't tried questioning Katherine Galloway. His pretty landlady seemed open when he'd first arrived, but since the arrival of her mother, she'd changed—become closed and reserved. Of course, with a mother like Frances Cooper, who could blame her? Jeffery had kept to himself as much as possible since the woman's arrival, only taking meals at the house and spending the rest of his time in town or in his room. He'd looked forward to occupying the comfortable parlor of an evening, but butting heads with that strong-minded, sharp-tongued woman didn't appeal. Not even if it meant gaining the information he sought more quickly.

Too bad. He'd have enjoyed getting to know Katherine better. Her two children were well behaved and obedient and didn't lend stress to the atmosphere. Katherine appeared educated, and he missed discoursing on the great works of literature and poetry he so enjoyed. Maybe he'd stay around awhile this evening. Mrs. Cooper might retire early, and he'd have a chance to speak to his landlady. He smiled as he stepped up onto the boardwalk running the length of Front Street. That sounded like an excellent plan, and one he'd be happy to put into effect.

Katherine breathed a sigh of relief. The breakfast dishes were done, Mr. Tucker was out on an errand, the girls were in school. Once Lucy and Mandy had walked out the door, Mama had headed to her room, making it clear she wanted to read. All the better. Mama didn't care to be disturbed while she read, so Katherine could feel at ease making her way to the church. She removed her apron and folded it carefully, laying it aside, then donned her hat and slipped out the door.

The path from her home to the church wound between the outskirts of town on one side and the flower-strewn field where Mandy had picked her bouquet on the other. Katherine inhaled the alluring scent of rain-washed air. The light shower that passed in the night had settled the dust and perked up the flowers. Katherine waved at a woman who was hanging clothes on the line at the far edge of a yard. Even Mama's presence couldn't weigh Katherine down when the sun shone on her face and friends waited at her destination.

Three buggies were parked in front of the one-story white church. The townspeople were proud of their building, which sported a bell tower and didn't have to double as a school. The miners and businessmen, generous in their giving, had erected this fine house of worship.

Daniel had helped raise the walls, although he'd struggled with the work. He was more a man of letters than one to swing a hammer, but he'd wanted to do his part. She'd never understood why he'd felt it necessary to take summer work in a mine. It wasn't like they were poor. But he'd wanted more for their girls than what he'd had as a boy....

She pushed the memories back. No time for grief—she'd had enough of that in recent years. Today she planned to enjoy the two hours away from home. As the Good Book said, "Sufficient unto the day is the evil thereof." And, with Mama, Katherine knew trouble was one thing she could count on.

A voice rang out as her foot landed on the bottom step and Katherine turned. A tall, willowy young woman with flaming red hair stepped away from the hitching rail, grasped her calico skirt, and hurried across to where Katherine stood. "So glad I caught you before you went in." She drew Katherine into a fierce hug. "I heard your mother arrived last week, and I wasn't sure I'd see you today. Is everything all right?"

Katherine gripped her friend's arms and blinked back moisture. "Leah, you have no idea how much I needed that hug. Let's go in, and I'll fill in everyone at once." She opened the door, allowed Leah Carlson to enter ahead of her, then shut the door behind her.

A trio of voices greeted the two as they made their way across the sanctuary and over to a side room where the quilting frame waited.

Virginia Lewis waved a wrinkled hand, her weathered face breaking into a grin. "We hoped you ladies would make it today. Welcome!"

Twenty-year-old Ella Farnsworth raised her head and gave a timid smile. "Good mornin'." She shifted her weight to her other foot and laid a hand on her protruding belly.

Katherine moved close and gave her a gentle hug. "Is your little one causing discomfort, dear?"

A rosy flush colored the girl's face. "He's a bit cantankerous this mornin'. I think he's ready to see the world." She sighed. "But not near as ready as I am to see him."

Virginia laughed. "Why do you think it's a boy, Ella?"

She pursed her lips. "Guess the way he kicks and uses his knees and elbows all at the same time. 'Sides, Matt wants a son powerful bad."

Hester Sue Masters poked Ella with her elbow. "After birthin' four sons and two daughters, I'd have to say I agree with your Matt. Boys are easy to raise, compared to girls."

Katherine chuckled. "Guess I'll never find out, since the Lord blessed me with two daughters." She took her place behind the quilting frame, gazing at the colorful yellow, red, and white sunburst-patterned quilt they planned on sending to an orphanage. All the blocks were set, and the intricate stitching came next. She threaded her needle and admired the artful handiwork. "It's certainly coming together nicely."

Virginia straightened her spine and rubbed the small of her back. "I'm glad. Guess I'm not as spry as I used to be, and bending over this quilt for an hour feels like two. Not that I'm complaining. I love the fellowship with you ladies. But for the next quilt, I'm going to talk one of my granddaughters into helping so we'll finish more in the same amount of time. This fine stitching takes a toll on my eyesight."

Katherine patted the older woman's arm. "Your work is some of the best I've ever seen. Why, I don't think my mother could quilt any finer, and she was known for her exquisite creations back home."

Hester Sue drew the thread through a quilt square and narrowed her eyes. "I heard tell your mama has come to pay you a visit. She all settled in?"

"Oh yes. Settled and determined to stay." Instantly Katherine was appalled at the angry tone that colored her words. "I'm sorry. That was disrespectful."

Hester Sue snorted. "Not to my mind. You're speakin' from your heart. Nothin' wrong with that."

Virginia met the other woman's gaze. "I agree there's nothing wrong with a woman sharing her heart to her friends, but I also understand what Katherine means. The Good Book says we should honor our parents."

"I know it does, Virginia. But doesn't it also say someplace that parents aren't supposed to rile their children without reason? I don't rightly remember the whole verse, but I do know it's not all one-sided." Hester Sue drew in a deep breath and let it out slowly. "My pa riled us kids all the time when he got liquored up. Whipped us and hit our ma for no reason a'tall. A mean drunk, that's what he was, till the day he died. Not sure how you honor someone like that."

Ella raised her hand as though asking permission to speak. "I don't think the Bible says we're supposed to agree with what they do or even like it, but my mama always taught me we should respect our elders and forgive wrongs done to us."

Virginia poked her needle into the quilt and left it there. "You have the right idea, Ella. And it's not always an easy thing, especially when they don't deserve it. We've all met people who are hard to live with and get more crotchety in their old age." She patted the sides of her silver hair, which was swept back into a knot at the back of her head. "I have a head full of gray now, but when I was young, I always declared I'd not be one of those mean old ladies."

Katherine sank onto the stool behind her. "I wish Mama had made that decision." She almost hated herself for saying the words out loud, but if she didn't let them out in this safe place, she knew something worse would tumble out at home. "I don't know why Mama dislikes me so much."

Leah had been silent, listening to the other ladies share. Now she tapped her toe on the hardwood floor. "Are you sure it's you she dislikes?"

Katherine's head shot up. "What do you mean? I'm the one she criticizes."

"I was thinking …" Leah's head tipped to the side, her red hair glinting in the sun that streamed through the stained glass windows. "Maybe she's angry at someone else and takes it out on you. Was she a happy child? Do you know if she had a good marriage?" She pushed a wayward tendril out of her face. "I don't mean to pry, but sometimes when people have been hurt, it comes out as anger toward others."

Hester Sue shrugged. "Pa was downright mean. I don't think it's 'cause *he* was hidin' any hurts."

"But you never know, Hester Sue. Maybe his pa beat him, too." Virginia's calm tone flowed across the ripples of tension starting to form in the room. "Leah might be right, Katherine. Do you know much about your mother's past?"

"Not a lot. I know she worshipped her first husband, and it crushed her when he died. And my pa …" She clenched her jaw and hesitated. How much could she tell these women? Yes, she'd come to love and trust them, but would it do any good to air her family's dirty laundry? Yet she'd been carrying the burden for so long, and she longed to find a reasonable explanation for her mother's behavior— something that didn't point back at her, if possible. "I think she married my pa so she wouldn't be alone while raising my older sister, June. Then, after she found out Pa had a gambling problem and couldn't hold on to money, she lost all respect for him." She remembered something she'd heard her mother say years ago. "I don't think she got along with her own father either. I'm not sure, but I think he broke my grandmother's heart more than once."

A chorus of clucks and sympathetic voices surrounded Katherine, wrapping her in a cocoon of comfort.

"I see what you all are saying," she said slowly, "but I'm not sure Mama's past has much to do with how she treats me. From what I can tell, I've just never measured up to what she expected me to be—at least, not like June did."

Virginia slipped a slender arm around Katherine's shoulders. "We love you, child, and I'm guessing your mother does too. Maybe she has a hard time showing it, but you keep on praying and seeking the Lord, and He'll give you the key to unlocking her heart in His own time."

"That's right, Katherine." Hester Sue's brown eyes snapped. "Keep on prayin', but you mustn't feel you don't have friends. Anytime you need to talk, you come runnin' to us, you hear?"

Katherine smiled and nodded. "I'm so thankful for each of you." She leaned back over the quilt and stabbed at the fabric, trying to see through the tears clouding her vision. What she wouldn't give to have Virginia as her mother, or even Hester Sue with all her rough edges. She'd keep on praying, but somehow she couldn't imagine Mama's heart changing anytime soon.

Frances watched at the window as Katherine sauntered off the road and up the path toward the house. Frances had been puttering in the kitchen for close to an hour, making a special dish for their luncheon. Obviously her daughter hadn't cared to hurry home to her domestic chores, but they still needed tending. Another example of Katherine's flibbertigibbet ways—she needed to think things through before dashing off to wherever she had been all morning.

This boardinghouse was a huge undertaking, and if her daughter didn't do things right, she and the girls could end up in the street. Why, to Frances's way of thinking, Katherine didn't have nearly enough business to make expenses, much less earn the money to buy the necessities of life. Someone should set the girl straight and help her make wise decisions.

And she was just the person to make that happen.

Chapter Nine

Micah headed for the door that led down to the livery. "Did you make sure all the stall doors were locked?"

Zachary's jaw tightened. "Yes, Pa. I wish you wouldn't worry so much."

Micah nodded. "Good enough. Head to bed then." His son had worked hard lately, more than making up for the time he'd sneaked off with the Galloway girl. Of course, now that Micah had met Lucy at dinner three days ago, he could see why Zachary might be smitten with her.

Kind, quiet, and as pretty as her mother. He tucked the thought away. Emma had been the prettiest woman he'd ever known, and no one could take her place. Nor did he aim to go there.

He walked across the cramped sleeping loft to his bed, which was on the far end of the room, closest to the kitchen. The weather was beginning to warm, and the stillness of the air had kept him awake for several nights. Thankfully a wind had sprung up today, cooling the temperature in their upstairs quarters considerably. Maybe tonight he'd make up for the hours spent lying awake. He pushed his suspenders over his shoulders, then sat on his bed and tugged off his boots. Once undressed, he stretched out on the cool sheet.

Micah flopped over onto his side, relishing the feel of the bed. He was glad he'd asked Zachary to take care of things down below. Time to let the boy grow up and quit checking every move he made. Besides, sleep was dogging his trail, and he could barely keep his eyelids open.

Micah woke from a deep sleep, groping through leftover slivers of dreams he couldn't quite grasp. Had Zachary called and woken him from slumber? He struggled upright and listened, but nothing stirred. Maybe the terrifying nature of the dream had awakened him.

He probed the recesses of his memory. *Fire.* He'd been caught in a raging fire and couldn't find his son. Emma had appeared on the other side of the smoky veil begging him to hurry, pleading with him not to fail. But what had been burning? He shook his head, unable to grasp the fading image.

A drink of water would put him to rights, but he'd need to be quiet. No reason for both him and Zachary to be awake. He tip-toed across the room and into the adjoining living area. Something popped beneath his feet. He paused. There—the sound came again, louder this time. A horse in the livery kicking a stall? No, it didn't have the right tone. It wasn't a solid thump, but more of a crackle.

Suddenly the shrill scream of a horse rent the air. Racing to the door, Micah yanked it open. Smoke billowed in his face. Flames like those he'd seen in his nightmare licked at the wall near the foot of the stairway. For a second he stood frozen—had he fallen asleep on his bed and drifted back into the dark maze of his dream?

No. This was real. Too real.

"Zachary. Wake up. Hurry!" He sprinted across the room and shook his son's shoulder. "The livery's on fire, and we've got to get out."

Zachary bolted upright, his hair sticking out in tufts on top of his head. "What did'ya say, Pa?" The words were mumbled, and he scrubbed at his eyes.

Micah heaved the boy to his feet and hauled him toward the stairway, grabbing both of their boots as he passed the chair at the foot of his bed. "Run. Go find help. The barn's on fire." He yanked on his pants under his nightshirt.

Zachary's gaze widened. "Yes, sir. Aren't you coming?"

"Yes. Now hurry. No time to waste. I'll turn out the horses first." He shoved Zachary toward the open door and tugged on his boots, then ran down the stairs behind his boy, watching him until he disappeared. Thank the good Lord the stairs ended a couple feet from the back entrance, and Zachary escaped without harm.

Micah swiftly surveyed the scene. The flames he'd spotted earlier licked at a side wall and smoldered in a pile of damp straw. More flames crept along the floor following a trail of straw. He ran forward and kicked dirt across the blazing stubble. Maybe he could get this under control without too much problem.

He grappled with two choices: take time to turn the horses out, or fight the fire and hope to win before it got a firm hold. The stomping and neighing from the nearby stalls made the decision. He sprang into action. A couple of the animals belonged to boarders, and he couldn't chance their safety.

Running to the big front doors, he pushed them open, then jogged to the first stall. He swung it wide and stepped aside to avoid getting trampled by the frantic animal, but instead the gelding backed into the far corner, eyes wild and rolling.

"Come on, Roman. Out of there." Micah twirled a rope he'd picked up, hoping to encourage the gelding to run out the doorway, but the big bay reared and struck out at him. "Easy, boy. Come on." It took precious moments to edge around the horse and turn him toward the outside. Once the horse's head was pointed the right direction, Micah slapped Roman on the rump, sending him racing.

He ran to the second stall, tossing a glance behind him as he moved. The flames that had been smoldering in the straw had ignited full force and now blazed against the interior wall. The fire had climbed to the top of the stacked bales of hay and straw and licked at the ceiling timbers that supported the second floor. If help didn't come soon, Micah would lose everything he'd worked so hard for. How much time had passed since he'd sent Zachary on his way? Would he even know where to go in the dark, and would he be bold enough to pound on a stranger's door? *Please, God, don't let him try to run clear across town to his friend Lucy's house. It's too far.*

Another five minutes passed as he set the rest of the horses free. He flung his arm across his face, nearly retching from the thick smoke choking the air.

A shout sounded up the street, and footsteps thudded on the dirt outside the barn. "Jacobs, you in there?" Pastor Seth Russell stepped within the circle of light cast by the flames.

"Yeah. One more horse coming out. Stand clear." Micah opened the last stall door and chased the sorrel mare out of the barn. "Where's Zachary?"

"I sent him to ring the church bell." Pastor Seth called over his shoulder to three shadowy figures emerging from the predawn gloom, "Hurry, men. There's no time to lose. Get to the water trough."

Micah could barely make out the faces of the sheriff, a store-keeper, and another man he didn't recognize. He took a shallow breath and coughed. "You have buckets?"

Pastor Seth nodded. "Each of us brought one, and I sent some-one after burlap bags, but I'm not sure how much good they're going to do."

Micah peered in the direction the pastor pointed. The flames cracked and danced as they raced across the tar-coated ceiling, gain-ing a deep hold. Embers drifted through the smoky air, igniting piles of straw and hay. Micah dashed forward, eluding the pastor's extended arm. He had to save his tools. He couldn't afford to com-pletely start over.

"Jacobs, get out of there!" Seth's words echoed in his ears, but Micah ignored the plea. Only a couple more feet to his workbench. He yanked open the cupboard and reached inside for the big wood box that housed the implements of his trade. Tucking it under his arm, he swiveled as the church bell began to toll. A loud cracking caught his attention, and he glanced up. Just then a blazing timber, bowed under the weight of the flaming ceiling, crashed toward him.

Katherine donned a shawl and turned toward her mother and children. "I don't know why they're ringing the bell, but I might be able to help. Mama, you're sure you don't mind staying with the girls?"

Frances straightened to her full five-foot-two height. "Why would I mind? They are my granddaughters, are they not? Now go." She waved toward the door. "No sense standing here jawing about it."

Lucy grabbed a coat and jammed her hands into the sleeves. "I'm not staying here. I'm coming with you."

Katherine peered at her older daughter. Lucy's pale skin and wide eyes spoke volumes. "All right. But you're to stick close beside me at all times, no matter what. Is that understood?"

Lucy nodded and raced for the entry. "Hurry, Ma. They never ring the bell at night unless something bad happens."

Amanda tugged on the fringe of Katherine's shawl. "Ma? Why can't I come?"

Katherine bent over and whispered in her little girl's ear. "You need to stay and keep Grandma company, honey. You don't want her to be lonely, do you?"

Mandy's mouth rounded. "Okay, Ma. I will."

Katherine followed Lucy outside, trying to quell the nausea twisting her stomach. The bells had rung the day of the mining accident when Daniel died. *Please, God, don't let someone else's husband be lost.* As they picked their way carefully down the path to the road, gratitude for her mother's presence swelled in her heart. Somehow Katherine believed she must be there for whatever was happening, and Katherine wouldn't have felt comfortable leaving Amanda home alone.

Lucy picked up the pace the minute they hit the road. "Can't you walk any faster, Ma?" She lifted her chin and inhaled a deep breath. "I smell smoke."

Katherine sniffed and caught the odor of burning wood drifting on the wind. She clutched her skirt, pulling it well above her ankles, and raced after Lucy. They ran along the back edge of town, the sky glowing a dull orange against the horizon. Men's voices shouted above the din of the flames. They rounded the corner onto the far end of the main street. Lucy bolted forward, and Katherine grabbed her hand. "No. You're not to go near that fire!"

"But, Ma! It's Zachary's pa's barn, and they live upstairs." Her voice rose to a wail, and she struggled to escape. "Please, let me go see if he's all right!"

"Lucy." Katherine pulled the girl toward her. "Stop. We'll go together and see what we can discover, but you'll not leave my side. Promise me."

Lucy stifled a sob. "I promise. But hurry."

Frances paced the floor of the sitting room and stared at the clock. How long would it be before word came from town? She'd already tucked Amanda into bed, read her a story, and given her a glass of warm milk to entice the child to sleep, and still no sign of Katherine or Lucy. The bell had stopped ringing some time ago.

The hands of the clock said only thirty minutes had passed since her daughter and granddaughter had left, but it seemed like hours.

Maybe the timepiece had stopped working. She stepped closer and listened. Ticking. She sank into the comfort of a nearby chair, resting her head against the high wingback.

Katherine, Lucy, and Amanda were her entire world now. Nothing and no one else mattered. She'd had her differences with Katherine over the years, but she loved her girl with an unshakable passion.

If only she'd been able to accompany Katherine and Lucy to town ... but she knew her duty as a grandmother. Surely, whatever the problem was, it wouldn't reach its tentacles out and ensnare her two girls. She rubbed her hands against her forearms and shivered. First, her dear husband had died, then Katherine's father, then wonderful Daniel, and most recently, her precious June. *Please, God, let no one else in the family be lost this night.*

She doubted her heart could withstand another such loss.

Chapter Ten

Micah groaned and tried to get up, but his right shoulder wouldn't move. His thigh was bleeding, and something pinned his ankle. The end of the large rafter. It had fallen before he'd been able to leave and was resting across the lower part of his leg. His skin was on fire. He tried to push the rafter off his foot, but heat rose from the middle of the smoldering timber, which lay across his heavy leather work boots.

From the amount of pain, he guessed his leg could be broken and his shoulder badly bruised. And it looked like something sharp had raked his thigh. He placed his good arm across his mouth and attempted to breathe. At least the smoke wasn't as dense so close to the ground.

"Jacobs. Micah Jacobs! Can you hear me?" Pastor Seth's voice penetrated the smoke. "Are you all right?"

"Yes. But my shoulder hurts, and my leg is under a timber. It's too hot to touch, and I can't lift it. The rest of the ceiling doesn't look good."

"I'm coming in and bringing help." The pastor and Jeffery Tucker, the boarder who lived at the Galloway house, emerged through the gloom, each carrying a bucket of water. They dumped it on the burning wood that pinned Micah's ankle, sending trails of steam into the smoke-saturated air. Jeffery placed a shovel under the beam and hoisted it off to the side.

Seth leaned over, a damp cloth pressed against his mouth. "Let's get you out of here before this ceiling comes down around our heads." He beckoned to the man at his side. "Tucker, grab his other arm and help me hoist him up."

Micah grunted his thanks and winced as the pastor drew him to his feet. "Tucker." He emitted a long, wracking cough, his eyes streaming with tears. "Grab that box of tools?" He gestured at the box that had caused him to return. Even after hurting his leg, he had no intention of leaving it behind.

Tucker didn't question but scooped up the wood container. "Pastor, need any help?"

"We're good. Go." Pastor Seth kept his arm across Micah's back. "I hope that whatever is in there was worth risking your life for, man. Put this over your mouth." He pushed the wet cloth into Micah's hand. "Thank the good Lord you're alive and not more seriously hurt."

Micah stifled a harsh reply and did as he was told. If the Lord were truly good, He'd not have allowed his barn and home to burn. Now he had nothing. No wife, no job, and no home.

Katherine moved forward, still holding Lucy's hand. "There. I see Leah. Let's ask if she knows anything." They moved away from the line of men that raced from the nearest watering trough to the livery with buckets. One man frantically pumped the water while others dipped their pails and dashed back to the burning building. It appeared to Katherine to be a lost cause. The roof was engulfed and starting to cave.

Leah turned as Katherine and Lucy paused beside her. She drew them both close. "It's awful. Someone is still inside. I saw two men go back in."

Katherine wrapped her arms around herself. Visions of Daniel's body being carried from the mine overwhelmed her. Had Micah and Zachary perished in the living quarters upstairs, or had the townspeople spotted the fire in time for them to be saved? The memory returned of Micah smiling at her the day he'd driven his wagon past the boardinghouse. Sorrow tore at her heart. She'd entertained them in her home only three days ago, and now they might both be gone.

She brushed a tear from her cheek. "Do you know what happened?"

Leah shook her head. "Nobody does. Someone rang the bell, and everyone came running. When I got here, the fire had climbed the walls, and the men were dousing the closest buildings to keep it from spreading. There wasn't much they could do to save the livery."

"You live a half mile from town. How did you get here so quickly?"

Leah rolled her eyes in disgust. "Hunting for Pa again."

A shout went up along the line, and three men rushed toward the gaping doors. A man ran out the door lugging a large wood box. Close behind, a smoke-blackened figure leaned heavily on another man as they emerged from the barn. Eager hands whisked them from danger, but not before Katherine caught a glimpse of Micah Jacobs. Where was his son?

Jeffery peered back at the crowd as he deposited the box of tools on the ground a dozen strides from the barn. Looked like the pastor could use a hand with Jacobs. He hustled to the injured man's side and helped him hobble to a stump a good distance from the blaze.

Micah lowered himself with a grunt. "You got my tools?"

Jeffery nodded, irritated that the man cared so much for his tools and so little for his near brush with death. "Yes. The box is beside the water trough. I'll fetch it before I go." He was more than ready to get back to his bed since the townspeople seemed to have things under control. When the bell had rung its warning toll, he'd raced from the boardinghouse where he'd been trying to work. Sleep had been elusive earlier in the evening, but now he was drained and ready to drop.

"Tucker?" A hand touched his sleeve.

"Yes?" Jeffery met Jacobs's gaze. "You need something else?"

"No. But I didn't have a chance to thank you properly for helping rescue me." The man wiped a smoke-blackened hand across his face, leaving a dark streak on his cheek. "I've been so worried about my boy and my home that I forgot my manners. Forgive me."

Shame over his earlier thoughts knifed across Jeffery's conscience. "No need to thank me. You would have done the same."

Micah gave a curt nod. "Doesn't change the fact that you're the one who went into that fire. Thank you. Let me know if I can help you in any way."

"Think nothing of it. I'll go see if I can find your boy." Jeffery stepped away and scanned the crowd. No sign of the young man who'd come to supper with Micah the other night. Hopefully, the boy escaped the building in time. Zachary's death wasn't something Jeffery would want to use in his work, even if the rest of this night might be good fodder. All tiredness dissipated as blood rushed through his body in eager anticipation. He hadn't brought a tablet and pencil, but he'd not forget, even if he had to stay up half the night to write it all down. He mustered a smile. Nobody had been seriously hurt, and he was thankful for that, but there was nothing like a tragedy to get people talking.

Chapter Eleven

Pastor Seth shouted above the din. "Somebody bring water over here for Jacobs and rouse the doc if he's not here already."

Embarrassed, Micah held up his hand. "I'll be all right. They've got enough on their hands fighting my fire."

The pastor peered into his face. "It's your livery, but it's not *your* fire. We're a community, and we stick together." Seth dropped onto one knee when the silence lingered. "You seem like you're carrying a mighty big load beyond your loss here." He waved toward the smoldering building where flames still licked the wood and thick smoke boiled into the night sky.

Micah stiffened, trying to remember that this man had saved his life. He'd lost his livelihood and his home, and very possibly his son's carelessness had caused this fire. Another month or so into the summer with drier conditions and the entire town could've gone up in smoke. What *wasn't* bothering him might be a better question to ask.

He lifted his head and met the pastor's eyes square on. "Nothing I care to talk about." He bowed his head again and stifled a cough with his sleeve. "Have you seen my boy? Zachary went to get help and ring the bell, but I haven't seen him since I came out. Can you find him for me?"

The pastor nodded, then rose to his feet. "Of course. But remember, Micah, even when things look bleak, God's light can illumine the darkest corner." He pivoted and began to head across the street.

"Maybe," Micah muttered. "But right now I need to know my son is safe."

"Mr. Jacobs!" A girl's shrill voice penetrated the hum of voices on the street and Lucy Galloway skidded to a stop beside him, wringing her hands. Katherine Galloway followed a step behind her daughter, and another redheaded woman he didn't recognize stopped beside her. "Are you all right? Where's Zachary?"

"You haven't seen him either?" He tucked his injured arm against his side, grabbed hold of the hitching post rail with his good hand, and dragged himself to his feet, stopping to lean against the post to steady himself.

Katherine touched his arm. "You're hurt. Has the doctor seen you?"

He pulled away, frowning.

Her hand dropped to her side and she stepped back, a wave of red suffusing her cheeks.

A sense of desolation swamped Micah. So many people, all eager to help, but none of them able to understand the depth of his anxiety and inner turmoil. "It doesn't matter. I've got to find Zachary." He set his teeth and planted his foot on the ground, determined to search this entire town if he had to. Searing hot agony tore through his body. Biting hard on his lip to keep from crying out, Micah fought to relax his jaw before he drew blood.

His good foot swung out quickly, taking his weight, and he tried again. One more step. He could do this. One at a time. Pain lanced up his leg and he swayed, then started to pitch forward.

Katherine clutched his shoulders, and he caught a whiff of rosewater as his nose buried itself in her soft blond curls. She held on, allowing him to catch his balance.

The redheaded woman hurried to his other side and grasped his good arm. "Maybe you'd best sit down, Mr. Jacobs." Her firm voice brooked no nonsense, and with Katherine's help, they settled him on the edge of the boardwalk.

Katherine slowly released her hold, leaving him alone again in a sea of people. Those scant moments she'd held him the anxiety had lessened and he'd felt comforted and … what?

Connected.

For the first time since Emma's death, he'd once again experienced a true connection with another human being.

He ran his hand over his face. Foolishness. His emotions were getting the best of him. "Please." He met Katherine's compassionate gaze. As a mother, surely she'd understand. "Can someone try to find Zachary?"

A shock went through Katherine at the raw pain swimming in Micah's eyes. She wanted to hug him again and reassure him all would be well, but that wouldn't be seemly. Besides, who was she to promise his son would return safely when her own husband had died in a tragic accident? All she could do was pray and try to offer comfort if this didn't end well, but her heart longed to do more.

The ring of people jostling behind her quieted and someone bumped her arm. Lucy squealed and jumped forward. "Zachary! You're all right."

The boy smiled at Lucy, then knelt beside his father. "You're hurt." The words were strained and laced with alarm.

The anxiety eased from Micah's face, leaving it relaxed and almost at peace. He held out his uninjured arm and drew his son into a fierce embrace. "When you didn't come, I feared you'd gone back into the house." A shudder shook his frame. "Where have you been all this time?"

Warmth flooded Katherine's soul as the blacksmith held his boy. How many men would publicly show this kind of affection to a nearly grown son? In her humble estimation it took a strong man who knew his own worth to do so.

Zachary eased away from his father and rocked back on his heels. "After I rang the bell, I tried to find the doctor, but he wasn't home. By the time I got back, the livery had caved in, and flames were shooting everywhere. When I didn't see you, I feared the worst."

He shot a look at Lucy, then hung his head. "I kind of got sick for a couple minutes and didn't move." The boy turned back to his father. "Then Pastor Seth found me leaning against a tree and told me you were safe." His face contorted in a grimace. "How bad are you, Pa?"

Micah grunted. "Twisted my ankle is all, and my arm is throbbing. I think I'll be fine."

"But your leg is bleeding too."

"It's only a cut. I'm sure it won't amount to anything."

Katherine touched Zachary's shoulder, and the boy swiveled toward her. "We're thankful you and your father are safe, but I think he's hurt a little worse than he's willing to let on." She hated to challenge Micah in front of his son, but if she remembered anything about men, she knew Micah's pride might not allow him to admit his level of pain. Sure as anything he'd probably try to hobble his way back home....

Then she realized he didn't have a home. Neither of them did.

She plunged forward. "The doctor needs to look at you."

Zachary scowled. "The doc isn't home. Someone told me he's tending a man at a mining claim and might not be back before morning."

Katherine nodded. "That settles it, then. Both of you are coming to the boardinghouse with me."

Micah's mouth gaped, and he snapped it shut. Go home with her? Why ever would he want to do that? He shifted his weight and grimaced as his shoulder and ankle gave him sharp reminders. Good thing he'd worn lace-up boots or—if the ache and swelling were any indication—he'd probably have had to cut the boot off later.

Zachary placed his hand on his arm. "Pa?"

"Yes?" He knew what was coming. The boy was smitten with Lucy and would push him to stay there till they could find a new place to live. Well, he wouldn't think of it. No, sir. It wasn't fitting ... Katherine Galloway being a single, attractive woman and all.

"Why did the barn burn down?" Worry clouded the boy's face, and his voice trembled.

Micah swallowed the harsh lump in his throat and scrambled to find an answer. He had little doubt his son had left a lantern burning, but this wasn't the time to speak the words. Not with strangers standing around. "I'm not sure. We may never know."

Zachary nodded slowly, but the confusion lingered. "Do you think …?"

"Let's not worry about it now, Son." He turned to Katherine, anxious to get the boy's attention off the fire. "You have a room at your boardinghouse available then?" Suddenly he realized the cash money he'd stashed in his room would've burned with the rest. If he was lucky, he might find a handful of silver after the charred boards cooled. "I'm sorry. I can't take charity."

Her brows rose a fraction. "Yes. I have several rooms available right now. Please don't worry about payment. That's what neighbors are for."

He tried not to scowl. "I won't come unless I pay my way, and until I start working again, that won't be possible."

"I'm sure we can work it out when you're feeling better."

"I'll expect to sign a note and reimburse you. I won't change my mind."

"Fine, Mr. Jacobs." The warmth in her voice faded. "I'd hate to have your pride get in the way when you're hurt, so I'll agree to take your money. The doctor can see you there."

"Like I told you before, I don't need a doctor. Can't everyone let me be and quit worrying?"

Katherine gripped Lucy's arm. "I'll go on ahead and get your room ready." She stalked off, her posture stiff.

Micah shook his head. What in tarnation put her in such a huff? A man had to keep a bit of pride intact, didn't he? From the look of things he'd offended Katherine Galloway yet again.

Hopefully his leg wasn't broken and he could start rebuilding soon. In fact, living in a tent sounded downright pleasant compared to the alternative.

Lucy tugged against her mother's grip, anxiety mixing with anger at the distance they were putting between her and Zachary. She hadn't even gotten a chance to speak to her friend, and now Ma was storming home with a bee in her bonnet. At least she knew Zachary was safe.

"Ma!" Lucy dug in her heels a block away from home, dragging her mother to a halt.

"What?" Ma swung around and glared, yanking her wrist from Lucy's grip.

"What's got you so riled? You were rude to Mr. Jacobs, storming off like that. And you didn't even tell Miss Carlson good-bye."

Her mother's breath rushed out in a whoosh. "Leah. Oh, my gracious. I can't believe I left her standing there with that man."

"That man? Ma, he was injured and almost died in the fire, and he was worried sick about Zachary." Lucy didn't care that her voice raised a notch or two. She'd take the scolding for being disrespectful if it came to that, but Ma needed to hear what she had to say. "You got mad at him for nothing."

Ma rounded on her. "You don't know what you're talking about, young lady. I offered him a place to stay, and I didn't intend to charge him, not after he'd lost his home *and* his livelihood. But no, his pride won't let him accept kindness. He'll pay me or not come. Then when I suggest the doctor stop to see him, he throws that in my face as well."

Lucy took a step back, a step away from her mother's anger.

Suddenly, Ma slumped and waved her hand. "I'm sorry. Let's walk back to the house like two civilized people."

The silence stretched as they strolled at a more dignified pace through the moon-drenched night, toward the brightly lit boardinghouse.

Lucy peeked at her mother. She no longer strode with her chin up but with lagging steps. Pity surged through Lucy's heart, and she wanted to hug her. Was Ma thinking about the night Pa died? Was that why she wanted to help Mr. Jacobs and Zachary, because she hadn't been able to help Pa? But she shouldn't get mad at him for not accepting charity. Lucy didn't know many men who would.

"Ma?"

"Hmm?" Ma slipped her hand into Lucy's.

Peace flowed through Lucy, and she squeezed Ma's fingers. "Nothing. I love you, Ma."

"I love you, too, Luce girl."

"Are you going to stay mad at Mr. Jacobs?"

"I reckon not. Unless he gets cantankerous or his pride flares up again. Then I might." She grinned and Lucy giggled, then sobered.

"It was real nice of you to offer to let them stay. I feel bad they lost their home and the livery." Her stomach lurched. After losing Pa, the most important things in her life were her home, mother, and little sister. Losing any of them would tear her heart out. No wonder Mr. Jacobs was cranky. "He was awful nice to Zachary when he came back. I was worried he might shout at him for being gone so long, but he only hugged him. I thought for a minute he was going to cry."

Her mother didn't speak, only gripped her hand a bit harder. Lucy knew what that meant. Ma wanted some time to think and not talk, which was all right with her. She had a lot to think about herself. Part of her wanted to shout for joy that Zachary was coming to stay at their house, but the other part was a little concerned.

Grandma hadn't seemed to like Mr. Jacobs very well, and before tonight, Mr. Jacobs had been really nice to Ma. What if Grandma was mean to him? She frowned and almost pulled her hand away but knew Ma would question her if she did. Scuffing her toe against the dirt as she walked, Lucy stared off into the night.

They had enough upset at their house as it was, ever since Grandma had come. What if Mr. Jacobs went back to being really nice and Ma started to like him too much? It wasn't that Mr. Jacobs wasn't a decent man from what she could tell, but he was *Zachary's* pa—she didn't want him for hers.

Chapter Twelve

Home never looked so good, but Katherine couldn't go to bed yet. She opened her front door as the clock on the mantle chimed midnight, and Lucy yawned. Patting her daughter's back, Katherine smiled. "You'd best go right up to bed, sweetie. Morning's coming all too soon."

"Yes, Ma. Are you coming?" Lucy placed her hand on the newel post at the bottom of the stairs.

"Soon. I'll see if Grandma is in bed or waiting up. I need to thank her for staying with Amanda."

"All right. Good night."

"'Night, honey." As she watched her elder daughter climb the staircase, she couldn't thank God enough that she and Lucy had such a wonderful relationship, quite unlike hers and her mother's. But Katherine had worked hard to keep the doors of communication open with Lucy and bathe her actions in love— not something she'd experienced from her own mother while growing up.

Katherine simply absorbed the quiet for a minute. Closing her eyes, she took a deep breath, trying to release all the worry, fear, and irritation that had assailed her this night. So much had happened since leaving only an hour or two ago. Micah Jacobs's home and business had burned to the ground, and she'd invited him and his son to live here. Of course, she did run a boardinghouse, so it wasn't as though she'd done anything immoral, but tongues might still wag. It didn't appear that the man truly appreciated what she'd done, either. If she could do it over again, she was certain she'd make a different choice.

A sudden image of the pain she'd seen reflected in Micah's eyes drew her up short. How could she deny someone who'd lost so much and had no place to go? She couldn't and regretting the offer wouldn't accomplish anything.

What would Mama think?

Not that it was Mama's business.

After all, Katherine *was* a grown woman who could manage her own affairs, wasn't she?

Katherine brushed a loose curl from her forehead and headed toward the kitchen. Weariness settled in. It was past time for bed, but she'd promised Micah and Zachary a room. Thankfully she had clean bedding in the downstairs room already and didn't need to do much but fill the water pitcher and turn down the covers. Surely Mama had gone upstairs after tucking Amanda in, but she'd best check.

She stepped through the doorway of the dining room and peered into the kitchen. The light was dim and nothing stirred— only shadows danced on the walls.

A chair scraped across the floor. "Katherine? I did not hear you come in. Are you and Lucy all right?" Mama rose from the far end of the table where she'd been sitting in the deepest shadow.

Katherine pivoted, placing her hand over her rapidly beating heart. "You gave me a start. I thought you'd gone to bed long ago."

A strange look flitted across the older woman's face, then quickly disappeared. "You have been away longer than I expected. I was not able to sleep."

Irritation? Or worry? But why would Mama be troubled about her and Lucy? They hadn't been in danger. Besides, her mother rarely showed emotions that indicated she cared. On the other hand, Lucy was her granddaughter, and she may have been anxious for her sake.

"I'm sorry if we worried you."

"Nonsense." Frances drew herself to her full height and frowned. "I simply could not sleep with all the commotion in town and you out wandering the streets. What happened? Why did they ring the bell?"

"You remember Mr. Jacobs and his son, Zachary, who came to dinner a few nights ago?"

"Of course. I am not in my dotage, Katherine. What do they have to do with anything?" Mama scowled.

Katherine motioned toward the table. "Would you like to sit down?"

"No. Tell me what happened and I will go to bed."

"The livery burned down."

Mama placed her fingers over her mouth. "They didn't die, did they? How awful."

Katherine's heart twisted at her mother's expression. She shouldn't have been so blunt. She should've started by telling her no one was hurt. Why didn't she think before she spoke? It was one of the many things Mama had chastised her for over the years. "No, I'm sorry. They're both safe, but their home was above the livery, and they lost everything. Mr. Jacobs may have sustained a broken leg."

A man's voice halting a team of horses sounded outside the window.

"I didn't expect them so soon." Katherine ran to the window and peered out. "I invited Mr. Jacobs and his son to stay in an empty room. What was I thinking standing here talking?"

Her mother harrumphed. "That is exactly what I would like to know. What *were* you thinking asking that man and his son to stay? If he has lost his business and home, it is likely he will not be able to pay. You cannot run a charity and hope to feed your family, Katherine. I always said you were too impulsive, and now you have proven it again." She strode toward the hallway without looking back.

Katherine balled her hands into fists, wanting to scream. Should she go after her mother and try to explain? It wouldn't make a difference, as Mama wouldn't listen anyway.

Instead, she uncoiled her fingers and pasted what she hoped would pass as a smile on her tired face. Time to greet her new boarders and get them to bed before the rooster crowed his early morning song.

How did life get so complicated? First Mama arrived, and now Katherine had to contend with a pride-filled man. Two people with prickly skin living under her roof, and from what she observed when Micah and Zachary came for supper, Mama wasn't cheerfully disposed toward the Jacobs. *Please, God, let things calm down and not get worse.*

Then a precious memory of the tender moment she had shared with Lucy surfaced. At least she didn't have to worry about her daughter now that she'd made it clear Zachary was not allowed to court her. Or had she? Katherine tried to remember. She'd planned on talking to Micah about his son. It had never happened.

A knock sounded on her door. Katherine's heart sank. She'd invited that young man to live here without setting any boundaries concerning her daughter.

Chapter Thirteen

Micah eased himself up off the pillow and groaned. His ankle throbbed, and mush seemed to have replaced his brains. He sucked in a lung-full of air, and pain shot through his chest, ending in a hard cough. He fought to regain his breath.

Once his breathing returned to normal, he glanced around the room. Bright morning sunlight streamed between gauzy white curtains that flanked a window near the foot of his bed. This didn't look like his room. He caught a faint whiff of lavender and smiled—it didn't smell like his room either.

Memories trickled in as he admired the flowers artfully arranged in a vase on the tall oak bureau on the far side of the window. He'd injured his ankle when a beam fell on him during the fire.

Fire? Micah fell back against the pillow. His home and business had burned last night and Zachary ...

He sat up so fast a wave of dizziness nearly pitched him to the floor. Why couldn't he remember if Zachary was safe? Panic rose in his throat, threatening to choke him. He grabbed the blanket covering his body and tossed it aside. "Zachary? Where are you?"

Feet padded on the hardwood floor outside his room, and the door flew open. A blond vision with pink cheeks and swirling skirts swept into the room. Katherine Galloway halted, regarding him with wide eyes. "Mr. Jacobs, I heard you call. Are you all right?"

A twinge of embarrassment tugged at Micah as he drew the sheet to his chin. He licked his dry lips. "Where's my son? Is Zachary all right?"

Katherine's posture relaxed. "He's fine. I put him to bed in another room, as you were tossing and turning, and I didn't think he'd sleep." She smoothed a wayward lock off her forehead. "I believe he's still sleeping. Zachary was very worried about your injury and convinced he was somehow to blame."

Micah struggled to recall something outside of his grasp. "How did the fire start?"

Katherine's brows rose. "You don't know? Everyone's been asking the same thing, wondering what happened. We were all waiting for you to wake this morning, hoping you could tell us."

Beads of perspiration formed on Micah's forehead. "No. I remember turning out the horses and the beam falling." He narrowed his eyes and concentrated. "I was worried Zachary might have gone back inside—ah, yes. He found me after the pastor got me out." Another memory surged to the fore, and he stiffened. "You told me I could stay here and …" He hesitated. "I'm afraid I didn't show any appreciation for your kind offer. I hope you'll forgive me."

Her expression softened. "There's nothing to forgive. I may have been a bit … prickly … last night. Fear has that effect on me, I'm afraid." She backed toward the door, her slender fingers wrapping around the knob. "I'll leave you alone now, and let you rest awhile longer. If you'd like, I'll bring you coffee and breakfast soon."

Micah pushed himself a few inches off the mattress and winced. "I need to get up and see what's left of my home and business."

Frances Cooper stepped up beside Katherine, a glower puckering her wrinkles. "You will do no such thing, young man. Not if you hope to get well enough to provide for yourself again."

"Mama, please!" Katherine gaped at her mother, and a wave of crimson stained her cheeks. "Mr. Jacobs has no need to rush back to work." She placed a gentle hand on her mother's arm. "Come, let's get breakfast started. I agree that our guest needs to rest. Please, Mr. Jacobs, don't try to get up until after the doctor has seen you."

Conflicting emotions swirled through Micah. How could a mother and daughter be such complete opposites in temperament and behavior? Katherine Galloway resembled her mother in coloring and bone structure, but that was where the similarity ended, from what he could tell during the little he'd been around them. One was abrasive and appeared to delight in dishing out her opinion and remarks with a free hand, caring little who heard or how the remarks might affect the listener. Her daughter, while certainly not a doormat—as evidenced by her prickly attitude the evening before—maintained an air of genuine caring. "All right. I'll stay here for now, but I'd appreciate you sending Zachary in as soon as he wakes."

"Certainly." A smile flitted so quickly across Katherine's face that Micah wasn't certain he'd seen it. "Come along, Mama. I could use your help in the kitchen."

Frances allowed herself to be led away, but her voice drifted back clearly. "You have not wanted my assistance before. Of course, I am happy to help, as I know you have a hard time keeping up. In fact, I have a plan that I am certain will please you."

Micah strained to hear more but the voices dimmed as the footsteps receded in the distance. Somehow he couldn't imagine much that woman shared would bring pleasure to anyone around her.

Katherine kept her back ramrod straight as she walked in front of her mother toward the kitchen. Knowing Mama, if she let her discouragement show through bowed shoulders she'd hear about it in not-so-subtle words. Her chin jerked up at another thought. *Why* should she be discouraged? After all the little comments her mother dropped, she should be irritated, not depressed. In fact, she *was* irritated—and frustrated and tired, all rolled into one tangled ball.

A plan that would please her, indeed. And since when did she have a hard time keeping up where her home or children or business were concerned? Well, there was no help for it. Mama would say what she wanted to say, whether Katherine cared to listen or not. She'd been taught since her earliest memory to respect her elders and never talk back. That had always been the way of things and probably would be until the day she breathed her last.

Stepping across the threshold into the spacious kitchen, Katherine reached for her apron, which hung from the corner of the cupboard where she'd tossed it not long ago. She removed a sturdy bowl from the tall corner cabinet and placed it on the painted countertop, then slid out a drawer to remove a tin of flour.

"What do you want me to do, Katherine?" Mama cast a glance around the room.

Katherine sent a swift prayer heavenward in hopes the subject that would please her had somehow been forgotten. How blessed it would be spend an hour with Mama without some type of rebuke or criticism. "Maybe you could crack and whip a dozen eggs for me. I'm making biscuits and gravy, and we'll have scrambled eggs on the side."

"Only a dozen? You are feeding eight people this morning, what with that man and his son you have taken in, as well as your own family, Mr. Tucker, and that traveling salesman who stopped in last night."

"We have another boarder? When did he arrive?" Katherine's hands paused in kneading the dough.

"Late last night while you were gone. In all the excitement I forgot to mention it. I gave him one of the rooms on the second floor. He is leaving after breakfast." Frances plucked the wire basket of eggs from the back corner of the cabinet and set them carefully on the counter. "You need more rooms, more sheets, and new towels. You have this great big kitchen and a dining room that is only occasionally full. How do you expect to hold onto this house if you don't make enough money?"

"I'm doing fine, Mama. The towels are only two years old, and the sheets are holding up all right. As for new rooms, adding on costs too much. Besides, we're not full every night, so I don't see it as an issue."

Frances cracked an egg on the edge of the stoneware bowl she'd set in front of her and tossed the shell into the nearby box of scraps.

Katherine grimaced but decided to hold her tongue. Telling Mama that the refuse bin was only for food scraps would ruffle her feathers. Better to pluck them out later when she wasn't looking.

"I told you I have a plan. Don't you want to know what it is?" Another shell landed in the box, and Frances grabbed a fork and commenced beating the eggs.

"Certainly." Then Katherine pinched her mouth shut to keep everything else she wanted to say from spilling out.

"You do not sound terribly interested."

"I'm sorry. I suppose I'm a little distracted with all that's happened. Please, tell me."

Frances set down the fork. "I have some money set aside. I am going to invest in your business and help you run this place. I am sure with my help it will prosper beyond what you could accomplish yourself."

Katherine struggled to comprehend her mother's words. Invest and help run the boardinghouse? Take over all decision-making was more like it. From her mama's expectant expression Katherine could tell she expected the news to be greeted with joy and approval. She gritted her teeth. Why couldn't it be enough that she'd given her mother a home? Why did she have to swoop in and try to take control of every part of her life? The next thing she knew, Mama would be disciplining her children and giving orders to the guests.

No. This had to stop somewhere. But how to tell Mama when she obviously thought she was doing Katherine a favor? The problem was, Mama's favors always came with a price.

Frances's smile faded as the silence stretched and her daughter made no move to break it. What was wrong with the girl? Didn't Katherine understand what a generous offer she'd made? You certainly wouldn't think so based on the set of her shoulders or the grim look on her face. "Aren't you going to say something? I would think you could at least thank me for taking an interest in your boardinghouse and wanting to see to your needs, not to mention my granddaughters'."

Katherine dipped her head and dusted her flour-coated hands on her apron. "Yes, of course. Thank you for your"—a fraction of a second passed—"kind offer."

Frances tried her hardest to give a winning smile. "So you accept? We will make your business a success together."

"I'm afraid not, Mama. I'm not ready to expand yet, and when I do, I'd like to manage it on my own. This boardinghouse was Daniel's dream, and I want to honor his memory in how I conduct my business."

"And you think it would *dishonor* his memory to have me involved—is that what you are saying?" Pain ripped at her heart at her daughter's reply. Katherine never appreciated her efforts to help.

Of course she would do things the way Daniel had wanted—within reason, of course. She had loved her son-in-law dearly. As far as she was concerned, marrying him was the only truly sensible thing Katherine had done in her life. Well, besides giving birth to Lucy and Amanda, but that was as much Daniel's doing as Katherine's.

Katherine reached out a hand, but Frances took a step back. "I'm sorry, Mama. I didn't mean to hurt you. Maybe we can talk about this another time when I'm not so distracted."

"So you can turn me down again, you mean?" Frances wanted to bite her tongue at the confusion and hurt reflected on her daughter's face, but she dared not retract her words. Katherine needed to think before she made such rash remarks and coddling her would not help that to happen.

Katherine's expression turned cold. "If that's what you think, Mama, we'll not talk about it again."

"Grandma?" Amanda skipped into the room and came to a halt at the end of the cupboard. "What are you fixing for breakfast? I'm awful hungry."

Frances drew the little girl into her arms, struggling to push back the ache in her throat and praying her words would come out sounding normal. "Scrambled eggs, and they will be ready soon. Go wash your hands." She gave her a little push, but the child didn't budge. "Hurry up. There's to be no dawdling, Amanda." She'd spoken more sharply than she'd planned. She hated the idea of hurting Amanda. Drawing in a deep breath, she nudged the child toward the sink again.

Katherine took a step toward her, dropping her voice to a whisper. "Just because you're upset with me is no reason to be short with Mandy. Please don't treat her the way you did me growing up. You'll break her heart."

Frances recoiled as though she had been slapped. Treat Amanda the way she had treated Katherine as a child? Whatever was the girl talking about? Coddling was not her way, but she had always loved her children, even if she didn't simper over them like some women she'd known. "I have done nothing wrong, and I will not have you correcting me." A tiny stab of guilt shot through her heart at the untruth of her words, but she could not take them back—would not take them back. Straightening her shoulders, she faced her daughter. "I am your mother, not your child, and I deserve your respect, if not your love." She took off her apron and tossed it on the counter. "I do not seem to be hungry. I believe I will go to my room to lie down for a bit."

"Mama, wait."

Frances didn't look back or slow her pace. Her daughter needed to understand she could not speak to her in that manner whether Katherine thought she had cause or not. Besides, there was no way Frances would ever allow anyone to see the moisture that threatened to spill over onto her cheeks.

Katherine stared at her mother's retreating back and fought her tears. She didn't know if she wanted to laugh, cry, or scream—maybe all three. But the puzzled look on Mandy's face steeled her nerves. No time to give in to her emotions when her little girl was confused over her grandmother's behavior. Fear rose as she recalled Mama's harsh tone. *Exactly* what Katherine had heard most of her life, but that voice had never been leveled at her daughters—until now.

"Mama?" Amanda tugged on her sleeve.

Katherine bent over and embraced the girl. Her daughters never called her *mama* unless they were distressed. *Ma* had always been their favorite name. "What is it, honey?"

"What's wrong with Grandma? Is she mad at me?" Amanda's chin quivered.

"No, Mandy. She's not upset with you at all." Katherine smoothed her daughter's hair and kissed her forehead. "We were talking about something before you came in, and I think Grandma may have been a little worried, that's all. It's nothing important. Grandma loves you very much."

The little face cleared. "I love her, too, but sometimes she acts so sad. I'm going to find something to cheer her up." With those parting words she scampered from the room.

Katherine stepped back to the stove. Her boarders would expect breakfast soon, and she still needed to fix a tray and take it to Micah Jacobs. At least the children didn't have school today, so she needn't worry about getting them ready and out the door.

Why did life have to be so difficult? All she'd ever wanted from Mama was love and acceptance. She rolled those two words around in her mouth, tasting to see what it would feel like should those qualities suddenly appear in her mother. Katherine shook her head, unable to even imagine that happening. Time to busy her hands. She slid a tray of biscuits inside the oven.

Mama loved her in her own way. At least, Katherine hoped that must be true, even if Mama didn't show love with hugs and kind words. So what was it she longed for? Would it satisfy her if her mother gave her hugs or demonstrated her love in other physical ways? It would help, but Katherine knew for certain the ache would remain.

What then? Approval? Yes. That came closer. Mama didn't approve of anything she did. Most of her comments were hurtful. She probably had the notion she was helping by "explaining" a better way to do things, but from where Katherine stood, it seemed her mother thought she never did anything right.

Acceptance and approval shouldn't be hard for a parent to give. It certainly hadn't been for *her* since Mandy and Lucy were born. But mercy was her strong suit, not Mama's. Mama saw merciful people as weaklings and shunned them.

Shunned.

Another action her mother would never believe she used with her daughter, but Katherine knew better. Mama had always found opportunities to point out where she believed June excelled over Katherine, and not once in her memory had Mama accepted a physical demonstration of love. She shook her head. No sense in wading through the muck any longer; she'd come out stinking to high heaven, and no good would come of it. Time to put this nonsense to rest and get on with her life. Mama would never change. Katherine simply needed to make the best of it.

Or go crazy.

She chuckled at the picture that popped into her head of her wandering around babbling incoherently, then she sobered. Once, when she was young, her father had taken her to town, and a crazy man had ambled down the street. His funny laugh, dirty clothing, and long beard scared her, and she'd shrunk back against her father's legs. Papa stooped and hefted her into his arms, stroking her hair and telling her not to be afraid. The poor man didn't have anyone to love and care for him.

Katherine's fear turned to sadness. No one to love him. It had been years later before she understood. It wasn't necessarily the lack of love that made him the way he was; he had something wrong with his mind. But she'd never forgotten the pang of dread that lingered for months after. If Papa didn't love her, would she be crazy like that man?

All she could do was give her situation to the Lord and let it go. A smile tugged away her tension. Thankfully *He* was bigger than Mama.

Chapter Fourteen

Frances wanted nothing more than to clomp up the stairs to her room, but she swept along instead, careful to walk with dignity and poise. No need to stomp, as much as she would love to show her displeasure. She would find a way to make Katherine understand the depth of her hurt as well as change her daughter's perspective about allowing her to invest in the boardinghouse.

Of all Katherine's recent foolish notions, this might be the worst, thinking she could take care of an injured man on top of caring for her girls and the other boarders. Didn't she see she needed help?

Young voices drifted from the open door of the upstairs parlor most often used by the family or children. Lucy must be visiting with someone. That area could've housed another room, but no, Katherine insisted on including a small sitting room away from the bustle of the downstairs living area. Another waste, to Frances's way of thinking. Daniel had catered to his wife a bit too much.

She paused next to the door, arrested by the sound of a young man's voice. More like a boy, but with an occasional crack that showed he'd recently taken the step from boy to young man. Who could Lucy be talking to? They didn't have any children lodging here.

Frances picked up the hem of her skirt. Time to see what her granddaughter was up to. Her foot lifted from the floor, then she halted so quickly she almost stumbled. What had Lucy just said? She inched closer and turned her ear toward the open door.

"You can't tell Ma." Lucy's words jerked Frances upright. "Or your pa. Promise?"

"Why would I tell anybody you like some boy at school? Besides, we already promised to keep each other's secrets, and I haven't spilled the beans yet. Why don't you want your ma to know?"

"Ma's already worried you want to court me, and she thinks I'm too young. I told her we're only friends, but I'm not sure she believed me."

Frances held back a smile. It may have been a lifetime ago, but she remembered her first crush on a boy at school. Her smile faded. Pa hadn't approved and had ended her daydreams with a willow switch after he'd caught her and her beau walking hand in hand through a meadow.

Zachary's words caught her attention again. What had she missed by letting her thoughts wander?

"I think that's a great idea, Lucy."

"Are you sure?"

"Yes, but won't it worry your ma?"

"It's not like we'll do anything. If she thinks I'm a little sweet on you, she won't find out about Jonathan. You don't need to act different. I'll just smile at you when she's looking. There's nothing wrong with smiling, is there?"

A long pause ensued, and Frances leaned forward. What were those children doing in there? Time to put an end to this nonsense and …

"I guess not. As long as neither of us fib. Pa won't tolerate lying, and I'd hate to disappoint him."

Frances relaxed and took a quiet step back. All was well; she could go to her room. Three strides down the hall, though, she stopped. She had seen the look on Mr. Jacobs's face when Katherine left his room this morning, even if her daughter had not. Yearning. He may not know it yet, but he was falling for Katherine, and Frances did not intend to let that happen. The man had no prospects—his business and home were destroyed—and she didn't want him thinking he could camp out here living off her daughter indefinitely.

Frances concentrated. The children's conversation gave her an idea, and she hurried down the hall. It might provide a way to convince Katherine to cut Zachary and his father's stay short. She wouldn't have to lie either, but ... this could work. Yes, indeed.

Micah shifted his weight on the bed, struggling to get comfortable. White-hot needles burrowed their way into his ankle, and he'd swear his heart was trying to pound its way out through his toes. If he hadn't gone back for his box of blacksmith tools, he wouldn't be in this situation today. But he'd already lost the barn and his home; he couldn't abide the idea of his tools being destroyed, as well. Of course, most of his tools were metal, but their wood handles would require time and work to repair. He gave a snort of derision—but probably not as much time or work as his ankle would need.

He threw off the sheet covering his chest and scooted up against the pillow, punching it into a ball beneath his shoulders. Losing his business and home cut deep, but it could have been worse—he could have lost Zachary. One funeral in the past two years was enough. He couldn't endure another loss without going mad. Maybe not mad, but after Emma's death he'd pretty much lost his faith. If God took Zachary away from him, too, he didn't know what he'd do.

"Pa?" Zachary stuck his head around the door frame, his hand clutching the frame so hard his fingers turned white. "You all right?"

"Come on in." Micah choked back his emotions. Men didn't cry. Well, maybe they did in the dark with no one around to hear, but he'd be ding-blasted if he let his son see tears. He blinked rapidly and held out one arm. "I'm fine. Nothing some rest won't cure." He patted the edge of the mattress and shifted over a couple inches, trying not to wince. "Sit. It's good to see you. I woke up worried."

Zachary sank onto the spot next to his pa and ran his gaze over his father's face. "What were you worried about?" His eyes darted away and lit on something across the room. "The barn." The words came out as a bare whisper. "I'm sorry, Pa."

Micah placed a finger against his son's jaw and pressed, bringing the boy's focus back around. "Not the barn or our home. I couldn't remember seeing you last night, and I had a moment of panic thinking maybe …" He let his breath whistle out between his teeth. "Maybe I'd lost you."

The blood drained from Zachary's face and tears pooled in his eyes. "It was my fault. You must hate me, Pa. Maybe I shoulda stayed upstairs, so you wouldn't know."

Terror coursed through Micah. He didn't care whose fault the fire was, as long as his son was alive. But those words—hearing Zachary wish he'd died so his pa wouldn't be disappointed in him? Had he let the boy think he didn't love him these past months since his mother's death? He dropped his hands to Zachary's arms and gave him a quick shake. "Stop that. I don't ever want to hear words like that from you again, do you hear me? Not ever!"

"But, Pa! You don't know what I did." The tears spilled over onto Zachary's cheeks and wended their way to his chin.

Micah reached up to brush the moisture away. "All that matters is we're both safe. We have each other. Nothing you do will make me love you any less." He waited, but Zachary bowed his head. "Look at me, Son."

Zachary sniffled and scrubbed at his nose but met Micah's gaze. "I thought you'd hate me for burning down the barn."

Micah closed his eyes. He'd been afraid of this—had known it might be the case. Only seconds before Zachary had come into his room, he'd recalled going to bed wondering if the boy had put out the lanterns in the stable. "What happened?"

"I set a lantern on a stall divider, but the closest horse was two stalls down. I forgot the lantern was there until I woke up later. I should've gone down and put it out, but I was too tired. One of the horses must've kicked a wall, and it fell off."

Truth struck him full force at his son's words. All this time he'd been worried Zachary might be to blame, when it was his fault, not the boy's. "It's as much my mistake as yours. I can't let you take all the blame."

Zachary straightened. "You didn't leave the lantern there, Pa. I did."

"Yes, I know that, and you were wrong not to follow the rules and make sure each light was doused." He hated having to chastise his boy, but sometimes facing a problem helped a child take responsibility and did more to relieve guilt than making light of it would. Telling Zachary it didn't matter would be lying, and that was something he'd taught his son never to do. "I wish you'd followed instructions and been more careful, but it's still not completely your fault."

Zachary's brows scrunched together. "I don't understand. You didn't do anything wrong."

"But I did. Before I fell asleep, I wondered if you'd remembered to care for everything, but I was too tired to check. Instead of following through, I slid into bed and went to sleep. If I'd done what God was nudging me to do, this never would've happened."

Katherine balanced the breakfast tray in front of Micah's open door. A murmur of words drifted out, and she hesitated—might she be interrupting? But food was best eaten hot, and she hated to waste it. She stepped into the open doorway and halted so quickly she almost upset the mug of coffee.

Micah sat propped up against his pillow with his son wrapped in his arms. She thought she detected a hint of moisture on the man's cheek as his forehead pressed against the boy's dark, tumbled curls.

A sense of reverence rose within her and she edged backward, not wanting him to catch her staring. Micah cried while holding his son. How many men would act with so little restraint? She couldn't even conceive of Daniel doing so.

If only she'd followed her earlier prompting and returned to the kitchen. Katherine's heart ached at the tender scene, evoking memories of Daniel with the girls—how she missed her husband and the love they'd shared.

She caught her breath as another emotion surfaced.

Longing.

To once again know the tenderness of a man's embrace. Oh, to be held the way Micah held his son, with his strong arms wrapped around her shoulders, gathering her close to his heart…. Her feelings threatened to swamp her.

How foolish. She didn't even know this man. Not beyond the surface acquaintance, at any rate, and she certainly wasn't looking for a husband. Micah was handsome enough, and from what she'd observed, gentle and oft-times considerate of others. But it didn't matter if he proved himself perfect. The man had recently been widowed and had made it clear he had no desire to accept her offer of a temporary home—he'd done so out of necessity. Micah Jacobs had no interest in her, and she certainly didn't in him.

But something about him tugged at her heart, and it scared her. She hadn't been attracted to a man since Daniel died. Maybe it hadn't been such a good idea to invite Micah to stay here, but what other choice was there? With his business destroyed, money would be scarce, so staying at the hotel would cause additional hardship. She'd made the right decision, but she'd need to be careful to guard her heart against any further intrusion.

She lifted her chin. Time to get on with the business at hand.

Katherine took a determined stride through the door, clearing her throat as she walked. "Pardon me for interrupting, but I've brought breakfast. Zachary, the others are waiting in the dining room, if you'd care to join them." She didn't wait for a response but busied herself setting the tray on the chair closest to the bed.

Taking a step back, she inadvertently stared into the depths of Micah's eyes, his lashes dark with moisture. She captured her bottom lip between her teeth. What could she possibly say to this man who openly displayed his love for his son? She struggled to force words past the lump in her throat.

Micah patted his son's shoulder. "You heard Mrs. Galloway. Breakfast is ready, so you'd best hurry."

"Yes, sir." Zachary stood and tipped his head toward Katherine. "Thank you, ma'am, for letting us stay here." He rushed from the room.

Micah lay back against his pillow with a warm smile. "I'm sorry to put you to so much bother."

"It's nothing to worry over. I'm happy to help with anything you need." Katherine slid the chair close to the bed, then handed him the plate. "Can you reach the coffee all right?" She kept her voice steady, wishing she dared ask what caused the tears.

"Yes, it's fine. Thanks." Lifting the mug, he took a long swallow before lowering it. "We won't stay any longer than we need to. As soon as the doctor says I can get out of this bed, we'll find somewhere else to live."

Had Micah read her mind? Katherine stepped to the window, opening the curtains and allowing sunlight to stream in. "No need. This room wasn't being used." The words came out flat, almost emotionless, not at all what she desired, but she couldn't let him see how he stirred her emotions. She swiveled and mustered a smile. "I'm happy to help. There's no reason for you and Zachary to leave." She wrapped her fingers in the folds of her skirt and tried to keep her voice light. "I'd best get back to the kitchen, or I'll have a revolt on my hands."

"Zachary can bring anything more that I need. You have enough work to do."

Silence settled over the room, and Katherine backed toward the door, suddenly unsure of what else to say, like a young girl fumbling for the right words on her first day at school. Turning, she hurried from the room. Maybe she'd ask Zachary or Lucy to collect the tray when Micah finished. Yes, keeping her distance from Micah Jacobs would be a very sensible plan.

Chapter Fifteen

Jeffery Tucker stared at the newspaper, trying to concentrate. Why didn't someone answer that door? He'd finished supper and retired to the parlor, hoping no one would join him. All he wanted was a little peace and quiet after the hubbub of the day. It had been eight days since Jacobs and his son moved in, and the amount of activity seemed to have doubled. This was the second time someone had knocked. For that matter, why would a person continue to hammer when it clearly stated this was a boardinghouse? Most people just walked in and asked for the proprietor.

There appeared no help for it. He laid the paper aside and propelled himself with long strides toward the insistent knocking. Whipping open the door, he fixed a scowl on his face, intending to educate the person on the niceties of boardinghouse etiquette.

A petite young woman cowered behind a matronly lady at least twice her age—and twice her width, since the older woman's bulk almost hid the younger. Dark brown ringlets peeked from under the younger woman's bonnet, falling several inches past her shoulders. Her hand clutched a large locket, which hung around her neck on a gold chain. Her wide blue eyes caught his attention, but the sheer panic in them caused the harsh words to die in his throat.

The stout woman slowly lowered her fist and surveyed him from head to toe. "Are you the owner of this establishment? I say, you certainly took your time answering. Not the way to run a successful business." She planted her hands on her hips. "Well, are you going to open the door and ask us in or stand there gawking?"

Jeffery, startled back to his senses, bowed as he stepped aside. "Pardon me for my ill manners, ma'am." He nodded toward the younger woman and offered a smile. "Miss. Please, do come in. I'll see if Mrs. Galloway is about, if you're inquiring about a room."

"Mrs. Galloway, is it?" The matron stood in the spacious foyer, allowing her gaze to sweep over the furnishings. "Isn't there a Mr. Galloway? I'm not accustomed to dealing with a woman on matters of business."

"I'm afraid Mrs. Galloway is widowed, ma'am. But she's a capable person, and I'm sure she'll care for your needs."

Katherine Galloway appeared in the arched doorway that led to the rest of the house. "Thank you, Mr. Tucker. I appreciate your kind words." She stepped forward. "Pleased to meet you, ladies. I'm the proprietor."

Something akin to relief mixed with a surprising amount of disappointment washed over Jeffery when he realized there was no need to linger. The young woman standing in the hall had lovely eyes and a gentle demeanor—she might be worth getting to know. But the strident tones of the older woman chased him from the room. If they stayed, Jeffery was sure he'd find another place to live. Shades of Katherine's mother. A shudder coursed through him. This female seemed cut from the same cloth.

Another thought struck him and tipped his mouth up in a grin. On the other hand, he might garner new material for his project

when those two met. Sparks would fly—he'd wager his last dollar on
the fact. Yes, indeed, staying might not be such a bad plan after all.

Katherine repressed a smile as Mr. Tucker hurried away, certain she
understood what had caused the man to flee. The rather imposing
female standing in her foyer, arms akimbo, was enough to intimidate
the bravest of souls. But fear didn't so much as tickle Katherine's
consciousness; after all, she'd been raised by Mama.

"Were you looking for lodging?" She peered beyond the pair.
"Did you bring any bags?"

"Humph." The matronly woman snorted. "Of course. Why else
would we come to a boardinghouse? Our luggage is outside with our
driver."

Any number of reasons crossed Katherine's mind, but she bit
back a retort. "May I ask your names and have you sign my guest
book?"

"*I* am Wilma Roberts, and this is my niece, Beth Roberts." She
beckoned the girl forward. "Don't stand there with your mouth
open, Beth. Act like the lady I raised you to be."

The young woman snapped her lips closed and shuffled closer.
"Yes, ma'am. I'm sorry." The whispered words appeared to mol-
lify Mrs. Roberts, as her grim expression faded to one of tolerant
patience.

"That's better, sweetheart. Why, a good-looking young man
answered the door, and you didn't so much as nod or smile. How do

you expect to find a husband that way?" She rounded on Katherine, shaking her head. "Beth's a little shy, but she's a good girl."

Pity flooded Katherine's heart. The girl, who looked no older than seventeen, was as timid as a newborn fawn. She directed a warm smile at Beth, then returned her attention to the aunt. "Would you care to share a room with your niece, Mrs. Roberts, or do you require two rooms?"

Mrs. Roberts's mouth formed a small circle, giving her a comical look. "Why, neither. We would like a suite, if you please. With a drawing room separating two private rooms, and a bath."

"I'm sorry, but that's not possible. I don't have any suites or private baths."

"I beg your pardon?" Mrs. Roberts's bulk quivered with indignation. "I will pay extra, if that is what it takes. I am sure the lodgers who reside in your suite can be convinced, with a little persuasion, to take a different room."

Irritation chased away the last remnants of Katherine's amusement. *The gall of the woman.* "No, ma'am, you misunderstood. My boardinghouse has no suites, but even if we did, I'd not ask someone to give up their rooms for any amount of money."

"Oh. I see." The furrows between the woman's eyes relaxed. "Then give us the best two rooms you have that adjoin, and we will have to make do."

Katherine shifted her weight. She'd been on her feet all day, running errands, caring for Mr. Jacobs, fixing meals, and trying to placate her mother. As much as she could use the money from extra boarders, she wondered if this woman would be more work than she was worth. There seemed no help for it, however; she'd do the best she could, but she'd hazard a guess Mrs. Roberts still wouldn't be pleased even if she were given the best rooms in the house. "Will there be anything else, Mrs. Roberts?"

"I was directed to your establishment as being one of the best in town, and since it's late, we will stay. But perhaps we'll look around tomorrow to find something a bit more ... suitable."

At the moment Katherine would love to see them leave. She didn't relish the idea of a second opinionated woman running rough-shod over her household. "You're welcome to look, of course, but I'm afraid you won't find anything with suites available, other than The Arlington Hotel, which is very expensive. The other two hotels are mostly used by miners coming in for a day off or a night on the town, and those don't cater to ladies. There is one boardinghouse besides mine, but it doesn't take single women." She wished she *could* direct them elsewhere. "I'm afraid I can't even offer you two rooms that are connected. The best I can do is offer rooms on the same floor, but you'll be sharing a bath."

"Sharing a bath? That is *not* acceptable, Mrs. Galloway." Mrs. Roberts drew herself up and peered over her spectacles and down her rather long nose. "What do I need to pay to acquire a private bath?"

Katherine almost shook her head and laughed but caught herself in time. Apparently this woman thought money could solve every problem. "Unless you have the funds necessary to build one, there's nothing I can do. We have one bath on the main floor. In your room, you'll have a washstand, basin, clean cloths, fresh water daily, and a mirror above your bureau, but that's the best I can offer."

"Since I have no choice, I will take the rooms." The matron huffed and turned toward the door. "I'll have the driver bring in our bags."

Katherine held up a hand. "Wait, please. I need to acquaint you with our rules, and *then* you can decide if you still care to stay."

"Rules? What an antiquated idea. I must say, I have stayed in some of the finest establishments back East, and the owners went out of their way to accommodate us. Why bother your lodgers with rules?"

"Antiquated or not, I have certain things I require if you choose to stay."

Mrs. Roberts grimaced, then gave a sharp nod. "All right, Mrs. Galloway, if you feel the need."

Katherine glanced at Beth, wondering what the young woman was thinking. Downcast eyes and stooped shoulders spoke volumes regarding her relationship with her aunt. Poor dear. Any personality that had tried to sprout over the years had more than likely gotten trampled before it took hold.

"First, I don't allow drinking in my establishment. Second, you have a niece who's single, and a town full of unmarried men, many who are looking for wives. A gentleman caller may be seen in the parlor but may not go beyond that room."

Mrs. Roberts's nostrils flared. "I resent the implication."

"I'm not implying anything, madame. I say the same to any single woman who chooses to reside here. Now, for the rest." She wondered if what came next would be better received. "I have two daughters. One is thirteen, the other six, and both are well behaved. However, this is their home, first and foremost. My mother, Mrs. Frances Cooper, lives here and occasionally has charge of the girls if I'm away. They will try not to bother you, but I don't expect them to stop being children. Is that acceptable, Mrs. Roberts?"

"I suppose it has to be, whether I find it acceptable or not. As long as your children aren't allowed in our rooms, that is, and aren't overly boisterous."

"They know never to enter a guest's room. But we can both make a decision tomorrow."

"Both? What do *you* need to decide, Mrs. Galloway? Isn't this up to me?"

"This is my home, and I fear you might not be happy here for any length of time. While the income I receive from boarders is important to me, peace in my household is more so."

Shock and indignation struggled for prominence on Mrs. Roberts's face. For the first time since their arrival, she didn't appear to have anything to say.

Katherine mustered a smile and allowed her words to settle. "Please, have the driver bring in your bags, and I'll show you to your rooms. Breakfast is served at seven o'clock, if you care to rise early enough to join us. If not, there's a nice café in the hotel where they serve meals most of the day."

Mrs. Roberts stared at her as though she'd lost her mind. *As well she might*, Katherine thought ruefully. Truly, she hated the idea of losing the income from renting two additional rooms, but she'd meant what she said. Katherine stepped to the front door and swung it open. A man sat slumped in the seat of a wagon, appearing for all the world to be asleep. "Driver?"

His head snapped up, and he shook himself. "Yes, ma'am. You ready for these bags?"

"Thank you, yes." Katherine waited till he clambered down and hoisted a bag onto one shoulder, tucking another under his arm.

"Follow me." Nodding at the driver, she headed down the hall. *Lord, grant me strength. Two strong-willed women under my roof is two too many.*

Chapter Sixteen

Katherine tied the strings of her bonnet and slipped out the door the next morning, praying she could avoid more confrontations with Mama and Mrs. Roberts. She hadn't decided if both women keeping to their rooms through breakfast boded well or ill for the day.

She'd kept so much bottled up since the last time she'd met her friends at the church. If she didn't talk to someone soon, she'd boil over. It would be sheer joy to spend time in the company of her friends again.

Birds twittered and sang as she hurried down the dirt road leading to town. Katherine inhaled a fresh breath of morning air and cast a glance at the Powder River, which meandered beneath the footbridge. Large fir trees flanked the water's edge, allowing only a smattering of sunlight through the branches, but a cool breeze stroked her skin, giving welcome relief. They were into the third week of June and already too hot for comfort. She was thankful the willow trees cast their welcoming shade over both her home and the church.

Katherine gazed at the exquisite stained glass window set in the roof peak at the front of the Methodist church, not far below the bell tower. She walked through the front door into the sanctuary, enjoying the fact that the builders had added a similar work of art on each side of the building, creating a sense of reverence and beauty.

Women's laughter rang across the sanctuary. Katherine's brows puckered in a sudden memory. She hadn't seen Ella in church this past Sunday and had forgotten to ask how the young woman was faring. It was only a month before her baby was due. Hopefully she wasn't feeling poorly or encountering problems with the pregnancy.

Katherine crossed behind the wood pews and entered the side room. Four cheerful faces swiveled her way, each one lit with a welcoming smile. Relief welled up in Katherine, and she hurried to Ella's side, gathering her into a hug. "I'm glad to see you. I worried when I didn't see you in church on Sunday. But you look the picture of health." Drawing back, she kept a light touch on Ella's upper arms and gave a gentle squeeze.

A flush tinted Ella's cheeks, and she ducked her head. "It was Matt's doin'. He insisted I stay at home and rest. He's been fussin' at me the past couple of weeks, sayin' I'm doin' too much."

Hester Sue thumped the flat of her hand against her hip, making everyone jump. She chuckled. "Good for him. Train 'em young, and some of these men will turn into right good husbands. You snagged a keeper, Ella."

Virginia tucked a strand of silver hair into the bun at the base of her neck. "Matt's doing a good job taking care of you."

"But he has his own work. He doesn't need to be waitin' on me, fixin' me breakfast, and totin' the water just because I'm expectin' a child. Why, women give birth every day. I surely don't want him resentin' me or the babe before it comes."

Leah reached a hand across the corner of the quilting frame and patted Ella's shoulder. "Nothing you can do would make that man resent you. I've seen the way he looks at you. My stars, I wish a man would look at me that way someday ... but I'm afraid my time is past."

Hester Sue emitted a cross between the bray of a donkey and a smothered laugh. "Past? Why, honey child, you got plenty of time to find you a man. What are you, a whoppin' twenty years old?"

"I'm afraid I saw that birthday a couple of years back, Hester Sue." Leah pushed her needle through the edge of a patchwork square. "I'm almost twenty-two, an old maid by anyone's standard."

Katherine rolled her eyes at her friend. "You are not an old maid, Leah. Just because a man hasn't caught your eye yet doesn't mean you won't marry."

Leah laughed. "You mean *I* haven't caught a man's eye, don't you?"

Ella cradled her belly with one hand and stroked the top of it with the other. "Baby's kickin' somethin' fierce." She scrunched up her face, then blew out a long breath. "Whew. He's feisty today."

"I think men are scared of you, what with you bein' so pretty. I've seen men turn and stare when you walk down the street. Maybe they don't know how to go about talkin' to you."

"Yep, they's plumb tongue-tied." Hester Sue chuckled. "Kinda strange, though, with all the single miners floatin' around town. You'd think one of them would propose."

Leah didn't reply. Katherine studied her, trying to read beneath the seemingly calm exterior. She didn't want to embarrass her friend, but something seemed to be bothering her. "Leah?"

"Yes?" Leah jabbed the needle into the fabric, making the tightly drawn quilt bounce.

Ella giggled and placed her hand on the wooden edge to steady it. "Whoa, there. Better take it easy, Leah, or this quilt might jump right out of the frame."

"I'm sorry, ladies." Leah dropped her needle. "I don't know what's gotten into me lately."

"I think it's time for a cup of tea." Virginia stepped over the threshold, waving in the direction of the sanctuary. "I know we usually get our work done first and visit after, but maybe this time we should reverse the order. I'll be right back with a tray."

Katherine could hear her footsteps headed toward the back wall where a teapot simmered on a potbellied stove.

Hearty assent rose from each woman, and they moved to the cluster of chairs in the corner. After they'd all been served, Virginia turned her attention back to Leah. "Come now, dear, tell us what the trouble is. I've rarely seen anything get you down."

Leah hunched one shoulder. "I wasn't completely honest when I said I haven't caught a man's eye."

Katherine jerked upright, almost spilling her tea. "Do you have a beau you haven't told us about?"

"No." Leah shook her head, making her red curls, clasped in a ribbon, dance around her shoulders. "But I've had two men approach me recently, and, well, I haven't appreciated their remarks."

Hester Sue narrowed her eyes. "What you tryin' to say, love? Sounds to me like we need to organize us a necktie party if men are treatin' fine ladies like you with disrespect."

Leah lifted a shoulder. "We're neglecting our work, and we haven't much time to finish."

Virginia pursed her lips, deepening the wrinkles on each side. "People are more important than projects, my dear. We want to help if we can." She glanced at Hester Sue and smiled. "Although I'm not entirely ruling out that necktie party should the need arise."

A light laugh escaped Leah's mouth. "Sorry, ladies, but the picture of the four of you dropping that 'necktie' over some man's head and hoisting him off the ground makes me laugh. Not that I don't think you incapable of protecting a friend, but I hardly think it'll come to that." Her eyes roamed from one face to the next, finally resting on Katherine's. "I've shared with you that my father ..." She seemed unable to finish.

Katherine laid her hand on her friend's knee. She knew exactly what Leah referred to but wondered if the others did. It wasn't something they'd discussed in this group, but if Leah hadn't wanted them to know, Katherine doubted she would mention it now. "Yes. He falls into a melancholy mood at times and drinks more than he should."

Leah nodded. "That's being charitable, but yes."

Murmurs and understanding sighs followed.

Leah waited a minute before continuing. "I think he mentioned that his spinster daughter couldn't find a husband while drinking at the saloon."

"I'm so sorry," Virginia murmured. "It may be wise to stay home for a few days." Then her face brightened. "But I do have another idea."

Leah leaned forward. "I'd love to hear it."

"We can pray."

The words dropped into the quiet like flower petals falling in a gentle breeze, releasing their fragrance. Smiles lit the women's countenances. Silently they held out their hands, linking each heart in a circle and lifting their voices to the One who could change, heal, and protect. Each petitioned the Father on her friend's behalf, then Leah finished with words of thanksgiving and praise.

Raising tear-dampened cheeks and eyes filled with peace, she whispered, "Thank you. I love you all so much. I don't know what I'd do without each of you in my life."

As one, they rose, set aside their teacups, and walked back to their places around the quilting frame. Needles were poised above the squares, and thimbles worked to push the sharp instruments through the colorful fabric.

Leah broke the silence. "It's your turn, Katherine. How are things going at home with your mother? And how is Mr. Jacobs doing? I've despaired for the poor man and his son, losing their home and business. Do you know how long before he'll be back on his feet?"

Katherine smiled. "Let's see … which one of those questions do you want me to answer first?"

Hester Sue piped up, laughter dancing through her voice. "The one about Mr. Jacobs. Now that there's a fine-lookin' man. And just the kind I like—one who don't talk a lot. I stopped in there to have him look at my wagon wheel a couple weeks ago. Couldn't a-been more courteous and didn't try to make me feel stupid for drivin' it with the wheel wobblin'. My pa woulda chewed me out something fierce, and even my Arthur mighta scolded a mite for not noticin' it sooner, but not Mr. Jacobs. He's as nice as could be."

Katherine gave a slow nod. "Now that you mention it, I have to agree. I've never heard him raise his voice to his son, even when he had cause."

Ella's dimples showed in her cheeks. "Sounds like my Matt. He's always patient with me."

Hester Sue chuckled. "Matt's still smitten, Ella. You two only been married a little over a year."

Virginia tapped her fingers against the wood quilt frame. "Makes no difference how long you've been married, dear. A man's character shows up mighty fast if something angers him. I'd say both Mr. Jacobs and Ella's Matt are cut from the right kind of cloth."

*Uh-huh*s and *Yes, ma'am*s echoed around the room.

Katherine straightened after finishing the last row of stitches on her square. "As for Mr. Jacobs's health, he's doing better. The doctor is to stop by this morning to dress the burn and leave a pair of crutches. Mr. Jacobs can start using them today if the swelling is down."

"How long do you think he and his son will stay at your place, Katherine?" Virginia asked.

"I'm not sure. I've told him he's welcome for as long as he needs lodging, but he seems determined to leave and make his own way."

Hester Sue tsked. "Sounds like a man. Stubborn and proud. Ain't likely he'll find any place better or more reasonable than yours, though. Did he say anything about tryin' to rebuild?"

"I think he wants to, but with his injured ankle, it's going to be hard. Besides …" Katherine wondered how much she should say but decided to plunge ahead. "… I'm not sure he'd have the funds to rebuild. He's only been in town a short while, and from what I heard, he bought the livery outright. I can't imagine he has a lot of cash to put up a new building." She shrugged. "Of course, I could be wrong, but he seems a little sensitive about the subject of money."

Hester Sue snorted a laugh. "What man isn't? Another place pride can take hold, if a man ain't careful."

Leah wove her needle through the patchwork and pushed it back up, then plunged it in once again. "I wonder if the townspeople might help."

"How?" Multiple voices echoed the word.

"I'm not sure. Maybe a barn raising or something? The pastor might be able to put that together."

"A barn raising might be a good idea," Katherine said. "I'm not sure how Mr. Jacobs would take it, as I've never seen him attend church, but I can't imagine it would upset him too much to have help."

"Who knows?" Virginia's eyes glinted with a spark of anticipation. "It might be a way for God to bless him and draw him to Himself. Let's make it a matter of prayer this next two weeks and see if the Lord opens a door."

Yes and *Good idea* chorused from the group.

"And how about your mother?" Leah repeated her question from earlier. "Have things improved?"

"Not a lot. She thinks I should expand—build more rooms to bring in added income. It's not that I'd be against that, but she wants to invest and …" Katherine was loath to say more.

Hester Sue nodded understanding. "The Good Book says we're not to be a debtor to any man. But would it be bad if your ma helped you out, since she's living there now?"

"I turned her down." The words came out flat, almost harsh. "She made it clear she'd expect to be involved in making decisions.

The next thing I know, she'd take over completely. It's what she does. She can't help it, and I'm having a hard enough time dealing with her suggestions now. She doesn't think I cook the right type of meals or have enough linens, and she wants to know everything about my finances. If she invested money, it would be unbearable."

Ella's sympathetic voice came from across the quilting frame. "How did she take your decision?"

"Not good, I'm afraid."

"And how are *you* doing?" Virginia leveled a compassionate gaze her way.

Katherine's hands stilled for a minute. "I'm not sure. A bit overwhelmed at times, I suppose. Wishing Mama had only come for a short visit, then hating myself for being selfish. Gout causes her pain, and she was lonely after my half sister passed away, but knowing all that doesn't make her any easier to live with."

Virginia nodded. "I understand, and I don't think you should feel guilty. All you can do is love her the best way you can and leave the rest up to God. Does your mother's attitude cause any problems for your girls?"

"I don't think so with Amanda, as Mama tends to dote on her, although she has spoken to her sharply a couple of times. But, overall, Lucy is the one I worry about. She's spoken disrespectfully to Mama once, and I've had to caution her about her tone a time or two." She laughed ruefully. "I'm guessing she thinks I'm weak, based on a comment she made."

Hester Sue quirked her brows. "What kind of comment?"

"She says I let Mama walk all over me and that I should stand up to her more. I explained that she's my elder and the Bible teaches us to respect our parents, but I could tell by her attitude she believes I let Mama go too far."

Leah jabbed at the quilt square as though she had a personal grudge against it. "What is it about our parents, that they can't let us live our own lives without interference?" Her head snapped up, and she gave a sly grin. "Maybe we need to do a little matchmaking and find a husband for your mother."

Several of the women chuckled, but Katherine shook her head. The comment had done much to lighten the mood. She was grateful the attention had drifted away from her response and attitude toward her mother, but she wasn't comfortable delving too deep into that subject at the moment and was happy to tread a different path.

A sudden thought sent a twinge through Katherine's heart. She'd forgotten all about her two new boarders—Beth and her obnoxious aunt. All she could do at this point was hope and pray they'd decided to find another place to stay by the time she returned home. And what in the world were people like them doing in Baker City, anyway?

The women tidied up the room and said their good-byes, promising to stay in touch and meet again in two weeks. On the walk home Katherine decided it didn't matter what Mrs. Roberts expected or decided. If the woman didn't behave herself and agree to abide by the rules of the house, especially as it pertained to common courtesy, she wouldn't be given a choice—as much as Katherine hated to do so, she would ask them to leave.

Chapter Seventeen

Micah would not be stuck in this room another second if he could help it. He rocked back on the bed and tucked his shirt into his waistband. He rolled forward, grabbed the crutches the doctor had left propped beside the bed, and gripped the handles situated in the middle of the wood contraptions. Why hadn't he allowed the doctor to demonstrate how to use these tomfool things?

Pride. Pure and simple. He shook his head. No time to moan about what might have been. He needed to get out of this bed and start tending to business.

Now what had the man said? Place the top with the curved wood under his arms and grip the handles. Didn't sound too hard, even with a bum leg and sore shoulder. Micah scowled at the offending appendage, willing the throbbing to subside. According to Doc, the burn would heal but might leave a scar. Like Micah cared about something so foolish. At least he hadn't broken any bones, and the doctor said he could hobble around a bit today as long as he didn't overdo it.

Where is that boy of mine when I need him?

"Stop it, Micah." He grated out the words, hoping the sound of his own voice would snap him out of his doldrums. Katherine had told him when she'd brought breakfast that Lucy and Zachary were doing chores while she attended a meeting at the church.

At least his son was pulling his weight—more than he could say for himself since they'd arrived. Well, that would end right now.

Micah grasped the crutches so firmly his fingers protested, but he didn't care. He wouldn't let these sticks get the best of him. By the time Katherine Galloway got home, he'd be swinging around this house, and he'd show everyone he could take care of himself.

Hoisting himself off the bed, he balanced precariously, his good foot on the ground, his injured leg raised. Doc told him he couldn't put any weight on it yet, as the deep cut, as well as the burn, troubled him. He had to admit it looked ugly, but a little pain and soreness weren't going to keep him abed.

Gritting his teeth, he planted the crutches ahead of him, resting his weight on his armpits and his good foot. He grinned. *Nothin' to this.* Keeping a tight grip on one crutch, he gingerly reached for the doorknob. *Simple. Can't understand why I worried.*

Swinging confidently through the door, he set his left foot on the floor and swiveled to grasp the handle and close the door behind him. But as he twisted, the crutch under his right arm tottered. Too late he realized it wasn't braced far enough away from his body. The doorknob bounced out of his fingers and he waved his arm in the air, trying to gather himself and regain his balance. No good. He pitched to the side and the floor rose up to meet him.

Landing on his injured leg was going to hurt like fire.

Lucy and Zachary entered the house and headed for the linen closet, Lucy leading the way. "Ma's going to be happy we got the clean bedding off the clothesline." She tossed a smile to the boy beside her. "Looks like a thunderstorm might be rolling in. Thanks for helping."

Zachary shrugged. "I didn't have anything else to do, with Pa laid up in bed. Guess I should go see how he's doing after we put these away."

A crash, followed by a loud groan, emanated from somewhere up the hallway. Lucy jumped, dropping her pile of sheets. She stared at the clean linens scattered on the floor. "I'm in trouble now.... What was that noise?"

Zachary tossed his blankets aside and took off running down the hallway. "I think that's Pa!"

Lucy scooped up the sheets and deposited them on top of the blankets. Zachary was already turning the corner, so she dashed behind him. Was Mr. Jacobs hurt? She picked up her pace and scurried around the corner, then skidded to a halt.

Zachary was on his knees over his father, who lay sprawled across the floor, one crutch under his body, the other lying a couple of yards away. "Pa? You all right? What happened?"

Another groan was the only response. Zachary looked up, eyes wide. "What should we do?"

Lucy gripped her hands together. "I'll find Grandma or Mr. Tucker. You stay with your pa."

Zachary nodded but didn't reply, just hovered over his father.

Lucy raced along the hallway. She and Zachary could probably lift Mr. Jacobs, but they didn't know what was wrong. Grandma wouldn't be able to lift Mr. Jacobs. But Mr. Tucker could, and he'd surely know how to wake him. She flew up two flights of stairs and skidded to a stop in front of his door, rapping on it sharply. "Mr. Tucker, are you there? We need your help." She waited a minute, but nothing happened. Raising her fist she pounded, desperation making her hit the wood harder than she'd planned. It rattled under her knuckles but still didn't open.

Giving up, she ran down to the second floor, praying someone else would be home. Steps sounded, and a door flew open. A woman Lucy presumed to be Mrs. Roberts stuck her head out of her room and scowled. "What is the meaning of that racket?"

Lucy's heart rate calmed a bit at the sight of an adult, even one as grumpy as Mrs. Roberts. "We need help. Zachary's father has fallen."

The woman moved out into the hall, smoothing the lace collar at her throat. "I don't know what you're going on about. Your mother promised you children wouldn't cause trouble, and here you are banging on doors first thing in the morning. Believe me, I'll let her know about your rude behavior as soon as I see her."

Lucy wanted to scream, and she would have if she thought it would help. Instead, she stomped over and peered directly into the woman's face. "I *said* Mr. Jacobs is hurt, and we need help. It is *not* early in the morning; it's half-past ten. Mother has gone to the church, and Mr. Tucker isn't home. You have to come help me. Right now." She engaged the fiercest look she could muster.

Mrs. Roberts drew back. "Well, I never!"

"Ma'am, I am not trying to be disrespectful, but Zachary and I need help." Lucy softened her tone a bit. "Please."

"Doing what? And who is this Zachary you keep referring to?"

It was all Lucy could do not to roll her eyes, but she worked to keep her voice even. "He's my friend who's staying here with his father, Mr. Jacobs. Their business and home burned down, and Mr. Jacobs was injured. He must have tried to get up just now, but he fell in the hall. Would you come?"

"Why didn't you say so?" Mrs. Roberts leaned back inside her room. "Beth, I'll be back as soon as I can. You go to your room and stay put, you hear?"

"Yes, ma'am," a muffled voice answered from somewhere inside.

Mrs. Roberts grasped a handful of her dark blue skirt in each hand and lifted it off the floor, revealing stocking feet with no shoes. "Lead the way, young woman, and hurry it up."

Lucy darted toward the stairway, relief flooding her heart. Right now all she wanted was her mother back home to see to the problem, but grumpy old Mrs. Roberts would have to do.

Frances struggled to finish dressing and groaned. She'd skipped breakfast this morning due to another flare-up of gout and a pounding headache. Katherine had been kind enough to bring her tea and toast before she'd left for her meeting. After nibbling at the food, she'd set it aside and relaxed into her bed. She'd fallen into a pleasant doze when a loud banging from the second floor woke her and scared ten years off her life. And she could ill afford to lose a decade. Rubbing the ache in her temple, she hobbled to the door and swung

it open, ready to lambaste the inconsiderate idiot making the confounded racket. She almost fell flat on her face before she made it
two yards down the hall.

"What in the world?" She tried to focus her bleary vision to see
what she'd tripped over. A large stick lay across the floor as though
placed to bring about someone's downfall. Her own, no doubt. Was
that young-man friend of Lucy's playing a prank?

A deep moan made her stiffen, and she moved her gaze to the
prostrate form several yards beyond. "Mr. Jacobs?"

The man's son, who'd been hunkered beside him, leapt to his
feet. "Oh, Mrs. Cooper! My pa's hurt bad. Lucy went upstairs to find
Mr. Tucker, but she's not back yet, and I'm not sure what to do."

Frances took in the scene in a glance. The fallen man lay with
his eyes closed and sweat drenching his forehead. It looked as though
Mr. Jacobs must have taken a nasty fall and hit his head. She stepped
forward and leaned over, placing her fingertips on his shoulder. "Mr.
Jacobs. Can you hear me?"

His eyelids twitched, then slowly opened. "Mrs. Cooper?"

Before she could reply, thundering feet pounded down the stairs
and Lucy came bounding up the hall with a rather large woman
following her.

Frances eyed the woman as she lumbered at a much slower pace
in Lucy's wake. Who was this person, and why in the world would
she wear dark blue velvet on a morning that promised nothing but
a steady increase of heat? The matron appeared to be younger than
Frances was, though a liberal sprinkling of gray hair displaced what
had once been a drab brown. And ... mercy! The creature wasn't
wearing shoes! Her rather large feet were clad only in stockings.

Frances looked the woman up and down. "And who, might I ask, are you?" She stared at the stocking feet peeking out from under the skirt. "I would think you might be a bit more careful about how you dress in public."

Lucy halted next to Zachary. "Grandma, Mr. Jacobs is hurt. This is no time to worry about how someone is dressed."

Frances tossed one last glance at the newcomer, then turned her attention to Lucy. "Yes, of course. We are forgetting Mr. Jacobs." She bent over the fallen man again. "Mr. Jacobs, can you hear me? Wake up, now."

The man rolled his head and blinked but didn't respond.

"Is he going to be all right, Grandma?" Lucy nervously bounced from foot to foot.

"He does not appear badly hurt. I think he got the wind knocked out of him when he fell."

Zachary patted his father's cheek. "Pa, can you hear me?"

Micah licked his lips. "Yes. Give me a minute."

Frances nodded. "You see, just like I told you." She pivoted toward Lucy. "Now who is this woman?"

Lucy glanced from one to the other. "Grandma, Mrs. Roberts and her niece arrived last night. They're staying in two of the rooms upstairs."

"Two?" Frances frowned. "Would it not be more appropriate for your niece to stay in your room, so you can act as her chaperone?"

"Well, I never." Mrs. Roberts huffed and crossed her arms over her ample bosom. "If I have the money, then I don't see it's any business of yours."

"Of course, *if* you have the money." Frances surveyed her up and down. This individual certainly didn't *look* like someone who had money to throw around. Frances wasn't up on the latest fashions, but she'd swear that dress hadn't been in vogue for at least five years. "Did you pay my daughter in advance?"

"Grandma!" Lucy planted her hands on her hips.

Mrs. Roberts snorted. "I can see I'm not needed here. I'll get out of your way and return to my room."

Frances straightened and mustered a smile. "As you wish. I certainly do *not* care to keep you from anything important."

"No!" Lucy practically shouted the word. "We need help. Zac and I don't know if his pa will be all right, and all you two want to do is bicker."

Frances jumped, and the pounding in her head doubled. "What is wrong with you, child? Please quit shouting. I have been nursing a sick headache all morning. Besides, Mr. Jacobs is not dead; he opened his eyes, moved his head, and spoke. He has an injured leg, and that is certainly not fatal."

Lucy gritted her teeth. "We need to get him up and back to bed, but since you haven't been well, I don't think you should help lift him."

Gratefulness spread through Frances. What a thoughtful granddaughter she'd helped raise. "That is very considerate of you, dear."

Mrs. Roberts swiveled, a triumphant gleam in her eyes. "Are you asking for my help, Mrs. Cooper?"

Frances lifted her chin with a jerk. "Certainly not. I am sure we can manage."

Zachary touched his father's arm. "Pa?"

The injured man slowly moved his head back and forth. "What happened?"

"You fell. Lucy, Mrs. Roberts, and I are going to get you up and back to bed. Can you help if you have your crutches?"

The man struggled to push up on one elbow. "I'll make it."

Zachary gripped his right arm, and Lucy scurried around to his other side and grabbed the left. Mrs. Roberts swooped in, plucked the crutch that had been underneath him off the floor, and held it in front of her like a weapon keeping the enemy at bay.

Frances was not certain what she could do at this juncture but was determined that woman would not usurp her authority in this house or with these children. "Leave this to me, please." She put out an arm to keep the odious woman from moving forward.

Mrs. Roberts simply grinned, stepped around her, strode to the door, and pointed. "Is this his room, young man?"

Zachary nodded. "Yes, ma'am." He kept an arm across his father's back and lifted as the man struggled to his feet.

Mrs. Roberts swept open the door. "Here you go, sir. Careful now. Go slow. You don't want to fall again." Shooting a look over her shoulder, she ushered the trio into the room and shut the door sharply in Frances's face.

Katherine, mouth agape, watched from the hallway as Mrs. Roberts shut the door on her mother. Why, the look of outrage on Mama's face was almost comical, like someone who'd been bested but couldn't conceive of how it had happened. After having tangled with Mrs. Roberts herself, Katherine could commiserate with Mama and would have had she not also tussled with her mother more than once. She was thankful she'd made the decision to ask the Roberts women to find a new place to lodge.

"Mama?" She walked forward and touched her mother's shoulder.

"Mercy me!" Mama jumped as if shot and whirled. "What are you doing, sneaking up on me like that? You liked to have scared me half out of my wits!"

Katherine took a step back. "I'm sorry." She nodded toward the door. "What's going on here? Why is Mrs. Roberts in Mr. Jacobs's room?"

Mama harrumphed. "That old biddy waltzed right in here and took over like she owns the place. I do not know who she thinks she is, but I am going to give her a piece of my mind when she comes out, that's what."

"Let's calm down, shall we?" Katherine took her mother's hand and drew her several feet away. "Is something the matter with Mr. Jacobs?"

"He apparently fell while trying to get up. Lucy ran upstairs to find Mr. Tucker and beat on his door so loudly I came out to see what had happened. I found Zachary on his knees beside his father and the man was quite insensible. I woke him and was attempting to get him on his feet when that … that … *woman* stormed down the stairs after Lucy and bullied her way in."

"So she's taking care of Mr. Jacobs? Where are Lucy and Zachary? Why didn't someone come to get me?"

Mama glared. "The children are in his room, as well. As I thought, Mrs. Roberts was not capable of helping the man up. Lucy and Zachary did so, while *she* waved that stick in my face and kept me from assisting."

Katherine didn't reply but walked to the door, rapped twice, then pushed it open. "Is everything all right, Mr. Jacobs?"

Her eyes grazed over the two children standing on one side of the bed and landed on Mrs. Roberts, who was tugging the blanket up under Micah's chin. A tender look encompassed the woman's face, and a gentle smile tipped the corners of her mouth. "There you go, dear boy. You relax now, and we'll leave you alone." She waved toward the door. "Everyone needs to leave so he can get some rest."

Katherine appreciated the sentiment but resented her boarder ordering her out of the room. She allowed Mrs. Roberts and Lucy to walk past her but stopped Zachary as he came abreast of her. "What happened, Zachary?"

The boy raised weary eyes to hers. "I'm not sure. Lucy and I brought the bedding in off the line and were headed to put it away when we heard a crash and Pa cried out. I guess he was trying out his new crutches. He fell on his bad leg, and the pain must have knocked him out, 'cause it took a while to wake him. Then your ma and Mrs. Roberts came to help and, well …" He shot a look at the partly open door and waited until the heavyset woman disappeared from view before dropping his voice. "Your ma and Mrs. Roberts had words and kind of forgot about my pa, so Lucy and I got him up and brought him back here. Mrs. Roberts opened the door for us and helped us get him in bed. Pa drifted to sleep by the time the covers were pulled up. Think we should get the doctor to come back again?"

"Yes, probably, but we'll let your father sleep for a while first. You and Lucy did well, Zachary. Do you want to stay here and sit by him or come out with us?"

"I'd like to stay, if you don't mind."

"Of course. I have business to attend to, but it would be good if you were here." Katherine stopped by the bed and gazed at the sleeping man. A flutter began in her stomach and traveled all the way up to her throat.

What was she feeling? Pity? Or attraction? The latter wasn't acceptable. She didn't need the added complication of a man in her life. But there was nothing wrong with feeling sorry for Micah—he'd lost so much, and now this …

Realizing she had things to tend to, she stepped away from the bed. "I'll be back later to check on him, Zachary."

Quietly closing the door behind her, Katherine headed down the hall. She needed to talk to her mother, but right now she'd deal with Mrs. Roberts.

Lucy waylaid her at the foot of the stairs. "Is he going to be okay, Ma? It scared me something awful when we found him and couldn't get him to wake up. I was afraid he was dead." Her face was pale, and her chin quivered. "Like Pa." The words came out in a whisper.

"Oh, honey." Katherine hugged her daughter. "This was nothing like your pa. Mr. Jacobs fell, but I'm sure he's going to be fine after he rests. We'll have the doctor come and check on him to be sure, but I don't want you to worry." She drew back and smiled, pride swelling her heart. What a brave, sensible girl she'd raised. "You did a good job taking care of things. I'm proud of you."

Lucy ducked her head. "Zachary helped too. It wasn't only me."

Katherine nodded. "I understand that, but you—not Zachary—were in charge since Grandma had a headache and wasn't feeling well."

"Why don't you like him, Ma? You never say anything nice about him, and he's my friend." Lucy's voice broke; then she fled down the hall.

Katherine stared after her daughter. What had just happened? She hadn't said a thing about disliking that boy; she'd only tried to emphasize that Lucy had done a good job taking responsibility for the events of the morning. Why was it so hard to get along with her daughter from one minute to the next? Ever since Lucy was born, Katherine had looked forward to the time when they could be friends. She laughed to herself. She should have known that was foolish. Parents couldn't be friends with children while raising them; they had to maintain structure, discipline, and accountability. Moving into the realm of friends would muddy the waters too much, and with a young girl in her teens, there was also the matter of emotions bouncing around like a rubber ball on a hardwood floor. Lucy would probably forget all about this and be totally fine by supper.

Katherine exhaled, knowing she still had an unpleasant task to tend to. Mrs. Roberts. The woman had apparently been rude to Mama—although that had to be taken with a grain of salt, knowing her mother. Mrs. Roberts might have overstepped her bounds, although from all appearances she'd only helped Lucy and Zachary care for Micah. What a pickle. Mama obviously didn't like their new boarder, and though Katherine could ill afford to lose the income, it appeared she'd made the right choice about the pair finding new lodging soon.

Trooping up the steps, she paused in front of the room she'd given to Mrs. Roberts. She hesitated, working to form the words

she'd use, then discarded the effort. Much would depend on the
woman's attitude when she opened the door. She raised her hand
and knocked, then waited several beats before trying again.

Heavy footsteps sounded on the far side, and the door swung
open. Katherine's gaze was met by red-rimmed eyes above puffy
cheeks.

Katherine started. Mrs. Roberts was either coming down with
a cold, or she'd been crying—but that didn't seem to fit the image
she had of the matron. "Mrs. Roberts? I wondered if you might
have time to talk. We could sit downstairs, or in the small parlor
down the hall if you'd like."

The older woman took a handkerchief from the pocket of her
dress and blew her nose. "No need. Come in. I have been expecting
you, and I'd appreciate the privacy my room offers."

Katherine was nonplussed, but she stepped across the threshold anyway and waited.

"Before we go any farther, how is that young man faring? Do
you think he'll recover?"

Katherine experienced a tinge of surprise at the question. She'd
come expecting a confrontation and instead found a woman who
appeared to have been crying and who asked about someone else
before discussing her own complaints. "He's sleeping, and I've
sent for the doctor to make sure he didn't do any further damage
to his leg, but I believe he'll recover. Thank you for asking."

The older woman nodded and moved across the room to an
overstuffed chair. She motioned to it and waited for Katherine to
sit, then perched on the end of the bed nearby. "I am afraid I had
words with your mother. She took an instant dislike to me for

some reason." Mrs. Roberts sniffed, and Katherine's heart started to soften ... until the haughty expression Mrs. Roberts had worn the previous evening reappeared. "And, I have to admit, I have no fondness for her. But in spite of her rude behavior, Beth and I will stay here for the time being. That is, if you can assure me that Mrs. Cooper will mind her own business and won't interfere with mine."

Katherine stiffened, and any sympathy she'd formed quickly dissolved. "I'm afraid I can't give you any such assurance, madame. My mother is her own person and won't be controlled by anyone, least of all me. But, regardless, I can't agree with your decision to stay. I have given it much thought and feel it's best for all involved if you find a new place to lodge as soon as possible."

"I beg your pardon?" Mrs. Roberts shook her head sharply as though trying to clear the unpleasant words from her ears. "I can't have heard you properly. *I* am the injured party here, not you, or your mother. *She* is the one who accosted me, not the other way around. If anyone is in the wrong, it is Mrs. Cooper. Why should my niece and I be asked to leave?"

Katherine sent up a swift prayer for wisdom and tact, something that eluded her in the presence of this woman. Why did some people have to make life difficult for everyone around them? She could well imagine that her mother hadn't been kind or considerate to Mrs. Roberts, but that didn't condone the other woman's behavior. "I simply feel it best. Let's leave it at that, shall we?"

Mrs. Roberts snorted. "No, we shall not."

"If you insist." Katherine extended her hand. "I must consider the welfare of my entire household over any one individual, or in your case, any two. It would seem that you won't be happy here unless we adapt to your needs, and that's not something I'm willing to do—not if it means making an uncomfortable atmosphere for my family and other boarders. Is that clear enough?"

Mrs. Roberts's hands fell to her sides. "Quite. We will pack and be off within the hour." Desolation colored her tone.

Guilt stabbed Katherine but this had to be done, and it behooved her to be strong and follow through. "There is no need to rush. Take as much time as you need, and if you'd like, I can send Lucy to one of the hotels to see if they might have a wagon available to transport you and your belongings."

"No, thank you. I do not care to be beholden to you or anyone else in this place. Beth and I will make do on our own." Mrs. Roberts strode to the door and opened it. "Now, if you will excuse me, I have work to do."

Micah woke slowly, trying to orient himself to his surroundings. Shooting pain traveled from his ankle to his thigh and back down again. Ah yes, he had attempted to get out of this bed. How stupid could he be, trying to walk with crutches? Maybe if he had waited till he were stronger, it would've been easier, but now he'd probably be in bed even longer.

His gaze landed on Zachary, sitting with his head tilted back against a Queen Anne chair, his body relaxed. Tenderness filled Micah's heart at the sight of his sleeping son. What a mess he'd made of things, getting hurt over a toolbox. Now he couldn't provide for his family and had to rely on the charity of strangers.

Well, maybe not strangers, exactly. His thoughts drifted to the last time Katherine had visited his room. She'd surprised him by delivering breakfast herself. He'd assumed Zachary or Lucy would arrive with his tray, but a fresh-faced, smiling Katherine had stepped through the door, breathless from hurrying—or so he assumed. He'd hated how unkempt he must appear. It had been days since he'd had a bath or a shave. He ran his hand over the scruff on his chin. Katherine hadn't stayed long, but the scent of lavender had lingered in the air afterwards.

Zachary stirred and sat up. "Pa?" He struggled from the chair. "You doin' all right? We were some worried when we found you out cold in the hall."

Remorse hit Micah hard, and he added *worrying his son* to his list of current transgressions. Nothing seemed to be going right lately, and he had no one to blame but himself. Unless he counted God. Frustration niggled at his heart. God could have kept all of this from happening—his wife's death, his home and business burning, even losing his balance and falling. That wouldn't have been too hard, would it?

"I'll be fine, Son. You didn't have to stay with me."

"I wanted to. Doc Sanders is on his way. Mrs. Galloway sent for him."

Micah frowned. "Don't need to see him again. I can't afford all these doctor bills. He was here this morning when he dressed the burn and gave me the crutches."

"Mrs. Galloway says you fell pretty hard and might've hit your head or hurt your leg worse."

"Well, she's not in charge. When the doctor gets here, I'll tell him he can head back home."

Zachary looked uncomfortable. "You sure, Pa? You always told me we shouldn't be uncharitable when people try to do something kind for us. Ain't that being uncharitable?"

Condemnation hammered his conscience. Couldn't a man be grumpy for even five minutes without someone ragging him about it? "Don't say *ain't*, Son." He wasn't ready to apologize yet.

Zachary hung his head but not before Micah caught a glimpse of hurt. "Yes, sir."

"I'm sorry. I had no call to growl at you, or at Mrs. Galloway. She's right. Doc Sanders should probably look at this leg again. I hit the floor pretty hard trying to work those confounded contraptions."

Warm brown eyes lifted and met his. Then a small smile crept across Zachary's face. "What happened, Pa?"

Micah hoisted himself up against the pillow and winced. "From what I recollect, I went one way and those sticks went another." He gave a deep-throated chuckle. "Guess they didn't care to dance any more than I did."

Zachary erupted in a laugh.

Micah joined in. He hadn't felt so good in days. Seeing the pain and confusion in his boy's eyes had stung, especially knowing he'd planted it there.

From now on, he'd do better at this parenting business. He didn't have much choice, seeing he was the only one Zachary had left, but he'd be hornswoggled if he'd keep falling down on the job like he had lately.

A second later, when Doctor Sanders strode in, black bag in hand, Micah's lips were still twitching with amusement. A blond vision floated in behind the doctor, and a jolt hit him hard. Had his heart been damaged during the fall? He couldn't imagine any other reason it would jerk to a stop, then race forward again, when his landlady entered the room. No reason at all.

Chapter Eighteen

Dinner last night had been a rather subdued affair after Micah's setback, although Mama danced around like a Banty rooster when she discovered Mrs. Roberts and Beth had departed earlier in the day for one of the hotels.

While Katherine had busied herself around the kitchen stacking clean plates and wiping down the front of the pie safe, the doctor had examined Micah. Doc had insisted Micah keep to his bed for at least another two days but had assured them the fall hadn't done any lasting damage.

Now that this morning's chores were done, it was the perfect time for baking pies. Her boarders had a fondness for apple, and with a surplus of dried apples in the cellar, she could afford the luxury.

A knock sounded at the front door. Katherine placed the last dish on the stack on the dining room sideboard and wiped her hands on her apron. She hurried to the foyer at the front of the house. Gripping the knob, she opened the door, ready to give a warm greeting.

Her smile faltered and died as soon as her gaze rested on the woman standing on her porch.

A deep flush stained Mrs. Roberts's cheeks, and she clutched her reticule against her midriff. "Good day, Mrs. Galloway. I wonder if I might have a moment of your time."

Katherine hesitated, then swung the door wide and stepped aside. "Of course. Please come in." She waited until the older woman strode past, suddenly grateful Mama had excused herself after breakfast to rest in her room. "Would you care for a cup of tea?"

"No, thank you." Mrs. Roberts's normal bluster didn't appear to be present, and her red-rimmed eyes glimmered with a hint of tears. "I do not care to put you out."

"It's no trouble at all. In fact, I finished cleaning the kitchen and was thinking of sitting for a minute before I started my baking. The kettle is on. Please join me?"

Mrs. Roberts hesitated, then gave a quick nod. "I suppose it might be a bit more private in the kitchen."

Katherine led the way down the hall. Why had Mrs. Roberts returned? She'd not been gone twenty-four hours—why, Katherine hadn't even stripped the beds in those rooms. The last thing she needed today was another confrontation with this obnoxious woman....

Suddenly she was ashamed of the direction her thoughts had taken. *Forgive me, Father. I have no right to judge.*

She plucked two of her best china cups and saucers off the sideboard and poured the fragrant peppermint tea she'd been steeping. Last fall, Lucy had discovered a patch of peppermint growing along the Powder River. They'd dried a large bundle and stored it in the pantry. "Sugar?"

"No, thank you. This smells wonderful." Mrs. Roberts's hand trembled as she lifted the cup, took a sip, then set it back on the saucer. She ran her finger around the rim of her teacup for several seconds. "Please, may Beth and I return and stay here?"

Katherine jerked and slopped tea over the side of her cup. She plunked it onto the saucer. "I'm sorry. Let me clean this before it stains the table." As she busied herself wiping the tea and rinsing the rag, she wondered: What had possessed the woman to come back after she'd been asked to leave yesterday? She hated to hurt Mrs. Roberts further by rejecting her request, but after all that had happened, she couldn't imagine it a good idea to allow them to return. Sinking back into her chair, she gripped the handle of her cup and waited, hoping she'd misunderstood.

Long seconds passed. The color in the older woman's cheeks became more intense. "I see it's no use." She pushed back her chair and rose. "Forgive me for being a nuisance. I will not take any more of your time. Thank you for the tea." She turned to go.

"Wait." Katherine sprang from her chair and extended a hand. "I've forgotten my manners. Please don't leave yet. I truly do want to understand."

Mrs. Roberts clasped her reticule in front of her like a shield. "Understand what, Mrs. Galloway?"

"Why you're asking to return when you left yesterday to find lodging elsewhere." Katherine refrained from tacking on the rest—that Mrs. Roberts had been *asked* to leave with the expectation she wouldn't return. "Won't you sit down again and explain?"

Mrs. Roberts paused. "As you wish." She slid into the chair as gracefully as a woman her size could but sat as mute as a block of granite and just as still, her hands entwined in a knot on top of the table.

Katherine touched the older woman's fingers across the flat surface. "Mrs. Roberts?"

"Oh." She sighed loudly. "I'm sorry. Yes?"

"You were going to explain your request."

"Yes. Indeed." The fingers twisted, the agitation quite opposite of what Katherine had expected from their earlier encounters. "I came to apologize."

Now it was Katherine's turn to be mute. She simply stared, unable to take in the meaning of those four simple words. "I see." But she didn't. Not really. She tried again. "May I ask what, exactly, you've come to apologize for, and what it has to do with your request?"

"Everything," Mrs. Roberts blurted, her fingers worrying the clasp of her reticule. "The hotel is horrid. The food is dreadfully expensive, and they only had one small room with a narrow bed for the both of us." Waving an expressive hand in front of her bodice, she continued, "As you can see, I am not a small woman. Poor Beth almost ended up on the floor before morning, and neither of us got much sleep." She sucked in a harsh breath. "And when I complained, the odious little man at the front desk told me one of us could sleep on the floor!" She gave a laugh tinged with hysteria. "Can you imagine me doing that?"

Katherine couldn't say that the words provoked a pleasant image, but she kept her opinion to herself. "I'm sorry you had such a difficult time, Mrs. Roberts, but I can't alter my decision about you staying here. If anything, I'm even more certain you wouldn't be a good fit for my boardinghouse."

"But you do *not* understand." Mrs. Roberts flopped back against the wood spindles of the chair. "I can't afford to stay anywhere else."

Katherine raised her brows. "I beg your pardon? Didn't you inform me when you came that you've stayed in some of the nicest establishments on the East Coast? They're far more expensive and lavish than my modest abode."

"Yes, of course they are." Mrs. Roberts's words held defeat and a sob hovered on the last word.

Katherine winced. Mrs. Roberts was nothing if not blunt. But the last thing she wanted was anyone else to hear and come running to see what the problem was—especially Mama. "Shh, it's all right. Why don't you take a sip of your tea and allow yourself a moment to relax?"

Mrs. Roberts clutched the handle of her teacup with shaking hands, raised it to her lips, then set it back carefully on the saucer. "I'm sorry. I'll try to control myself."

Katherine waited for her to continue.

"I lost a lot of my money a number of months ago." A blush crept up her neck. "Never mind how right now; suffice it to say someone I trusted took advantage of me. It left me in a rather precarious situation, and I came out West, hoping to somehow improve my position."

Katherine had a good idea how the matron hoped to improve her position, and it had to do with Beth, but she kept the uncharitable thoughts to herself. It wasn't uncommon for a parent or guardian to arrange a marriage for their daughter or niece to a wealthy man in hopes of filling the family coffers. But Beth wasn't Katherine's responsibility, and she had no right to comment on the matter, even if she didn't agree. Besides, it was possible the young woman might find a man to care for who could provide for both of the ladies.

Mrs. Roberts dropped her gaze. "I see you don't approve." Then she raised her clear brown eyes. "Well, neither do I, but I don't want my niece placed in servitude in some rich man's home, nor do I want either of us to land in the poor house."

"I'm not sure what that has to do with me," Katherine said.

"Oh, dear, I *am* making a mess of this, aren't I?"

"I don't know, Mrs. Roberts." Katherine shrugged. "I don't see any reason why it makes sense for me to allow you to return here."

"Before I came today, I planned on begging your forgiveness for my behavior. Then when I got here and you were so kind … well, I guess my troubles tumbled out instead." She leaned forward, her face drawn with anxiety. "I know I can be difficult at times. Demanding, even. My sister used to tell me that all the time. Not that it mattered. But in my heart, I knew she was right. I tend to run roughshod over people when I want my own way."

She scooted her chair back and picked her reticule off the floor. "I do not expect you to accept my apology; I can see I've already turned you against me. That's my fault, not yours. Besides, I certainly couldn't promise to be perfect if we returned. I'm not, you know. I'd probably say and do things that would offend you once more, and you'd have to ask me to leave again. I hoped that I could show you how sorry I am, and you would give me another chance. But I won't press you. I'm sure Beth and I will find something. Good day, Mrs. Galloway, and thank you for your kindness in listening."

Katherine sat, unsure what to say or think. This was the last thing she'd expected. Part of her wanted to accept the woman's decision to leave and hurry her out the door, but deep in her heart she knew her heavenly Father wouldn't be pleased with that attitude. When she and Daniel had started this business, they'd talked about the ways they might be able to help people—a ministry of sorts, as well as a source of income. Now she had a chance to minister to a woman who was obviously hurting, and all she wanted to do was run the other way—or hope Mrs. Roberts did. She offered a quick prayer for strength. "You can stay."

Mrs. Roberts's mouth gaped. "I beg your pardon?"

Katherine squirmed. It had been hard enough saying it the first time, but it seemed there was no help for it. "You and Beth may return." She held up her hand to stop the gush of words she knew was coming. "I'm willing to do this on a trial basis. We'll say a week, then talk again. I appreciate your apology, but as you said yourself, you can be difficult and demanding at times. I'm not sure that will easily change, and I'm not willing to subject my family or other guests to fits of temper or histrionics."

"I understand." Mrs. Roberts gripped her reticule as though it were a lifeline. "I promise I will try to behave and not complain— too much." She gave a little chuckle. "It won't be easy, but I *will* do my best."

"That's all I can ask. None of us is perfect, Mrs. Roberts, and I don't expect you to be, either. But I do ask that you try to get along with the other guests—and with my mother."

Mrs. Roberts placed her hand over her heart and a whoosh of air exited her mouth. "Oh, my. I had forgotten your mother."

"Is she going to be too big of a problem for you?" Katherine rose from her chair.

"No." The older woman shook her head vehemently. "I'm certain I can abide—er, I mean, be kind—to Mrs. Cooper." She grimaced in the semblance of a smile. "At least, I will try."

"That's good enough for me." Katherine smiled warmly in return. "And since you've been so honest with me, I'll do the same. My mother is not the easiest person to live with. I have trouble with her myself at times. I don't expect you to put up with her needling you, but I do ask that if it gets too unbearable, you simply walk away. Can you do that?"

"Yes. Certainly. Thank you." Mrs. Roberts rushed around the table and threw her arms around Katherine. "You won't regret this. I promise."

Katherine stood still, not sure how to respond. Right now she didn't know what she'd regret, but one thing she did know—it wasn't going to be pleasant facing Mama when she learned that Wilma Roberts had permission to return.

Chapter Nineteen

Frances sat at the supper table, her stomach burning as though she'd swallowed poison instead of the dinner her daughter had served. Not that she'd tasted any of it with that woman sitting across from her, looking like a cat that had lapped up the last few drops of cream from the milk pail before the dairy wife whisked it away.

The insufferable creature. Mrs. Roberts—not the poor cat. At least a feline had an excuse for its behavior. Mrs. Roberts did not. She was supposed to have left and not return. Why had Katherine allowed the pair access to the boardinghouse again?

Of course, Frances had been in her room most of the afternoon with another headache and hadn't spoken to Katherine. More than likely they came back for something they'd forgotten and Katherine, charitable soul that she was, had invited them to supper. Hopefully she'd remember to charge them for their meal.

She pasted on what she hoped would pass as a smile. "So, Mrs. Roberts, you could not find any place that served as fine a meal as my Katherine's? I would have thought the hotel dining room would be an easier place to eat since it is so much closer to where you are living now."

A hush fell over the table, and all eyes turned toward the woman in question. Mr. Tucker seemed particularly interested and … what?

Amused? Why would he be amused? Frances frowned. She hadn't said anything even the least bit comical.

Of all things. If Wilma Roberts didn't positively beam with happiness—or was it preening satisfaction? The woman's face was wreathed in smiles. "Why, I assumed you knew, Mrs. Cooper. Beth and I moved back—not long after luncheon, in fact. We're very grateful Mrs. Galloway saved our rooms and invited us to stay again. You must be very proud to have raised such a considerate, generous daughter."

It took all of Frances's willpower to control herself. She bit the inside of her cheeks, certain her head would explode. Katherine had invited *these* people to move back in? What could she possibly be thinking? Why, Wilma Roberts had been positively rude during their last encounter, and Katherine had assured her they'd moved out.

Frances harrumphed. "Oh, yes, *very* proud." She cast a withering glance toward her daughter, who was sitting at the head of the table. "You have no idea." Focusing back on the cheerful woman, she continued, "Why did you feel it necessary to return? Weren't you able to find adequate lodging in town? I am sure a woman of your means can afford something far finer than our modest establishment."

Mrs. Roberts's face sagged. Her mouth opened, but no sound issued forth.

Ah, that got to her, didn't it? Something was afoot here that would bear digging into. "You *can* afford better, can't you, dear?"

"Mama, why don't we talk about this later and allow us to finish our meal?" Katherine picked up a tray of raised biscuits and handed them to Lucy, sitting on her right. "Pass these down, dear. I'm sure Mr. Tucker or Beth would like another while they're still warm."

Beth ducked her head. "No, thank you, ma'am. I've had plenty."

"Nonsense." Her aunt reached across her, plucked a biscuit from the plate, and set it in front of the girl. "You're too thin as it is. No man wants a wife who appears to be ready to expire. Eat up, now."

Frances narrowed her eyes. "Your niece said she is not hungry, so why force her to eat? She looks perfectly healthy to me." She did not, but the last thing Frances cared to do was agree with Mrs. Roberts. Her high-handed treatment of the young woman was ridiculous. Of course, Mrs. Roberts was obviously poorly bred and didn't understand good table etiquette.

"Well, I never." Mrs. Roberts's face darkened and her eyes flashed.

"Mama! Mrs. Roberts. Please!" Katherine's words cut across the charged atmosphere.

Amanda gazed from her mother to her grandmother and back again. "Why is everyone so angry? What's wrong, Grandma?"

Frances melted at the apprehension on the little girl's face. "Oh, honey, it's all right. Grandma is not angry at anyone. I was only helping Mrs. Roberts. Don't worry, sweetie." She caressed Amanda's hair. "I think there are cookies for dessert. Would you like to go to the kitchen and bring them back in?"

Amanda's expression cleared, and she looked toward her mother. "May I, Ma?"

"Yes, dear, go ahead." Katherine's gaze flickered to Frances and lingered there. "I'll be in to get the coffee in a moment."

Jeffery Tucker absorbed the scene in silence, wondering if he should excuse himself or stay in case more fireworks flared. It was always possible he could use this scene as fuel for his work. He settled back in his chair and surveyed the table. Too bad Jacobs was still laid up in his room with that bum leg. Another male perspective might bring a bit more balance to the conversation, but Mrs. Galloway had done an adequate job stepping in between the two combatants. That mother of hers was a corker. She seemed to have an opinion about everything and expected others to agree or move out of her way. Must have been hard for her children and husband to live with—assuming the man had stuck around very long.

He placed his forearms on the table and addressed Zachary. "When will your father be able to join us?"

Zachary jumped as though he'd been poked. "What? Were you speaking to me, sir?"

"I was, but pardon me if I startled you. I didn't realize you were gathering wool." He'd seen the boy's gaze resting on Mrs. Galloway's older daughter, Lucy, in the past, but tonight he seemed dumbstruck by the newest addition, Beth. The young woman was closer to his own age than Zachary's, but the boy probably didn't realize it.

Warm color suffused Zachary's face. "Uh, I ..." He squirmed in his seat. "What did you ask, Mr. Tucker?"

Lucy giggled and placed her hand over her mouth, but not before Zachary shot her a frown.

"I wondered how your father is faring after his injury and when the doctor will allow him out of bed."

"Oh." The boy relaxed. "Soon, I hope. He's getting pretty restless, and I'm not sure he'll be willing to stay in that room much longer." He cast an apologetic glance at Lucy's mother. "Not that he's complaining, mind you. It's just that he's used to being active and doing for himself."

Mrs. Galloway nodded. "I understand, Zachary. No need to worry about my feelings. I can only imagine what your father is going through, and I certainly hope he's allowed to get up in the next day or two." She nodded graciously. "Excuse me. I need to go see to the coffee in the kitchen."

As soon as Mrs. Galloway had left the room, Mrs. Roberts tapped her fingertips on the tablecloth. "Mr. Tucker, isn't it?"

He sat up straighter. "Yes, ma'am, at your service."

She surveyed him from the top of his head, down over his shoulders, and to the tips of his fingers. "You don't look like a man who's seen many hours of hard labor. What brings you to Baker City? Certainly not mining."

The table went still, and every set of eyes swiveled toward him. He'd been able to avoid this question since arriving by turning the conversation back on the person doing the asking. "No, not mining, ma'am. And you're correct. I wasn't born to manual labor. How about you and your lovely niece? What brings *you* to this fair city?"

"That's not good manners, Mr. Tucker, to avoid my question. What type of work do you do? Or are you a wealthy man here hoping to find a wife, with no need to work?" She assessed Beth before fixing her attention back on him.

"Hardly." He tried to laugh, but it came off as more of a grunt.

Mrs. Cooper smirked. "Mrs. Roberts, you certainly do not mind asking pointed questions of others. It sounds as though you might be fishing for a rich husband. Are you looking for one yourself, or perhaps for your niece?" Her probing eyes flicked toward the young woman, who wilted into her chair.

Mrs. Roberts looked as though she might choke.

Jeffery wanted to laugh, but pity at the poor woman's discomfiture kept him silent.

"Who wants cookies?" The high-pitched voice of Amanda entering the room broke the silence and swung the focus to the plate of fragrant molasses cookies balanced between her small hands.

He jumped up and hurried toward her. "Let me help. We don't want any of those treats sliding onto the floor, do we?"

"No, sir. Thank you, sir." She handed over the tray with a grin. "You can have the first one. Grandma, Ma wants to know if you could bring more. She's getting the coffee."

Mrs. Cooper nodded and rose from her chair.

Placing the plate on the table, Jeffery plucked a cookie from the edge. "I'll go see if I can help too." He sauntered from the room. They'd all been saved by a child bearing treats. From now on he'd make sure not to engage nosey women in conversation if he could avoid it.

Katherine thanked Mr. Tucker for his offer but sent him back to the table. She needed a few moments with her mother. "Mama? Can you stay here, please?"

Mama pivoted, the second plate of cookies gripped in her hands. "What is it? I need to take these to the dining room."

"I think they have plenty for now, and I'd like to speak with you."

Mama plopped the plate onto the counter. "Well! You did not think it important to tell me you had given in to that woman's demands and invited her to move back here?"

Katherine tucked a wayward strand of hair behind her ear and silently counted to five. Just like Mama. Turn it around on her before she had a chance to say a word. The last thing she needed was a fight. "She didn't demand anything, and I didn't invite her, she asked. In fact, Mrs. Roberts was very humble and apologized for her behavior. I thought it only charitable to accept her apology and give her another chance."

"Humble? Ha! More than likely an act she put on to get back into your good graces—and obviously, one that worked." She shook her head. "I would think you would be more discerning, Katherine. You let people pull the wool over your eyes far too often. If you keep this up, you will lose business you can scarce afford. It is obvious the woman is destitute. Did you see the way she avoided my question about her circumstances?"

"My business is fine, Mama. As for being destitute, Mrs. Roberts paid a full week in advance, and we'll decide if she stays longer when the week is up." Katherine spoke the last words without thinking, and her heart dropped when satisfaction flitted across her mother's face.

"Ah, so you only agreed to a week. Good. Well, I guess we will have to see if she can hold her tongue and control her temper for a week, then, won't we?" She picked up the plate of cookies and hobbled out of the room.

Chapter Twenty

Micah swallowed the last of his morning coffee and set it back on the tray Katherine held. "Thank you, Mrs. Galloway. That was an excellent breakfast."

"I thought we agreed you'd call me Katherine?" She quirked a brow.

"I recently realized it may have been a hasty decision. Somehow it seems rather disrespectful to call my landlady by her first name."

"I'm afraid I'm in the habit of thinking of you as Micah, not Mr. Jacobs. But if that offends or worries you, I suppose I can make the effort to change." A mischievous smile tugged at her lips.

Micah relaxed. "If you have no objections, then it's fine … Katherine. At least when we're talking in private."

"Good. Now, how about getting you back on your feet? It's been three days since your fall, and Doc Sanders said you could try again today, if you wish."

A mirthless chuckle broke from his throat. "Oh, I wish. In fact, I insist. If I stay here much longer, I'll have bed sores on top of the burned skin and banged-up body." He winced. "Pardon me. That was rude and thoughtless. You've been very kind to offer this bed and our rooms."

She waved an airy hand. "Nothing to apologize for." She held out the crutches. "Here you go. Take it slow and easy this time. See if you can make it to the sitting room."

He reached for them and his fingertips brushed hers. The tingling that ran up his arm almost made him jerk back, but he controlled the urge. What was it about this woman that affected him so? It would soon be two years since he'd lost his wife. Many men remarried within that space of time, but he hadn't been able to even look at another woman that way—until now.

Katherine Galloway was not only a fine-looking woman, she was kindhearted, generous, and from all he could tell, a hard worker to boot. Her children adored her, and Zachary seemed to get along with her, as well. He shook his head. What was he thinking? She'd made it plain she was a successful businesswoman with no need for a man. "Thanks. I think I've got it from here." He tucked the crutches under his arm and swung forward, working to keep from gazing at her again.

"So, what's been happening in town since I took to my bed? I've gotten snippets out of Zachary, but not much." He wasn't typically so talkative, but his nerves were getting the better of him with Katherine walking so close. He felt shy and bumbling all at the same time. Emma had never affected him this way, but they'd known one another since grammar school.

"I think the church is planning a social next month, and the mines appear to be doing well, if you can judge by the number of men who come into town on the weekends." She paused in the doorway to the parlor and waited for him to hobble past. "Maybe you'd like to come to church with us some time and attend the social?" Pink tinged her cheeks and she hurried on. "With Zachary, of course. I mean, you're both welcome to join our family."

"Thanks. I'll think on it, but I'll probably pass on attending church." He settled into a wingback chair. "Looks like I made it without taking a tumble this time. Where are the children? Zachary didn't come to my room this morning."

"I gave them permission to take their fishing poles down to the Powder River to see if they can catch anything for dinner. Mandy's been begging to go, and Lucy and Zachary promised to watch her."

"Ah, that's good." The words drifted off into silence, and the room seemed to close around him. He cast about, wondering what he might talk about to keep her close, but nothing came to mind.

"Here comes Mrs. Roberts and Beth." Katherine tipped her head at the two women entering the room.

Micah's heart sank clear down to the toes of his work boots. The last thing he wanted was to be cornered by two women he didn't know. Maybe he could claim to be tired and head back to his room—but the prospect of lying in that bed and staring at those walls was not pleasant. Better to take his chances out here and hope they didn't stay long. "Ladies." He nodded and forced a smile.

Mrs. Roberts swooped across the room—at least, she tried. Her deep green skirts flared around her ample figure. "Beth, dear, come along and meet this nice gentleman." She stopped in front of him and waited for her niece to catch up. "We haven't been formally introduced yet, I'm afraid."

Katherine moved forward, and her pale yellow dress rustled. "I'm sorry, I didn't realize. Mrs. Roberts, allow me to introduce Mr. Jacobs. You've met his son, Zachary." She turned toward Micah.

"This is Mrs. Wilma Roberts and her niece, Beth. She's the one who helped the children get you back to your room when you fell. They'll be lodging here for the coming week."

"Or more." Mrs. Roberts's voice boomed. "At least, that's our hope." She extended her hand and gripped his with surprising strength. "It's good to see you up and around again."

She settled into a brocade chair across from his and motioned Beth to take the one alongside. "It appears you're on the mend now." She indicated the crutches. "Now tell me, young man, what do you do for a living? Are you a miner, or something else?"

Startled by the abrupt question, he cast a glance at Katherine, who gave a gentle smile.

"I need to do some mending and start dinner preparations ... if you'll excuse me." She inclined her head and walked from the room.

Micah felt as though his lifeline had been yanked from his hands. What was wrong with him? He could certainly carry on a brief conversation with this matron and her niece on his own. Now what had she asked? "Mining? No. Although I've dabbled at that in the past. I own a livery stable in town. Or, at least, I used to."

Her look of expectancy changed to one of disappointment. "Used to? Did you go out of business?"

"No. It burned to the ground a few weeks ago." The words came out clipped and hard, and he turned his head to the side, not wanting her to see the pain that surely must show.

She sat back in her chair. "My dear man, I'm sorry. Do you plan to rebuild?"

He hunched a shoulder. "I'm not sure."

"What a pity. I pray your circumstances improve." She reached across the short space and touched Beth on the shoulder. "We really should be going. I want to walk to the general store to see if they can match a button I lost. Good day, Mr. Jacobs."

Beth stood and gave a small curtsy. The shy gaze she fixed on him was warm and full of sympathy. "I do hope you're able to rebuild your business, Mr. Jacobs, and that your leg heals soon."

Micah relaxed at the kindness evident in the younger woman's voice. "Uh, thank you, Miss. Much appreciated."

He watched them leave, wondering where Mrs. Roberts's questions were leading. Was she hoping to find a rich husband for her niece, or was she genuinely concerned? Either way, she'd apparently gotten her answers. Just as well. The last thing he needed was someone pushing a girl into his path hoping for a match.

He hoisted himself up and tucked the crutches under his arms. He needed to get out of the house. Thankfully his lungs hadn't been seriously damaged by the smoke. Fresh air sounded good, but Micah wasn't sure he'd be up to navigating the rutted road leading to town. Not to mention his throbbing leg and waning strength.

Footsteps thumped up the stairs leading to the front door. A knock sounded, and then the front door opened seconds later. "Hello? Mrs. Galloway? Anyone at home?"

Micah hobbled toward the spacious foyer, recognizing Pastor Russell's voice. Normally he wouldn't be interested in visiting with the town preacher, but this man had helped pull him out of a burning building. The least he could do was be hospitable until Katherine appeared. It was, after all, her home, not his. Pain knifed his chest as he remembered he had no home but this one—at least for the moment. "Pastor. In here." He shimmied around the end of the divan and limped his way to the open archway.

The pastor appeared, hat in hand. "You're the man I wanted to see. How you doing, Jacobs?"

"Tolerable, Pastor Russell. In the absence of the landlady, I'll escort you back to the parlor and offer you a seat, if you'd care to come. Or better yet, I was thinking of sitting on the porch in one of those wicker chairs. I've been hankering to get into the open air."

"Seth, remember? We don't stand on formality around here. Or Pastor Seth, if you insist. And the porch sounds fine."

The man followed Micah's thumping crutches across the foyer, then stepped in front of him to open the front door, waiting for him to pass through. Following Micah, the pastor lowered himself onto a chair. "Glad to see you up and around."

Micah sank into a chair and propped his crutches beside him. He'd lived so much of his life in the outdoors, doing a man's work, that it was a relief to be out of the house. He inhaled the fragrance of the air, freshly washed after last night's thunderstorm. "Today's the first time I've been out of bed since the accident. Well, other than a few days ago, when I tried and tipped over."

The pastor's mouth twitched. "Oh?"

"Took a tumble while learning the ropes with these sticks. I think I've got the hang of them now, as long as no doors or rugs get in the way." He allowed a chuckle to slip out.

"I'm glad you can joke about it. You do any real damage?"

"Set me back a day or so, but Doc says I'm on track again. I think I'll be able to toss these things soon. The swelling's going down, and the dressing on the burn only has to be changed every other day."

Pastor Seth rotated his hat through his fingers. "Good. So, Jacobs, what are your plans?"

"I'm not rightly sure." Micah bowed his head, then met the man's steady gaze. "I'll be honest. I don't have the money to rebuild. I was thinking I'd see about renting room in a barn on the edge of town, if I can find someone willing. The town needs a blacksmith, even if I don't have the means for a full livery. I still have my team of mules and my horse. At least my wagon was parked away from the building and wasn't destroyed. I can rent it out to those who need it, and do some smithy work as soon as I'm able. That's about as far as I've gone in my planning."

"Those all sound like fine ideas." The pastor nodded slowly. "Have you thought about asking your friends to help you rebuild?"

Micah's muscles tensed. The man meant well, he knew that, but the idea of asking for help soured him to his very core. All his growing-up years, Pa had taught him to be self-sufficient, never beholden to anyone. If anything, he needed to find ways to give back to the community and those around him. That's what a man did. He shook his head. "I can't do that. For one thing, I really don't know many people yet, and for another, they have their own work and responsibilities. No one wants to be burdened with another man's problems."

"But that's what the community is for. We're a body, and we need to operate as such. The Bible says that just like a body isn't only a foot or an arm, the church isn't made up of one kind of person. We all have talents and gifts. We all look after the other—step in when someone is hurting."

"I'm not part of your church, Pastor Seth. I'm not trying to be rude, and I hope you'll forgive me for being frank, but I have no desire to be part of any church."

"I'm sorry you feel that way, but I'm not going to give up." The pastor grinned. "I have a bit of a stubborn streak myself."

Micah's shoulders relaxed a mite. "Your choice, I guess. But don't expect me to show up on the church's doorstep anytime soon."

"Before I go, would it be all right if I pray with you?"

Micah clenched his teeth. The last thing he wanted was to hurt this man who'd done nothing but try to do good, but he couldn't string him along. Honesty right up front was best. "I don't think so. God's done me no favors these past two years, and I can muddle through life as well on my own. But thank you for offering." He reached for a crutch. "I think I need to lie down for a spell. Would you like me to call Mrs. Galloway? I'm sure she'd be pleased to see you."

Micah wanted to bite the tip of his tongue. That hadn't come out right. Now the preacher would think he wasn't pleased to see him, and he hadn't meant that at all. But probably better to let it lie than scramble to explain. He'd dug a deep enough hole as it was, and trying to fix it might plant him that much deeper.

Lucy leaned her elbow on the grassy bank, letting her line dangle in the water. She was glad Mr. Jacobs had been up and around for a couple of days now, so Zachary could go fishing with her. They hadn't caught anything the last time they'd come, so Ma allowed them to come again, so long as they brought Mandy along too. But she'd done nothing but fuss about not catching a fish the last time they came.

The line gave a light jerk and she sat up straight, her fingers clutching the pole. Another tug and she snatched it back hard. "I've got one!" She jumped to her feet and took a cautious step backward, lowering the tip of her willow stick till it almost touched the water.

Mandy dropped her own homemade pole on the bank and came running. "Let me see, Lucy! How big is it? Can we keep it?"

Zachary hovered over her shoulder. "Easy now. Don't pull too hard. Walk a couple steps and pull him on in. You don't want your line to break."

"I know. I've been fishing since I was younger than Amanda." Lucy worked the pole back and forth, then eased it forward until she felt the fish tire. After a couple more minutes of allowing it to dart around, she steadily walked back until she could see the trout rise to the surface. It rolled on its side and its blue-green underbelly glistened, the bright sunlight reflecting on its prominent pink stripe. *It must be well over a foot long.* For an instant, a pang of regret struck her at hooking such a lovely creature, but she shook it off. If they caught enough, Ma would fry trout for supper. Her mouth watered at the thought of the fried potatoes and onions she'd serve on the side.

Enough playing this fish; it was time to land her prize. She snapped her pole back, knowing her catch was exhausted and would be easy to land. At the exact moment she pulled, though, the trout seemed to get a second wind and plunged forward, pulling against her line. The string broke and the sudden release of weight sent Lucy stumbling backward. Her fish disappeared under the surface.

"Oh no, Lucy! See what you went and did!" Mandy sent up a wail that could probably be heard all the way home. "Why'd you pull on the line so hard? You always tell *me* not to do that."

Lucy tossed her pole on the ground and plopped down next to it. "Hush, Mandy. There's no need to shout."

"Yes, sirree. I wanted to eat that trout. He was a whopper. Ma's going to be disappointed." Amanda sank to her knees and clutched the broken end of the line, gazing at it as though staring at it hard enough could bring the fish back.

"Then I guess we'll have to try again." Lucy ruffled the little girl's hair and grinned. "Maybe you'll catch the next one and show me the right way to land him."

Zachary sank onto the grass beside them, a rusty can in his hand. "Want me to put another hook and worm on for you? I don't mind."

Lucy eyed the can that was packed with moss and worms they'd dug right before they started fishing. This was the part she hated—threading the worm on the hook. Pa had taught her how when she'd been Mandy's age, but she'd never had the heart to teach her little sister. Ma didn't like to fish, and they hadn't gone out often since Pa died. That was one thing she enjoyed about Zachary, besides the fact she could talk to him so easy. He loved to fish, too, and didn't make her feel like a sissy for not liking to bait her own hook. "Thanks."

Mandy scooted closer. "Can I watch?"

Zachary shrugged. "Sure, I can teach you." He finished tying off the hook then plucked a worm from the can and began threading it on.

"Ouch! Doesn't that hurt?" Mandy inched away but her gaze stayed glued to the worm. "I don't think I want to do that."

Zachary didn't look up. "Naw. They don't have feelings."

"Is he dead?"

"Nope. They have to wriggle around so the trout notice and want to eat them."

Mandy shuddered. "Why would anything want to eat a worm? They're yucky."

Lucy laughed and reached over to tickle her little sister. "Not to fish, silly. To them it's like eating a stick of candy."

"Eww!" Mandy wrinkled her nose. "No, it's not. Will you put a new worm on for me, Zachary? I don't think I want to learn."

Zachary grinned. "Yep, doesn't bother me." He worked in silence for another minute, then helped Mandy get situated on the bank. "This is a good spot. I'll bet you catch a big one. But be sure you keep a close watch on your line and ..." He dropped his voice to a loud whisper while casting a glance at Lucy. "Don't jerk on it hard if you get a nibble."

"Okay, Zac. I won't." She beamed at him and then turned her attention to the tip of her pole.

Lucy came up next to him and gave him a playful push. "Don't jerk on it hard, huh? I suppose you're going to remind me of that whenever we go fishing?"

"I might." He laughed and snatched up his pole.

"You'd better not, or I might have to tell your secret." She gave him a sly look.

He kept walking, stopping a short ways upstream at a still pool. "I don't have any secrets, so I guess I can keep teasing you."

"No? I saw the way you looked at Beth last night."

He turned a startled face her way. "I didn't … I don't …"

Lucy sobered at his distress but let him squirm a little longer, like a worm on a hook. She finally relented. "I'm sorry, Zachary. I was joshing. I won't say anything, I promise. You've never told anybody my secret, and I won't tell yours."

He heaved a big sigh. "Thanks. But it's silly 'cause she's way older than me. I think she's kind of pretty, but I feel sorry for her that her aunt is trying to marry her off. Beth doesn't seem very happy to me."

Lucy nodded. "I know. But you're almost fifteen. How do you know she's way older?"

He looked thoughtful. "I dunno. I guess I figured she must be at least seventeen."

"Why don't you ask her?"

He jumped backward like he'd been slapped. "No, sir. Not me."

"Want me to find out?" She almost giggled at his discomfort but chose not to. Zachary had become her best friend, and she wouldn't hurt him for the world. She felt bad about all the horrible things he and his pa had been through and wanted to help. If that meant talking to the quiet girl who'd come to live at their house, she'd do it.

"I don't want her to think I'm chasing her."

"I won't tell her. I can be friendly and find out without her knowing you're interested."

"You sure?" The furrow in his brows made a deep crease at the top of his nose. "Besides, I'm not really *interested*."

"I know what I'm doing. She'll never figure out a thing. I promise."

"Thanks. I'm not glad our house burned down, but I'm sure happy your ma invited us to stay at your boardinghouse. At least till we figure out what we're gonna do for a place to live."

"Me, too." Lucy nodded, then squealed. "Mandy's got a fish! Hold on Mandy, don't let it pull you in!" She tossed her pole to the side and sprinted toward her sister, wondering how in the world she'd keep the promise she made to Zachary. She'd never been much good at making friends with girls, and Beth Roberts had to be one of the shyest girls she'd ever met.

Chapter Twenty-One

Frances fanned herself with a newspaper. She wouldn't be surprised if she were having a heart attack. Should she hobble out of the parlor as fast as her gimpy foot would allow, or stay and battle it out with the old biddy who had just entered the room? Luncheon was over, midday was fast arriving, and the tea she had brought to the parlor lured her into staying.

Wilma Roberts looked as proud as a peacock sporting a new crop of tail feathers—and, in Frances's opinion, her voice would rival the bird. She was too plump for the ruffles, flounces, and folderol embellishing her person. The costumes might be tolerable, but her manners were far from it. No, indeed. The woman had obviously *not* been taught from *Godey's Lady's Book*.

All of this was Katherine's fault, and Frances planned on letting her know as much. Life was not the same since the arrival of Mrs. Roberts a number of days ago. Frances picked up her teacup and took a sip, watching as the odious woman slouched her way across the room. Humph. Poor posture. More evidence of an unfortunate upbringing.

She straightened her own carriage, then set her cup aside and folded her hands in her lap. Staying here seemed the best option.

After all, if she got up now and abandoned her post, it would appear as though she were fleeing the room. This was her home, and she would not allow anyone, least of all Mrs. Wilma Roberts, to drive her from any area in which she chose to relax. She'd take this up with Katherine later. Right now she had a battle to wage. If she played her cards right, she'd venture she could convince this woman to depart before nightfall.

Frances forced a smile, for smile she must if she hoped to win. "Good day, Mrs. Roberts. Where is your lovely niece?" In her way of thinking, the girl was as shy as a field mouse, if not as drab, but it wouldn't do to say as much to the girl's doting aunt.

Wilma Roberts stopped, eyes widening. "Why, Mrs. Cooper! I declare. You were so quiet I didn't know you were here. You gave me quite a start." She clapped a hand over her heaving bosom as though to emphasize her words.

Frances snorted. The creature had seen her the second she stepped into the room. Mrs. Roberts hoped to ignore her, pure and simple. "Well, some people do not see the need to talk every minute to make themselves known." She snapped her mouth closed. That was not what she'd planned to say, but the woman only had to flap her lips to irritate Frances.

Mrs. Roberts's jaw dropped.

Frances lifted her chin. Better make haste to repair the breach before she lost her opportunity altogether. "Pardon me. I did not mean to appear rude."

Mrs. Roberts appeared to search for a suitable reply as she slowly walked to the divan facing the chair where Frances sat. She motioned toward it. "Do you mind if I join you?"

Frances abhorred lying, but there were times it was better than speaking the plain truth—as much as she'd love to do so at the moment. "Certainly not. You live here as well as I do." She waved toward the tray on the low table beside her. "Katherine brought tea earlier and it is still quite hot. Would you like me to pour you a cup?"

"Thank you, yes." The matron settled back against the divan cushions with a low groan. "My feet are about to drop off, and my knees feel as though they will not hold me up much longer."

Something akin to sympathy tickled Frances's conscience, but she shot an arrow through it before it had a chance to take hold. She would not cater to any weakness where this woman was concerned, even if Mrs. Roberts *did* suffer from pain similar to her own. She carefully poured the tea from the Limoges china pot she'd brought from her home. "Why, what have you been doing that is so exhausting?" She kept her tone light.

"Beth and I have been traipsing around town. The dear girl insisted on going down to the stores in hopes of meeting interesting people."

"Indeed." Frances would love to tell this woman what she thought of that. It was clear to anyone who met the young woman that she'd rather cower in her room than encounter a stranger, but the comment played right in to where she'd hoped to lead. "I am very surprised you decided to move back to our humble boardinghouse."

"Really? We find it a delightful place, Mrs. Cooper."

"But it is so dull for a young woman of your niece's age." She held out the rose-sprigged cup and saucer. "Be careful. It is still quite warm."

"Thank you." Mrs. Roberts placed the saucer on her knee and balanced it with her fingertips.

"How old is your niece? Seventeen? She appears rather young."

"Oh my, no. She turned twenty last winter."

"Ah. Old enough for a serious beau back home."

Mrs. Roberts squirmed, and her fingers whitened around the teacup handle. "I'm afraid not. She was at a girls' school prior to heading West and hasn't met any suitable young men."

"Poor dear," Frances crooned. "I am afraid she will not find one here, either. The only men who usually board with us are traveling salesmen or poor schoolteachers. Not that I know from personal experience, as I have not lived here long, but from what I hear, all the wealthy patrons frequent The Arlington Hotel. It was the first two-story brick building built in Baker City, and millionaires have stayed there for weeks at a time. Can you imagine?"

"I had no idea." Mrs. Roberts was positively drooling, and her teacup tilted precariously.

"You really need to move to the hotel, my dear." Frances lifted her cup, letting her words settle in the air.

Steps sounded at the arched doorway, and Katherine hurried into the room. "Oh, there you are, Mama. I checked your room and didn't find you. I hoped you were feeling better."

Frances glared at her daughter. She'd interrupted at the most sensitive point of the conversation. "I am fine. We are having a cup of tea and a nice chat."

Katherine looked as though she might laugh. "A nice chat?" she echoed in an incredulous tone. "Good. I'm glad to see the two of you have made up."

Mrs. Roberts set her cup aside. "What's this I hear about you not feeling well, Mrs. Cooper? Have you been ill?"

Frances didn't know whether to laugh or cry. They might never get back to their topic of conversation. But at least she'd planted the seed of an idea and could only hope it would take root and grow. "I said I am fine. There is nothing to worry about at all."

Katherine moved closer. "It didn't sound like nothing earlier."

"Can't a woman keep anything private around here?" Frances thunked her saucer and cup onto the side table, not caring if she slopped the remaining tea or chipped the china.

"I'm sorry, Mama. I didn't realize it was a secret. I think most of us are aware you've been struggling lately."

Frances poked a finger toward Mrs. Roberts. "*She* did not know, did she?"

Mrs. Roberts's brows knit in a fierce scowl. "Well, I never." She struggled to her feet. "No. I did not. Nor do I care. And here I thought you wanted to make up and be friends. I guess that's what I get for making assumptions and trying to return kindness for that ... that ..." She eyed Katherine and closed her mouth. "And I will *not* be following your suggestion, Mrs. Cooper, as it appears you are not to be trusted." Mrs. Roberts nodded at Katherine, then swept out of the room without a backward glance.

Katherine sank onto the spot the matron had vacated. "*What* did you suggest? Did you somehow mislead her, Mama?"

Frances couldn't believe what she was hearing. "That is utter nonsense!" Now her daughter wanted to chastise her as well? She would not allow herself to be subjected to this kind of treatment. "Poppycock, that is what it is. The woman simply misunderstood my attempt to give her sound advice—that is all. Nothing to go on about, if you ask me."

"What kind of advice?" Katherine cocked her head.

"Oh, about her niece, if you must know."

"Yes?"

"I do not know why I must explain every conversation I have with someone else."

"I'm trying to keep peace between my boarders and family members. I can't have paying boarders antagonized, Mother. As you pointed out not too long ago, we need the money."

"Oh, bother." Frances waved a hand in front of her face. "I was not antagonizing anyone. I simply asked how old the girl is. When she told me Beth is twenty, I asked if she has a beau at home. The woman said she does not and has not met anyone since leaving school. So I told her she is not likely to meet anyone here and should move back to a nice hotel, where there are plenty of wealthy patrons."

"Mama." Katherine simply stared.

Frances shrugged. "There is nothing wrong with suggesting she move. I am sure she would be happier elsewhere, and it is obvious she wants the girl to find a husband. I offered a solution. I cannot imagine why she would take offense at something so practical."

"Practical?" Katherine leaned forward, gripping her hands in her lap. "Can you truly tell me you said it because you care about Mrs. Roberts or Beth? Or would it be closer to say you want them out of your hair?"

"Of course, it is not going to hurt my feelings if they decide to move, but that is beside the point."

"Is it, Mama?"

"Certainly." She winced as she got to her feet. "I am not going to sit here and be reprimanded any longer. It is not your business what I think or say. I am your mother, after all, not your child." There. She would not tolerate being scolded by her own daughter over something as trivial as recommending a better place for those people to live. It wasn't like she'd done anything sinful, for heaven's sake. Nor would she apologize to Wilma Roberts. Not today and not ever.

Katherine blew out a loud sigh as she exited the parlor on Mama's heels, not caring if Mama heard or not. She'd come very close to speaking her mind but had held back, knowing the words and tone would come out disrespectful. But more than anything, she'd wanted to light into Mama and make her understand how cruel her actions had been. If Mrs. Roberts's revelation about their lack of finances hadn't been given in confidence, Katherine would have made sure Mama recognized the inappropriateness of her comments.

Not that it would've made much difference. Her mother wrote her own rules. Saying something about Mama's health probably hadn't helped, and she wished she'd kept quiet, but she'd assumed everyone in the house was aware of Mama's affliction. After all, she'd stayed in her room more than once while others gathered in the parlor to talk, and she'd missed meals due to headaches or aching feet. Katherine exhaled. When things calmed down a bit, she'd make sure to apologize for that slip, but right now she'd better see if she could repair the damage. Of course, Mrs. Roberts probably wouldn't storm out and take her business elsewhere, but the last thing Katherine wanted were ill feelings or strife coloring the atmosphere in her home. That would not do at all.

She walked past Micah's door. The poor man had looked like a trapped animal when Mrs. Roberts and Beth accosted him in the parlor, and he hadn't ventured there since. Maybe she'd check on him after this errand was finished. She trooped up the stairs to the second floor and tapped on Mrs. Roberts's door.

Nothing. No rustle of skirts or footsteps. Maybe the woman was visiting Beth in her room. She moved to the next door and knocked.

"Yes?" Beth's timid voice barely penetrated the wood panels. She opened the door a crack, peeked out, then smiled and swung it wide. "Mrs. Galloway. I was worried it might be Mrs. Cooper come looking for Aunt Wilma."

The young woman's smile was contagious, and Katherine gave one in return. That was the most words she'd heard Beth string together since she'd arrived. "Is your aunt at home, dear?"

Beth shook her head. "She went for a walk to clear her head. I'm afraid she was a little upset when she left. She slipped down the back stairway so she wouldn't meet your mother in the parlor."

"I see." Katherine hesitated, not wanting to pry but still concerned about the elder Roberts's state of mind.

"Forgive me for my poor manners." Beth took a step back. "Won't you come in? I don't think she'll be gone long, and you're welcome to wait."

"I'd love to visit, but I'm not sure how long I can stay. I have supper preparations to start in the kitchen, and I imagine I'll hear your aunt when she returns."

"Oh. I see. Well, I don't want to keep you." A crestfallen expression blanketed Beth's features.

Katherine stepped forward and touched the girl's arm. "I'd be happy to chat for a few minutes. We haven't had a chance to get acquainted since you arrived." She left other words unsaid but could tell by the young woman's expression that she knew exactly what she meant—the poor girl rarely got a chance to speak when her aunt was around.

"Thank you, Mrs. Galloway." The pinched look smoothed. "Would you care to have a seat?" She motioned toward a damask chair that flanked one side of the window and waited until Katherine sat before sinking into its twin, adjusting the hem of her skirt to cover her ankles.

A hush settled over the room, and Beth cast her gaze from object to object as though seeking a topic of conversation. *Poor dear.* Katherine could only imagine how she felt trying to entertain a stranger on her own. Had she ever encountered this type of situation before? According to Mrs. Roberts, the young woman had attended a girls' school before heading West. Better to help her along than to let the silence become uncomfortable. "How do you like our little city, Miss Roberts?"

"Please, won't you call me Beth?" Her hand rose to touch the ruffle of lace at her neck. "I have no friends here, and it sounds so dreadfully formal for everyone to call me Miss Roberts."

"Beth, then." Pity filled Katherine's heart at the timid entreaty in the girl's trembling voice. She could only imagine what her dear Lucy would go through if she were uprooted from her home environment and sent off cross-country with a loquacious aunt to an unfamiliar town—for the obvious purpose of marrying her off to a rich man. "I realize you only arrived a short while ago, but are you settling in nicely?"

"No." The word came out in a whisper. "I am not. I'm horribly homesick." Beth bowed her head and covered her face with her hands.

"Oh, my dear! I had no idea." Katherine wasn't sure whether to rise and try to comfort the girl or to stay seated and hope she continued talking. "Have you told your aunt?"

The dark curls bobbed an affirmative, but no sound came forth and Beth's face remained covered.

"And what does she say? Is she willing to take you back home?"

The curls shook, and Beth dropped her hands, revealing pale cheeks. "That's the last thing she'll consider."

"May I be so bold as to ask why not?"

"Mrs. Galloway, if I tell, you must promise not to speak of it."

"Of course. You have my word." What could be so horrible at home that Mrs. Roberts would keep the girl from returning? A memory stirred. The woman had mentioned losing part of her money when she'd asked to come back to the boardinghouse.

Beth clasped her hands in her lap. "Thank you. Somehow I knew I could trust you." She raised tear-dampened lashes and met Katherine's eyes. "I left the man I love behind. Aunt Wilma thinks he's not the right man for me, and she seems determined to keep us apart."

Chapter Twenty-Two

Heavy feet clomped down the wood hall and Beth jumped to her feet, her arms wrapped protectively around her waist. "Please don't say anything to Aunt Wilma. Promise me?"

Katherine rose slowly. "As you wish. You told me very little, and it's not my place to repeat anything you tell me in confidence. You have my word."

The girl's arms dropped to her side as the door flew open.

"Beth? Are you here?" Wilma Roberts stepped inside. "Oh! Hello, Mrs. Galloway. I didn't realize you were visiting my niece." She cast a look between the two. "Is anything wrong?"

Katherine moved toward the older woman. "Not at all. I stopped by to see you several minutes ago, and Beth kindly offered me a seat, as she thought you might return any moment. I hope you had a good walk, Mrs. Roberts."

"Quite." The tension melted from her shoulders. "What did you want to talk to me about?"

"My mother." Katherine's words were biting, and almost immediately she wished she could take them back and try again. She hadn't meant to sound so harsh. "That is, I worried that Mama upset you earlier. I'm afraid she has a rather"—she groped for the right words—"brusque personality at times and isn't always aware of how she sounds."

Mrs. Roberts's brows shot halfway to her hairline. "Humph. That woman knows exactly how she sounds, my dear, and says exactly what she means." She tossed her parasol on the bed. "I must say that is the only thing I have found to admire about her thus far."

Katherine knew she must look like a fish gasping its last, so she closed her gaping mouth. "I beg your pardon? You admire her after the way she treated you?"

Mrs. Roberts waved her ring-bedecked hand in the air. "Not at all. Well, I should say, I don't appreciate the underhanded way she behaved, but that's not what I meant. Your mother is blunt, but she is not afraid to say what she thinks. I like that. Too many people hide their feelings behind falsities. Now take me, for example. I come right out and ask people a question if I want to know something. I don't beat around the bush and hint. Mrs. Cooper and I have that in common, I believe. Although I will admit I wish she'd learn to couch her opinions with a bit of courtesy and grace."

Katherine hardly knew how to respond and shot a glance at Beth. The young woman shrugged but didn't offer a comment.

"Yes, indeed. And something else. I am quite ashamed that I wasn't aware your mother had been ill. I have a family remedy that might help. I took a walk trying to clear the cobwebs and hoping to remember exactly what it is. Once I can recall it, I will be sure to share it with her. She'd like that, don't you think?"

"I …" Katherine tried to get a grip on her whirling thoughts. She'd come hoping to calm Mrs. Roberts's ire and keep her from doing anything hasty that might cause more distress in the household, but the woman had taken a walk hoping to remember a family remedy that would help her mother? Maybe she hadn't made a mistake about letting this odd pair move back to her home, after all. "Forgive me for appearing rude, but you took me by surprise. I thought I'd find you angry and hurt at my mother's behavior."

"Oh, that. Piffle. I was quite upset at first, and had I not made a promise to you to try to hold my tongue, I would probably have said something I'd later regret. But once I had time to think about things, I realized the poor old dear must be lonely for companionship. All she needs is a friend to pour out her troubles to, and that'll put her sour spirit to rights."

Katherine didn't know whether to weep with relief or laugh hysterically at the picture Mrs. Roberts had painted. She couldn't be further from the truth. Mama would never pour out her troubles to anyone, least of all to Wilma Roberts. And if Katherine didn't set things straight quickly, there'd be even more hurt feelings in the future. "Um … Mrs. Roberts?"

"Yes?" She waved toward the chair Katherine had recently vacated. "Forgive my manners. Please. Sit down again."

"No. I can't stay, but I must tell you something." She paused, unsure how to continue.

"Go on. I'm listening."

"You're very kind to want to help my mother, but I'm not sure it's a good idea to try." She inwardly groaned. That hadn't exactly been what she'd wanted to say, but it certainly was the truth.

Mrs. Roberts narrowed her eyes. "And why would that be, might I ask? Surely everyone needs a friend."

"Yes, I'm sure you're correct." Katherine hedged, wondering how in the world she'd explain without heaping more hurt on this kindhearted woman. "It's just that Mama isn't like everyone else. She's always been a loner in many ways, and I'm not sure …"

"Not to worry, my dear." Mrs. Roberts smiled, a dimple in her left cheek peeking out. "I know how to deal with women like your mother. Kill them with kindness, that's what."

Katherine reached for the door. All she wanted was to get out of this room and to the safety of her kitchen. "That's very good of you. But I hope you won't be too disappointed if things don't work out. As you mentioned earlier, Mama has a mind of her own, and she can be a bit unpredictable." *And that's being charitable.* "Now I'd best get back to work. I have baking to start before supper."

"Give it time, Mrs. Galloway. Your mother and I will end up being fast friends, you will see."

Katherine gave a weak wave toward Beth, feeling as though she'd swallowed an egg whole. Trouble was coming; she knew it. And there wasn't a thing she could do to prevent it.

She slipped out and headed down the hall, then paused on her way downstairs. Lucy could help with supper preparations, and Amanda was old enough to set the table. Swinging toward Lucy's room, she tapped on the door and poked her head inside. Nothing. But she was sure she'd heard her older daughter's giggle. Picking up her pace, she rushed forward, hearing it again, louder this time. The door to Zachary's room stood cracked a couple inches and Katherine halted, her hand over her heart. Surely her daughter wasn't alone in a boy's room; she'd taught her better than that. Giving a quick rap on the door, she opened it wide and gaped.

Lucy jumped back from Zachary's embrace, a horrified look clouding her features. "Ma! What are you doing here?"

The blood pumped through Katherine's veins like fire blazing a trail to her heart. "I won't let you make the same mistakes I did at your age." She gripped her daughter's arm and yanked her toward the hall.

"I didn't do anything wrong." Lucy's words rose in a wail. "Let me explain!"

Katherine's voice shook, and she willed it to settle. "Out." She pointed at the door, then swiveled toward Zachary. "I'll thank you to keep your hands to yourself if you live in my house." It was all she could do not to grab him by the scruff of the neck and haul him to his father's room, but she couldn't continue to react out of anger. She would not imitate her mother. No, she'd wait and speak to Micah when her emotions calmed.

The color drained from Zachary's face, and he gave a short nod.

"But, Ma—" Lucy's eyes pooled, and she stepped toward her mother.

"Out, Lucy. Downstairs to the kitchen." Katherine waited for her elder daughter to leave the room and shut the door behind her.

Lucy met her at the bottom of the stairs, her stormy face set. "I can't tell you what I was doing because I promised Zachary to keep it a secret, but I didn't do anything wrong, Ma."

"That's not enough, Lucy. I can't have you making promises to boys and doing things I don't approve of."

"You're not being fair." Lucy whirled and raced for the front door, slamming it behind her.

Katherine started forward, but by the time she reached the foyer, she'd reconsidered. Memories from the past threatened to swamp her. There were things Lucy needed to hear, but they'd have to wait. There was no sense in making this situation worse, and her daughter was too upset to listen to reason. First her mother caused problems and now her child. What in the world was next?

Micah slowly made his way to the breakfast table the following morning, thankful he could now care for his own needs. He'd appreciated the care of others when he needed it, but sitting at the table made him feel less of an invalid. Doc said the burns were healing nicely, and the pain had lessened, so Micah no longer lay awake the entire night. He'd almost given in when Doc Sanders had first offered laudanum, but in the end he managed to resist the lure of the medicine that would dull the pain—and dull his senses right along with it.

Mrs. Roberts scooted back her chair, stood, and pulled his out. "Well, dear boy. How's your leg today?"

"Tolerable, thank you. But you didn't need to get up."

Apparently Mrs. Roberts didn't listen to directions. When she made her mind up, she was like a bull intent on breaking a fence to reach green grass. Oh well, better to let it go. He reached behind him, placed the crutches against the wall, and slid into the chair she drew out for him.

"No bother at all, Mr. Jacobs." Her joyful smile creased her cheeks. "We were all talking about an upcoming social in a couple of weeks."

Zachary brightened. "Can we go, Pa? Mrs. Galloway is going to bake pies for it, and everyone is welcome."

Mrs. Roberts cleared her throat. "And my sweet Beth will be baking pies, as well." She addressed the silent girl sitting beside her. "Won't you, dear?"

Red raced into Beth's cheeks as the gaze of everyone at the table swiveled toward her. She placed her hand over the base of her neck and ducked her head. "I'm sure Mrs. Galloway won't want me in her kitchen, Aunt Wilma."

"I've already spoken to her about it."

Katherine nodded and sent Beth an encouraging smile.

Her aunt rushed on as though she hoped to convince the girl before she fled. "As long as you get your baking done before she needs to start, and leave the kitchen clean, of course." She faced Mr. Tucker across the table. "Beth learned to cook at the boarding school she attended back East, you know." The words came out with a simper. "She got very high marks. Are you planning on attending the social, Mr. Tucker?"

Micah covered his smirk with his hand. If a man could turn green, Jeffery Tucker did so quite nicely. "Uh, I'm not sure, ma'am."

Sympathy for the man welled in Micah's chest. Being cornered by this woman was not a pleasant experience. Beth was little more than a child. Certainly not the type or age Mr. Tucker would be interested in. His gaze shifted to Katherine Galloway sitting at the head of the table. Not that he had any personal interest in marrying again, but if he ever did entertain the idea, a woman with wisdom and grace would be far preferable to one recently out of boarding school.

Zachary placed his palms flat against the table. "If Pa comes, I'll be there, Mrs. Roberts. I've saved a little money from chores, and I'd be pleased to buy one of Miss Beth's pies."

Startled, Micah stared at his son. No mistaking the admiration coloring Zachary's words. Could the boy be smitten with the young woman? But she had to be, what, three or four years older than him, didn't she? He frowned and studied Beth. Not the slightest hint of flirtation showed. In fact, if anything, she appeared a bit shy and embarrassed.

Maybe he'd imagined the interest in Zachary's voice. But at almost fifteen it was possible a pretty woman could turn his head. Something to watch out for. However, he'd been certain his son was infatuated with the Galloway girl. He cast a quick look Lucy's way and didn't note any jealousy. He gave a mental shrug. Matchmaking, or an understanding of the subject, wasn't something he had a hankering for. He'd best turn his thoughts elsewhere. "Mrs. Galloway?"

Katherine's eyes widened. "Yes, Mr. Jacobs?" A hint of a smile touched the words.

"I seem to remember you mentioned going to the general store today. I'd like to come with you, if I may. I've waited long enough to see the remains of my livery and pick up a few things at the store." He regretted the gruffness that roughened his voice and cleared his throat, hoping to lighten it.

"Certainly, Mr. Jacobs. I take my horse and wagon when I go to market, so I don't have to carry my supplies back. I'd be happy to give you a ride."

"Much obliged." He dipped his head briefly but didn't remove his gaze. Such lovely blue eyes—almost like the color of a mountain lake on a calm day, restful and pure. He wrenched his attention away before everyone noticed him staring.

The rest of the meal passed quietly, as the diners dug into their food. Micah tried to repress his growing anticipation. His heart rate increased as he imagined sitting next to Katherine on the wagon seat. Of course, that was mostly due to anxiety over seeing his burned home and business for the first time since the fire, he was sure of it. Yes, his excitement about the trip was solely an eagerness to see if anything had survived.

It wasn't acceptable for it to be anything else.

Chapter Twenty-Three

Talk about stubborn men! Katherine clenched her hands around the reins as Micah struggled to get up into the wagon on his own. The obstinate man had refused her offer of help in spite of his apparent discomfort. Just because he could manage around the house with the aid of crutches didn't mean he had the strength or ability to hoist himself onto the seat.

"Everything all right?" She wanted to fuss over him now that he'd settled himself but knew he wouldn't accept it. Besides, he wasn't her husband, her beau, or even a close friend. Time to grab these wayward thoughts and corral them before they galloped away. Besides, she must speak to him about his son. More than likely, by the time she finished he would never want to ride with her again.

"I'm fine. Nothing to it." But the slight panting belied his assertion. "I'm just glad to be out of the house." Worry flickered in his eyes. "Sorry. I'm grateful you offered us rooms, but it's hard being dependent on—" He paused, then continued, "Others."

Katherine shook the reins and clucked to her mare. "You were going to say 'a woman,' weren't you?" She shot him a quizzical look, hoping she didn't sound as amused as she felt.

He hung his head for a moment, then lifted it. "I'm sorry. I'm so used to caring for women—first, my mother after my father passed, then my wife, Emma. I guess it feels wrong, somehow, having it the other way around."

The tension eased from her shoulders. "I understand. Is your mother still living?"

"No. She passed away when Zachary was three. I think she pined for my pa so much that it weakened her heart. She was never the same after he died."

"I'm sorry." Katherine wished there were more she could say, but the mention of Zachary's name renewed her anxiety.

Micah adjusted his bad leg against the footrest. He peered at her with a slight smirk. "At least you still have your mother."

"Yes." She stifled a groan, then allowed a chuckle. "And she makes her presence known daily." She sobered. "Seriously, I'm very thankful I have her in my life, but at times …"

"She can be difficult. So I've noticed." He tossed her a grin. "Not that I'm complaining. I must say, she managed to raise a very nice daughter."

"Why, thank you." Warmth suffused Katherine's body, and her palms grew damp against the leather reins. She'd better concentrate on her driving and not the man beside her, or they'd be in trouble. If only Lucy and Zachary weren't so young and hadn't chosen to break the rules. Attraction drew her to Micah, but the relationship forming between her young daughter and his son wasn't acceptable. In her heart she knew it would place a wall between any chance she and Micah might have of growing closer.

They crossed the bridge over the Powder River, the wagon wheels clattering against the wood boards. A black raven flew from an overhanging branch, screeching his displeasure at being dislodged.

She reined the horse to the left and onto the dusty main street, taking in the Elkhorn Mountains towering above the town. She loved this settlement, with the two mountain ranges to the east and the west and the river running through the middle. The wide valley extended for miles, allowing ranchers and farmers to raise cattle and crops that helped sustain the miners and residents.

"Where would you like to go first?" She slapped the reins against the mare's rump, then turned toward Micah.

"What? Oh, sorry." He ran a hand over his head. "Wherever you're going is fine."

"But you wanted to see …" She didn't finish as she caught a glimpse of pain etching deep lines around his mouth. "I'll be about an hour or so. Will that be enough?" She scrambled to decipher what had happened. Why had he changed his mind about going to the site of the livery?

"Yeah. Thanks."

"Whoa, Gracie." Pulling the mare to a stop, she waited. "Will you be all right, Micah?" Katherine touched his arm, and he jumped.

"Sure. I'll be happy to get down and stretch this leg a mite." He hitched himself to the edge of the seat and twisted his body, gripping the side rail and easing down onto the step. "I don't reckon I'll go far." He reached back up and pulled the crutches off the seat. "Not this trip anyway." Shooting her a grim smile, he tucked the crutches under his arms and hopped away.

Micah wanted to kick himself a minute later for not having Katherine drop him off in front of his old business and home—even more, for allowing her to see his discomfort. He was a grown man, for pity's sake, not a child who couldn't handle a little tragedy in his life. Why had he told her he wouldn't go far when the burned-out building four blocks away beckoned him? Surely he could make it that distance without too much trouble.

Glancing around, he took in the people strolling the boardwalk in front of the stores and the wagons rattling past on the dirt street. He'd forgotten how good it felt to be out in the sun and standing on his own two feet. A wry grin formed—well, sort of on his own feet.

"Jacobs! Good to see you in town." The voice of Pastor Seth came from close by. "You drive yourself in from Mrs. Galloway's place?"

Micah shook his head, leaned his weight on one crutch, and extended his other hand as the man strode up. "No. Mrs. Galloway had some shopping to do so I hitched a ride. I was considering moseying on down the street."

"Ah." The pastor cocked his head in the direction Micah indicated. "Care if I walk with you?"

Micah shrugged. "Sure. I'd appreciate the company after being cooped up so long. If you think you can stand visiting with me yet again." He grinned.

Pastor Seth laughed. "Not sure about that, but I'll try." He gestured toward the crutches. "When do you get rid of those?"

"Doc says soon, but it can't be soon enough for me. I'd dump them now if I could, but he's worried the cut will split open again if I put too much pressure on it. Another day or two, I reckon."

"Good. You put any more thought into rebuilding?"

"That's about all I think about these days." Micah slowed his pace and shifted his balance. At least he'd gotten the hang of moving quickly, and since his arms were strong from swinging a blacksmith hammer so many hours a day, it was no chore to carry his weight with his arms and one leg. "But no, I haven't made any decisions yet. Still no idea where I'll come up with the money, but I'll make it happen somehow. I've got to." He tried to keep the desperation out of his voice but knew he'd failed when the pastor regarded him with compassion.

"Something will turn up, Micah. I'll be praying about it, as well. God's not going to let you down."

"Right." This time Micah didn't try to hide the sarcasm. "That would be a first." He shook his head. "Sorry. It's not your fault. You've been decent and kind since I met you, and I appreciate it. But I don't feel the same way about God. He's let me down more than once in past years, so I have no reason to believe He won't again."

Pastor Seth nodded. "Sure, I suppose we all feel that way from time to time. God doesn't always answer our prayers the way we hope and sometimes it seems as though He's ignoring us. But I can assure you that's never the case."

Micah planted his crutches and pulled to a halt. "Then He made an exception for me when He allowed my Emma to die and left me to raise our son alone. Not trying to be rude, Pastor, but I don't think I'm in the mood to visit the site of yet another disappointment. I think I'll head back to the store."

"Wait, Jacobs." Pastor Seth placed a hand on Micah's arm. "I know it appears that way, but believe me when I tell you life will get better. God hasn't abandoned you."

"Whatever you say, Pastor. Now I need to go. Good day to you."
He headed back the way they'd come as fast as his crutches would
take him. A twinge of guilt mixed with some bitterness. The pastor
was only trying to encourage him, but the words stung all the same.
He was tired of hearing from do-gooders that God cared and hadn't
forgotten him. He didn't believe it, and no amount of preaching
would change his mind. Maybe he shouldn't have been short with
the man, but he wanted Pastor Seth to understand once and for all
that he didn't care to discuss the subject. Hopefully this would end
all the foolish talk about God taking care of him and seeing him
through this current calamity.

He settled into a chair against the wall of the mercantile, content to watch the traffic go by and the people traipsing up and
down the street. Katherine had picked a busy time of day to do her
shopping but all the better for him. At least it kept his focus off his
troubles.

And he had another pleasant ride with Katherine to look forward to, so the day could only get better from here.

Katherine exited the store, content with her purchases and anxious
to return home. Hopefully Micah would be close by and they could
head out now that the wagon was loaded with her provisions. She
looped her reticule over her wrist, noticing the difference in weight.
She'd spent more than she'd planned, but with the increase of boarders, her pantry was low and must be restocked. A small movement

pulled her attention to the side, where a chair was tipped back against the wall. Micah Jacobs sat with his eyes closed, his crutches resting beside him.

How could she wake the man without startling him? She'd been longer than the hour she'd promised and worried he might be tired, but his evident exhaustion pricked at her heart. She leaned toward him and spoke in a whisper. "Micah?"

The man's eyelids quivered but didn't open.

"Mr. Jacobs?" She said it a little louder this time, but there was still no response. Taking a chance, she touched his shoulder.

He jumped, and the front legs of his chair thumped down on the boardwalk.

She drew back. "I'm so sorry. I didn't mean to surprise you."

He scrubbed a hand across his eyes and focused on her face. "Katherine. I didn't hear you walk up. I was resting for a moment."

"Of course." She fought a smile. "The clerk has finished loading my purchases. Are you ready to return home?"

"Sure. Whenever you are." He grabbed the crutches and slowly eased to a standing position. "Guess I got a little stiff sitting so long."

"I'm sorry I kept you waiting."

"No matter." He swung to the edge of the boardwalk and made his way to the wagon.

"Did you accomplish what you'd hoped in coming to town?" As soon as she said the words, she wished she could retract them. Hardness settled over his features again. How had she forgotten the pain she'd witnessed less than two hours before?

"I got out in the sun and on my own two feet, so I guess I did." He mumbled the words, then headed toward her side of the wagon.

"Let me give you a hand." Leaning his crutches against the driver's box, he took her arm and assisted her onto the seat.

"Why, thank you, Micah." Her breath caught at the touch of his hand on hers, and she wished he didn't have to remove it to go to his own side of the wagon.

Grabbing his crutches, he made his way to the rail where the horse stood, untied him, then limped to the side and hoisted himself up onto the bench. The muscles in Micah's shoulders and upper arms bulged as he tried to avoid using his leg. Katherine averted her gaze, afraid he'd catch her staring. She waited until he got situated, then picked up the reins and released the brake.

Silence settled around them as the horse pulled the load up the dusty street. She longed to bring up the subject nibbling at her thoughts since last night, but how could she do it without troubling Micah? He already seemed burdened, but he had the right to know about his son's behavior. Drawing in a deep breath, she mustered her courage. "I have something I'd like to discuss with you."

He turned his head. "All right. But if you're wondering what I'm planning to do about my business and home, I don't know. But as soon as I figure it out, I'll make other living arrangements."

His brusqueness shocked her. "Why in the world would you think that?"

Micah hunched one shoulder. "I ran into the pastor today, and that's all he wanted to talk about, so I figured it was probably bothering you as well."

"Oh. I see." She didn't but saw no sense in pursuing the subject. It was apparent something the pastor said had hit him wrong, and she'd probably only add fuel to the fire by saying anything more.

"No, that's not what I had in mind." She wished she could think of something else to talk about besides Zachary, but nothing surfaced. Better to stick with her original plan, get it over with, and pray he wouldn't be upset.

"I apologize for being gruff. Guess I have a lot to work through right now. Go on. I'm listening." He settled his frame against the back of the bench.

"It's about Zachary."

He shot bolt upright. "What about him? What's wrong?"

"Oh, dear, I didn't mean to worry you. I guess I should have said it's about Lucy and Zachary."

Micah slowly relaxed again. "What about them?"

"I'm concerned about some behavior I observed last night before supper." She held up her hand to forestall his questions. "I'll explain. Just give me a minute. I was looking for my daughter and heard her laughter coming from Zachary's room. The door was partially open, so I pushed it the rest of the way and stepped in. Lucy jumped back, but it was clear Zachary had been holding her in his arms."

"What?" Micah choked on the word and then sputtered, "I don't believe it."

Katherine waited until they'd crossed the bridge, then reined Gracie to the side of the road and pulled her to a halt. She wound the leather reins around the brake handle and swiveled toward Micah. "See here, Mr. Jacobs. I'm telling you what I saw, and I'm not accustomed to making up stories."

He held up a hand and shook his head. "That's not what I meant. Simply that it's hard to believe my son—my boy—with a girl—"

"He's not that young. He's fifteen, isn't he?"

"Yes. Well, almost. Next month." His voice dripped with confusion. "What did they say? Did you talk to him about it?"

"No. I told Lucy to get to the kitchen, and then I walked out. I assumed Zachary would tell you about it before I had a chance to." Katherine had been trying to keep her anger from showing but couldn't contain it any longer. "Lucy denies anything happened, and I suppose I'm willing to believe that, but I don't like it. It's been obvious to me from the start that Zachary is smitten with Lucy, but I told her some time ago that she's too young to court. She assured me she and your son are only friends, but after what I saw, I don't believe it."

"Did she explain what happened?"

Katherine gave a slow nod. "She said it wasn't a hug. That she was helping Zachary with something, but she promised to keep it a secret. And, if you must know, I can't for the life of me think of anything she could be helping him with that involves hugging. I'm worried. I can't have Zachary inviting my daughter into his room and making inappropriate advances toward her."

Micah's face hardened. "They're children, Katherine. You seem to be taking this a bit far."

"Really?" Katherine stared at him for several seconds, then plucked the reins from around the brake and slapped them against the horse's rump. "Let's get home, Gracie."

The mare broke into a trot that sent Micah rocking against the seat. "I'll talk to Zachary, but I still think you're upset about nothing."

"My daughter was in your son's room, and his arms were around her." She kept her tone level, but it took all the effort she could muster. Why didn't this aggravating man see how dangerous this situation might be? Two young people alone in a bedroom—even if the door had been slightly open—wasn't something to be taken lightly.

"Yes," he said with an edge. "She was in his room; he wasn't in hers. Have you thought of *that*? Besides, I'd like to know what's wrong with my son. If he did care for your daughter, would that be so terrible?"

Katherine whipped her head toward him. "I didn't say there is anything wrong with Zachary. That wasn't my point at all." Her body began to tremble with barely suppressed frustration and anger. "I can't believe you're implying this is Lucy's fault. She's only thirteen!"

"Yes, but obviously old enough to know better, and she still chose to enter his room. I'd say your anger is a little misguided if it's all pointed at my son. And I'm more than a little upset on his behalf, that you apparently feel he's completely to blame."

Katherine gaped, then closed her mouth with a snap and turned back to her driving. She wouldn't argue with this impossible man any more. But from now on, she'd keep an eye on his boy.

Micah gritted his teeth to keep from saying anything that he shouldn't. Right now he wanted off this wagon and out of Katherine Galloway's house—and life. Of all the infernal, insufferable, frustrating women, she took the cake. Why did she have to be sweet, pretty, and generous so much of the time, then do this complete about-face and accuse his son of improper behavior? And just when he'd started to think he might be able to open his heart a crack to another woman. Well, it was a good thing he'd found out before anything happened. The last thing he needed was another broken heart.

Exactly what did she have against Zachary that she believed he wouldn't be suitable for her daughter? Micah hated to think that it had anything to do with his own poor circumstances, with the loss of his home and business. Most likely, he'd not have much to pass on to his son if things didn't turn around soon. But he'd never have believed Katherine would be so petty as to feel that way. Was it because he wasn't as educated as her? Did she think his family beneath her?

No, this wasn't about him, and he shouldn't try to make it into something it wasn't, but it stung all the same. His son was a fine, upstanding young man, good enough to court any girl he chose, and Katherine should be able to see that on her own.

The silence hung as dense as quicksand pulling at his boots, ready to suck him under if he so much as glanced at the woman who sat ramrod straight beside him. When the wagon drew to a stop in front of Katherine's small barn, Micah clambered down from his perch as fast as his injured leg would allow. Good manners demanded he scoot around to Katherine's side and assist her as she stepped down, so he headed that direction. To his relief, her small feet touched the ground as he came around the back. She reached up to loosen the reins from the brake and her skirt lifted an inch or two. He quickly averted his gaze. "Want me to lead the mare to the barn?"

"No. Thank you. I have a man who does the afternoon chores. He'll unhitch Gracie and put her away."

"What can I take into the house for you?" He chafed at standing outside talking when all he wanted was to get inside to find Zachary.

He'd get to the bottom of what happened if he had to squeeze it out of the boy.

"Nothing." She gave a pointed look at his crutches. "It wouldn't be easy to juggle those and a box of supplies. But I appreciate the offer. Lucy will help."

"All right. Thank you for the ride. I'll go find Zachary." He hated that they sounded like polite strangers who'd only met, but it couldn't be helped. She'd accused his son of luring her daughter into his room and behaving as less than a gentleman, and until Micah heard the details for himself and made his own judgment, he'd keep his distance.

He didn't look back over his shoulder as she tarried outside, even though everything within him shouted to do so. This woman tugged at his emotions more than she ought, and he didn't like it. As soon as he could make other arrangements, he'd move. No way could he allow himself to get entangled in a relationship with someone who didn't trust his son.

Chapter Twenty-Four

Frances marched to the kitchen, hoping to find Katherine alone. The wagon had pulled in, the front door slammed, and then Mr. Jacobs stomped up the hall toward his room. The man had mastered the art of stomping while using crutches, something she had never thought possible. She smirked. Maybe he and Katherine had a falling out while on their jaunt to town.

She had almost forgotten the plan she'd conceived several days before when she overheard Lucy and that boy talking, but right now might be a good time to put it in place. After all, it couldn't hurt to give Mr. Jacobs an extra nudge out the door. Not that she had anything against him personally, but with him having no home or prospects, Katherine should be discouraged from looking his direction.

Katherine glanced up from unpacking a crate of provisions and smiled. "Hello, Mama. How are you feeling today?"

Frances wavered, her conscience pinching. Why did Katherine have to be so kind and friendly? It would be so much easier if she were grumpy or disagreeable. Frances pushed those thoughts away. She did not plan on lying, and this was for her daughter's own good. Katherine had an admirable existence in this house with her girls, and she did not need a man lugging his troubles into her life. "*I* am fine, thank you. Did you get everything you need?"

"Yes, I think so. Would you care for a cup of tea? The kettle is hot, and I'm about finished and ready to sit."

"That sounds good. I will get the cups." Frances removed two of Katherine's special sprigged china teacups, which she reserved for tea with family, and placed them carefully on the table. Her daughter only used these for special occasions, but they so rarely had time to take tea alone together.

She slid into her place. Katherine poured hot water from the kettle and sat across from her with a sigh.

"Long day, my dear? Or is something bothering you?" Maybe she could find out what had transpired between her daughter and Mr. Jacobs before launching into her own tale.

Katherine hesitated, as though trying to decide whether to confide in her mother or not, then slowly shook her head. "Nothing I want to talk about at the moment, Mama."

"Oh. I see." The words came out sharper than Frances planned, but Katherine's words pricked. Why couldn't the girl ever talk to her about things that mattered? It was either surface chatter or irritation at some imagined wrong she had committed. Katherine never shared any confidences or secrets. Frances pressed her lips together. No sense in starting yet another disagreeable scene. That wouldn't accomplish her purpose. "Very well, you are entitled to keep your own counsel, of course."

"I didn't mean—"

"Nonsense. Do not give it another thought." Frances lifted her chin. "Do not let a fussy old woman's words bother you."

Katherine's brows rose, sending another shaft of annoyance through Frances. The girl acted like she never spoke kindly to her, for goodness' sake! Of course she did, but she spoke plainly, too, and it ought not to bother Katherine when she did.

But enough of that. It was time to say what she had come to say.

Frances fingered the handle of her teacup. "I have noticed that Lucy and Zachary have been spending a lot of time together."

Katherine nodded but didn't reply.

Not the response Frances hoped for, but she pressed on. "You know, I was interested in my first husband when I was her age. Thirteen is not too young to start thinking about a girl's future, and Zachary seems like a fine young man. Maybe you should consider allowing him to court her." There, the words were out, and all she could do was hope they had the desired effect.

"Lucy is too young to court, and I'd appreciate it if you don't plant that idea in her head." Katherine set her cup on the saucer. "You haven't already said something to her, have you, Mother?"

Mother. Ha! The only time her daughter used that word was when she was overly annoyed. "No, of course not. My goodness, Katherine, you act like you want her to be an old maid all of her life. The girl is young, pretty, and will certainly have boys calling soon. You must realize that."

"Yes, but she's only thirteen and still a child. I have no intention of allowing her to court until she's at least fifteen."

"You have a perfectly acceptable young man living under your roof who appears to be very interested in Lucy, and if my eyes do not deceive me, she might even return the sentiment. Why are you being so stubborn?"

There, she hadn't come right out and said she believed or knew Lucy liked the boy. Not exactly. A little coloring of the truth for the good of all concerned. If Katherine believed they were interested in one another, that might be enough for her to ask them to move. Frances sat back, working to keep a satisfied smirk from spreading.

"I am not being stubborn. I am being Lucy's mother." Katherine pushed her chair away from the table and rose. "And I do not care to discuss this further. I have work to finish."

"Whatever you say, dear. I think I will go along to my room to rest for a bit. But you might want to check on Mr. Jacobs. He seemed upset about something when he came in. I hope his leg is not acting up and causing him to feel poorly again."

She left the room to the sounds of pans clanging and jars clanking as Katherine put the rest of the supplies away. Guilt washed over Frances as she walked to her room. Had what she'd accomplished been worth the price she paid in evoking Katherine's anger and displeasure? Well, her own mother hadn't approved of her most of the time, and they'd never been close friends, so what could she expect with her own daughter? She often wished for a closer relationship with Katherine, but she'd had to content herself with June. Maybe getting that man and his son out of the house and letting life return to normal would help. Frances sighed, not sure the Jacobs' leaving was the answer, but only time would tell.

Katherine wasn't sure how she'd gotten through the past couple days after her talk with her mother. She still wasn't convinced Mama hadn't encouraged Lucy in her behavior toward Zachary, regardless of what she'd claimed. Not that Mama had ever outright lied to her before, but there had been times Katherine suspected she'd shaded the truth in a certain direction when it suited her. After what her mother had shared, she was thankful she hadn't confided about the episode between Lucy and Zachary. That would pour fuel on the fire, for sure.

Today, Katherine couldn't get her morning work done fast enough to suit her. Micah had been taciturn at breakfast, Lucy had refused to speak, Zachary appeared to be embarrassed, so she could only assume his father had spoken to him. The only person who didn't seem to notice the tension was her precious little Mandy, who'd chattered throughout each meal. She talked about the fun she'd have with her friend while Mama quilted with the ladies today. Katherine winced at the memory, wishing Mandy hadn't mentioned the group in front of her grandmother.

Anger bubbled inside, and it took all Katherine's effort not to slam the pots and pans. She'd known it wouldn't be easy having her mother live here, but the years of being apart had softened the bad memories. Since Mama arrived, they'd come rushing back. So many harsh, hurtful words had bruised her young heart, with no tender touches or hugs to balance the pain.

All Katherine could think about at this minute was getting out of the house and off to her quilting session. The ladies were nearing the completion of the quilt and had decided to meet an extra day this month. Thank the good Lord it was today. Everything seemed to be tilting sideways in her world. Maybe her friends could help bring her back into balance.

Drying her hands on a towel she surveyed her kitchen with satisfaction. The bread dough was rising in a large bowl beside the stove and would be ready to punch down when she returned.

"Mandy? Are you ready to go, honey?" Katherine stopped at the door of the parlor and smiled. Her little girl sat on the floor playing with a doll.

"Yes, Ma. Can I take my dolly and the clothes Grandma made for her?"

"Of course. Hurry and let's go."

Mandy carefully folded and placed each item into the bag her grandmother had provided for safekeeping, then jumped to her feet and held out her free hand. "I'm ready. Carrie will be so happy to see Verna." She waved her stuffed doll in the air. "She doesn't have one with a real head and glass eyes."

Katherine leaned down to Mandy's level. "Are you sure you should take her, then? We don't want Carrie to feel bad that she doesn't have something as nice as you do."

"Oh, it's all right." The little girl spoke in a wise, serious tone. "She has a doll with real hair, and my doll's head is naked."

Katherine choked back a laugh. The porcelain-headed doll was a replica of a newborn baby, and the artist had painted tiny tufts of hair on its head rather than applying real strands. "Well, as long as you girls are both happy, I guess that's what matters."

"We are, Ma. And I don't even mind that Carrie's doll has long hair." She placed her petite hand into Katherine's, and they set off out the front door.

After dropping Mandy at her friend's house a block or so away, Katherine sighed with contentment and struck out at a brisk pace for the church. She slipped into the building, drawn by the chattering voices and laughter echoing through the open door. This was as close to heaven as she was apt to get today or anytime soon.

Each head turned and faces lit with smiles as she walked into the side room. Voices lifted in greeting and Virginia, standing the closest, offered a warm hug. Katherine melted into her embrace, holding the older woman for several seconds. Virginia stepped back and swept her a quizzical glance. "Is everything all right, dear?"

Katherine inhaled a long, cleansing breath. "It is now. I needed to get out of the house and be with friends who love and accept me."

Leah cocked her head. "Your mother again?"

Katherine gave a dry laugh. "Something like that, I guess. But truly, I don't want to dwell on my problems today. Leah, are things getting any better with your father?" She took her place behind the quilting frame and positioned her thimble on her finger, then held up her needle and ran the thread through its eye.

"Yes, I think he's forgotten all about his efforts at the saloon." She wrinkled her nose.

Hester Sue poked her needle through a colorful square of the sunburst quilt. "Ain't no man worth his salt should do a thing like that. No offense to your pa, Leah, but someone needs to knock some sense into that man's noggin. Why, you're as fine a lady as they come."

Leah held out her sun-kissed hand. "I'm certainly no city lady with soft hands and white skin." She rubbed her fingers against her cheek. "I wish these confounded freckles wouldn't pop out every summer."

Virginia patted the younger woman's shoulder. "Your freckles give you character, and your skin has a positive glow. I wouldn't worry overly much about little things like that, if I were you."

"I declare, any man worth keepin' won't give a lick about freckles, or brown skin over white." Hester Sue jabbed at the cloth beneath her fingers, then ran the needle back up through the square. "Mark my words, girl, the good Lord will send along the right man, and you'll be glad you waited."

Leah rolled her eyes. "It's not like I have much choice in the matter, ladies. I don't have many eligible men beating my door down wanting to marry me. I'll probably be single forever."

Virginia shook her head. "I doubt there's much chance of that, dear. You're much too pretty to stay single forever, but it's all in the good Lord's time."

Leah brightened and turned to Katherine. "Enough about me. Tell us what's been happening at your house. I heard you have new boarders—beyond Mr. Jacobs and his son—so your house must be nearly full now?"

"Yes. There's Mr. Tucker, a single man who's in town on business. And you know about Mr. Jacobs, Zachary, and my mother, of course, so that leaves Mrs. Roberts and her niece, Beth."

Ella tugged her needle through the fabric and pushed it in again before looking up. "I met them both in the store not long ago. The girl is lovely, but she didn't say a word. But as I recall, her aunt didn't leave much time for anyone else to talk." She giggled. "Do they have business that brought them to our town?"

"I'm not certain, but it seems Mrs. Roberts might be hoping to catch an eligible bachelor for her niece and marry her off if possible."

Leah snorted. "Good luck to her is all I can say." She eyed Katherine. "Sounds like you have your hands full as well as your house."

"Yes, but if I have anyone else needing a room, I'll put a cot in Micah's—I mean, Mr. Jacobs's—room and move Zachary in there." Heat crept into her cheeks, and she prayed the ladies wouldn't notice.

Hester Sue's head whipped up, and she cackled. "Micah, is it? Well now." She winked. "Want to tell us about it, dearie?"

Katherine shook her head. "There's nothing to tell."

"Come now, you used his Christian name, so that must mean somethin'."

"We're just friends. We decided it might be simpler to not be so formal." Hearing the words, she realized how weak they sounded, but she had no idea what else to say. "That is, we were friends of sorts until recently. Now I'm not so sure."

The women put their work aside and turned their full attention on Katherine, each one intent and alert. Finally Leah asked, "So, what happened?"

Katherine settled onto the stool behind her, sticking her needle into the quilt and leaving it there. "I found Lucy in Zachary's room and confronted them. Lucy claimed she was helping Zachary with something, but she wouldn't tell me more. I'm convinced the boy is smitten with my daughter, and she's too young for courting. So I had a talk with his father on the way back from town."

Ella's mouth formed a small O. "You went to town together? You and Mr. Jacobs?"

Hester Sue smirked. "No, she didn't go with Mr. Jacobs; she went with *her friend* Micah."

"No, I mean, yes … it's not like we're courting or anything. I simply took the wagon to the mercantile for supplies and gave him a ride. He's still on his crutches for a while. That's all it amounted to, I assure you."

"Oh." Ella's face fell, then lit up. "But you had a day together, and it was lovely." She patted her swollen belly. "It's been some time since I've had any real romance in my life, so hearin' about the possibility in someone else's makes my knees a little weak."

Katherine stifled a chuckle. "Believe me, Ella, there was no romance involved on this trip, nor will there ever be between Mr. Jacobs and me. Especially after our talk." She sobered. "He was none too happy that I accused his son of inappropriate behavior toward my Lucy. In fact, he implied it was as much her fault since she was in Zachary's room, rather than the other way around."

Virginia's gaze was direct. "I'm afraid you can't really fault his reasoning, dear … at least not if you're fair and looking at it from his point of view."

Katherine's indignation rose, but she pushed it aside. She loved this woman and knew Virginia would never say or do anything with the intent to hurt. "Would you explain, please?"

"Mr. Jacobs may have felt you were attacking his son's virtue unjustly." She held up a finger when Katherine started to protest. "Hear me out. I'm not saying Lucy did anything wrong, and she's a young girl who didn't think through the impropriety of going into his room. Was the door open or closed? Do you think they were trying to hide anything?"

Katherine thought for a moment. "Not at all. The door was open, but not wide enough for me to see in before I pushed it the rest of the way. I heard her giggling and the two of them talking before I entered."

"Has Lucy ever lied to you that you're aware of? Do you have reason to believe what she told you—that nothing happened?"

"No, she's never outright lied. Like any child, she's probably skirted the truth a bit when it served her purpose, but if asked a direct question, I believe she's told me the truth."

"Then if she told you Zachary wasn't doing anything wrong," Virginia pondered, "you ought to believe her."

Katherine sighed. She probably should have talked to these wise ladies before jumping on Micah about his son and embarrassing Lucy and Zachary, but seeing them together in his room had shocked her. "Yes, I suppose. But it still wasn't right they were together, unchaperoned, in a bedroom. Mr. Jacobs needed to be aware of that fact."

"I agree; he did." Virginia nodded, and the other women followed suit. "I'm merely pointing out it may have been totally innocent, and that Mr. Jacobs isn't at fault here."

Katherine frowned. "I know he's not, but he *is* Zachary's father and responsible for his son."

"To a point, yes, but just like you can't be everywhere at once watching your children, neither can he. Let me ask you a question. What if he'd been the one who walked in on those two? Do you think he'd have the right to be incensed and come to you, demanding you take action against your daughter?"

Katherine's hand went to her throat. "Putting it that way, I suppose I can see how he'd feel. In fact," she caught her breath as she recalled the last words he'd spoken, "he thinks I was judging Zachary because I believe his son isn't good enough for my daughter. I've made a mess of things, haven't I?" She bowed her head. The past weeks with her mother's shenanigans, the advent of Mrs. Roberts, the bickering between the two women, Micah's accident, and now this business with Lucy and Zachary, left her feeling completely drained.

Virginia patted her hand. "Not at all, dear. Have you prayed about this? You might consider apologizing to Mr. Jacobs."

A sick feeling lodged in Katherine's stomach. She hadn't prayed much about anything lately, she'd been so busy. When had she slipped so much in her daily walk with the Lord?

"Not like I should have, I'm afraid. I appreciate the reminder, Virginia." She was skirting the suggestion of apologizing to Micah, but that one needed a little more consideration. "I know you're right about how Mr. Jacobs must have perceived my words."

Why was she being so stubborn about agreeing to apologize? She was so tired of the battles going on in her home that left her feeling battered; maybe she simply wanted to be right this once.

Whatever the case, Katherine knew she was wrong. The last thing she desired was her relationship with the Lord suffering as a result. She must make this right, and not only for Micah's sake.

Someone tapped at the portal of the open door, and all heads swiveled that direction. Katherine covered her mouth with her fingertips.

"Hello, ladies. Katherine has told me so little about this group that I decided to come see for myself what I was missing. I found my way down here, and I would dearly love to get acquainted. Introduce me to your friends, will you, Daughter?" Mama stood in the archway, smiling, her eyes pinned on Katherine's, looking for all the world like a cat that cornered a canary.

Chapter Twenty-Five

Frances swept her gaze over the faces of the five women gathered around the quilt frame, each frozen in place, staring at her as though she were an apparition come to haunt them. At least one of them looked to be her age, so she couldn't imagine not being welcome. After all, church quilting groups were typically open to anyone who wanted to attend and could handle a needle, and that was one area where she excelled.

A flutter of nerves attacked her spine and almost set her to shaking during the silence that seemed to stretch without end. Had Katherine gossiped about her, and were her friends aghast that she had shown up unannounced? Maybe she should march right back the way she'd come, before one of them opened her mouth and dismaying words tumbled out. She had rarely been wanted in many small groups she'd attended before, so why should this one be any different? Slowly she pivoted, reaching for the door frame with a trembling hand.

"Mrs. Cooper?" The oldest woman in the room stepped from her place and moved forward, her hand extended. "I am Virginia Lewis. You must be Katherine's mother. We are so happy to meet you. Please, won't you come in and join us?" She grasped Frances's hand in both of hers, giving it a warm squeeze.

The rest of the women came alive and moved toward them. Friendly voices were raised in welcome, and smiles creased nearly every face. Every face, that is, but for one.

Katherine's.

Her daughter's expression of shock had turned to one of fleeting anger that just as quickly smoothed over into careful acceptance. Had Frances even seen that flash of anger, or had it been something more akin to hurt? But why should her daughter be grieved because her mother came to a church quilting group?

Maybe she'd misgauged Katherine's reasons for hiding her attendance and walked in where she wasn't needed, much less wanted. The other women seemed welcoming enough, but for all she knew, it could be an act.

People had set her up to be disappointed before, offering friendship and then withdrawing it as soon as they got better acquainted. She had learned years ago to put her prickles to the forefront to keep from being disappointed. At least she knew what to expect that way and didn't chance opening her heart only to have it stepped on.

She lifted her chin and sniffed. And she would put up a wall again here, since it appeared she wouldn't be welcome for long—not if Katherine had much to say about it.

Micah placed his foot on the floor and grinned at the doctor. "Feels good. I'm happy to get rid of those sticks."

Doc Sanders pointed across Micah's bedroom to the open door leading into the hall. "Not so fast. Let's see you walk first; then we'll decide."

Micah took a tentative step, then another, lengthening his stride with only a slight limp as he walked into the hall, turned, and came back again.

"How's the leg feel?"

"Not bad. Sore, but I guess that's to be expected." He slowed to a halt a couple paces in front of the doctor.

"It is. Any burning in your muscles or tightness?"

"No, just a little stiff."

"Good. The gash is healing well, and the stitches are holding. The burned area has covered over nicely and doesn't appear in danger of infection, so I think I can release you from some restrictions. Of course, I expect you to be sensible, and I'll want to see you again in a week or so to remove the stitches."

"How much do I owe you, Doc? I'll need to make payments, but I'll get you the money, you can count on that."

Doc Sanders waved in dismissal. "I'm sure I'll need your services in the future. As many trips as I make out to the ranches and up to the mines with my buggy, work always needs to be done on a wheel or a harness. I'll take it out in trade, if it's all the same to you."

The tension went out of Micah's spine. He hadn't realized how worried he'd been about his inability to pay this bill on top of what he owed Katherine for board. "Thank you, Doc. Much obliged. You say the word, and I'll take care of whatever you need."

"Fair enough. Keep those crutches handy in case you overdo and that leg weakens, but I think you'll be fine if you're careful."

He plucked his black bag off the dresser and headed out the bedroom door.

"Thanks again, Doc," Micah called as the man disappeared down the hall. No sense in sitting in his room all day, now that he'd dumped his second pair of legs.

Then his smile drooped as the memory of last week's talk with Katherine rushed back. Zachary had denied any wrongdoing when Micah cornered him but refused to say more than Lucy was helping him with a project. It didn't appear to have anything to do with school, and the boy wouldn't tell him any more. In fact, he'd appeared a bit embarrassed when pressed, but not guilty or sullen. Micah hadn't been able to make head or tails of it and finally allowed it to drop, but not before he'd made it clear that his son was never to be alone in a bedroom with a female again.

Micah stepped into the parlor and glanced around. He'd half feared that the Roberts woman or her niece might be in evidence, but he was happy to see it empty for a change. Not that he had anything personal against the pair, but he didn't care to be the object of affection Mrs. Roberts set her cap for—or rather, set Beth's cap for.

A pinprick of disappointment hit him at not finding Katherine; then he remembered something about her visiting the church this morning. He wandered toward the kitchen on the chance he might be wrong. Not that he wanted another confrontation, but he'd have to face her sooner or later, and it might be easier without others around.

As he neared the doorway into the kitchen he heard a girl's giggle and paused. Zachary's muffled laugh followed right after, and Micah picked up his pace. He halted in the doorway and stared at the sight of his son clutching Lucy in his arms, for all the world appearing as though he were hugging her.

Lucy gripped Zachary's hand and drew him forward. "You can do this, silly. Keep your hand on my waist and move your feet with mine."

"Zachary!" a man's voice bellowed, making Lucy jump clear of Zachary's arms, her hand going to her heart.

Mr. Jacobs stood nearby, horror blanketing his face. "What do you think you're doing? Get away from that girl this instant!"

Zachary scrambled backward and tripped over a chair leg, sprawling onto the floor. "Pa! What are you yellin' for? You liked to scared us to death." He pushed up onto his knees and glared.

Lucy caught her breath as Mr. Jacobs's expression rapidly changed to anger. What was he thinking, anyway? They weren't doing anything wrong, and they weren't hiding in a bedroom this time, either.

"Mr. Jacobs, Zachary isn't doing anything bad." She hurried to her friend's side and bent over, offering her hand while directing a worried glance at his father. "Zachary, are you hurt? Come on, I'll help you up."

He scrambled to his feet. "I'm fine." He scowled at his pa. "Everybody keeps yelling at us! First Lucy's ma and now you."

Mr. Jacobs rubbed his forehead. "Why don't you tell me what's going on, then?"

"I don't really want to, Pa, but I guess I don't have a lot of choice." He tossed a look at Lucy, raising his brows, and she gave a slight nod. "Lucy is teaching me to dance. Or, at least, she was trying to whenever I wasn't stepping all over her feet."

"Dance?" Mr. Jacobs looked from one to the other of them. "Whatever for?"

Lucy tried to muster a smile, although her insides still trembled at his bellowing. "Because he wants to ask someone to dance at the social next week."

"Yeah, Pa. I don't know anything about dancing, and Lucy promised to help me."

"So why hide in your bedroom to do it?" Mr. Jacobs frowned. "If it was innocent, you shouldn't slip away in secret to learn."

Zachary shrugged. "Guess I didn't want Beth to find out. Her aunt isn't good at keeping secrets ..." A slow red stain worked up his neck to his cheeks. "That is ..."

"I get it, Son." Mr. Jacobs nodded. "Mrs. Galloway worried something fierce when she found you." He swung his gaze to Lucy. "And from what I understand, you didn't tell her the truth, either."

Lucy dropped her head and scrubbed her toe against the wood floor. "No, sir. I didn't."

"That's not her fault, Pa. She promised me she wouldn't tell. I shouldn't have asked her to do that."

"I see." He looked squarely at Lucy. "I'd say Miss Lucy has been a good friend, if she kept her word at the risk of getting in trouble."

"Yes, sir. The best friend a fella could ask for." Zachary beamed.

Lucy's heart melted into a puddle at the admiration in Zachary's tone, and a tiny spurt of envy toward Beth sprouted in her heart.

Katherine slowed her pace, thankful her mother seemed content to walk in silence and wondering yet again why Mama showed up uninvited today. Not that the group was closed to outsiders, but she hadn't shown much interest since arriving in town. Katherine sorted through her memory to find the exact words Mama had used when she'd arrived over an hour ago. *"Katherine has told me so little about this group that I decided to come see for myself what I was missing."* She made it sound as though the meeting had been kept hidden on purpose.

In her heart Katherine wanted to deny it, to shout to the skies that her time with her friends was sacred and she had no obligation to invite anyone, much less her mother. But she knew better. She *had* deliberately slipped out of the house more than once, hoping Mama wouldn't ask to come along, and always breathed a sigh of relief when she didn't. But why should she invite her? Mama didn't know these women and didn't need to take part. Her eyesight and hands weren't what they used to be, and while she might add something to the work they did on the quilt, she probably wouldn't enjoy it. Standing too long would bother her feet and ankles, and … Katherine caught herself.

Excuses. Every one.

What if Mama came today because she was lonely? The idea had never occurred to Katherine before. Her mother had never seemed like someone who needed friends, but was that fair? Everybody needed at least one friend in their life. What would her own be like if she didn't have Leah and the others?

Destitute, but for her two daughters.

Katherine gazed at the diminutive woman limping along beside her. They'd never been friends. Not ever. Not that she hadn't tried, but Mama had squashed that notion early in Katherine's childhood....

Her best friend in the whole world had moved away. She'd asked Mama to play dolls, hoping to fill the void. "I am your mother, Katherine, not your friend. You need other people too much, and you might as well get over that. It will only cause you more hurt." She'd never asked her mother to play dolls or anything like that again.... The pain still pricked to this day.

Katherine blinked and focused on the present. "I didn't know you were coming, or I would have brought the wagon so you didn't have to walk. Would you like to lean on me?" She extended her arm.

"Certainly not. I am not an invalid, you know." Mama sniffed and made an effort to walk the following strides without limping. "Besides, if I had mentioned I wanted to come, you wouldn't have let me. I know you did not want me there. I saw it on your face as soon as I entered."

Katherine wanted to deny the accusation, but she hated to lie. Maybe it was better to stay silent rather than acknowledge the charge. On the other hand, silence would only bolster Mama's belief and possibly cause more hurt. "I'm sorry you feel that way." It was the best she could do in the circumstances, but she still doubted it would be enough.

"Humph. Doubtful. But it does not matter now." Mama looked the other way.

Katherine saw moisture glistening on her mother's eyelashes. She touched the older woman's arm. "I didn't mean to hurt you. Please forgive me if I did."

"I said to forget it. And do not worry; I will not impose again."

"You're welcome to come anytime. The ladies were happy to meet you, and I'm sure they'd want you to return."

"But you would not, is that it? I am not dense, Katherine, and I do not care to continue to discuss it. Let it go."

"All right, if you wish." Katherine shook her head, burdened at the pain she'd caused but not knowing what else she could do to make it right. The ill feelings between them had continued for so many years Katherine didn't know how to break the cycle. Although, truth be told, she'd not realized before that her mother sensed there *was* a problem. Mama had always gone on her way, saying what she pleased, seemingly without thought or realization of anyone else's feelings.

Had something happened today to change that? She wasn't sure, but from now on it appeared she must be more careful. As difficult as Mama could be, she was still Katherine's parent. As long as God kept her on this earth, she would have to find a way to honor her—or at least to honor her position, even if she found it difficult to respect or love the woman.

Chapter Twenty-Six

Jeffery felt like he'd moved into a hornets' nest comprised of stinging words and biting women. He settled on the porch bench and put his feet up on the rail. He had a lot to consider, and the house was too busy for his taste, especially since Mrs. Roberts and her niece moved in two weeks ago. Heading to town wasn't an option, as he was almost dead on his feet from the long hours he'd spent staring at his blank notebook last night, and if he stretched out on his bed, he'd fall asleep and accomplish nothing.

He'd come to this area due to its proximity to the Oregon Trail, but also because he'd heard that Baker City was a thriving town bursting at the seams with miners, ranchers, and everyday folks.

Little good it had done him thus far.

His dreams of reaching acclaim had so far come to naught. He managed to hide his aspirations from inquisitive people who'd asked about his business, which was just as well. How embarrassing that he'd found so few people willing to share their stories and so few exciting incidents to flesh out.

It wasn't like he hoped to pen a thousand-page saga of the West. No. He simply desired to depict the lives and happenings of real people in a way that easterners would find fascinating—but not with a bunch of silly fiction…. Although, he must admit, he'd love to have his book read like a novel but gain acceptance beyond what some people were beginning to call the "penny dreadful." Dreadful indeed. His book would exude excellence, if only he could figure out what to write.

Maybe it was time to return to the newspaper business. His savings were rapidly disappearing with little to show for his time and effort, and he wasn't willing to ask his family for help. And beyond that, he'd developed a loneliness he hadn't expected. Yes, heading back East seemed the best option, if things didn't turn around for him soon. He wasn't suited to work in the mines or on a ranch.

He lowered his feet back to the porch floor. If something didn't give him an idea or direction soon, he'd brush the dust off his clothes and head home to Cincinnati—and pray he could stay out of the grip of his father.

Frances woke the next morning in agony, barely able to move her swollen ankles and feet. She fell back against her pillows and groaned. She had so hoped to spend some special time with Amanda today. The past week or so she'd sorely neglected both granddaughters, and she wanted to make up that time.

It was no use trying to mend the relationship with her daughter; it appeared to be too far gone for that. But if it were within her power, she would not allow the same wedge to be driven between herself and Lucy or Amanda. However, based on her level of discomfort today, spending time with them wasn't an option.

She rubbed her stomach as it lurched and roiled. Oh dear, she didn't need indigestion—or worse—on top of the gout. The smell of bacon fat and potatoes frying for breakfast wasn't a bit enticing, but further sleep would probably evade her. She reached for her Bible on the nightstand and plucked her spectacles from the open page where she'd laid them the night before. At least she could do something productive if her stomach would allow it.

A half hour later there was a tap at her door, and Frances set her Bible aside. Her strained eyes would not have allowed much more, regardless. "Yes? Is that you, Katherine? Come in."

The door swung open, and Wilma Roberts strode into the room.

Frances struggled up higher against her pillow and winced. "What?"

"You're still in bed?"

Frances set her jaw and glared. "Why is it any business of yours?"

Mrs. Roberts planted her fists on her hips and glowered right back. "Your daughter is worried. When you didn't come for breakfast, she asked me to check on you."

"If she was so worried, why did *she* not come herself? She certainly did not need to send *you*." Frances tried to keep the sarcasm out of her voice but knew she'd failed miserably. Her stomach hurt, her legs and feet throbbed, and if she wasn't mistaken, a fever was setting in—and she was stuck talking with the one woman who tormented her as much as her gout.

"Katherine was busy serving her guests, and I offered. There's no reason to take offense." The frown faded, and Mrs. Roberts took a step forward. "Why, you look terrible."

Frances stiffened. "That is rude. *You* do not look perfect either." Sweat trickled down her brow.

"Oh my. That's not what I meant at all." Wilma approached the bed. "You poor dear. Are you sick? You appear to be in distress."

"*I* am fine. I need to go back to sleep, and I *will* as soon as you leave."

Wilma peered over her spectacles at Frances. "Are you sure you're all right? Would you care for some breakfast?"

"No." The word came out fast and sharp. The thought of food made her stomach misbehave. "Not now, thank you." She hoped the softer answer would satisfy the woman, so she'd be on her way.

Instead Mrs. Roberts touched Frances's forehead. "I believe you have a fever." She reared back on her heels. "I'm getting your daughter."

"Please do not. As you said, she is busy and I am fine. Simply overtired." She settled lower on the mattress, turned her head, and deliberately closed her eyes. "I am going to sleep now. Good-bye." Frances listened. She didn't hear Mrs. Roberts so much as stir. After several long minutes, she opened her eyes and turned to face Mrs. Roberts again. "Why are you still here? Go back to your own breakfast and leave me to rest."

"I've already eaten." The woman headed for the door. "I'll be back. You stay put."

Frances groaned. "No! Do not come back, I tell you!" But the door quietly closed behind her obnoxious visitor.

All Frances wanted was to bury her head under the covers and sleep, but with her body on fire, kicking the covers off might be a better idea.

Slapping her hand against the blankets, she shoved them down to her ankles. "'Stay put.' Like I could get out of this bed and go anywhere even if I wanted to." She grumbled the words out loud, not caring if anyone heard. Why would Wilma Roberts bother? Did she plan to torment Frances with her insufferable presence, or did she have some other torture in mind? Whatever it was, Frances did not care to find out. When Mrs. Roberts returned, Frances would order her out of her room—if she had the energy.

She hitched her nightdress up to her knees, reveling in the cool air caressing her skin. She would get out of this bed, if only the swelling and throbbing would go down, and her stomach would settle a bit. All her life she had detested people who used physical infirmity as a ploy for attention, and she made no bones about voicing her opinion to those who had done so. Now she wondered if she'd been fair to those who might have truly been in distress.

Maybe spending time discovering the root of the trouble before labeling them *lazy* would have been more sympathetic. Well, it was too late for that now.

She'd half expected Wilma Roberts to chastise her for not being up earlier to help Katherine in the kitchen, but she had seemed genuinely concerned.

"Here I am, Mrs. Cooper!" The light voice in the hallway gave Frances only a second's warning to pull the cover back up to her waist. Mrs. Roberts shoved the door open farther with her shoulder and entered, bearing a tray in her hands. "Coffee, cold water, a damp rag, and some dry toast with a bit of honey on the side. And Katherine will be along with a lightweight cotton sheet to replace that woolen blanket."

Frances gaped at the beaming woman.

"I'll put this on your bureau for a moment while we get you all set." Mrs. Roberts puttered to the side of the room and set down the tray. "Here comes your daughter. We'll get you cooled off in no time."

Katherine walked in holding a clean, folded sheet and wearing a concerned expression. "Mama? Mrs. Roberts says you're ill. What's wrong?"

Frances swallowed her hot retort. Wilma Roberts had a lot of nerve, giving orders and marching in like she owned the place. She ought to give her a piece of her mind and run her right on out of here. But her gaze traveled to the tray of hot coffee and cool water on the bureau, then over to Katherine holding that inviting, lightweight sheet. Maybe she could tolerate Mrs. Roberts's presence for a couple more minutes.

"I am only a little tired. That is all. But I can get up if you need me. I was going to spend some time with Amanda today, but it seems I overslept." She bit her lip, troubled that she wasn't telling the complete truth, but hating the idea of *that woman* knowing her private business, even if she was being considerate this morning. Frances still wasn't sure she could trust Wilma Roberts's motives, and she would not set herself up to get criticized should she be proven right in her suspicions.

Katherine clucked her tongue. "I'm sorry, I should have checked on you when you didn't come to the dining room."

"No need for that." Frances tugged at the blanket, wincing as it bumped her foot.

Katherine leaned over her and lowered her voice. "Is the gout acting up again, Mama?"

Frances glared at Mrs. Roberts, daring the intrusive woman to speak, but she didn't appear to have heard. She gave a slight nod. "Yes."

"Ah, no wonder. Are you up to eating a bite of the toast and coffee Mrs. Roberts brought in?"

"I am not sure. You can leave it if you would like."

Katherine nodded. "Let's put the sheet on instead of this blanket, shall we?"

Mrs. Roberts cleared her throat. "I'll step outside if you're concerned with modesty, Mrs. Cooper, but let me assure you that nothing you have is news to me."

Frances narrowed her eyes. "And what is that supposed to mean?"

"I know you have gout, and I also know you may have a fever, although I admit it might only be that you are overheated from being too stubborn to take that blanket off since I arrived. And you are wearing a nightdress that covers you from your neck to your ankles, so there is absolutely no reason for this degree of modesty. We are both women well advanced in age, and we certainly don't need to play games."

"Well, I never!" Frances sat bolt upright. "My good woman, I do not play games. Stay if you must. I do not give a whit one way or the other."

Katherine gently drew the blanket down to the end of the bed. "Oh, Mama." She gasped. "I had no idea it was so bad." She grimaced at Frances's swollen joints. "I'll bring a pan of cool water so you can soak your feet."

Frances shot a look at Mrs. Roberts, then nodded. "I suppose it might help. Thank you." She tacked on the last two words with an effort, hating that the smug woman was hearing her private business and observing her discomfort.

Besides, Mrs. Roberts was a paying guest and shouldn't be asked to do their bidding. Couldn't her daughter have abandoned her work for a brief minute rather than send this annoying stranger? Apparently not. Now Katherine was trying to compensate by bringing the sheet, but she'd only made matters worse by exposing Frances's affliction.

Katherine hurried out, leaving Wilma Roberts standing nearby. Why, the woman almost looked like she cared, gazing at Frances with something akin to compassion. "I would like to help. I have no desire to censure you, or make you more uncomfortable, if that's what you believe."

"I suppose it is." Frances met her gaze head-on. "You must admit, we have not been on the best of terms since you arrived."

Mrs. Roberts crossed her arms over her chest. "Humph. I don't seem to remember causing the problem." She let her arms fall to her side. "There I go again, letting you get my back up instead of holding my tongue." She dipped her head. "I apologize for my temper."

"I beg your pardon?" Frances wrinkled her nose and almost laughed. Why in heaven's name would Mrs. Roberts apologize? Frances had done her best to drive the woman and her annoying niece away. Not only did she persist in staying, she continued to surprise her with occasional spurts of kindness. Amazement at the woman's declaration warred with irritation. Under different circumstances she'd have enjoyed another sparring match. "Never mind. We'll let it go this time, shall we?" She pointed at the tray. "If you insist on staying, you might as well make yourself useful and hand me that damp rag." She took it and wiped her forehead and cheeks, sighing as the cool water touched her warm skin. "Thank you."

"Coffee or a glass of water?" Mrs. Roberts raised a brow.

"Water first, I think. Then the coffee." The next moments passed in silence as Frances drank the water, then took sips of the strong black coffee.

Katherine carried a large basin of water into the room. "Here, Mama. This is deep enough to cover your feet and your ankles. Can you sit up?" She set it on the floor in front of the bed.

Mrs. Roberts hustled over to Frances's side. "Let me help." She extended her hand. Frances hesitated, then gripped it, allowing herself to be helped to an upright position. The woman slipped her other hand under Frances's legs and ever so gently swung them to the edge of the bed. "Tell me if I'm moving too fast or if I jar you."

The woman's tender touch surprised Frances. "I believe I am fine.... Th-thank you."

Moments later she sat with her feet soaking in heavenly cool water, her nightdress hitched almost to her knees. Relief flooded her heart as some of the heat drained from her body. She ducked her head, a little ashamed at her recent behavior toward both Katherine and Mrs. Roberts, but she had no idea how to let them know without humiliating herself further, so she chose to keep silent. Surely they'd understand how good this felt and know they were appreciated without her having to spell it out.

Katherine looked from one woman to the other. "I need to go check on Amanda. I left her drawing pictures at the kitchen table, but I promised I'd help her make cookies this morning. I hate to leave you, Mama, but I'll check on you in a little while."

"Oh, fiddlesticks. I will be perfectly all right now that I am cooled off a bit. You go about your business and do not worry about me." She waved at her daughter and nodded at Mrs. Roberts. "You, too. I am sure your niece is in need of your companionship, so do not stay on my account. I cannot imagine you would want to sit around playing nursemaid to an old woman, anyway."

"Nonsense." Mrs. Roberts plopped down in a chair. "I have no intention of leaving you alone. I'll stay until you want to get back in bed, then help with that sheet. And if you want that toast and honey, or a refill on your coffee, I shall take care of that as well."

Katherine thanked Mrs. Roberts and hastened out the door. Frances blinked rapidly, unsure why her eyes moistened without her consent. This woman sounded positively eager to stay around in spite of the way she'd been treated.

Frances didn't understand it at all, but she didn't have the energy to figure it out. "I suppose I might nibble at that toast if you have a mind to hand it over." That was the best she could do, but gratitude and wonder simmered deep in her heart. Wilma Roberts had offered an olive branch—maybe not of friendship, but at least a truce—and Frances intended to grasp it. At least for today. She would wait and see what transpired tomorrow ... and how long this truce lasted.

Chapter Twenty-Seven

Katherine shook her head in wonder as she headed back to the kitchen. Who'd have thought Mrs. Roberts would take so much time for Mama? Why, they'd nearly been enemies since Mrs. Roberts's arrival. For the life of her, Katherine couldn't understand what had changed. Mama certainly hadn't put out any effort to win over the other woman.

Now where had Mandy gone? Katherine stopped in the doorway of the dining room and examined every inch of the room. Sometimes her little scamp liked to hide in a corner and then jump out to scare her. A smile tipped the corners of her mouth. With the house full of boarders, she hadn't spent enough time with either of her girls, and she missed their giggles and secrets. Her smile faded. Not that there'd been many giggles lately from her Lucy. Her elder daughter had kept her share of secrets. She heaved a breath. Well, the girl was thirteen—a difficult age for the best of girls—and Lucy had always been one of the best.

A tap sounded at the front door and Katherine lifted her skirt, hurrying down the hall. Still no sign of Mandy, but she had to deal with a visitor. She swung open the door.

Pastor Seth stood on the porch, his hand gripped by that of her younger daughter.

Mandy tugged him inside. "Ma, Pastor Seth has come to visit, and he'd like some tea and cookies."

The pastor's face wrinkled in consternation, and Katherine stepped back, stifling a chuckle. "Don't worry, Pastor. I know you didn't ask Mandy for anything. She's been begging for a tea party for the past two days, and I haven't had time to accommodate her. I'm sure she sees you as the perfect opportunity."

He gazed down at the girl. "I'd be happy to stay for tea, Miss Galloway, if you're inviting me to your party."

Her blue eyes widened as she smiled up into his, then she turned to Katherine. "He called me Miss Galloway, Ma." Her little chest swelled, and her chin lifted. "I am a lady now." She took his hand again. "Come on, Pastor. We'll go sit in the parlor, and Ma can serve us tea."

Katherine choked as she tried not to laugh, then waved the two toward the archway of the parlor. "Please go right in and make yourself at home. The kettle is on, and as Amanda mentioned ..."

Mandy's head jerked up. "I am Miss Galloway, Ma, not Amanda or Mandy. I am having a tea party, 'member?"

"I beg your pardon, Miss Galloway. You take Pastor Seth and find him a seat. I'll be right along." She whispered to the pastor, "I hope you weren't in a hurry to get somewhere."

"Not at all." He gestured toward the kitchen. "Take your time. I'll visit with my charming hostess."

Katherine chuckled to herself as she headed toward the kitchen. Pastor Seth never ceased to amaze her with his gentle, caring ways. Minutes later she returned to the parlor with a tray of molasses cookies, her china teapot, and three cups. She'd hesitated over bringing one of her best cups for Mandy but decided to chance it. The little girl would be so thrilled at being treated like one of the grown-ups, and Katherine would hate to disappoint her during her first official tea party.

She set the tray down on the low table in front of the divan and poured the tea, offering sugar and cream. Mandy eyed the entire proceeding, chattering to the pastor and handling her cup with care. Katherine waited a little longer, allowing her daughter to carry the conversation, before interrupting, casting a quick smile at her visitor. "Mandy, honey, the pastor came to talk to me about something. Since we're finished with our tea, I think we need some time alone. Would you wait in the dining room? You can get your papers and pencil out of the drawer."

"Sure, Ma. Would you like me to take the dishes?" She set her cup and saucer carefully back on the tray.

"No, but thank you for offering. We'll leave it for now, and I'll bring it when I come."

Mandy gave a dainty curtsy to Pastor Seth. "I'm so glad you could join us for tea, and I hope you can come again." The words were spoken with the air of an adult. Pride swelled in Katherine's heart. Her baby was growing up.

The pastor stood and bowed. "I wouldn't have missed it for anything, Miss Galloway. You have been a wonderful hostess."

Mandy giggled, waved, and skipped out of the room.

Katherine turned back to her visitor. "Thank you for going along with her. I think this has been one of the highlights of her young life. I had no idea how much she'd enjoy it, or I would've made an effort to invite someone over sooner."

His face lit up. "My pleasure. I don't get to spend enough time with the little people in our congregation. As you expected, I am here for a specific purpose. I'm glad I caught you alone—well, except for Amanda, of course."

Katherine nodded, waiting for him to continue.

"Did Mr. Jacobs mention that I spoke with him in town last week?"

"Yes, he did." She let the words stand. Since she'd returned from her quilting meeting, she'd not been able to find time alone with Micah to apologize. Between Mama's bouts of illness and the work that needed to be done in the house, the time had flown by with little contact other than meals. When the pastor left, she'd seek out Micah and deal with her poor behavior.

"I offered to walk to the site of his business with him, but we never made it that far. I'm afraid I upset him by asking about his future intentions."

Her head snapped up, not sure what he might be referring to. "Intentions?"

"Where his business and home are concerned. I wasn't sure if he'd raised the necessary money or manpower to rebuild either one, but it appears he hasn't—and it only frustrated him that I asked." The pastor sighed. "He must be feeling pretty desperate at this point, being beholden to you for a home and not able to pursue making a living. So much of a man's self-worth comes from providing for his family."

"I had no idea." The words came out in a low whisper. She'd sensed something was wrong but had plowed ahead, determined to get her grievance against Zachary out in the open. How selfish and unkind could she be?

The poor man must have felt bombarded on every side. He'd probably been working up the courage to see his business and home, and then anxiety, or something akin to it, had stopped him. Then he'd walked with the pastor, who'd questioned his plans, and afterward she'd scolded him about his son. If only she could turn back the clock and undo the harm she'd done.

She suppressed a shiver. "Mr. Jacobs has been rather withdrawn since we returned from town." She wanted to say more, to confide in this kind man, but didn't feel it was her business. "I wish I could do something."

The pastor laced his fingers together between his knees. "That's why I came. I have an idea, and I need your help to put it in place."

Micah entered the parlor in time to see the pastor shut the front door behind him and Katherine turn away with a smile. A sharp stab of unease hit him. Had Pastor Seth called on Katherine for personal reasons? From what he'd learned, the man wasn't married and might be looking for a wife. As a man of faith, he'd be a perfect fit for Katherine. Micah backed up a step, hoping she hadn't seen him. Maybe she'd head down the hall and not come back into the parlor. The last thing he wanted was another confrontation with an angry woman.

She paused, almost as though sensing his presence, then slowly pivoted and looked him full in the face. Her lips parted as if in surprise, then she relaxed and smiled again.

Micah's breath caught in his throat. He'd forgotten how beautiful she was. He tipped his head. "Katherine." He couldn't seem to force anything else out.

"Micah." She breathed the word so quietly he wasn't sure he'd heard. Then she extended her hands and moved across the parlor toward him. Stopping a mere stride from him, Katherine seemed to come to herself and clasped her hands. "I hoped I'd see you today."

No anger in her tone, no irritation. In fact, she sounded almost eager and … happy. Not at all what he'd expected. "Oh?" What a dunce she must think him, speaking in one-word sentences and standing there like a dumb ox.

"Would you wait for me a moment? Mandy went to the dining room after having a tea party with the pastor, and I need to check on her and let her know I'll be along soon."

"Certainly."

She disappeared with a rustle of her skirt. Was that kindness in her eyes, possibly even tenderness? Micah shook his head, hoping to clear it, then realization dawned. Pastor Seth had told her about their encounter. The fear of being pitied rose in him again. He wanted Katherine's friendship, maybe even her affection, but the last thing he'd tolerate was pity. Not from her, or the pastor, or anyone else. Not today and not ever.

Katherine's heart pounded as she moved back up the hall to the parlor and the man who waited there. Thank heavens for the excuse to step away and gather her composure. She hadn't expected to see him so soon after her talk with Pastor Seth, and certainly not without preparing something to say. The pastor's suggestion had thrilled her, and it would be hard to keep any hint of it out of the conversation, but she must remember the purpose of her discussion with Micah. Setting things right between them was of utmost importance. If only she could quell her nerves and ease the trembling in her body.

She quickened her pace, half afraid he'd disappear before she got there. He'd said almost nothing when she'd asked him to stay, and his blank expression told her little. Would he accept her apology and understand, or turn away in disgust that she'd blundered so badly? Katherine paused before stepping through the open door.

Micah stood with his back to her, staring out the front window, his hands clasped behind him. What a fine-looking man he was. The well-defined muscles in his upper arms showed through the fabric of his linen shirt, and his dark head angled to the side, as though deep in thought. She wasn't accustomed to seeing him without the crutches but was thankful for his sake that he'd finally left them behind.

She cleared her throat so as to not startle him. "Micah?"

He turned with a slight grimace. A pain in his leg from standing too long, or apprehension and displeasure at having to deal with her again? "Do you need to stay with Amanda?"

"No. She's happily absorbed in her drawing. Won't you have a seat?" What was wrong with her that she spoke to him with such forced formality, like they were two strangers starting their acquaintance all over again? "How is your leg? Is it bothering you today?"

He took a seat. "It's tolerable. Aching a little but getting better, so I can't complain."

Relief swept her—not that he'd been in pain, but knowing the effort of swiveling might have caused the distressed look a moment ago. "I'm glad." She sank onto an upholstered chair. Where to begin? This was harder than she'd imagined it would be. "I need to ask your forgiveness." There. It was out and couldn't be taken back. Not that she wanted to, but she hadn't planned on blurting out the words.

His hands gripped his knees. "I beg your pardon?"

Katherine slumped against the chair. He didn't look at all happy or receptive. She hoped he didn't hold a grudge so deep he wouldn't forgive her. "For what I said to you on our way back from town."

"About what, exactly?"

Annoyance pricked her, followed by apprehension. Was he purposely being obtuse, or had their conversation meant little or nothing to him? Maybe she'd blown this whole thing out of proportion, and there was no need to even bring it up. But too late now, the deed was done. She must get this out in the open, or things between them might never return to normal—although she wasn't certain what normal was anymore.

"For accusing Zachary unjustly. I didn't give you a chance to speak to him, nor did I find out what was going on before I assumed the worst. I was wrong for talking to you the way I did. I hope you'll forgive me."

The stiffness in his back relaxed. "Of course I forgive you. And I hope you'll do the same for me."

Surprise jolted her upright. "For what? You were upset with me for pointing a finger at your son. I don't blame you at all."

He shook his head. "No. I said some unkind things about Lucy and her possible intentions in coming to Zachary's room. I was out of line, and I'm sorry."

She nodded. "Thank you. I wasn't expecting that, but I appreciate it so much."

A smile tickled his mouth. "I found out what they were doing."

"You did?" She clasped her hands and raised them to her chin. "Can you tell me?" She didn't care to assume anything and wouldn't make the mistake of trying to force this man to say or do something.

A chuckle broke free. "Lucy has been secretly teaching my son to dance. I caught them practicing in the kitchen yesterday, and they spilled the beans."

"Oh, my!" Katherine gaped, then realized what she must look like and composed herself. "I had no idea. Why didn't Lucy tell me herself?"

"Zachary said he'd made her promise not to tell, and she kept her word—at her own expense, I might add. Even when she knew we were both angry. I have a lot of respect for someone who keeps their word."

"Thank you for saying that, Micah." She could hear her own voice tremble. What a blessed relief to have everything out in the open. But even more than that, to be friends with Micah Jacobs once more.

Micah studied the woman seated nearby. The way she'd said his name sent a thrill of pleasure through his heart. He couldn't believe he'd been thinking about leaving this place and not looking back. Now it would take something mighty big to force him out. It had been over two years since he'd experienced this type of happiness. "I meant every word, Katherine. You should be proud of your daughter."

She nodded. "I am. I think your son is a special young man, as well."

He closed his eyes briefly. What an amazing woman. Humbling herself and asking his forgiveness when she didn't know how he'd respond, then taking all the blame instead of placing it on his son. "So the pastor came to have tea with Amanda? That was kind of him. It's not often a grown man has time to spare for a child."

She nodded, but her expression closed and her gaze shifted from his. "Yes, very kind."

Micah tensed. Had he said something wrong, or had his first impression been accurate after all? Could Pastor Seth have come courting Katherine? "I imagine it gets lonely for you, being a widow all these years."

She looked mystified. "Not really. Why do you ask?"

"I don't know. I thought maybe you and Pastor Seth …" He hadn't meant to be so bold, but better to find out the truth now than open his heart and then have it trampled.

"Oh, my. Me and Pastor Seth? You thought he'd come calling on me?" She shook her head, loosening a gold curl from her bun and sending it bouncing at the nape of her neck. "No, he came to discuss"—she hesitated as though struggling to find the right word—"church business, that's all."

"I see. Well then …" Micah had no idea where to go from here. How foolish that he'd said anything at all. She'd think him an idiot who didn't know how to carry on a normal conversation.

"Would you care for some coffee or tea?" Katherine scooted forward on the edge of her chair as though she planned to jump from it and flee to the kitchen.

"No, but thank you." He got to his feet. "I should let you go. I imagine Amanda is wondering where you are, and I'm sure you must have work to do."

She stood as well. "I do, but you're welcome to come to the kitchen." Katherine said it swiftly, turning her head as she did.

"I think I'll see what Zachary is up to, but thank you for your kindness." He hated this. Ever since he'd brought up the subject of the pastor, the atmosphere changed. What was going on here that he didn't understand, and why had she retreated? Precisely when they'd made progress toward being friends again, or maybe even more, she'd taken a step back. He couldn't imagine what he'd done wrong, or what the pastor had to do with her behavior, but something didn't set right.

Chapter Twenty-Eight

Lucy walked down the hall toward her grandmother's room, carefully balancing the tray of dessert and coffee. Ma was checking on Grandma, who had only picked at the food on her supper tray. A tasty piece of cake and Lucy's cream-laden coffee might entice her to eat a bit more.

She neared the room and paused, wondering if Grandma was sleeping after her difficult day. Ma said her ankles and feet were giving her more pain than usual, and she'd been running a light fever again this morning. Three days was a long time to spend in bed. Tiptoeing forward, Lucy pushed open the unlatched door with her foot and waited a moment. A voice drifted out, and she released her breath. Good. Grandma must still be awake.

"Katherine, I am telling you, Lucy cares for that boy, and you are being unfair not allowing them to court." Her grandmother gave a loud harrumph. "But you always were too harsh with those children. Daniel did a good job parenting, but unfortunately, he is gone. I am so thankful I came here. I can bring some balance into their lives."

"I am the one who needs to make the decisions concerning Lucy and her prospects. She's too young to decide such things. I agree that Zachary is a fine young man. If they are still interested in one another in a couple of years, that will be another thing entirely."

Lucy stood unmoving, not sure if she should back up and flee to the kitchen, or stay and listen some more. Curiosity won out and she decided to stay put—at least for another moment or two. After all, they were discussing her future, so she had a right to listen.

Grandma's voice rose in pitch and Lucy winced, withdrawing a little. "I declare, you are too stubborn for your own good. I have half a mind to talk to Lucy myself."

"Now, Mama, we've discussed this, and you need to leave the parenting to me. I appreciate that you love my girls, but they are *my* responsibility."

"One that you do not always handle well, if you ask me."

Why didn't Ma tell her to stick to her own business? Lucy wanted to burst into the room and tell Grandma to leave her mother alone—and shout at Ma to quit being so nice. Ma never said rude things to Grandma no matter what she did.

On the other hand, Lucy had to admit Ma *was* a little stubborn. After all, Lucy was thirteen and if she did like Zachary as more than a friend, she was old enough to at least think about courting. Her anger flared, first at her grandmother, then at her mother. Why did Grandma have to treat Ma like she was stupid? And why did Ma treat Lucy like she was a baby? She was sick of it.

Grandma could do without her cake and coffee. Lucy was in no mood to take it to her. She crept backward, careful not to bump the tray on the doorpost.

One thing she knew. If those two kept going at it, she didn't want to keep living here. It was bad enough having Grandma snipping at Mrs. Roberts and Beth. If Grandma and Ma kept this up, Lucy would move away and live somewhere else. That would show both of them she could control her own life.

Katherine exited her mother's room without looking back. She'd come so close to snapping at Mama when she'd criticized the way she raised the girls that it scared her. Discord had played too big a part in her life with Mama, and she was determined it wouldn't continue within the confines of her home if she could help it.

But if things kept going this way, she wouldn't be able to help it much longer. She'd let fly and say things she shouldn't. At least things no respectful daughter should say. She was tired. Bone weary of the constant barrage of negative comments and thinly veiled innuendos.

Did her mother actually think she was helping? If only she could understand the hurt she caused and that it pushed Katherine further away. Instead of teaching her something as Mama probably hoped, it made her that much more determined to go her own way—if nothing else, to prove she wouldn't be bullied. Katherine tried to compose herself. There was no point in allowing this emotion to boil over onto any of the guests or her girls. Somehow she had to keep Mama from frustrating her so much, but she didn't know how.

Maybe taking a cup of tea in the parlor would help calm her nerves, especially since Mama wouldn't be there baiting Mrs. Roberts. That kindhearted woman had sacrificed hours waiting on

Mama since she'd taken to bed, although how she managed to keep her composure Katherine couldn't imagine. It was almost certain her mother didn't appreciate the effort Mrs. Roberts made and highly doubtful she'd be able to keep her comments benign.

Minutes later, Katherine carried a tray with a pot of coffee and tea into the parlor, pausing at the threshold to survey the room. Jeffery Tucker sat at a desk, his back toward her, hunched over a tablet, quill in hand. Mrs. Roberts leaned against the back of the divan, eyes closed and lips slightly open. A snore emanated from her mouth. Beth sat with her head bent over a book, its pages lit by a kerosene lamp on the round, cherrywood table.

Katherine started as her gaze moved to Micah. He lounged in Daniel's overstuffed chair, the one her husband had frequented while reading his paper. Micah didn't have a paper spread across his legs, but the same dreamy expression she'd seen on Daniel's face blanketed his features. What could the man be contemplating that took him to such a faraway place of delight or inspiration?

Pleasure darted through Katherine at the realization that Micah had stayed in the parlor that evening, and a sudden longing swept over her. It had been so long since she'd had the pleasure of a man's company, much less anything more intimate. It wasn't the first time she'd daydreamed of sitting close beside Micah, sharing a cozy chat or even ...

Katherine pulled her thoughts back, ashamed at where they were headed. Not that there was anything wrong with a kiss or feeling a man's strong arm around her shoulders, especially for a widow of her age, but she had no right to think that way where Micah was concerned.

She set the tray on the sideboard once inside the door. "Would anyone care for tea or coffee?" She kept her voice low, hating to wake Mrs. Roberts. The poor woman had been at Mama's beck and call so much of the day she must be exhausted. "Are the children still upstairs?"

Micah looked up. "I believe Lucy said she, Amanda, and Zachary were playing a game. Should I call them back down?"

Katherine shook her head. "Not at all; they're fine. It will be their bedtime soon, but we'll let them play for a bit while we have our tea." She picked up the pot. "Would you care for a cup, Mr. Jacobs?"

"None for me, thank you. I had a second helping of your delicious cake and two cups of coffee after supper."

She made the rounds, pouring a cup of coffee for Mr. Tucker and tea for Beth. The young woman lifted it to her nose and inhaled. "Ah, peppermint, my favorite. This is precisely the tonic I needed tonight. Thank you, Mrs. Galloway." She took a sip, then set it aside to tug the sleeve of her dress back down over her wrist.

"Has your aunt had a difficult day?"

"She was up quite early, unable to sleep for worry over Mrs. Cooper." She touched the locket at her throat. "When I finish my tea, I'll wake her and insist she go to her room."

Katherine settled herself in a chair not far from the desk where Mr. Tucker sat bent over his tablet. "May I ask what has you so consumed, Mr. Tucker?"

He jumped, dropping his quill, and slowly turned. "By Jove, I think I've finally got it."

Micah leaned forward. "What's that, man? Did you lose something?"

"No, I believe I've finally found it." Mr. Tucker ran his hand over his sandy hair, ruffling the waves into even more disarray than usual. "The idea I have been seeking ever since I arrived." He looked up, brown eyes alight with excitement. "I can't tell you about it, though, as I have not fully developed the notion yet. But I must say, I think I am on to something."

Katherine smiled, happy to see her normally reticent boarder so animated. "Can you give us any hint as to what you're about, Mr. Tucker? We would certainly like to celebrate with you, if we may."

He regarded her blankly, then swift color rose up his neck. "I don't ... I can't ... I did not mean to say ..." He passed his hand over his face and groaned. "Forgive me. I know I must sound like an imbecile. I was so engrossed in my work I wasn't even aware I was speaking aloud, or that others were in the room who would hear me." He pushed back his chair, stood, and tucked his notepad under his arm. "I must go to my room now and think this through some more." He tipped his head. "I bid you all good night." Without a backward glance he strode from the room, leaving a weighty silence behind.

Beth stared at his retreating form as he disappeared through the door leading to the stairs. "I am completely at a loss as to what he was talking about."

Katherine chuckled. "You are not alone, my dear." She turned to Micah. "Mr. Jacobs, can you cast any light on the mystery?"

He lifted a shoulder. "Not a bit, I'm afraid. What does the man do for a living? Do you know?"

"I have never asked him directly," Katherine murmured. "I should have, I suppose. I assumed him to be a businessman of some sort, based on the type of reading he enjoys. Not to mention the time he spends in town and the hours sitting at that desk. But this is the first time he's offered a comment of any sort. I'm as mystified as you as to why he wouldn't elaborate."

"Well, I won't worry about it too much tonight." Beth set her teacup down on the saucer and covered a yawn with her fingertips. "I believe it's time I woke Aunt Wilma." She scooted over on the divan and touched the older woman's arm. "Auntie?"

Mrs. Roberts sucked in a deep breath and held it for a long moment, then released it in a loud, rolling snore.

Beth turned pink right up to the tips of her ears. "Oh, my! She would be so embarrassed." She turned a distressed face to Katherine. "Should I wake her?"

"Let me try." Katherine stood and made her way to the woman's side. "Mrs. Roberts, Beth needs you."

"What is the trouble?" Wilma sputtered. Pushing a lock of graying hair out of her eyes, she peered at her niece over the top of her spectacles. "Beth, did you drift off to sleep while I was resting? I swear I heard someone snoring in quite an unladylike racket, if you must know."

"Yes, Auntie. I mean, no, Auntie. I've been reading, not sleeping." Beth closed her book and held out her hand. "But my eyes are quite tired, and I would love to have you walk me to my room, if it's not too much trouble."

"Certainly, dear girl. I shall make sure you get there safely." She got to her feet, swayed for a couple of seconds, then steadied herself.

Beth slipped an arm around her aunt's waist. "Thank you. That will make me feel much better." She dipped her head at Katherine and Micah. "Good night. We'll see you at breakfast."

Katherine followed the two with her gaze. "Beth is such a dear," she told Micah. "When she first came, I wasn't sure if she even *had* a mind of her own, but honestly, I think she takes care of her aunt as much as Mrs. Roberts takes care of her. She'll make some man a fine wife one day."

Micah cast a brief glance at the two exiting the room. "Yes, I think she will."

Katherine's heart jolted at the words. Could he be smitten with Beth Roberts but unsure how to proceed? Surely not. The girl was twenty and old enough to marry, but a little young to mother a fourteen-year-old son. Katherine tried to squash the sharp prick of jealousy as being beneath her but didn't quite succeed.

Well, there was nothing like being direct. "If you're interested in Miss Roberts, you should approach her aunt. It's not my business, but I think Mrs. Roberts would be open to a suit from a fine man like you."

"What?" He stared at her, mouth open. "You think *I* am interested in Beth Roberts?"

Katherine's stomach unclenched at his obvious surprise, and relief swept through her. Maybe she'd misjudged his earlier dejection. "I thought perhaps … you seemed distracted when she left."

He laughed. "It had nothing to do with her. I was focused on other matters."

"I'm quite a good listener." She cocked her head to the side and sent him a tentative smile. "When I'm not scolding, that is."

Micah relaxed into his chair. "I'm sure you are, but I would hate to bother you with my troubles."

"Nonsense. As long as we don't get interrupted by the children, I would love to spend a few minutes talking. But I don't want to pry if you'd rather not discuss it."

"It is not a secret or anything terribly personal. I'm anxious about my business and home, I suppose. Some of the pastor's questions got me to thinking again. I still have no idea what I'll do, although I plan to fight through and get my business going again if it's the last thing I do."

Katherine nodded as waves of guilt washed against her conscience. Was it fair to keep the truth from this man, when he'd admitted his distress? Maybe she could hint at Pastor Seth's plan. No, that wouldn't be right. And it might make Micah feel he was an object of pity. Both sides warred in her thoughts, making her almost dizzy with the effort. "I see. I wondered after he mentioned seeing you in town if that might be the problem. You seemed a bit distracted when you got back into the wagon."

His features hardened. "So he did discuss me with you." It wasn't a question, but a flat-out declaration, and not one he appeared to appreciate.

She shook her head. "Nothing negative. Just that he'd had occasion to ask about your plans and to express his concern for your future."

"I do not want your pity, Katherine." The words were stark. Blunt.

Katherine blinked. *Your pity.* He'd made it quite personal. She pushed up from her chair and went to stand at the window, looking out into the dark and weighing her words. "I'm sorry. I didn't mean to hurt you." She kept her back to him, not even certain he'd heard her words.

The room was silent for a minute. Then a step sounded behind her. "You didn't hurt me. I'm sorry I snapped at you."

She turned and gazed up into his concerned green eyes. He reached out and touched her hair, then let his hand settle tenderly on her shoulder. Tingles stole down her arm and she smiled, not wanting to move, not caring to break the tenderness. Praying it would last a little bit longer.

"Katherine." The word slipped out on a sigh. He drew her toward him and wrapped his arms around her, pulling her close.

A woodsy fragrance tickled her nostrils. She relaxed against him, savoring the moment and the gentle strength of his arms. It had been too long since she'd been held like this, and it seemed like a small touch of heaven. Her cheek lay against the rough fabric of his shirt and somehow her arms had crept around his waist.

"This feels right. I'm not sure if it is or not, but I don't want to let go." He touched her chin and tipped it up.

She held her breath, wondering if he would kiss her, and praying he might. But deep inside she knew Micah was too much of a gentleman to kiss a woman without some type of commitment. Yet his hug ignited a fire in her soul, even if he didn't take it any further.

"Maybe I am presuming too much, but I want you to know that I am starting to care for you."

Her heart leapt at his declaration. "And I for you, Micah. I think I've been feeling it for a while now, but wasn't certain you felt the same."

"That's good. I've been worried it was pity instead."

She shook her head, surprised at his words. "Never. I admire so much about you."

He stroked her hair, then traced a finger from her cheek to the corner of her mouth, his gaze resting there. "I'd best be careful. It's been a long time since I held a woman like this, and I don't want to do something I shouldn't. Besides, we have our children to consider."

His touch sent a wave of longing coursing through her body, but his words were like a dash of cold water on her hot cheeks. "Micah, I'm not sure a relationship between us is wise—not if there's a chance Lucy and Zachary are interested in one another. Our children's welfare must come first."

Micah bobbed his head. No words came—but the intense look filling his eyes as they held hers for another long moment said it all. "We will consider that. But there's something I must do before you go." He bent over and touched his lips to her cheek, just an inch or so from her lips, then placed another on the other side, lingering for a moment. "I'll not take advantage again, Katherine, and I hope you'll forgive me for being so bold."

She closed her eyes, afraid to look at him. More than anything she'd wanted to turn her head a fraction and allow her lips to meet his. She stayed still for a minute longer, not trusting herself to move deeper into his embrace, her desire was so strong.

"Ma!" Lucy's high-pitched shriek filled the room. "I can't believe you are kissing Mr. Jacobs!"

Katherine jumped back, one hand flying to cover her pounding heart.

Zachary's mirthless laugh followed Lucy's words. "And *they* have been scolding *us* about you teaching me to dance and spending time alone together. Ha." He threw his father an angry look. "You are a hypocrite, Pa." He took a step backward, then dashed to the door.

A shadow loomed over Lucy, and Mama stepped into the soft glow of the kerosene lamplight, glaring at Katherine. "I cannot say I disagree with the boy." She swung toward Micah. "I have been holed up in my sickbed and come out to find you sparking my daughter in the dark. A fine example you are setting for your young ones."

Lucy backed toward the doorway. "You aren't my pa and you never will be, no matter how many times you kiss Ma." She ran, leaving silence cloaking the room.

Chapter Twenty-Nine

Micah's heart was ready to explode as Katherine fled after her daughter. So many emotions swirled inside that it was hard to separate one from another. He couldn't believe how close he'd come to smothering her with kisses—how desperately he'd wanted to—and what fierce control it had taken to resist. Her demeanor told him it wouldn't have offended her, and the way she'd leaned into his embrace spoke volumes about her own desire.

Part of his mind revolted at the idea that they were being selfish. He wanted to race after Katherine and assure her that Lucy and Zachary would be fine, whatever they decided to do, but his heart kept his feet planted firmly on the floor, unmoving. They were parents first and foremost, and nothing should come ahead of their children's well-being. But why did it have to hurt so much? First he'd lost Emma, and now that he'd discovered Katherine cared for him as well, it about killed him to let her go.

He needed to find his son and explain, but first he had to deal with the woman who stood at the edge of the lamplight glaring over the top of her spectacles. He gritted his teeth, trying to contain his emotions. "Mrs. Cooper, I'm afraid you got the wrong idea about what you saw tonight."

"I do not think so, young man. It is quite clear what you are after."

"I beg your pardon, ma'am? I'm not after anything."

"Balderdash. Of course you are. You lost your own place of business and home, and you see the perfect opportunity to walk in here and take over what Katherine's built up for herself and her children." Her glare intensified even further. "But you have met your match, Mr. Jacobs. You will not be taking advantage of anyone while I am alive to keep it from happening."

"I care for your daughter, Mrs. Cooper."

"And I do not choose to believe that, Mr. Jacobs. Now, good night to you." She headed for the door, then swiveled to drill him with her gaze once again. "And if you know what is good for you, you will find another place to live as soon as you can."

Katherine raced up the stairs after her daughter, gripping the banister with one hand and raising the hem of her skirt with the other. The last thing she needed was to twist her ankle or fall on the stairs, adding injury to the upset of being accosted downstairs by her daughter and mother.

Part of her raged against the injustice of the judgment Zachary, Lucy, and Mama had delivered, while the other part shriveled with embarrassment at having been caught in Micah's embrace. How could she explain that to her daughter when she didn't fully understand it herself yet?

It was all too new, too tender and fresh. She'd had no time to analyze her feelings after the near kiss they'd shared. The kiss she'd wanted more than she cared to admit.

She reached the top of the stairs and paused. What would she do if Lucy asked her about her sentiment where Micah was concerned?

A sudden thought hit her. She'd left Mama down there with Micah, and Mama looked fit to be tied. It was becoming more obvious her mother didn't care for Micah, and Katherine sickened at the thought of what that might mean for her future. Mama planned on making the boardinghouse her permanent home and with her not-so-subtle dislike, which she rarely kept covered, Katherine couldn't imagine how anything lasting could develop between herself and Micah.

She wanted to rush back down the stairs and step between them but stopped herself. Lucy was her priority right now. Micah was an adult; he'd have to fend for himself. And she needed to trust God with their future. But she still released a small groan at what Micah faced downstairs. Somehow she doubted he'd had many encounters that prepared him for dealing with Mama.

Katherine stopped outside Lucy's door and tapped. She hadn't expected an answer but tried again. "Lucy? I'd like to come in."

The door cracked open, and Mandy peered out, her eyes round and worried. "Lucy's on her bed crying. What's wrong with her, Ma?"

Katherine swooped the little girl into her arms. "She's sad about something, but she's going to be all right. How would you like to sleep with me tonight, sugarplum?"

Mandy squealed and bounced in her arms. "Yes, yes, yes!" She suddenly stilled and cast a look toward the bed on the far side of the room. "Can Lucy come too?"

"Not this time, honey. I need to talk to Lucy. Would you take your nightdress and go to my room? I can help you when I get there if you need me to." She set her younger daughter on her feet.

"No." Mandy shook her head. "I don't need help. I'm old enough to do it myself. Can I get under the covers and wait for you there? And can I take my dolly with me?"

"Of course." Katherine plucked Mandy's nightdress from the wardrobe hook and held it out. Mandy carefully draped it over her arm and tucked her doll under the other. "I'll stay awake till you get there, Ma."

"All right, sweetie." She kissed the girl's pink cheeks and watched her walk from the room.

Sobs continued from underneath the covers.

"Lucy?" Katherine halted by the bed. "We need to talk about this."

"There's nothing to talk about. Please go away."

"I'm sorry, I can't do that. I'll stay here all night if I have to. We are going to talk. Mandy has gone to my room for the night, so we're alone."

"Where's Grandma and Zachary?" The blanket muffled the words, but Lucy's head didn't poke out.

The question sent a stab through Katherine's heart. She had no idea where the boy had disappeared to and hated to consider what her mother might be doing or saying. "I'm sure they're fine. Mr. Jacobs will talk to Zachary, and your grandmother is probably back in her room by now. I imagine she came down for a cup of warm milk before heading to bed."

Lucy threw off the blanket. "No, ma'am. She walked down the stairs behind me and said she was coming to check on you, because you hadn't been upstairs for such a long time."

"Figures." Katherine muttered the word.

"What did you say?"

"Nothing important. Will you sit up, please?" Katherine perched on the edge of the bed and waited for Lucy to scoot up against the pillows. "I'm sorry for upsetting you." She still hadn't decided exactly what to say but sensed her daughter needed to hear an apology, at the very least. The girl had been shocked at the scene she'd walked in on, even if nothing improper had happened.

"Why were you kissing Mr. Jacobs?" Her voice rose. "That was awful, Ma. He's Zachary's pa, and Zachary is my best friend. How could you do that?"

"We weren't kissing, Lucy. He gave me a hug and a kiss on the cheek, that's all."

"That's not what it looked like to me." She narrowed her eyes. "Are you lying to me?"

Katherine straightened, shocked at how closely her daughter's words echoed her own from a few days before. "Is that what you think?"

"I don't know what to think." Lucy smoothed out the sheet beneath her trembling fingers. "You didn't believe me when I told you nothing happened in Zachary's room, and I was only teaching Zachary to dance."

"I know, and I'm sorry. Mr. Jacobs told me. It was wrong of me to jump to conclusions and not listen to you."

"But why did you? It's not like I've ever given you a reason to not trust me. You acted like we did something terrible."

Katherine wondered how much to say. Honesty would serve her best. "You're old enough to understand, and I suppose I should have explained before this, considering."

"Considering what?" Lucy raised tear-dampened lashes and peered up at her.

"Your age, and the fact that you could be seriously interested in a young man."

Lucy heaved a sigh. "Ma."

"All right. But you're old enough that your feelings could become more before long."

"I thought we were talking about you."

Katherine placed two fingers under Lucy's chin and raised it an inch. "No. Right now we're talking about you; then we'll get back to me. You asked why I didn't trust you and didn't listen, and I'm going to explain. Part of it has to do with your age, and part of it has to do with me." Her stomach did a somersault, but she pressed forward. "I was only fifteen when I first met your father. Almost sixteen, but not quite."

"Really?" Lucy perked up at the mention of her pa. "I didn't know that."

"Yes, and it didn't take me long before I knew I was falling for him. Hard."

A dreamy smile covered Lucy's face. "Pa was easy to love."

"Yes, he was. But we were alone one time when Grandma wasn't home, and things got a little out of hand." How much detail should she give to a girl her daughter's age? Yet she'd gone this far. In for a penny, in for a pound. "We weren't betrothed yet, and I let him kiss me. In fact, Mama had barely given us permission to court, and I wasn't to be alone with him."

"But he kissed you anyway?" Lucy's brows scrunched together. "When Grandma said he couldn't?"

"She didn't *exactly* say he couldn't kiss me, but I knew it was wrong."

Lucy shrugged. "He kissed you one time. You ended up marrying him. So it doesn't matter, right?"

"It was more than one time. He kissed me that once, then a second time, then a third, and before long, it was hard to stop. I got so swept up in the desire of the moment that I didn't want to stop. Your father was three years older than me, almost nineteen at the time, and very much a man. I'm afraid he didn't want to stop, either."

Lucy's mouth formed an O. "What happened?"

Katherine entwined her fingers in her lap. "Thankfully, nothing, because we heard the front door open, and Mama arrived. I jumped back, straightened my hair, and sat on a chair across the room."

"Did Grandma find out?"

"No, she never did."

"Then why does it matter now? What does that have to do with me teaching Zachary to dance in his room?"

"Because of what could have happened between your father and me. We didn't plan that first kiss, or the second or third or fourth. We didn't plan to get so swept up in passion that neither of us wanted to stop at kissing."

A blush rose into Lucy's cheeks. "Ma. That's disgusting."

Katherine smiled. "No, honey, it's perfectly natural. But it gives me hope that you still think of it that way."

Lucy wrinkled her nose. "You don't need to worry about me. I still don't see why you're telling me this."

"You were alone and unchaperoned in Zachary's room, and from what I could tell you'd just stepped out of his arms. I had no idea how long you'd been there, or what had happened. My thoughts immediately went to your father and me, and how close we'd come to crossing a very important line. In fact, we did cross a line, as we weren't married or even promised to one another."

She prayed her daughter would understand. "Kisses and physical affection should be saved for the person you know you're going to marry. Even then, you only give them after a commitment to marriage has been made. It's not right or proper to allow those types of liberties during a courtship. And anything beyond a kiss or two should be saved for marriage. Does that make sense?"

Lucy nodded slowly. "I think so. You were afraid I was kissing Zachary when we weren't courting or betrothed, is that right?"

"Yes, exactly." Katherine smiled, thrilled that Lucy appeared to accept her explanation.

Lucy's brows lowered. "Then you and Mr. Jacobs must be betrothed, 'cause he was kissing you when I walked in."

Chapter Thirty

Micah shaded his eyes from the morning sun, surveying the monumental job he had avoided so long. He brushed his arm across his forehead, wiping away the rivulets of sweat. He wished it were that easy to erase the disappointment reflected in his son's gaze when he'd followed him outside nearly two weeks ago. It seemed impossible so much time had passed since he'd held Katherine. On the other hand, it felt like a lifetime. Their paths had crossed a number of times since, but there'd been no opportunity for a private talk.

Maybe it was just as well, as she appeared to struggle with looking him square in the face—but that might also be due to the watchful eyes of her mother. He didn't know, and he'd about given up trying to figure it out. At least his leg was sufficiently mended to accomplish some work.

He tossed another burnt board from his ruined livery stable onto a pile, wishing for the thousandth time he had the courage to attend the social and dance later this afternoon. The idea of having an excuse to hold Katherine in his arms again, if only for one dance, made his mouth go dry and his heart pound.

"Hey, Jacobs, I thought I'd lend a hand for an hour or so, if you've a mind to let me." Pastor Seth strolled up to the wood keg where Micah was pitching the nails and pieces of metal.

He jerked upright, clutching his hammer to keep from dropping it. "Howdy, Pastor. Sorry. I didn't see you standing there. It's pretty dirty work. I'm afraid you'll be black as a coal miner if you chance it."

Seth shrugged and rolled up his sleeves, exposing strong forearms that had seen their share of sun. "Last time I checked, soot washes off."

Micah wasn't sure what he'd expected, but most preachers he'd known were not accustomed to physical labor. He grinned and pointed at a pile. "I've made some headway, but if you want to toss those boards onto my wagon, that would be fine. I've pulled all the nails so they should be safe. I'm keeping any usable boards, but those aren't worth saving."

The pastor pitched in without another word.

Minutes later Tom Collier from the hardware store sauntered over, tugging on a pair of leather gloves. "This a private party, or can anyone join in?"

Pastor Seth waved a hand at the back wall of the building. "Dig in. Jacobs wants everything removed."

"Brought my own tools." Collier plucked a hammer from a loop on his hip. "One of the advantages of owning a hardware store, doncha know?" He chuckled and strode to the back wall.

Before the hour struck seven, more men arrived, each acting as though he'd just been wandering by, but from the pleased expression on the pastor's face, Micah doubted that was the case. He wasn't sure if he should be grateful or embarrassed, but as the men dove in, the rubble that would have taken him all day to remove disappeared in a fraction of the time.

Micah tossed the last nail from a board into the barrel and walked over to Seth. "Want to tell me how this came about?"

Seth grinned and winked. "Nope, don't think I care to. You getting hungry yet?"

Micah took off his hat and scratched his head. "I brought a pail with a sandwich and an apple, but I'm afraid I don't have enough for everyone. By dinnertime we'll be done, and the men can head on home."

Seth tipped his head back and chortled. "Somehow I don't think the ladies will want all this soot tracked into their houses, but that's not going to be a problem."

Micah lifted an eyebrow. "Huh?"

The pastor planted a firm hand on each of Micah's shoulders and turned him around. "Look there at what's coming up the street."

The rumble of wagons and the chatter of women's voices reached Micah's ears. He'd been so engrossed in his work he hadn't noticed the increase in the late-morning traffic. Four wagons, each pulled by a team of horses, rolled toward him. Two were filled with women and boxes, while the other two were piled with lumber. His jaw sagged. *What in the world?*

Seth slapped him on the back. "Better shut that mouth, Jacobs, before it fills with dust. You want to be able to taste all that good food the ladies are bringing."

Micah swung around and grabbed the man's arm. "Tell me what's going on here." He focused on the first wagon. Katherine sat on the front seat proud and tall, her face beaming as she clutched a small box on her lap.

The teamster driving one of the lumber wagons pulled off to the side, wrapping the reins around the brake and jumping to the ground. "Where you want this unloaded, Jacobs?"

Micah tightened his grip on Seth's arm. "I didn't order that lumber, and I can't pay for it." He wanted to shake some sense into the well-meaning reverend. This was getting out of hand, and he had to bring it under control.

Seth laid his hand over Micah's fingers. "I know you can't, and so does he." He nodded toward a big, blond-haired man wearing dungarees held up by a pair of suspenders. The man was striding in their direction. "That's George Mayfield, the owner of the mill outside of town. Talk to him, why don't you?"

Micah groaned. The pastor meant well, but he'd gone too far. It was one thing to accept some hours of help from the townspeople, but another thing entirely to accept lumber he couldn't pay for. He stepped forward. "Mr. Mayfield, I'm afraid there's been a misunderstanding." He dropped his voice as the man drew to a halt. "I appreciate the thought, but I didn't order these supplies. I'm sorry you went to the trouble, and I'll pay for your time as soon as I'm able."

The man slid his thumbs down the inside of his suspenders and then ran them back to the top. "I was hoping we could make us a trade, Jacobs."

Micah's thoughts whirled but couldn't settle on what Mr. Mayfield was saying. The happy chatter of women, the neigh of a horse, the ringing of hammers against boards, and the thump of boots as men unloaded boxes of food and set planks on sawhorses distracted him. Cloths were thrown over the makeshift tables, and plates and flatware were unwrapped as he stood there and gawked.

"Uh, Jacobs?" George Mayfield rocked back on his heels and grinned. "Want to wait and palaver about this after dinner? Looks like yer attention is on the food those ladies brung us."

Micah started and blinked, ashamed that he'd ignored the man. "Forgive me, Mr. Mayfield. I reckon this is a lot for me to take in. I wasn't expecting help today, and now …" He waved toward the bustle of activity in front of what had once been his livery. "Well, now people show up, and you bring lumber, and I'm not sure what to think." He turned, working to gather his disjointed thoughts. "You said something about a trade?"

"Yes, sir, I did at that." Mayfield jerked his thumb over his shoulder. "I got stacks of lumber out at my mill, but I also got two broke-down wagons, a harness wanting repair, a busted wheel, and three horses in bad need of shoes. I'd planned on bringing the work to you 'bout the time your building caught fire, then you was laid up and couldn't work. I'll admit, I'm doing this as much for myself as you, but I hope you won't hold that a'gin me. You'd be doing me a service if you'd consider it."

Micah shook his head. "You're saying you want to trade all this lumber for work? But there's enough here to frame up a whole new building."

"Yep, and more coming for the siding, along with a load of shingles, if you'll take 'em."

Micah held up his hand. "Whoa, now. No, sir. That's too much. I'll owe you more than the work you mentioned."

Mayfield shrugged. "Makes me no never mind, Jacobs. I've got a tally of it all back at my office. Believe me, I'll not be shy about asking you to work when I need it. I run a business, and something is always breaking down at the wrong time. I lost my smithy a couple of months ago and figured on replacing him till I heard you'd come to town. My work alone will keep you busy for the next month. 'Course, it don't all have to be done back-to-back, if you get other folks needing your time. Long as you fix that harness and a couple of my wagons, and shoe the horses, that'll tide me over for a mite." He stuck out a beefy, work-hardened hand. "Is it a deal?"

Micah grinned and stretched out his arm. "Yes, sir, I'd say it is. I can't thank you enough."

Mayfield heaved a sigh. "Don't be thanking me too fast, Jacobs. You might be cussin' me by the time we're finished."

"I hardly think so." Micah watched the man stride back to the wagons. A surge of joy and gratitude swelled to the point where he was sure his heart would burst. All of this was Seth's doing, he knew it. He searched for the pastor, and his heart jolted again. Katherine stood only feet away, her blue eyes ablaze with joy—and something else—as they met his. He wanted to race forward, swoop her into the air, and swing her around, but he clamped his arms to his sides and froze. He'd promised Katherine to respect their decision to put their children first and hoped Mrs. Cooper's attitude toward him would change. If it killed him, he'd keep that promise.

Even from the distance that separated them, Katherine could see the fire that lit Micah's eyes as soon as he saw her … and then, just as quickly, faded. His hands clenched into balls, and his body stiffened.

Had she offended him somehow, or had he discovered she'd helped plan this day and resented her for it? She prayed he wasn't humiliated by something one of the men had said. Or was refusing to swallow his pride and accept the supplies offered.

She wanted to run to him and pour out a dozen questions—things she'd been longing to ask for the past several days. What had happened between him and Zachary that night the children discovered them in the parlor? Did he regret the declaration he'd made about caring for her and wish he'd kept silent? She moved forward when a step beside her made her pause. *Oh dear.* She'd forgotten Mama and Wilma Roberts had insisted on coming along.

"Katherine, where do you want these pies?" Mrs. Roberts tapped her on the arm. "Oh, I see you are staring at Mr. Jacobs. Well, if you ask me, he certainly is a fine-looking specimen."

"I wasn't staring at him, Mrs. Roberts. You can place the pies on the end of this table. Is Lucy making herself useful?" She turned her back on the man in question, but not before she saw him pivot away.

"Yes, as is little Mandy. Fine girls you have raised, Mrs. Galloway. They do you proud."

Katherine drew a breath, thankful she'd derailed the conversation. "Thank you."

"Yes, indeed. But it is not good for a woman to spend the rest of her life alone. When I first arrived at your boardinghouse, I had hoped Mr. Jacobs might be interested in my Beth, but it appears he only has eyes for you. And according to what I've seen …" Her voice raised a notch and she bumped Katherine with her elbow. "… the feeling is mutual."

Heat rose in Katherine's cheeks and she dipped her head, hoping the eagle-eyed Mrs. Roberts wouldn't notice. "I can't imagine where you've heard that, Mrs. Roberts. Mr. Jacobs and I are only friends."

"Ha, that is not what a certain little birdie told me."

Katherine forced herself to relax. "It is never good to listen to gossip."

"Oh, it wasn't gossip, my dear. It came straight from your mother."

Katherine blinked. She hadn't expected Mama to talk. In fact, she'd assumed Mama would want to bury the episode. Nothing had been mentioned over the past week or so other than an occasional cold stare or sharp grunt. "Are you implying my mother was conveying good news or ill tidings, Mrs. Roberts?"

"Oh, certainly not good news, my dear. In fact, if I didn't know better, I would think she was hoping to start a bit of a scandal and force Mr. Jacobs to move. I told her it was an ill wind that would blow no one any good, and she would do well to keep her own counsel. I reminded her that you are a grown woman and a pretty one, at that. Your two girls could use a father, and I'm sure it wouldn't upset you having a man around the house."

The matron beamed. "She and I have gotten quite close since her illness. That is, when she's not angry with me over one thing or another, but that is happening less. I am still convinced the only thing that ails her is that she needs a friend, and I am determined to fill that role for as long as I am here." She lifted her head and smiled. "She may not appreciate it yet, but she will. Mark my words."

Katherine patted the woman's arm, thankful the subject had swung to her mother. "I'm sure she will, and you are a saint to keep at it, Mrs. Roberts. Now, if you will excuse me, I need to find my girls."

"Not at all. In fact, I should see how Frances is faring. I left her sitting in the shade and instructed her to stay off her feet. We don't want gout sending her back to bed."

Katherine slipped away, but not before peering over her shoulder in the direction Micah had gone. Disappointment rocked her when she saw the spot where he'd stood was vacant. But it might not be a good idea to seek him out anytime soon. She didn't want tongues to wag. The last thing she needed was the town setting them up as a courting couple. What had her mother been thinking, and what, exactly, had she said to Mrs. Roberts? Katherine didn't know, but she intended to find out.

Micah stared at the gathering throng of people. He hadn't expected the dance to take place in the square outside his new building, but the general consensus was to stay here rather than move to the usual location. He ran a hand over his freshly washed hair and rocked back on his heels. Butterflies danced in his stomach, feeling as though they had razors for wings. He hadn't been this nervous since he'd given Emma a handmade Valentine's card the year he turned thirteen. *Emma*. He waited for the sharp pain that always arose at the memory of his wife, but he only experienced a tender sadness. Incredible. He'd never forget Emma—didn't ever want to forget. But how could this new feeling for Katherine have done so much toward helping him heal?

More men had arrived after the lumber was delivered, and the sounds of hammering and shouts of encouragement rang in the air. In no time at all, the walls were up and the second-floor joists spanned them. The workers all promised to return on Monday to finish the framing, including the roof. Micah still wasn't positive he'd use the upper story for a home, but it would come in handy no matter what he decided.

The work the men had accomplished astounded him, as well as the compassion poured out by this town. More specifically, by Pastor Seth. He'd been God's hands extended these past weeks, and the framing of Micah's new building proved he'd done so again.

How could Micah possibly remain angry at God when his heavenly Father continued to express His love in such tangible ways? Sure, he still had questions and concerns and knew he'd need to sort through his feelings of loss and abandonment, but for the first time in two years he saw a ray of hope.

People he didn't know had spent hours helping—not only on his building, but setting up tables and food for the social this evening. The early evening air remained warm, and the sun wouldn't set for another three hours, giving plenty of time for socializing.

Micah's palms grew damp at the thought of dancing with Katherine. He hadn't danced for years and would probably step all over her dainty shoes if he tried, but the lure was too great to resist.

But first, he had to find her. He scanned the swelling crowd of colorfully dressed people, hoping to spot her dark gray dress and blond hair. Women sashayed in on the arms of their husbands or beaus, and children ran screaming and giggling, weaving among the tables. A group of men cleared a space in his new building while another set chairs in a circle around the outer walls. It appeared they were placing benches outside the big double doors.

Katherine had been in evidence during supper, but he hadn't enjoyed a minute alone with her—not with her mother glaring daggers. Katherine had sent him an apologetic smile followed by a shrug that sent his heart soaring. At least *she* didn't appear upset with him.

A blond woman in a powder-blue dress caught his eye, making Micah catch his breath. From a distance it appeared to be Katherine, but she'd been wearing a gray dress a couple of hours earlier with her hair drawn back in a knot. He turned and followed the woman with his gaze. Her hair was down, caught in a clip at her neck, allowing a riot of golden curls to cascade down her back. He hadn't realized how long those tresses were. Her trim hips swayed slightly, causing the full skirt to flow around her ankles. He shook his head, unable to tear his eyes away but hating to stare.

She paused, then stopped and slowly turned, raising her hand to touch a curl that framed the side of her face. Micah's heart lurched. Katherine. He'd never seen anyone so beautiful in his life.

Shivers ran up Katherine's spine. Someone was watching her. She turned and looked back the way she'd come. Micah stood on the far side of the small clearing, holding his hat in his hands, his mouth agape. Deep admiration shone on his freshly scrubbed face.

He must have returned to the house in the past hour or so, possibly slipping in and out while she took care of her own preparations in her room. Gone were the soot-stained clothing and old work boots. In their place were dark trousers, a white shirt, a five-button vest, and a neatly done tie. The clothes must be another kind gesture from Pastor Seth, as Micah didn't have the funds to replace what he'd lost.

Micah's hair shone, and his face was cleanly shaved. The muscles of his upper arms tightened the fabric of his thin cotton shirt, and Katherine's heart skipped a beat. He had never looked so handsome.

He wended his way between the people gathering in small groups and stopped a short stride away, bowing low and smiling. "I must say, you're lovelier than I've ever seen you."

She curtsied and laughed. "Thank you, kind sir. And I might say the same about you. But handsome, not lovely, if I'm to be perfectly accurate."

One corner of his lips twitched, then he extended his arm. "May I escort you, madam?"

She slipped her hand through his bent arm and thrilled as he drew her close. "Have you seen the children?" She hated to squelch the moment, but if she weren't careful, she'd forget caution and fall right into his arms. With the possibility that gossip might have already started, she needed to be vigilant—not to mention the added threat of Mama, who'd kept an eagle eye on almost every move she and Micah made recently. She hadn't seen her family yet and prayed she'd have time alone with Micah before they appeared.

They strolled toward the shade of a large, towering oak and paused close to its trunk, shadowed by the branches. Micah gestured to a bench. "Would you care to sit for a minute until the dancing starts?" He gave her a devilish grin that sent tingles through her. "I'm not the best dancer in the county, but I'd sure like to give it a try,

Katherine." His voice dropped low as he spoke her name. "I haven't been able to think of much else these past couple hours."

Katherine's breath caught in her throat. "I'm afraid I've had the same difficulty. I'd be honored to share a dance—or two." She took a seat and waited for him to settle beside her. "Now tell me, are things all right between you and Zachary?"

The light dimmed from his face. "As good as can be, I expect. We talked after he bolted from the room, as I'm sure you did with Lucy."

She nodded but didn't reply. She'd been longing to know how Zachary had responded ever since that night.

Micah leaned closer, and his shoulder touched hers. "He listened, but I don't think he liked hearing that I care for you, even if we remain friends." He frowned. "I tried to get him to open up about his feelings for Beth, but he was mute as a rock."

She gently probed. "You object that he might be interested in her?"

He hunched a shoulder. "She's five years older than he is."

Katherine touched his arm. "You're right, Micah, although he's nearly fifteen. Boys tend to develop an interest in women by that age, you know."

His face relaxed. "He seems smitten with her."

"Yes, Lucy mentioned that. But when she talks about Zachary she lights up, somehow. I'm afraid my little girl doesn't know her own heart. Sometimes she appears to root for Beth; at other times there's a bit of jealousy peeking out."

She furrowed her brows. Any serious relationship between herself and Micah could make it difficult for Lucy and Zachary. They couldn't allow that to happen, at least not until they were certain the children weren't interested in a relationship with one another. It had been hard enough for her to avoid a physical relationship with Daniel once she recognized she loved him. If they'd lived in the same house, it might have been nigh unto impossible.

Her heart sank at the thought. Lucy was only thirteen and needed to wait at least two more years before she was old enough to court. Katherine must stick with that decision, no matter the personal cost to herself.

She gazed up at Micah. "Our children's futures come first, before our own. And even beyond that, there's Mama."

He raised his brows a fraction. "What about her?"

How could she tell him the truth? The last thing she wanted was to hurt him, but she couldn't allow him to believe she didn't care or that the children's feelings were all that held her back. The Bible taught that truth set a person free. She surely hoped it would this time. She drew in a short breath. "She doesn't like you."

He chuckled, his eyes twinkling. "And you think you're revealing something I didn't already know?"

Katherine touched Micah's hand, and his fingers wrapped themselves around hers. "She's here to stay, Micah. Mama will live with me until God takes her home. I can't imagine trying to have any kind of future together unless she changes her way of thinking. It would be too difficult living with that level of animosity. It's hard enough now."

"I am not giving up and walking away. Your mother may be here to stay, but *I* am not going anywhere either, Katherine. Until then I'll choose to trust God is in control." The words were spoken quietly, with a deep reverence and conviction.

"I agree, although I will admit it's going to take a mighty big miracle where Mama is concerned. I just wish ..." Tears rushed to the surface.

He brushed a drooping curl from her face, tucking it tenderly behind her ear. "What is it? Please tell me?"

"I'm not sure ... It seems disrespectful somehow—"

"The way your mother treats you." The words were a statement, not a question, and said with such certainty they caused Katherine to start.

"I'm ashamed it's so obvious."

"I hate seeing the hurt she causes." A dark cloud swept over his features. "I want to ask how she could treat her own flesh and blood that way, but I doubt she would listen. It would probably make matters worse."

Katherine nodded. "Yes, more than likely. She has always treated me this way, but I still haven't figured out why she seems to have taken a dislike to you."

"I think she sees me as a drain on you—someone who can't pay his way and with a son to provide for. A man she assumes will never amount to anything." His profile looked set in stone. "But I'm determined to not let that stop me. I shall treat her with kindness, regardless of her actions. Our children won't be young forever, and I want your mother on our side when the time comes."

Katherine could swim in the warmth of his eyes and drown in the passion coloring his voice, never coming up for air. "Thank you for that. I've never figured her out, and I have wondered if I've been unfair at times. Yes, she is prickly and oftentimes unkind, but recently I've gotten a glimpse of a lonely woman with very few friends. I want to help her, but I have no idea how. She has never allowed me to get close, and that hurts as well. Mrs. Roberts has been working hard to befriend her, but Mama seems afraid to allow a relationship to develop." She wasn't sure if she was conveying the strength of her mother's fear.

Micah's jawline was firm, determined. "I'm sorry, Katherine, but I don't agree. She is a smart woman and should be able to see what she's doing when her tongue runs amok."

"Mama has her own set of rules. One is that she must be in control—and if I hesitate or don't always agree, she assumes it means I don't love her or that I'm angry. What she doesn't understand is that I have my own thoughts, my own desires, my own needs. It does not mean she's wrong or that I'm criticizing her, but we don't always have to agree." She heaved a sigh. "I so wish she could see that, but I doubt it will happen."

She shook her head in frustration, then touched his arm. "You said you are choosing to trust God. Does that mean you're no longer angry at Him?" Hope surged through her, and she didn't even care that someone might notice that he was holding her hand.

"Not as much. It's still hard for me to understand why Emma died, but I think He is starting to crumble the walls I've built. I have blamed God for everything that's happened over the past couple of years, growing bitter and closing myself off from good, caring people who tried to show me His love."

He waved his free hand toward the new building a short distance away. "God sent Pastor Seth to talk to me so many times, but it took the labor and sweat of the men of this community to show me that He hadn't forgotten me. It was love in action that broke me. I never expected anything like this. I have a ways to go in trusting Him completely, but I've made a giant stride in that direction."

She squeezed his fingers. "I am so grateful. What an amazing gift. He has given me second, and even third, chances before, as well."

Micah rubbed his thumb across the top of her hand, sending shivers up her arm. "You never know. If God can soften my heart, He's big enough to change your mother, too."

Katherine laughed. "I know, but when she's on one of her rampages, it's hard to remember that. I shall try, though. Truly I will. And I'll start praying for her more. I think I stopped doing that after she moved in with us. I didn't realize, until now, how long it's been since I truly asked the Lord to intervene in her life—in our lives."

A gentle silence settled around them, blanketing Katherine in peace. No matter what might come in the future, even if Micah could never share her life as more than a friend, she knew she'd be all right. Nothing could happen that would rattle her faith. Nothing and no one.

Chapter Thirty-One

Lucy wanted to shake some sense into Ma and Grandma, no matter how much she loved them. She walked with Zachary along the path leading to the Powder River, swinging her pole and scuffing her toe against the clods of dirt kicked up by a passing horse. She didn't feel like talking today, but being with Zachary was better than being stuck in the house. Grandma went around biting off anyone's head if they looked at her crossways, and Ma was too blamed nice to Grandma. Lucy didn't understand. Sure, respecting your elders made sense, but how far did you have to take that when your elders treated you with disrespect most of the time?

She hadn't been thrilled when she'd seen Ma dancing with Mr. Jacobs three nights ago, but it didn't bother her as much as she'd expected. It wasn't like he was a monster or anything. She grinned and kicked at another dirt clod. If she were honest, she'd have to admit he was handsome and kind, and he treated Ma nice. These past few days Ma had been happier than Lucy had seen her in a long time, and that was something, considering how much unhappiness Grandma caused.

Lucy scowled. She wished Grandma would go back to her old house and quit living with them. If she did, maybe life would return to normal. Ma would be happy again without Mr. Jacobs, and … Lucy stopped and peeked at Zachary trudging beside her. If Ma married Mr. Jacobs, that would make Zachary her brother. Would it matter, since he already lived at their house, and they were best friends? She shrugged. Probably not. But if that did happen, he'd better not think he could tell her what to do just because he was older.

Zachary cleared his throat and shot her a sideways look. "What you thinkin' about? You're awful quiet."

"Nothing much." Lucy heaved a sigh. "Would you bait my hook? Somehow I don't feel like killing a worm, even if it is for a good cause."

"Sure." He reached for her pole and sank down on the grassy bank. "Want to tell me what's bothering you? Is it my pa and your ma? I saw them dancing together at the social." He exhaled a sigh of his own. "Since I wasn't doin' too much dancing of my own."

"I'm sorry, Zachary. I couldn't believe Beth didn't come. Mrs. Roberts was fit to be tied when she decided to stay in her room. I can't imagine what's wrong with her. She didn't appear to be sick."

"I think she's tired of her aunt trying to push her to marry."

Lucy glanced at him, surprised at the depth of understanding in his answer. She'd always thought of Zachary as a boy close to her own age, but now he sounded more like a man. "You might be right. I know I wouldn't like it if Ma did that to me." She harrumphed. "Not that she's apt to. She's so worried about you wanting to court me, it's ridiculous." Lucy clapped her hand over her mouth.

Zachary turned a shocked expression toward her. "Your ma thinks I want to court you? Is that why she got so riled when she found you in my room?" He gave a shout of laughter. "That's funny."

Lucy stood over him, hands on her hips, and glared. "Thanks a lot, Zachary. I may not be the prettiest girl in town, but I don't think you need to laugh at the idea. Besides, it's not like I *want* you to court me." She dropped her arms to her side and plopped onto the grass. "I don't know *what* I want anymore. Except for Ma and Grandma to get along and things to go back the way they used to be."

He nodded. "Yeah, I understand. And hey, I'm sorry. I didn't mean anything bad by that. I never thought of you that way. You're my best friend, and I don't want that to change."

"I know. You're my best friend too." She leaned back on her hands and tipped her chin up, staring at the lazy clouds passing overhead. "I'm sorry you didn't get to dance with Beth."

He peered through narrowed eyes at the hook, then held it up with a flourish. "There you go. All ready. It's no big deal about Beth. She's too old for me anyway."

Satisfaction swelled in Lucy's chest, quickly followed by shame. She shouldn't rejoice over Zachary's disappointment—but she hadn't realized before how worried she'd been that she might lose his friendship if he continued to pine after Beth. "Yeah, I heard Mrs. Roberts tell Ma she's twenty. Why, she's practically an old maid. I can understand her aunt being worried about getting her married."

Zachary's head whipped up. "Twenty?" The word came out on a croak. "I thought she was seventeen, maybe. Whew."

Lucy choked back a laugh. No way would she let Zachary see her amusement; he'd be too embarrassed. "You still have me for a friend if you want."

"You told me you liked some boy at school."

She tossed her head, sending her blond braids flying. "Not anymore. Bella Mae caught his eye, and I don't want anything to do with him. Why, anyone who'd like that stuck-up girl doesn't deserve my attention."

"Is that what's been bothering you?"

"Naw. I didn't care about him that much anyway. I guess I'm mad at my ma and grandma. I'm so sick of the way Grandma treats Ma, and tired of Ma never standing up for herself the way she should. I'm telling you, Zachary, one of these days I'm going to make them sorry for making everyone around them miserable."

He pushed up on his elbow and stuck a blade of grass between his teeth, all thought of fishing apparently gone. "Like what? Need any help?"

Her mind scrambled, surprised at his offer. How much should she tell him of her plan? She didn't have it fully formed yet, and the last thing she wanted was someone trying to talk her out of it. Better keep it quiet for now. "I'm not sure yet, but I'll let you know when I do."

"Okay. So we goin' fishin' or what? It's kind of a hot, lazy day. Maybe we should wade in the shallow part of the river instead and get cooled off."

"Lucy! Zachary!" A distant voice drifted to them, and Lucy turned her head. Amanda stood on the edge of the water a hundred yards away, her skirt hiked up to her knees. "Look at me. I'm big enough to go up to my knees in the water all by myself."

Lucy sprang to her feet on the grassy slope as fear clenched her stomach. What was her sister doing here? She'd left her home baking cookies with Ma. Calm eddies in front of her sister were deceiving. Only a short distance out the bottom dropped into deeper, swifter water, too treacherous for a young child to handle. "No, Mandy. Wait for me. The water is too swift." Her little sister took a step forward. "Wait!" The word came out as a wail.

Mandy advanced another step as Lucy raced along the bank toward her, praying the little girl would listen and turn back. Mandy wasn't a good swimmer, and her heavy dress would pull her under if the current caught her. Lucy heard Zachary's footsteps pounding behind her and increased her pace, feeling his urgency. "Mandy. Don't go any farther. Stop!"

The words seemed lost on the child as she moved deeper into the river. She turned with a grin and waved. Then she seemed to totter, slowly rocking one way and then the other, the joy of moments before swamped by a horrified look. "Lucy! Help me!" With a final desperate cry she waved both arms trying to regain her balance, then fell into the river, disappearing beneath the churning water.

Chapter Thirty-Two

Zachary raced past Lucy and yelled over his shoulder, "Run home for my pa and your ma. Hurry, Lucy! And bring blankets."

Lucy hesitated only a second. Her own swimming skills weren't strong, but Zachary was like a fish in the water. He had absolutely no fear. If anyone could save Mandy, it was Zac. "You've got to save her."

He threw her a look, then sprinted toward the calm water a hundred feet down the river.

The last thing Lucy saw was Zachary kicking off his shoes and diving into the water.

She hiked her skirt to her knees and ran, thankful it wasn't far to the house. A sob ripped from her throat. She hadn't expected her little sister to follow them here. Ma would never have let her come alone. She must have slipped away when no one was looking.

Lucy picked up her pace, her feet flying over the uneven ground. Maybe she shouldn't have left—what if Zachary needed help and didn't reach her in time? *Oh, please, God. Help Zachary save Mandy. I'll never forgive myself if something happens.*

Seconds later she burst through the front door of her home and bolted down the hall to the kitchen. "Ma, Mr. Jacobs, come quick!

Mandy's ... fallen into ... the river." Her breath came out in pants, and she hoped they'd understand the disjointed words.

Ma came to the doorway, wiping her hands on her apron. "What's all the yelling about, Lucy? Your grandmother is trying to sleep."

She skidded to a halt. "Didn't you hear me?" Frustration pulsed in her chest. She didn't care if she woke her grandmother or anyone else. "Mandy followed us to the river and fell in. Zachary jumped in to save her. Come quick and bring blankets!"

Ma dropped the pan of cookies onto the floor, her face turning white. "She was here a minute ago." She hurried to the parlor. "Mandy, where are you? Mandy?"

"She slipped away when you weren't looking. Hurry!" Lucy whirled toward her mother. "Is Mr. Jacobs home? We need his help!"

Katherine rushed out, carrying two blankets and jerked open the front door. "He's gone to town. Can Zachary reach her in time?"

Lucy bit her lip so hard she almost cried out, wishing she could lie to make her ma feel better. She needed to trust that God would take care of her baby sister. "Zachary's a good swimmer."

Katherine grabbed her hand. "Hurry!"

Lucy pushed down the hard lump in her throat as she flew along beside her mother, trying not to trip over the skirt she'd bunched high above her ankles. "I prayed, Ma. I'm ... so sorry ... I didn't take better care ... of her."

"Not your fault. You did right. I should ... have watched her." Katherine gulped back a sob. "Too busy ... with my baking." She sucked in a harsh breath. "No matter."

"What?" Lucy's mind churned with possibilities. Did Ma think Mandy would be dead when they arrived? A shudder shook her, and she stuffed back more sobs. She must concentrate on where she was planting her feet.

"Nothing … important." Katherine panted out the words, then reached out and grabbed Lucy's hand. "Faster! I see the river."

Katherine wanted to rage and scream, but she didn't want to scare Lucy. Why would God let this happen? She'd already lost her husband.… Wasn't that enough? Lucy assumed Zachary was a strong enough swimmer to rescue Amanda, but what if he failed? What if her little girl died? She couldn't endure the thought. Wouldn't endure it. *You have got to do something, God. You cannot let this happen. Not again. Please not again.*

A shout went up from someone far ahead, and waves of relief washed over Katherine. Micah Jacobs was waving his arms above his head. "Over here, Katherine. Bring the blankets."

She dropped Lucy's hand and pushed forward with all her might. It had to be good news if Micah was here. If Zachary had been unable to save Mandy, Micah would be in the river as well.

Katherine slid to a halt on the grass and looked around wildly. "Where is she?" The words spilled from her mouth as she grabbed his arm. "Where's Mandy?"

"Hang on, Katherine. She's all right. Zachary flagged me down. He's with her in the wagon, but I think we should take her to see Doc." He slipped his hand around her shoulders and gently pulled her close. "She's awake, but she swallowed some water and got sick to her stomach. Come on." He nodded toward a towering oak. "Zac told me you were coming. I didn't want to start out for Doc's until you arrived."

Katherine sagged against him, thankful for his strong embrace. Then she yanked away and dashed forward, Lucy right on her heels. She could hear her older daughter's sobs and slowed her pace to embrace her. "Shh, it's all right, honey. Mr. Jacobs said Zachary got to her in time."

Lucy hugged her in return but kept pace with her brisk walk. "Thank you, God."

"Yes, indeed." Katherine whispered the words, ashamed at her own earlier lack of faith. "I'm so glad you prayed on your way home, Lucy-girl. My fear got the better of me, and all I did was rage at God, thinking I might lose Mandy."

Zachary sat in the back of the wagon with the little girl on his lap, rubbing her arms. Micah kept pace behind Katherine and Lucy, and Katherine wondered if he'd heard her admission. It didn't matter if he had—she knew he'd understand after his own spiritual battles. All she could do was give thanks that this had ended well.

Micah slapped the reins against the horse's rump and clucked, eager to return home after their visit to the doctor. Funny, he'd come to think of the boardinghouse as home in so short a time. He glanced at the pretty blond sitting beside him cradling her sleeping girl on her lap, and his heart swelled with joy. Katherine was much of the reason for this new emotion. After the narrow miss with Mandy, he'd come to realize how entangled his heart had become with her two girls, as well. He didn't know what they would do about a future relationship, but for now it didn't matter. The important thing was that Amanda was safe, and they were on their way home.

"She's sleeping sound." He spoke the words in a low voice so as not to wake the child.

"Yes. Doc said she'd probably sleep through the night due to the medicine he gave her. I still think we should have had him look at Zachary. We don't want him to catch a chill and sicken after being in that cold water."

"He's fine. Once he dried out and got warm at the doctor's office, he perked right up."

"I can never thank him enough for saving my girl, Micah. Never." A shudder passed over Katherine's slender form. She cast a look over her shoulder at the two older children riding in the back of the wagon. Zachary had a blanket wrapped around his shoulders while Lucy sat beside him, holding his hand. "She hasn't left his side once since she knew her sister would be all right."

"Yeah, I noticed. They care a lot about one another."

"Yes." Katherine let the single word fall and didn't say more.

Micah's heart lurched, and the hope that had been rising withered and dried like a tender shoot in the hot sun.

Micah gently took the sleeping child from Katherine's arms. He allowed his fingers to brush Katherine's cheek before he tucked Mandy against his shoulder and turned toward the house. All was right with his world, and he thanked God yet again for His provision and care. They'd had more than enough excitement for one day, and what they all needed tonight was peace and quiet.

He'd probably need to help Katherine with supper preparations, but undoubtedly Lucy and Mrs. Cooper would pitch in as well. Between them, they should whip things together in short order, then settle into the parlor and relax before bed.

Katherine stepped down from the seat and turned to the older children climbing out of the back. "Lucy and Zachary, would you take the mare to the barn, unhitch her, and give her some hay and grain?"

"Sure, Ma." Lucy grinned at Zachary. "But I'll make Zachary sit and watch. I think he's done enough for today."

"Hey, I'm no sissy girl." Zachary growled the words and Lucy broke into a laugh, poking him with her elbow. They led the mare toward the barn as Micah and Katherine stepped up onto the porch.

He waited for Katherine to swing open the door, then walked up the staircase with his precious burden.

Katherine passed the girls' room and stopped in front of her own. "I want to keep her with me tonight." She entered first and beckoned for him. "I'll sleep better if she's close."

Micah tried not to blush as he kept his eyes averted from Katherine's bed. With her mind on her little girl's condition, it probably hadn't occurred to her that she'd invited him into her room. As Katherine drew down the covers, he walked forward and gently placed Mandy against the pillow. Quickly he stepped back and retreated to the doorway, willing her to hurry. This evoked too many emotions he didn't care to deal with. But at present, Mandy's welfare was all that mattered. He needed to get a grip on his thoughts.

Katherine leaned over and placed a kiss on Mandy's forehead, then joined him across the room, joy lighting her face. "I guess we'd better head down. I'm sure Mama and the others are wondering what happened."

He swallowed the lump in his throat. "Yeah." The word came out with a rasp. "The children and I can set the table or peel spuds or whatever you need. Say the word."

"Thank you. I may take you up on that offer." She walked beside him toward the staircase.

They'd gotten halfway down the steps, Katherine behind him, when a sharp sound alerted him.

Mrs. Cooper stood at the bottom of the stairs, appearing so angry fire seemed to emanate from her mouth. "And what do the two of you think you were doing in Katherine's bedroom? I get up from a nap, find the house filled with smoke, the children missing, a batch of black cookies in the oven, no supper on, and you come traipsing down pretty as you please like nothing is wrong."

She aimed a glare that should have dropped him in his tracks. "You ought to be ashamed of yourself, Mr. Jacobs, enticing my daughter to leave the straight and narrow. I hope you will have the decency to pack your bags and get out of this house before nightfall."

Shock at her mother's harsh words coursed through Katherine's body so hard her feet were unable to move. She couldn't deal with Mama's nonsense tonight. She had endured a sufficient amount of pain already. Thoughts and memories swirled, bouncing from one spot to the next in her head like a jackrabbit hopping through the brush, searching for a hole to hide in.

She wanted to scream and fly down the stairs. *Enough is enough, God!* There was no way she could take more, and it wasn't fair to ask it. Her daughter had nearly died today, and now the man she cared for was being attacked by her mother. Her mother, who didn't appear to believe in her daughter's sense of decency and right. Never in her life had Katherine so badly wanted to slap Mama and shake some sense into her. But all she could do was stand like a statue carved into the stairwell.

Chapter Thirty-Three

Frances gripped the banister post at the bottom of the stairs so hard she feared she'd break her hand. Right now she'd like to break that man's face—better yet, wipe the shocked, innocent look off it and drive him out of the house with a horsewhip. That's what her papa would have done if he had caught *her* in a compromising situation, and he'd not have thought twice about it either. She couldn't believe the hurt on Katherine's face. Frances had known something like this would happen if that man stayed here. She had done her best to thwart it, but evidently too little, too late.

"Grandma, what are you doing?" Lucy's high-pitched voice sent daggers through Frances's thoughts, bringing her back to the present. Her granddaughter stalked across the foyer with that Zachary boy on her heels. That one needed to leave as well.

"I am talking to your mother and"—she waved a dismissive hand at Micah Jacobs—"this person. It is not your concern. Find your little sister and go to your room. This is not a discussion that involves you children."

Rustling emanated from the parlor, and Wilma Roberts swept into the room. "Is there a problem, ladies? And gentlemen." She gazed from one to the other, then back at Frances. "I sent Beth to her room a couple minutes ago to freshen up for supper, but the house smelled like smoke, and it appeared no one was home."

"Quite so." Frances drew herself up straighter, appreciative of the fact she had an ally in Wilma Roberts. It was about time the woman proved herself useful.

Truth be told, she'd gone beyond what Frances expected in her attempt at friendship recently, and *this* gesture cemented it. Yes, indeed, when the household returned to normal, she would make it clear to Wilma how much she appreciated her efforts. "If you must know, my daughter has been ..." She paused, not sure how to proceed.

"Enough, Mrs. Cooper!" Micah Jacobs's words came out in a hard undertone, but they might as well have been a shout, there was so much force behind them. "I will not allow you to criticize Katherine. She has done nothing wrong. I insist you apologize."

"Humph." Frances glared up at the man, determined not to be the first to remove her gaze. "If Katherine is innocent, then I will lay the blame squarely where it belongs. At your feet."

He stormed down the stairs, causing her to blink twice and back up a step. "I have done nothing wrong either." His stern voice ground out the words. "If you had *asked* what happened rather than rushing to the most horrible conclusion possible, you would have your answer. Instead, you chose to believe the worst of your daughter, as I've seen you do time and again."

Lucy made an indecipherable noise beside her. "Yes, Grandma. Ma didn't do anything wrong, even if she won't say anything. And I can't get Mandy and take her to my room, because she's already asleep on Ma's bed. We just got back from the doctor's office."

Frances's chest constricted, and a lump lodged in her throat. "Doctor's office? Why? What?"

"Exactly the questions you should have started with, Mrs. Cooper." Mr. Jacobs scowled, then worked to school his expression. "I am not trying to be disrespectful, but you are completely out of line. Katherine is a fine, wonderful woman who doesn't deserve your vile accusations. She thought she'd lost Mandy today. Amanda followed Lucy and Zachary to the river and fell in."

He waved at his silent son standing beside Lucy. "My boy dove in and pulled her out before she drowned. I came along as he waded out of the river carrying her. We got her to cough up the water she'd swallowed so she could breathe again. Lucy had run for help, and when she and Katherine arrived, I drove them to the doctor." He drew in a deep breath and let it out slowly, as though trying to compose himself. "She'll be fine, but we just got home and were coming from putting her to bed—*not* from visiting Katherine's bedroom, as you assumed."

Frances placed a hand over her heart and moaned. The room swam, and everything started to grow dark. The last thing she heard before she hit the floor was Katherine's shocked voice. "Mama! Grab her, somebody!"

Katherine rushed forward on Micah's heels. He scooped the tiny woman into his arms. "Where should I take her? To her room or the parlor?"

"Her room. She'll be mortified if she wakes in the parlor and finds everyone watching."

Lucy stomped her foot. "Ma! I can't believe you. I heard every word Grandma said about you and Mr. Jacobs as I came through the door. You didn't try to stop her. Now you want to make sure she's not upset when she wakes up? At least Mr. Jacobs stood up to her, and it's about time. Besides, I'll bet she pretended to faint so she'd get all the attention." She spun on her heel and dashed up the stairs and down the hall, slamming the door of her room hard enough they felt the vibration all the way downstairs.

Katherine wanted to follow, but she knew it wouldn't do any good. Her daughter needed time to cool down and Mama required care whether Lucy understood it or not. She silently led the way to Mama's room and opened the door, then turned to Mrs. Roberts. "Would you mind helping me?"

"Not at all, dear. That's why I came." The older woman drew down the quilt. "Such a shame she doesn't see things more clearly. Always saying something she will live to regret. Never seeing the damage her words do to the ones she loves most. So sad." She peered with compassion at Frances.

Micah placed Mama on the bed and stepped back. "I'll go check on Zachary, and let Mr. Tucker and Miss Roberts know supper will be late."

Katherine nodded, her gaze still on her mother. "Thank you. But Mr. Tucker told me he wouldn't be here this evening." She turned to Mrs. Roberts. "Do you need to acquaint Beth with what's happening?"

"She's all right. The girl has a sensible head on her shoulders, as well as a fine set of ears. I'm certain she's already familiar with the circumstances and will make herself useful when needed." She raised a hand toward Micah. "Mr. Jacobs, if you happen to see her, ask her to heat the pot of stew and slice a loaf of bread left over from dinner. I think that will do fine for our supper, don't you, Mrs. Galloway?"

Katherine blinked, coming back to the business at hand. "Yes. Thank you." She gave Micah a tired smile as he exited the room, then focused on her mother, who stirred. "Mama, are you all right? What can I get you?"

Mama regarded her with a dazed expression. "Head hurts a little. Must have bumped it when I fell." She lifted a hand and touched a spot above her left ear.

Katherine's heart jerked. "Maybe we should call the doctor."

"No! No doctor." Mama clutched her sleeve. "I shall be fine after I rest. Not sure what got into me. I woke up. So worried when I smelled smoke … thought the house was on fire. Couldn't find anyone. Scared me. Alone. So alone." Her lids drifted shut.

"Mama?" Katherine touched her mother's forehead and looked at Mrs. Roberts. "What do you think? Should I call the doctor?"

"I'm not sure. She could need to sleep, is all. I don't know much about head injuries, but it makes sense she'd want to rest."

"Let's keep an eye on her for the evening and decide the next time she wakes." Katherine tugged off her mother's shoes. "Should we try to undress her, or wait?"

Mrs. Roberts shook her head. "Let's wait. She may not thank us for doing it now."

Katherine peered at her mother lying so still on the bed. Her chest rose and fell rhythmically, and a snore came from between her parted lips. She drew a quilt up to her mother's chin, then rested a hand on her forehead.

Mrs. Roberts waited at the foot of the bed. "I will stay with her while you take care of your family. And I must say, Mrs. Galloway, I admire the way you have dealt with this episode."

Katherine clamped down on her emotions, even though she deeply appreciated the kindness that prompted the words. "You heard what my mother said?"

"I'm afraid so, as did anyone who was in the house at the time. I am thankful Mr. Tucker wasn't present, for your sake." She gestured toward the still form. "And for hers. I'm afraid she stepped over a line tonight and embarrassed herself greatly. I feel sorry for her."

"Sorry? For my mother? That's hard to believe after the way she's treated you." Katherine didn't know whether to laugh or cry. She'd experienced this emotional conflict before when it came to Mama.

Part of her was so angry she was shaking inside, while the other part felt nothing but a deep, abiding pity for her parent. Love didn't enter into her emotions, even though she wished it would. She wanted to love Mama—and more than that, she wanted to feel loved.

But it was getting harder and harder to believe that was possible.

Frances lay with her eyes closed, listening for all she was worth. She must have drifted off for a second or two, but the words *"stepped over a line"* had jerked her from slumber. She tried to keep her face expressionless but almost sat upright when Katherine replied. She'd felt a slight sense of triumph that Wilma Roberts seemed to care, even though it irked her that the woman thought she'd embarrassed herself.

But Katherine. Her own daughter. There was no compassion or love in her voice. Had she truly earned that degree of contempt? Well, maybe she didn't hear contempt in the soft words, but there was surely no respect. The Bible commanded children to respect their parents. Or was that honor? It didn't matter. Katherine didn't show signs of either.

"Yes, I feel very sorry for her." Wilma's voice droned on, emphasizing those horrid words yet again. "Your mother doesn't realize how other people view her. If she did, I don't believe she would act the way she does."

Katherine snorted, something between a laugh and a choking sound. Frances couldn't be completely sure, but it sounded more like a laugh. "Then you don't know Mama very well. She has never cared what anyone thinks about her. She says what she wants, and it wouldn't matter if you wore a sign saying 'You are hurting me' around your neck. She would keep on doing it. People's opinions do not matter to Mama."

Frances almost recoiled at her daughter's cold tone. Did Katherine really believe she didn't care? She had winced at Wilma's words, hating the idea that people might talk behind her back or view her in any way but a positive light. All right, she would admit that some people's opinions mattered very little, but that certainly did not include everyone. Some folks were entirely too sensitive and got their feelings hurt too easily. It was impossible to make everyone happy. She must remember those points and make sure to bring them up to Mrs. Roberts the next time they had occasion to speak. That was, *if* she deigned to speak to the woman again.

"I am not positive that's entirely true, my dear. She wants you to believe that, and perhaps it could be true for the most part, but deep down each of us wants to trust we are loved, respected, and yes, even liked, by the people around us. I don't think your mother is an exception."

Frances's ears pricked at Wilma's astute commentary. She had put her finger on it this time. Respect. Of course that was exactly what Frances wanted and expected. It was her right. At her age, she should be respected and honored. No, she did not want everyone to love her or even to like her; there were too many people she couldn't be bothered to like in return. But respect and honor were entirely different matters.

"Well, she's not earned much respect from me over the years, I am sorry to say." Katherine heaved a deep sigh as though it pained her to speak the words. "I've tried to love her, truly I have. More times than I can count. But she makes it so difficult. She's full of sharp edges and flings out her opinion without a thought of what it might do. She has wounded me so many times I've felt like a battle-torn soldier who crawled back to his hole to die."

"I'm sorry, dear, but I can't say I am terribly surprised. Something in her life has turned Frances into a bitter, vindictive woman. It's too bad she can't take that pain and give it to her heavenly Father. That is the only way she will attain true peace or gain the respect she is so hungry for."

Frances lay motionless, barely able to breathe. They detested her. Both of them detested her. They thought she was an evil person with no feelings or regard for others. Her own daughter said she had wounded her to the point of wanting to crawl off and die. When had she ever said anything that could hurt that deeply?

Her mind flew backward in time to scant minutes ago when she had gazed up the stairs into those eyes so like her own and as much as called her daughter a harlot. She hadn't given her a chance—hadn't asked what had happened, just like Mr. Jacobs had stated. She jumped to the worst possible conclusion and been none too shy about speaking her thoughts.

She had always believed the truth needed to be spoken, and let the chips fall where they may. A tremor passed through her as she realized this attitude was exactly what the two women were discussing. They always said that a listener never heard good of herself, and she saw that clearly now.

Micah Jacobs alleged that Mandy had almost drowned and his son had saved her, and she'd blasted him for being in Katherine's room. Why, she'd even gone so far as to command him to pack up and leave. She would not have allowed him to carry her to her room if she had not still been weak and shaky from her fall. As it was, she had been embarrassed that he swooped in and plucked her off the floor.

She had seen the intense pain that flashed across her daughter's face at her words, at least before Katherine carefully cloaked it and dropped her gaze. And Lucy's angry words still rang in her ears. Not only had she hurt and disappointed her daughter, she somehow managed to do the same to her beloved granddaughter.

Frances wanted to moan and cover her face with the quilt, but that would only let them know she'd heard every word.

If only they would leave her alone so she could think. Grieve. Plan.

No. Planning had gotten her into too many pickles in the past that often ended in disaster. She hated to admit that, even to herself, but her behavior since arriving in Katherine's home was a shining example. She had planned from the beginning to get rid of Micah Jacobs and his son, and look what happened. That boy saved her sweet Mandy's life, and his father stood up to her in defense of the woman he apparently had come to care for deeply. That was worthy of respect, and more.

"If you don't mind, Mrs. Roberts, I shall take you up on that offer to stay with Mama while I go check on Mandy and Lucy."

"Not at all, Mrs. Galloway. I will be here when you get back. Never worry."

Oh, Katherine would not worry, Frances knew that as a certainty, but *she* would. The last thing she needed or wanted was Wilma Roberts staying in her room watching her with those eagle eyes. And her sharp tongue all set to unleash its vitriol on her head.

Frances bristled and bunched up her muscles, waiting until she heard the door close behind Katherine. Then she would give Wilma Roberts the razor edge of her tongue if she so much as tried to put her in her place.

The door clicked and she lay rigid, trying to form a response before Wilma Roberts had another chance to speak. Of course, there would be no reason for her to do so, as she assumed her patient to be unconscious.

Frances sagged against the mattress and replayed everything she had heard. Mrs. Roberts hadn't said a thing about putting her in her place. No, her last words were something about attaining peace by discovering what drove Frances to behave the way she did and turning it over to her Father.

She wasn't sure she could do that, but something about the suggestion held a mighty strong appeal. Maybe she would lie here quietly and study on the idea. Mrs. Roberts might not be so far off the mark this time after all.

Chapter Thirty-Four

Lucy slipped outside, intent on getting as far away from the house and her grandmother as possible and praying no one would see her. All she wanted was to run away and never return. That would fix them all. Grandma would feel bad she'd been so unpleasant to Ma, and Ma would finally understand she needed to stand up for herself.

She reached the end of the walkway and glanced in both directions. Going to the river didn't appeal, not after what happened to Mandy. Town wasn't a good idea either, since people there knew Ma and someone might tell.

"Lucy, wait up!" Zachary's voice almost made her jump into a nearby bush, he'd scared her so badly. She swung around and placed her finger against her lips. "Shh. Not so loud."

He halted. "What's wrong with you?"

She beckoned frantically for him to come forward but didn't reply. The window of the parlor was open, and someone could hear.

Zachary cast a look over his shoulder, then back at her. He pointed a finger at his chest. "Me?"

"Who else, silly?" She hissed the words between clenched teeth. "Don't just stand there. Hurry up."

He pushed his hands in his trouser pockets and sauntered forward.

As soon as he reached her side, she grabbed his wrist and dragged him along behind her. The barn would have to do for now. "Keep quiet till we get inside." At least he was able to obey orders and not squawk like a girl. That was one of the things she appreciated about Zachary.

"What did you grab me for?" Zachary shook his arm free and scowled. "Are you playing some kind of game?"

"It's no game, Zac. I don't want Ma or anyone else to know I'm out here."

"Why not? Did they tell you not to go to the barn?" He peered around suspiciously.

She rolled her eyes and sighed. Boys could be so dense. "No. I'm running away."

"Huh?" He scratched his head. "But it's almost supper time, and I'm hungry. Then it's going to be dark. Why'd you want to do something like that for, anyway?"

Her stomach growled, reminding her of the time, and she clamped her hand over it. "Guess I *am* a little hungry."

"Can't you wait to run away until tomorrow? I figured you'd want to take care of Mandy tonight."

The air went out of her lungs. "How could I forget Mandy?" Lucy almost wailed the words and slapped her hand over her mouth. She dropped her voice to a loud whisper. "I'm mad at Grandma and Ma for fighting all the time. I guess I should say at Grandma for fighting and at Ma for not fighting back."

"Huh?" Zachary plopped down on a pile of loose straw in the corner and stuck a piece between his teeth. "Say that again slower this time. I don't get it."

"Never mind. It sounded pretty stupid the first time."

"Well, maybe not *totally* stupid, but ..." His eyes twinkled, and he dodged to avoid her swinging hand. "Ha. You missed." He leaned back on the straw. "So what good would running away do, other than getting hungry, and cold, and not having a warm bed to sleep in tonight?"

"Mercy me, you ask a lot of questions."

He grinned. "That's what friends do."

She grabbed a handful of straw and shredded it, letting the tiny bits drift over her skirt. "I guess I hoped it would get their attention. Maybe if they both worried about me, they'd quit being mad at each other all the time."

"That kind of makes sense, I guess. So did you leave your ma a note so she'd know why you ran away?" He scratched his head. "Hey, Pa did a first-rate job tonight when he lit into your grandma, don't you think?"

Her shoulders sagged. "I can't believe I didn't think about a note either." Her fingers stilled, and she cocked her head as Zachary's words settled in. "Your pa did a wonderful thing the way he talked to Grandma. In fact, I think he's one of the finest men I've ever met. Except for my pa, of course."

Zachary nodded. "'Course. That's the way it ought to be. Your own pa always comes first."

Lucy smirked. "Even if your father ends up becoming my father? Do you think it would be all right for my pa to still come first in my heart?"

"Huh?" Zachary turned a stunned gaze her way. "My pa be your pa? I don't know what you're talking about."

"Now who's being stupid?" She tossed the straw at his face and ducked when he tossed some back. "I can't believe you haven't noticed."

"You mean that my pa is sweet on your ma? Yeah, I've noticed." He growled the words and hung his head.

"I was upset at first too. But after the way he stood up for Ma tonight, I could tell he really cares about her. Is that so bad, Zac?" Lucy's heart beat faster, and she almost held her breath. She didn't understand why she'd changed her mind concerning Mr. Jacobs, but the look on her mother's face made her realize how much Ma needed someone in her life who would stand up for her, no matter what. It appeared that might be Mr. Jacobs. Now it seemed her best friend in the whole world wasn't happy about it. If he didn't approve, then they couldn't become a family.

"I don't know if it's bad or not. I guess I'm not used to the idea, is all."

"So don't you like my ma?"

"I like her a lot. She's a whole site better of a cook than Pa, that's for certain."

Lucy gave a laugh, then clamped her lips together. "Forgot again." She motioned toward the door. "But I doubt anyone's looking for us after Grandma pretended to faint."

"You think she pretended?" Zachary struggled to sit up in the deep pile of straw. "What makes you say that?"

"I don't know. I could be wrong, since she did hit her head when she fell. But Grandma tends to be a bit ... dramatic at times. When she wants her own way, that is. I figured when your pa lit into her, then she heard about Mandy, she might have realized how wrong she'd been and didn't want to admit it. So fainting was an easy way to get out of it without having to apologize."

"I used to wish I had a grandma, but if that's what they do, I'm kind of glad I don't."

"Oh, they're not all that way." Lucy curled her lip. "Only the selfish ones."

Zachary pondered that for a moment. "So you were talking about your ma and my pa. Maybe it wouldn't be too awful if they got hitched. You think your ma loves him? I know he's been awful lonely since Ma died. I've worried about him lots of times. He'd get all moody and grumpy and wouldn't talk for days. Since we moved here, he's been different. 'Specially since he met your ma."

"Don't you remember when he had his arms around her? I saw the look on her face." Lucy nodded. "Yep. She loves him. For sure."

"So how come they haven't said anything to us? Don't we deserve to know first?"

"I dunno. Maybe they think we'd be upset. We *were* the other night, you know."

"Oh. Yeah. Guess so." Zachary wallowed the straw from one cheek to the other, then spit it to the side and clambered out of the pile. "Then we need to set things to rights."

Lucy stared at him. Had he lost his senses? "Whatever are you talking about?"

He held out his hand. "We've got to tell them to quit draggin' their feet and get married. My pa is lonely, your ma cares about him, my pa stands up for your ma, and she's a good cook. Sounds like the right decision to me." He tucked her hand under his arm and pulled her to her feet. "We'll do it together." He winked. "Remember, that's what friends are for."

Katherine worked to focus on what Lucy and Zachary were saying. "Would you please repeat that?" She carefully set her cup on the saucer, no longer interested in the fragrant mint tea. A swift glance at Micah showed he had a similar reaction—disbelief.

Zachary looked at Lucy, who gave a slight nod. He squared his shoulders and lifted his chin. "We think you two ought to get married. We know you care for each other—that's obvious as anything. I'm tired of eating Pa's cooking, and Lucy likes that Pa stuck up for her ma. It's as simple as that." He snapped his fingers and grinned, resembling a magician who'd pulled a rabbit out of a hat and expected a round of applause.

Lucy edged a bit closer to Zachary's side. "It's not just the cooking or Mr. Jacobs standing up to Grandma—although I'm grateful he did, and it makes me like him a lot." She aimed an admiring gaze at Micah, and Katherine's heart swelled. "Both of you have been so lonely since you were widowed, and we hate seeing you alone when you have each other. Of course, you have Zachary, Mandy, and me, too." She tossed them a saucy smile. "But somehow I don't think that's quite the same."

Micah cleared his throat. "But what about the two of you?"

Zachary scrunched his brows. "What about us?"

Micah didn't reply but sent an imploring look Katherine's way.

She knew exactly where he'd been headed. "We've thought for some time now that you two are sweet on one another, even though Zachary did seem interested in Beth. If that's the case, we're not sure it would be wise for us to, er, court ... or anything." She stumbled over the last words. After all, it wasn't like Micah had ever asked her to marry him. They'd only talked twice about a possible future together. Besides, even with the children's approval, there was still her mother to consider. And Mama had made it more than clear that she wanted nothing to do with Micah.

Lucy burst out laughing, causing Katherine to jump. "How many times do I have to tell you, Ma? We're friends. We aren't interested in courting."

Katherine turned her attention to Zachary. "Is that how you feel too?"

"Yes, ma'am. Sure do. Lucy and I even talked about it earlier. I made her mad 'cause I said there wasn't any way I wanted to court her. I didn't mean it in a bad way. But she's my best friend, and I don't want to lose that. Truly, she's more like my sister, but we get along, if that makes sense."

Katherine nodded slowly and glanced at Micah. "Yes, I think it does. I appreciate you explaining it so clearly."

Lucy's face brightened. "Good. So are you going to marry Mr. Jacobs, Ma?"

Once again she wanted to sink through the floor—or better yet, go crawl into bed for a week. This was all too much.

Micah thumped his son on the back. "We appreciate your concern, but there's another person to consider." He caught Katherine's eye, and her heart started to pound. Was it possible he meant her mother? If so, nothing would ever happen between them.

He continued in a firm tone. "I don't think either of you have eaten yet, and there's a pot of stew on the stove keeping warm. I'm going to walk Mrs. Galloway to her room. She's exhausted and needs to rest. The two of you clean the kitchen when you finish, all right?"

"Golly, Pa. Here we came in to help the two of you, and we get put to work. That's not fair!"

Lucy slugged him in the side with her elbow and hissed, "Shush. Your pa wants to talk to Ma. We'll clean the kitchen."

Katherine smiled. "Thank you, Lucy." She stepped over to Zachary's side. "And, young man, I have yet to thank you properly for what you did today. I imagine you're too old to hug, and it doesn't quite feel right to shake your hand, so I'm not sure how to convey what I feel. But when you saved my Mandy, you did me a service I can never repay."

"It wasn't nothing, ma'am." He dipped his head an instant, then raised it. "But a hug sounds nice. I haven't had one since Ma died."

Joy thrilled through Katherine as the boy gave her a quick squeeze. "Good night, then. And thank you for helping in the kitchen."

She walked from the room with Micah by her side, truly hopeful for the first time. Until she remembered Micah's words. He hoped to court her and thought he needed Mama's consent as well as the children's. Her heart plummeted, and she wanted to groan. Never in a million years would that happen, but from the determined set of Micah's jaw he intended to try.

Chapter Thirty-Five

Micah paced the floor and looked at his pocket watch for the hundredth time, wondering if it was too early to approach Mrs. Cooper in her room. Breakfast was over, and she hadn't appeared, but he'd expected that after her swoon last night. Actually, he was relieved she'd been absent, as he feared he might lose his temper if she spat any more ugly words at Katherine. He loved that woman so much, and he'd never again allow that type of disrespect if he had anything to say about it. He still marveled at the way love had sneaked up on him, then exploded into full bloom.

All this time he'd assumed Emma would hold his love forever. Now he realized she'd always have a special place in his heart, but it was time to move on.

Near panic gripped him for a moment. If Katherine would have him, that is. That thought left him quaking. He'd never boldly spoken of his love to Katherine or asked if she'd consent to become his bride. Should he have asked her first before approaching her mother?

No. He ran a hand over his hair. Mrs. Cooper's acceptance was one of Katherine's biggest concerns. If she didn't give her blessing on their union, he didn't know if Katherine would be willing to accept his proposal. He understood Katherine's misgivings, as he'd been the recipient of the sharp edge of Mrs. Cooper's tongue more than once in the past and living with it full time wouldn't be easy.

Besides, there was a proper order to all things. When he'd wanted to marry Emma, he'd gone to her father and asked for her hand. Katherine's father wasn't alive. The logical—if not preferred— choice was Mrs. Cooper. If only it didn't have to be this way…. But Katherine's mother would probably remain with her daughter the rest of her life. Even if Katherine did consent to marry him, he couldn't ignore her mother or cast her aside and have any hope of peace in the family.

He'd sent word to Mrs. Cooper that he would appreciate a bit of her time, and she hadn't refused. Should he have invited Katherine to join him? Of course not. He wouldn't consider it if her father were living.

He admitted feeling rattled, and he'd best get a grip. He was surely a big enough man to take anything verbal Mrs. Cooper dished out. At least, he hoped so.

Enough stalling. It was time to approach the dragon in her lair. He grimaced. Or the queen in her bedchamber, if kindness were uppermost in his thoughts. If she didn't chase him from her room in disgust that he'd entered her private domain.

He tapped on the door and waited, then tried again. "Mrs. Cooper? It's Micah Jacobs."

"Just a moment, please." The words quavered a bit, not at all like Mrs. Cooper. "All right, I am presentable now."

He stepped inside, expecting to see her propped against her pillows, but instead found her sitting, fully clothed, in the stuffed chair near the window.

She beckoned him forward. "I am sorry I do not have another chair to offer."

Right now he wished he had a hat in his hands so he'd have something to clutch. He felt like such a big oaf, standing in the middle of her room. The words he'd so carefully planned fled. "I'm fine, thanks."

She nodded. "All right." A couple seconds passed. "You wanted to talk to me, Mr. Jacobs?"

"Yes. I did. I do." He licked his dry lips and tried again. "Yes, ma'am. I came to see you about Katherine."

Her face darkened, and he winced but stood his ground. "Please. I don't want to hear anything more about what you think she's done wrong. There's been enough of that already."

"Yes, there certainly has." She lifted her head.

Confusion almost addled his brain. "I beg your pardon?"

"I was remembering my uncharitable comments the last time we spoke. My reaction now was no reflection on my daughter. Forgive me for the way I spoke to you last night, and please proceed."

Now he was completely flummoxed. He'd come in expecting at least a semblance of a battle, if not a full war, and she was asking for forgiveness?

He didn't want to bumble this even more. "I love your daughter. It might come as a shock, seeing as how Katherine and I have only known one another for a short time."

"Not at all. In fact, it would surprise me if you did not. Katherine is a very special woman."

All he could do was stare. He was certain his hearing had dimmed. "Did I hear you say she's special?"

"Yes, young man. I hope you think so as well, or you are not half the man I suppose you to be."

"Of course I do. Quite honestly, I didn't think *you* believed that. All I've seen and heard have convinced me of the opposite."

She nodded slowly, but no rage appeared, merely a tinge of sadness. "I can understand why you would say that. Now, you came in here to tell me something."

Micah straightened. "Yes. Of course." He couldn't think of any other way to phrase the words. "I want to marry Katherine and came to seek your permission, if not your blessing."

"I give them both, with gratitude that you would care to ask." Her lips smiled, but her eyes remained untouched. Only sorrow lingered in their depths.

"I beg your pardon, ma'am?"

"You heard me correctly. Now fetch that daughter of mine. I have something to say to both of you, and I plan on answering your questions as well." She waved her hand at him. "Go along with you, Mr. Jacobs. I am not growing any younger." The sharpness was back, but without its usual bite.

Micah turned and fled, certain that he'd dreamed the whole thing and worried she'd change into her old self by the time he returned. But a small part of him rejoiced in the words she'd spoken. Blessing as well as permission. Now if only Katherine agreed.

Katherine's heart nearly pounded out of her chest, and she thought she'd lose her breakfast before she reached Mama's room. Why did she need to accompany Micah there? Surely Mama had tormented him enough when he'd gone alone. Katherine had about given up on anything ever changing in her life, at least where her mother was concerned. Micah would do well to learn it sooner, rather than later. It saved a lot of heartache not setting up false expectations.

"Relax, Katherine. It's going to be all right." Micah touched her shoulder and nudged her into the room. "Trust God with this."

She almost laughed. The man who'd been angry and stubborn for years was preaching at her to trust God? Fine. She'd make an effort, but so much that pertained to Mama had gone wrong in her life that she was afraid to try.

Mama sat in her chair as though she were royalty, and Katherine choked back a laugh. Yesterday had been nothing but an act, based on the way her mother looked now. Fully clothed and sitting ramrod straight, as was her custom. "I see you're feeling better."

"Yes, a little more rested, although I still tire easily." She beckoned to Katherine and held out her hand. "Before Micah has his say, I need to have mine. You are wondering why I asked you to come when it appears I am perfectly able to walk to the parlor."

"The thought occurred to me." Katherine reluctantly took her mother's hand and tried not to wince. How awful that this gesture was so foreign she didn't know what to expect when it happened. She couldn't remember the last time Mama had hugged her or volunteered a gentle touch.

"Appearances can be deceiving, Daughter. I am fully dressed because Mr. Jacobs sent word this morning that he wanted to speak with me. I have remained this way because I believed I could better say what was needed if I wasn't huddled under my covers like an old woman on her deathbed."

Katherine felt as though she'd been slapped. "Are you saying you believe you're dying?"

Mama motioned her concern away. "Of course not; it was simply a figure of speech. Although I suppose we are all dying a little bit each day. I simply desired to be fully clothed to keep my courage up."

Katherine withdrew her hand from her mother's. "What do you need courage for? You didn't appear to be lacking in that capacity last night."

Her mother winced. "Do not think I am not well aware of the fact that I deserved that. That, and a lot more."

"I beg your pardon?" This was not what Katherine had come expecting to hear. Where was the woman who had raged at them for impropriety, then ordered Micah to pack and leave? It was a rare occurrence for Mama to take responsibility for *any* wrongdoing.

"You heard me, Katherine. I am still very new to this apology business, so please do not expect me to repeat myself when I admit I have been mistaken."

Katherine bit back a smile. The old Mama was back. "Fine. But if you'd care to explain, I'd appreciate trying to understand."

"Why don't you sit on the bed?" She turned and eyed Micah. "Mr. Jacobs, normally I would ask you to leave the room, but considering the circumstances and why you are here, I will allow you to stay. Please step over by the door and do not make any comments while we talk. Is that acceptable?"

"Of course." He moved to where she indicated and leaned against the wall.

Prickles of uncertainty ran up Katherine's spine. What was Mama up to? Only a small touch of her usual tartness had made itself known. There must be some hidden scheme underlying the supposed courtesy. How sad that her relationship with her mother was so colored by mistrust, but she couldn't change it at this stage of her life. She sank onto the edge of the mattress and rested her hands in her lap, trying to relax but ready for whatever might come.

Mama opened her mouth, closed it, then opened it again, but no sound came out. She shut her eyes for a moment, then tried again. "I owe you an apology. I have already extended one to Mr. Jacobs, but I should have done so to you first. You are my daughter. I am proud of you, and I love you more than anyone else in the world." She rolled her shoulders with a slight smile. "Gracious, that was not as painful as I expected."

Every bit of the tenderness Katherine had started to feel disappeared in an instant. As she had assumed, this was all an act. "So it's painful to tell me you love me, is that what I'm hearing? I must say, I'm not surprised. You've avoided doing so most of my life. I can't imagine what prompted you to start now." She pushed to her feet. "We're done here."

Micah stepped forward, but Mama held out her hand. "Wait. Please. You did not understand." Tears moistened her eyes. "I meant that I am not used to apologizing. I expected it to be ghastly, but it was actually quite cleansing. I am so sorry you thought I meant it was painful saying I love you. Not at all. Please forgive me." She choked out a laugh through her tears. "Now I have done it again, and it *is* getting a little easier. Soon I will be asking forgiveness of Mrs. Roberts, if I am not careful."

Katherine wondered what to believe. The tears appeared real, but she'd been fooled before. What she'd give to have Lucy's clear perception where Mama was concerned. "Why are you saying all this? Something doesn't feel right." She wasn't sure how to express her confusion but hadn't meant to be quite so blunt. "I'm sorry. I don't mean to criticize or accuse you of a falsehood. I simply don't understand."

"You have no need to apologize. In fact, according to Lucy, you have done far too much of that since I arrived."

Katherine grimaced, certain she knew what was coming. Rarely did Mama condemn anything the girls said or did, so Lucy's comment would likely be placed at Katherine's doorstep. "Lucy shouldn't have said that."

"Lucy should have said it, and I am glad she did. It was the first thing that started me thinking. And what you and Mrs. Roberts said in my bedroom last night hit me hard as well."

Katherine blinked. Mama had heard what they'd said? But she'd been asleep. They'd heard her snores. Shame washed through Katherine that she'd been gossiping about her mother, much less that she'd been overheard.

Micah shifted his weight behind her and his warm hand settled on her shoulder. Relief that he'd ignored Mama's order to stay by the door flooded her. He gave a quick squeeze. "Why don't you let your mother explain, Katherine?"

She relaxed against him as he moved closer behind her. "That's a fine idea. I won't interrupt if you want to talk, Mama."

"Thank you." Her mother nodded. "I see that I surprised you. I did not try to deceive you. But nor did I allow you to know I was awake. That was dishonest. I am afraid I am seeing many such places where I have erred over the years." Her face twisted; then she pressed on. "As I said, Lucy's disgust started my thought process, as did the shame that consumed me when I realized how unjust I had been in accusing Mr. Jacobs." She tipped her head toward Katherine. "And you, my dear. Especially in light of the wonderful service Zachary did for our dear little Amanda."

She placed her hand over her heart and shuddered. "I truly did weaken at the revelation of how close we had come to losing her, but I revived shortly after. I fell asleep for what appears to have only been brief moments after speaking to you and Mrs. Roberts. When I woke, I did not attempt to let you know. I will admit I wanted to listen, although several times it took all my willpower not to sit up and argue."

Katherine opened her mouth, but Mama waved her to silence. "Not yet. Please. There is more."

She drew in a deep breath. "Mrs. Roberts had more to say after you left the room, and some of it was quite pointed. She was right, as much as it pains me to admit it. I have buried years of resentment toward your father for his gambling, and I have taken it out on you. I saw him as a weak man, even though I realize now he loved us— especially you—dearly. Gambling was his one weakness, and I could not forgive him for it. I saw your neediness as a child and worried you would become like him."

She waved a ring-bedecked hand in the air. "Not gambling, you understand, but that you would make poor decisions. I wanted to guide and direct your steps. I never recognized what an amazing woman you have become." She smiled sadly. "And I must confess that part of me wanted you to need me. I assumed if you became infatuated with Mr. Jacobs, you might not want me around any longer. At the very least, you would never seek my counsel if you had someone else to turn to. I see now that my attitude may have kept you from that, regardless."

Katherine's eyes burned with unshed tears. This was too sudden, too huge, and too unbelievable. This couldn't be her mother speaking. People didn't change like this overnight. Had it been the shock of her granddaughter's accident on top of the things she'd overheard? She wanted to trust her mother's words, but a deep-seated fear gripped her. Katherine placed her hand over the strong fingers resting on her shoulder, needing the reassurance that something in the room was real. As much as she wanted to ask questions, she wouldn't. Not yet. Not until Mama indicated she'd finished.

Her mother eyed her closely. "It has always been easy to read you, Katherine, even when you keep your own counsel. Although I must say you have gotten better these past weeks at hiding your emotions. But they are apparent now. I have shocked you. You are having a difficult time believing I am telling the truth. Is that correct?"

Katherine tried to form the right words. Calling her mother a liar wouldn't do by far, but neither would admitting her own fear.

"Wait." Mama halted her once more. "I have put you in an untenable position. Something I have done too often in the past." She emitted a low laugh. "I am afraid I still have a long way to go, and I find I cannot force myself to apologize yet again. There is only so much I can bear in one morning, you understand."

She laced her fingers in her lap. "I cannot make you any promises other than I will *try* to change. It is easy right now with all that has happened. But I am an old woman, set in her ways with a lot of bad habits. I am certain I will lose my temper more than once in the future and say things I should not. I will probably meddle in your lives after you marry and anger you both from time to time. I hope you will see it in your hearts to forgive me and allow me to continue living here. I would like that very much."

Katherine bolted to her feet, appalled and sickened that her mother would put Micah in this position. "Marry? What *are* you talking about, Mama? I am most certainly *not* asking you to leave, and Mr. Jacobs *hasn't* asked me to marry him. I don't know where you got either idea. He must be mortified." She turned toward Micah. Instead of embarrassment, he wore a broad smile, adding to her confusion. "Micah?"

He took her hand. "Not a bit mortified. You must have guessed I wanted to speak to your mother about us."

"Yes, but you planned to tell her we want to court. She's jumped to conclusions and …"

"No, dear. She has not." He placed a tender kiss on her palm.

Her fingers closed after he removed his lips, hoping to capture the essence of his touch.

"You are the one who misunderstood. In fact, she gave me her blessing. I planned on asking you privately after the two of you had a chance to talk, but it appears this is the way it was meant to be."

The warmth of that kiss did strange things to her heart, not to mention the wild butterflies flitting about in her stomach.

Micah dropped to one knee. "I love you, Katherine. I had no idea I could love a woman again, certainly not with the passion I feel for you. Since the day we met in the street, I haven't been able to get your sweet face out of my mind. You've consumed my thoughts and even my dreams. I fought against it at first. It felt so disloyal to Emma. Then I realized she wouldn't have wanted Zachary and me to be alone. I believe she'd have given her blessing and loved you as well. I'm hoping—no, praying—that you love me a little, and it might grow into a deeper love as time goes on. Is it possible, Katherine? Is there any hope you'd consider marrying me?"

Katherine melted, and for the first time in her life forgot to care what Mama might think. All she could do was focus on Micah's handsome, strong face gazing up into hers. Joy exploded inside, sending a shaft of pure pleasure pulsing through her body. Wonder of wonders. He loved her.

Not only that, he'd stood up to her mother and then approached Mama, knowing she might not give her blessing. Why she had done so was still a mystery, but it didn't matter. Nothing mattered except this dear, wonderful man who'd boldly proclaimed his love for her, in front of her mother. Why did it all keep coming back to Mama?

She squeezed his hand and smiled, drawing him to his feet. "I would be honored to be your wife, Micah. I have known for weeks that I love you, but there were so many things that stood in our way. The children and ..." She glanced toward her mother.

Micah nodded. "Mrs. Cooper will always be a part of our family. I haven't had a mother for years, and I hope she can help fill that place in the days to come."

A smile crept over Mama's face, and she extended her hand. Micah reached out while keeping his other arm firmly wrapped around Katherine.

Mama breathed a sigh that sounded much like relief. "I would like that, Micah. I surely would. Thank you from the bottom of my heart for forgiving this foolish old woman and giving her another chance at happiness. Now go break the news to the children. That is, after you two have had a few minutes alone." She quirked a brow at Micah. "I see you understand my meaning, young man."

"Quite clearly." He released Frances's hand and drew Katherine toward the hall. Pausing outside the partly open door, he took her into his arms. Micah waited a heartbeat, then gathered her close and dipped his head. He kissed her gently, lingering longer than she'd expected, causing a shiver to course through her. Then he whispered in her ear, "That's a deposit on what's to come—if you will allow me to be so bold."

Katherine's heart galloped like a runaway colt, leaving her breathless. Lifting her hand she traced the firm outline of his lips with her fingertip. She gazed into his green eyes and smiled. "As long as it's only a down payment, I think that's quite acceptable."

She linked her arm through his and took a step toward the stairs, then paused, stricken. Mama. The door to the bedroom was still open. She had seen it all and hadn't raised a word of protest. Katherine thought of all the things her mother had said only

minutes earlier. Shame washed over her. Her mother had poured
out her heart and apologized for the first time in her memory, and
Katherine hadn't even responded.

Turning, she walked to the seated woman and knelt at her
side. "Thank you for everything you said. I know it wasn't easy
for you to apologize, but I appreciate it more than you know."
Leaning over, she kissed her mother's forehead. "I love you,
Mama." Katherine whispered the words, almost choking on the
emotion swelling inside. For the first time since childhood, she
meant those words.

"I love you, too, but I cannot promise to be perfect, Daughter."
Mama's voice cracked on the last syllable.

Katherine laughed, and she brushed away a tear that threatened to spill onto her cheek. "Nor I, Mama." She smoothed her
fingertips along her mother's hand. "But we'll both try."

Micah slid his arm around her shoulders. "I'm proud of you,
Katherine Galloway. I can't wait for our great adventure to begin."

"Soon to be Katherine Jacobs, I hope," she said with mischief.
"I'm not a believer in long betrothals, so I hope you aren't hankering to wait."

He tugged her toward the door. "We can head to the church
right now."

A laugh sounded behind them. "At least let me recover my
strength for a day or two. Besides, I believe you still need to collect on that 'deposit,' Katherine."

Warmth stole into her cheeks as Mama's laughter followed
them out the door, but Katherine's heart sang. Micah loved her,
and that was more than enough.

On top of it all, Mama had done the unexpected and not only apologized, but expressed pride in her daughter. For the first time in years her mother had shown her affection. And, beyond that, approval.

The two most important people in the world besides her daughters had declared their love. Her life and hope were restored once more. No longer would she need to wish on foolish dandelion fluff blowing on the wind. No, indeed. The Lord was her strength and her fortress, and His love and Micah's would take her over any obstacle that came her way.

... a little more ...

When a delightful concert comes to an end,
the orchestra might offer an encore.
When a fine meal comes to an end,
it's always nice to savor a bit of dessert.
When a great story comes to an end,
we think you may want to linger.
And so, we offer ...

AfterWords—just a little something more after you
have finished a David C Cook novel.
We invite you to stay awhile in the story.
Thanks for reading!

Turn the page for ...

- **Author's Note**
- **Great Questions**
- **A Sneak Peek at Book Two: *Wishing on Buttercups***

Author's Note

Why I Wrote This Story

Blowing on Dandelions is a work of fiction in a historical setting, but it closely parallels daily events in today's world. It is a book driven by emotion, centering on the pain and joy of the characters. Their story consumed me and wouldn't let go until it was written—in fact, it still hasn't let go. I want to share with you how the story came to be, so you can understand the depth of my passion. Hopefully, *Blowing on Dandelions* will bless you as much as it has me!

It all started several years ago, when I bumped into a woman I'd met in the past. Over the course of our time together, she let slip little comments about her relationship with her mother. Let's just say the comments were filled with pain and grief. Mama was alive, well, and still contributing to that pain and grief.

I could bear it no longer, and while giving her a hug, asked if I could pray with her that God would grant her peace and healing. Through barely contained tears, she refused. Not that she wasn't grateful, but she couldn't tolerate the thought of attaining some kind of peace, only to return home to the same situation and have it shattered—or worse, new shards embedded into her healed heart. I went home heartsick and unable to shake the urgency to pray for my friend. I sensed her deep level of hopelessness that her life and relationship with her mother would never change. I prayed every time her name came to mind, which happened frequently. I couldn't forget the despair in her voice the last time we spoke.

As I asked the Lord what my next writing project should be, He gently directed me back to those memories. I knew He was showing me, over and over, that thousands of women ache with the same need—for approval, love, and acceptance, just as they are—from their mothers. He directed me to tell this story.

At the time, I started writing *Blowing on Dandelions* as contemporary women's fiction, but after two chapters, I decided the book would be better received if set in the 1800s. It was a bigger challenge showing the depth of the heroine's emotions, as so much was demanded during that era in regards to respect and honor toward the older members of society, especially parents. Children didn't speak back to their elders and often repressed how they felt.

One night, while lying in bed (so many of my best ideas sprout there), I saw a picture of a woman sitting in a grassy field with dandelions in bloom, some gone to seed. She plucked one and blew on it, and the fluff drifted away on the wind. I heard this grown woman's little-girl heart wish that she could drift off to a place where she'd never again be hurt.

I couldn't draw from personal experience, since I have a wonderful relationship with my own mother and count her as one of my best friends, as I do my grown daughter. Nevertheless, I knew I must write this book. I'm a licensed minister (not a pastor) and lay-counselor and minister to women at our church, so I've had occasion to pray for and with many hurting women who have struggled and continue to struggle with such relational pain.

When I posted a request on my Facebook Reader's Group, asking for women who had experienced a difficult childhood with their mother (extending into adult life) who were willing to fill out a survey and answer some questions, I received a flood of responses. Many of the heartbreaking answers helped flesh out the mother in this story, as well as the way in which Katherine, the daughter, responds. However, none of the events depicted in *Blowing on Dandelions* is based on any direct information shared with me, and no confidence was broken, but the input from these women was invaluable.

I also asked several women to read my manuscript when I finished my final draft. Each found multiple places where they related at a deep level. My hope is that this book—set in a historical time period with a strong romantic thread—will minister to you today, dear reader, far beyond "the story." Whether you're a mother who's had a difficult time with a daughter or the daughter who's always struggled with her mother, I believe you'll find places where you can relate. As you step into the head and heart of the mother and daughter, I trust you'll discover nuggets of truth from both that will open your eyes to what others experience … and that you'll come to a place of healing and hope.

The end of this story might leave you with questions about two of the secondary characters, but don't shut the book at the end. The AfterWords section includes great questions for individual reflection and/or group discussion, as well as a sneak peek at the first pages of Book Two, *Wishing on Buttercups,* to tantalize you in the short months you'll have to wait between book releases.

What of my friend whose story inspired me to write this book? God has been working on her mother's heart. She's slowly changing, in tiny increments, and the relationship no longer sinks my friend into despair. She's experiencing hope for the first time in her life.

Not many things in life are easy, but I truly believe there is no relationship too hard or any heart too wounded for God to mend. But, yes, it does come to a matter of free will. God won't force any-one to change or conform to His image.

If we commit to pray for the person who has caused us pain, we can be assured that God will do His part and speak to their heart. So don't ever think that prayer can't work for *your* relationship or problem, even if you don't see results quickly or tangibly. God speaks to the heart. He is a God of miracles, and He is more than enough.

Always. Forever.

Amen.

Miralee Ferrell

Great Questions

for Individual Reflection and/or Group Discussion

1. What does Katherine long for in her relationship with her mother? Have you longed for the same things in your relationship with a parent? If so, when? Think of a life event—small or large—that symbolizes that longing.

2. Why do you think that the mother-daughter relationship is, in particular, so significant to both parties?

3. Lucy struggles to understand what respecting your elders really means. *"How far did you have to take that when your elders treated you with disrespect most of the time?"* she wonders (chapter thirty-one). What do you think? Do you believe that we should respect our elders? Why or why not? Are there lines that shouldn't be crossed? If so, what are those lines?

4. How do you handle critical comments that other family members make? Do you tend to let things slide, pretend they don't penetrate, or confront them head-on? Explain. When has a well-intentioned comment you've made gone awry?

5. Have you ever felt lonely, like Micah? How did you respond: by throwing yourself into a busy life, by going into a self-imposed exile (like Micah did the first eighteen months after his wife's death), or by doing something else? Why? What method(s) worked for you? Didn't work for you?

6. Have you ever felt angry at God for not sparing someone you loved? Have you come to grips with that anger? If so, how? If not, why not?

7. How were Micah and his son, Zachary, and Katherine and her mother, Frances, at odds with understanding each other? What did each think of the other, and how were they all incorrect in one or more way(s)?

8. Do you know any "prickly" people like Frances Cooper? What hidden hurts were behind Frances's behavior? What hidden hurts might be behind the prickly people you know? How might your awareness of those potential hurts change your own responses toward those people?

9. How does both the fire and Amanda's near drowning bring people together? How do they change Katherine's perspective toward Micah and Zachary? How might almost losing the person you struggle with transform your own perspective and relationship?

10. Frances tried to protect Katherine by making her tough so she could survive on her own, and also so she wouldn't make the same

mistake Frances had made of marrying again out of desperate need. When have you done things to "save" someone else out of good intentions? In what ways were your efforts understood? Misunderstood? How did your actions impact your relationship with that person? What small step could you take this week to begin breaking down the barrier between you and that other person?

11. Why did Katherine respond the way she did when she saw Lucy hugging Zachary? What memories do you tend to stuff far back in the past? How do they creep into your present? Your future?

12. When Frances passes out and is lying in her bed, she finds out— for the first time—what people truly think of her. If your friends and relatives were discussing you and didn't know you were listening, what would they say? How might those words change your actions toward others in the future?

13. Were you surprised when Wilma Roberts and Frances Cooper became friends? Why or why not? Have you ever experienced an "unlikely friendship"? Tell the story and what you both gained by your relationship.

A Sneak Peek at Book Two:

Wishing on Buttercups

Miralee Ferrell

Chapter One

Baker City, Oregon
Late August, 1880

Beth Roberts willed her hands to stop shaking as they gripped the cream-colored envelope. She hadn't heard from her magazine editor in months and had about given up.

Stepping toward a corner, Beth licked her dry lips. Dare she open it here? No one lingered in the lobby of the small post office tucked into the corner of the general store, and the clerk was working on the far side of the alcove stuffing mail into the slots. Glancing out the window at the bustling street of the small city that had become her home a few months ago, she scrubbed at the fabric covering her arm and wished her scars hadn't chosen this moment to itch. Only a handful of people knew her, so she shouldn't fear discovery.

Beth sucked in a quick breath and slid her finger under the flap. A folded page fluttered to the floor, opening as it landed. Her heart rate increased as a second piece of paper, long and slender, drifted several feet across the hardwood. They'd sent her another check.

Seconds passed while she stood frozen, unable to take in the renewal of her dream. She stepped forward, then crouched low to pick up her treasure.

Masculine fingers gripped the end of the check before she could snatch it up. Beth found herself staring into the twinkling brown eyes of Jeffery Tucker, a fellow boarder at Mrs. Jacobs's home. She bit back a gasp, fumbled for the nearby letter, and plucked it off the floor, praying he wouldn't ask questions.

She extended her hand. "Thank you, Mr. Tucker. How careless of me." Her stomach did a flip-flop as his gaze lingered on the paper, then lifted.

"Not at all, Miss Roberts. I apologize if I startled you." He offered the check, keeping those mesmerizing eyes riveted on hers.

Beth tucked the payment and letter into the envelope, then pressed it against her chest.

His brows drew down, erasing the warm smile as his gaze dropped to her hands. "Is everything all right?"

Panic gripped her, and she covered the scar on her wrist. Her loose sleeve had left her exposed, and she was sure he'd noticed. All she could think of was escape. "I'm fine. I must get home. Good day." She backed up two steps and bumped into someone behind her.

"Umph." Firm hands gripped her arms and kept her from falling.

Beth gasped and scrambled forward out of the man's grasp. "Mr. Jacobs. I'm sorry; I didn't hear you come in."

"Forgive me, Miss Roberts." Micah Jacobs removed his hat and bobbed his head. "If I'd known you planned on getting your mail today, I'd have offered you a ride. Zachary and I would have enjoyed your company."

"No need." Beth sidled toward the door and avoided his stare. If only the sun weren't streaming in the front window and illuminating everything in its path. "It's lovely now that fall has almost arrived. I enjoyed the walk." She smiled, then turned and dashed across the lobby. When she'd entered, the place was empty, and now it seemed almost every person she knew had been drawn to the post office.

Thank the good Lord Aunt Wilma hadn't appeared. At least these men were too polite to ask questions. Not so with her aunt. That dear woman would dig and pry until she obtained every last shred of information possible. Not that she wouldn't tell Auntie her news, but first she wanted to savor whatever the letter contained.

Beth bolted outside, keeping a tight grip on the envelope. She had no intention of revealing her secret to anybody, except to Aunt Wilma, of course, who'd been like a mother. Beth had made it this far without anyone else knowing, and she intended to keep it that way.

A shudder shook her at the memory of Jeffery Tucker's quizzical look after he'd glimpsed the check. Had he taken in the dollar amount and the signature of the sender? Would he recognize the magazine from back East? Probably. Although from what she knew of the mysterious Mr. Tucker, she surmised he had secrets of his own to guard. She could only pray he'd be charitable and keep his own counsel.

Jeffery worked to keep his expression carefully neutral. No need to encourage questions from Micah Jacobs or his son, Zachary. Something certainly had Miss Roberts flustered. She'd appeared self-conscious and worried at the same time. Did the check from the magazine contribute to her distress, or had he somehow disconcerted the young woman? Another thought struck him. Why in the world would the timid Miss Roberts have a check made out to someone else from a well-known women's periodical? Of course, he assumed it was a payment, and a large one at that. She may have been picking up the mail for her aunt, but he'd swear the check was made out to someone named Corwin, not Roberts.

Not that he had a right to pry—time to quit attempting to solve mysteries that weren't his concern. He'd come to town for another reason entirely.

He stepped up to the window. "Mr. Beal, any mail today?"

A tall, gangly man pivoted quickly, his Adam's apple bobbing. "Mr. Tucker. Yes, sir, there is indeed." He pushed his rimless spectacles up his nose and grinned. "An envelope from a publishing house back East and a letter from your family. Your father or uncle, perhaps? Hope they're both good news."

Jeffery bit back a groan. Too bad the timid Miss Dooley wasn't working today. She never snooped in patrons' business. Not so with Mr. Beal. He knew the comings and goings of everyone in town, all by inspecting the outside of their mail. "Thanks." He tucked the missives under his arm and tipped his hat.

"Not so fast there, young man." The clerk leaned close, his warm breath fanning Tucker's cheek. "You mailed a package to that same publishing house some weeks back. Does this letter mean they've made it into a book, or they're turning it down? If we're gonna have a famous author in town, I want to be the first to congratulate you." He stuck his hand across the divider.

Jeffery took the man's hand and shook it briefly, then backed away. "Sorry. I don't know what it might be, and I'm not famous for anything. Please excuse me."

He strolled from the post office without looking back, then halted a half block from the building. Micah and Zachary were standing in the lobby, a perfect target for prying questions from that obnoxious man. He'd better return and encourage them to leave or rumors would be flying through town faster than a rabbit fleeing from a prairie hawk. Of course, he'd never personally seen that type of chase, but he'd read about such things in his favorite dime novels.

He glanced at the envelope from his father and scowled. No telling what he might want, but based on his recent correspondence, it probably wasn't good. Jeffery's thoughts flitted back to Miss Roberts, and he grunted. Speculation about her behavior no longer seemed proper. He couldn't speak for anyone else, but his letter was only one of the things he'd prefer to keep private.

Beth slipped into the boardinghouse, hoping she could get to her room without being seen. Not that she disliked any of the other residents, but the letter from her editor begged to be read. She hadn't dared to stop along the way after her encounter with Mr. Tucker.

She'd made it to the foot of the stairs when the skin on the back of her neck tingled. Gripping the banister, she turned and peered over. "Aunt Wilma." She released the breath she'd been holding. "I didn't hear you come in."

Wilma Roberts crossed her arms over her ample bosom. "Why are you tiptoeing?"

Beth tried not to roll her eyes. Aunt Wilma never had a problem with subtlety. Maybe a change of topic would deter the dear woman from further prying. "Did you have a good visit with Mrs. Cooper? I hope she's not feeling poorly again."

"Frances is as strong as a horse. As long as her gout doesn't kick up, that is." Aunt Wilma narrowed her eyes. "You didn't answer my question."

"I'm going to my room to rest, Auntie. It's been a long day."

"What are you hiding?" The older woman took a step closer, and her eyes shifted to the handbag clutched against Beth's chest. "Did you get a letter?"

Beth glanced down. The corner of the envelope peeked out of her reticule. "It's nothing to worry about." She stepped onto the bottom stair.

Aunt Wilma raised her chin and glared. "Did that good-for-nothing rapscallion from Topeka have the gall to contact you after I told him to stay out of your life?"

"What?" Beth's thoughts spun, trying to keep up with the sudden shift in direction. "Brent Wentworth?"

"I'd prefer not to have his name spoken, but yes, that's the scoundrel I meant."

Fresh pain knifed Beth's heart. She'd worked so hard to forget the man who'd won her love a year ago. "I haven't heard from him since we left Kansas City." She waved a dismissive hand at her bag. "It's nothing to worry you, truly. Now I want to go upstairs, if you don't mind." She touched the small locket hanging on a chain around her neck, finding comfort in the contact.

It wasn't often Beth spoke to anyone in that tone, but she didn't care to linger. She trooped up the steps, thankful beyond measure that Aunt Wilma had secured two rooms when they'd arrived in Baker City earlier this summer. As much as she loved the woman who'd taken her in as a toddler, she could be quite overbearing at times.

Sinking onto the brocade-covered chair near the window, Beth pulled out the envelope. What if they no longer wanted her work? This might be the last check she'd ever receive. But even if it was, did the money they paid her really matter?

No. She had not spent a dollar of it since the first one arrived. Getting that initial contract for her illustrations had boosted her confidence, but only in a minuscule way. After all, every drawing was published under the name of Elizabeth Corwin rather than Beth Roberts.

The skin on her arm prickled again. How timely. The scars on her neck, arms, and legs were a constant reminder of the shadows that had dogged her from the age of three. What made her think an important magazine would see her worth if they knew her real identity? So far they appreciated her drawings, but let them catch a whiff of the mystery surrounding her childhood, and that would end. She'd decided early on that hiding her identity would serve her purposes the best.

Time to quit ignoring the inevitable. If her editor decided he no longer needed her work, she wanted to know. With trembling fingers she withdrew the letter and spread it on her lap, not yet daring to look closely at the check.

Dear Miss Corwin,

Please accept this draft as compensation for the recent illustration you presented, along with an advance payment against your future contract. Our periodical has experienced an expanding readership demanding more depictions of the Oregon Trail as well as life in the West. We're contracting to purchase a series of four illustrations of your choice capturing the westward movement and living in a town out West. Possibly something with a boardinghouse or cabin theme would be appropriate.

Our readers are quite taken with your art, and we trust you to provide us with more exceptional work. Please sign and return the agreement, and submit your first drawing no more than thirty days hence.

Yours most respectfully,

Byron Stearns, Editor, The Women's Eastern Magazine

Beth slumped against the chair, shock and excitement coursing through her body. Four illustrations of her choice, with a portion advanced. She'd assumed the check to be for the most recent drawing she'd submitted and hadn't noticed the amount. Her insides quivered so hard she almost felt sick. This couldn't be real.

Snatching up the letter, she read it again, savoring each word. They trusted her and liked her work. Their readers wanted more. Shivers of delight danced up her spine, chasing away the unease.

She grasped the check and held it to the light. One hundred dollars. "Oh my!" She placed her fingers over her lips to keep from shouting. This would keep her and Aunt Wilma in comfort for a couple of months. Then, as she scanned the document again, her heart plummeted, leaving her cold and shaken. Elizabeth Corwin. The check was made out to Elizabeth Corwin. How had she forgotten that detail?

It hadn't been a problem picking up her mail, as it came in care of Aunt Wilma. And there'd been no difficulty cashing the three smaller amounts when she'd lived in Kansas City, with a childhood friend and confidant as her bank teller. If he still worked there, she'd simply sign and send it to him. Opening an account here in Baker City without proof of her identity—or, rather, confirmation of her alias—could prove difficult. Of course, Aunt Wilma could vouch for her, but would anyone really believe her to be an upcoming illustrator for one of the largest magazines in the East? People in this town knew her as Beth Roberts, the quiet, shy young woman who lived with her aunt on the edge of town, and she'd prefer it remained that way.

She leaned back in her chair and a sigh escaped. If she didn't cash the check, would the magazine editor think she didn't want the contract? Surely not. She'd sign the agreement and get it in tomorrow's mail before they changed their minds. It would be legally binding whether she spent the money or not. After all, Auntie had plenty of money of her own and certainly didn't need her help. She'd tuck it away for now and quit worrying.

And while payment was nice, it wasn't the reason she sketched. When her pencil flew over the paper, creating new worlds and half-forgotten scenes, she knew what it was to truly be alive. Something inside cried to be released and nothing satisfied so completely as her work.

No one could understand the depths of insecurity she'd lived with all her life—the bottomless pit of fear and anguish that struck her every time the shadowy memories surfaced. The scars on her limbs … she had only vague recollections of where they'd come from, but a definite knowledge of what they represented. But all of that disappeared when she escaped into her chosen field.

Art. It drew her, calmed her, healed her, in a manner little else had ever done.

Somewhere along the way, a voice had started to whisper in the early morning hours while lying in bed. Often she thought it must be her own mind playing tricks, hoping to convince her the past didn't matter. She'd pushed it away at first, but it had persisted, pulling her into the warmth of its embrace. Trying to persuade her to accept—something.

Rising to her feet with new resolve, she neatly tucked the letter and check into the envelope. Tomorrow she'd sign the contract and place it in the outgoing mail. Right now she must make her way downstairs to supper and put on an unassuming face. How would she avoid Aunt Wilma's badgering questions? It didn't bother her to tell Auntie about the contract offer, but the world, including Aunt Wilma, must never see her uncertainty.

She touched a spot on her arm where the scars were prominent. Not knowing what exactly had happened in the past—or more precisely, why—had caused her so much pain.

And her early childhood was only a portion of what she'd had to endure. Beth's thoughts flashed to Brent Wentworth, the reason she and Aunt Wilma had left Topeka, Kansas. After years of guarding her heart, Beth had finally chosen to open herself to love. She'd been so certain she'd found a man who would love and accept her without conditions. She lifted her chin. Never would she make that mistake again.

About the Author

Miralee and her husband, Allen, live on eleven acres in the beautiful Columbia River Gorge in southern Washington State, where they love to garden, play with their dogs, take walks, and go sailing. She is also able to combine two other passions—horseback riding and spending time with her grown children—since her married daughter lives nearby, and they often ride together on the wooded trails near their home.

Ironically, Miralee, now the author of eight books with many more on the way, never had a burning desire to write—at least more than her own memoirs for her children. So she was shocked when God called her to start writing after she turned fifty. To Miralee, writing is a ministry that she hopes will impact hearts, and she anticipates how God will use each of her books to bless and change lives.

An avid reader, Miralee has a large collection of first-edition Zane Grey books that she started collecting as a young teen. Her love for his storytelling ability inspired her desire to write fiction set in the Old West.

"But I started writing historical fiction without even meaning to," Miralee says, laughing.

She'd always planned on writing contemporary women's fiction, but God had other ideas. After signing her first contract for the novel *Love Finds You in Last Chance, California*, she decided to research the town and area. To her dismay, she discovered the town no longer existed and hadn't since the 1960s. Though it had been a booming town in the late 1880s, it had pretty much died out in the 1930s. So her editor suggested switching to a historical version, and Miralee agreed, although she'd never even considered that era.

It didn't take long to discover she had a natural flair for that time period, having read and watched so many western stories while growing up. From that point on she was hooked. Her 1880s stories continue to grow in acclaim each year. Her novel *Love Finds You in Sundance, Wyoming*, won the Will Rogers Medallion Award for Western Fiction, and Universal Studios requested a copy of her debut novel, *The Other Daughter*, for a potential family movie.

Aside from writing and her outdoor activities, Miralee has lived a varied life. She and her husband have been deeply involved in building two of their own homes over the years, as well as doing a full remodel on a one-hundred-year-old Craftsman style home they owned and loved for four years. They also owned a sawmill at the time and were able to provide much of the interior wood products. Miralee has done everything from driving a forklift, to stoking the huge, 120-year-old boiler, to off-bearing lumber, to running a small planer and stacking boards in the dry kiln.

Besides their horse friends, Miralee and her husband have owned cats, dogs (a six-pound, long-haired Chihuahua named Lacey was often curled up on her lap as she wrote this book), rabbits, and yes, even two cougars, Spunky and Sierra, rescued from breeders who didn't have the ability or means to care for them properly.

Miralee and Allen spent just under a year in the San Juan Islands and lived in Alaska for a year, where she was actively involved in women's ministry. Later, she took a counseling course and earned her accreditation with the American Association of Christian Counselors, as well as becoming a licensed minister (not a pastor) through her denomination. She spends time each month in her office at church praying with and ministering to women, as well as occasionally speaking and filling the pulpit.

Miralee serves as president of the Portland, Oregon, chapter of ACFW (American Christian Fiction Writers) and belongs to a number of other writers' groups. She also speaks at women's groups, libraries, historical societies, and churches about her writing journey.

www.miraleeferrell.com
www.miraleesdesk.blogspot.com

Books by Miralee Ferrell

Love Blossoms in Oregon Series
Blowing on Dandelions

Love Finds You Series
Love Finds You in Bridal Veil, Oregon
Love Finds You in Sundance, Wyoming
Love Finds You in Last Chance, California
Love Finds You in Tombstone, Arizona
(sequel to *Love Finds You in Last Chance, California*)
The Other Daughter
Finding Jeena
(sequel to *The Other Daughter*)

Other Contributions/Compilations
A Cup of Comfort for Cat Lovers